click.*date*.repeat. *again.*

a novel

K. J. Farnham

Click Date Repeat Again

Cover design © QDesign
Edited by Leah Campbell and Barbara Malmberg
Formatting by Karan & Co. Author Solutions

more. *books*. by k. j.

Click Date Repeat

Don't Call Me Kit Kat

A Case of Serendipity

Visit kjfarnham.com for more information.

dedication

To the couple who inspired this book.

chapter one

Jess – 26
Location: Milwaukee
My Subscription was a Gift

Relationship Status: Never Married
Kids: No
Want kids: Undecided
Ethnicity: White / Caucasian
Body type: Curvy
Height: 5' 4"
Religion: Non-denominational
Politics: Middle of the Road
Smoke: Social Smoker
Drink: Social Drinker
Pets: Cats
Education: Bachelor's
Employment: Travel Industry
Income: 20,000-30,000

I'm not really sure what to say here, soooo . . . I like going to the movies, but no thanks to the popcorn. (Is anyone else annoyed when the kernels get stuck in your teeth?) I also like to read. Historical fiction novels are my favorite, and sci-fi is my least favorite. Crossword puzzles, Sudoku, a good game of Scrabble, and wine (any variety) are my favorite pastimes. (Drinking wine is a pastime, right?) I'm not a fan of extreme exercise or all-consuming professional sports. If you'd like to know more, drop me a line!

~

"Lookin' good, pretty lady," I say, bringing my hands to my hips and turning right for a side view in the mirror. It never hurts to give yourself an ego boost, especially when there's no one around to do it for you.

Mags, my lazy and overweight tabby, looks on from the bed behind me and meows as if I was talking to her. "What's up, Mags?" I ask, swiveling back for another front view. She silently stares at my reflection, almost like she's thinking the ten minutes of effort I've put into dolling myself up have been a waste of time. I don't disagree.

"Yeah, yeah, yeah," I lament as I dip into a front shimmy and dig a hand into my bra cups to give each breast a boost. "Trust me, you're not the only one who thinks online dating is a bad idea." She curls into herself for a nap, seemingly satisfied to know we're on the same page. "But I promised I'd give it a shot, and . . . I'm bored," I mumble as I turn and reach over Mags to grab my purse off the bed.

When I open the bedroom door, my other furry roommate, Savannah, scurries in, brushing against my jet black pixie capris. She's white and sheds like crazy.

"Seriously, Savannah?" I groan, rushing over to my dresser where a lint roller is always at the ready.

Checking the clock on my nightstand, I increase my rolling speed. If I don't head out the door as soon as possible, I might be tempted to change my mind about this impromptu date.

~

I'm on my way to Tiki Time when my phone vibrates. It's Chloe, my best friend, and the person who gifted me the three-month subscription to Yahoo! Personals for my birthday. I let the call go to voicemail and listen to her message as soon as I pull into a parking spot.

"Hey! Haven't talked to you in a few days so I'm just calling to see what's new. If you call back tonight, just make sure it's not during Survivor, *okay? Oh, and not after ten either . . . So, I guess just try to call sometime between*

eight and ten. Otherwise, I'll call you tomorrow. I can't believe you're going on your first date! I need to hear all about this guy! Talk to you later. Bye!"

I delete Chloe's message and chuckle at her excitement over my first date, which she thinks is tomorrow. Heck, when I emailed her about it last night, that's what I thought too. But then I'd had a message from this new guy, Coordinates Kyle, waiting for me when I logged into my Personals account this afternoon.

Hey there Jess,

Great tagline. I'm curious...who gave you the gift of online dating? I recently moved to Milwaukee from Homewood, Illinois, so in my case, it was my nosey sister Eileen. So who was it for you? Your mom? A co-worker? A best friend who insists you'll have more luck finding someone worthwhile online than in a sleazy bar? For the record, I have another nosey sister who thinks online dating is just as sleazy as meeting someone in a bar, and she'd much rather I meet a nice girl at church. Eileen swears this works though. She keeps sending me and nosey sister number two articles about the growing popularity of online dating, and I keep telling her popularity doesn't necessarily guarantee success. Interested in testing the waters with me?

Kyle

Kyle's message was a nice change of pace compared to most of the other introductory messages I've received over the last two weeks. With the exception of two guys, the rest have been bland variations of one another. Something along the lines of, "I read your profile and you seem like: a nice person/the kind of woman I'm looking for/someone I could get along with."

One of the first standouts caught my attention with a joke the day after I set up my account. It was actually pretty lame, but his unique approach won me over. We've been messaging back and forth ever since.

The other standout's introductory message focused on his love for being one with nature when he hunts and fishes. Granted, things with hunter guy didn't make it past two rounds of messages because he took offense to my asking if hunting with a rifle was kind of like cheating compared to using a bow. *Touchy-touchy.*

My luck getting past the first round of messages with most of the generic guys hasn't been great. I've deleted a few snore-worthy conversations early on, and several guys have abandoned ship without explanation.

Entertained by Kyle's message, I had clicked to view his profile.

~

Coordinates Kyle – 25
Location: Milwaukee
J.R.R. Tolkien anyone?

Relationship Status: Single
Kids: No
Want Kids: Yes
Ethnicity: White / Caucasian
Body type: Average
Height: 6' 8"
Religion: Spiritual
Politics: Liberal
Smoke: No
Drink: Yes
Pets: No
Education: Bachelor's
Employment: Professional
Income: 30,000-40,000

~

My first thought had been, "Six foot eight? Holy shit!" Then I proceeded to think about the logistics of dating someone that tall. At five foot four, I'd have to crane my neck to look up at him when we talk, and I'd have to stand on my tiptoes to hug or kiss him. And what if we had sex?

I decided that could be interesting, so I messaged him back.

Hey Kyle,

Thanks for the message. My tagline is a result of having a best friend who would probably get along great with your sister Eileen. Since online dating worked for her, she thinks everyone who's single should give it a go.

Testing the waters together sounds like a plan. But I do have a pressing question first . . . Why is your screen name Coordinates Kyle?

Jess

Between loads of laundry and cleaning up around my apartment, we exchanged nearly a dozen messages apiece this afternoon. In the first message, Kyle revealed that he's a mapmaker, hence his catchy screen name. After we cleared that up, the rest of our online conversation was a long string of questions and answers back and forth. Nothing too personal though. No ex talk, no deep dark secrets, and nothing about fetishes or kinky sexual fantasies (such as getting it on with someone who's over a foot taller than you). Instead, we shared other basics like where we grew up, favorite food/color/movie/type of music, etc. I was enjoying the virtual conversation enough that the online-dating skeptic in me faded into my subconscious—for a little while anyway. Then, as I ate tomato soup and grilled cheese for dinner, Coordinates Kyle messaged to see if I was up for a fufu drink.

"A fufu drink?" I replied.

"Yeah, you know, one of those drinks that looks all pretty and innocent but if you aren't careful it'll leave you passed out on the bathroom floor with your pants down?"

Actually . . . ahem . . . I'm quite familiar. Been there, done that.

"Tonight? Well, okay, sure . . . why not? You talked me into it. Why keep conversing via a computer screen and keyboard? Where did you have in mind?"

So here I am, two hours later, half a block down from Tiki Time, a cozy bar that specializes in ice cream drinks and exotic cocktails. Oddly placed, it's located in a residential neighborhood on Milwaukee's southeast side and nestled between single family homes. If it weren't for the neon multicolored martini glass in the front window, passersby would never guess it's a dimly lit, vintage cocktail lounge. Most women probably would have declined to meet someone for the first time in such an intimate setting, but Coordinate Kyle's reason for choosing it seems totally legit. He'd recently seen an article in *Milwaukee Magazine* that listed Tiki Time as having one of the city's most unique drink menus. Plus, I'm a sucker for liquored-up ice cream drinks.

As I make my way to the entrance, I laugh at the thought of how anxious Chloe was when she started online dating and met people for the first time. I think it was because the optimist in her thought there was a chance each guy could have turned out to be "the one." I, on the other hand, don't feel the slightest bit nervous. Instead, my mouth is simply salivating at the thought of the Vanilla Winter Russian I plan to order.

While I wait in line to speak with the hostess, I scan the foyer and bar area for Coordinates Kyle. At six foot eight, he should be easy to spot. While looking for him, my eyes adjust to Tiki Time's hazy reddish glow. Not only are the floor and walls red, but the bar is also lined with fuzzy red fabric reminiscent of Muppet fur. Judging by the décor, you'd never suspect the brilliance of their drink menu.

I step forward as the people in front of me are led away by a server.

"Good evening. How many in your group tonight?" the mild mannered blonde hostess asks as she repositions black glasses atop her nose. They're the kind of glasses people tend to wear as an accessory versus necessity. Her name tag says CORA.

"Just two. Me and . . ." I quickly scan the immediate area again. "I'm actually meeting a guy I met online."

She smiles broadly and squeals, “How exciting!”

“Yeah, I guess,” I say, chuckling. “We just started messaging back and forth this afternoon, so hopefully he doesn’t turn out to be a closet whack job. Although, I’m sure the odds of that are probably pretty high, right? I mean, considering the type of people who are lurking about online.” I say lurking with little air quotes, laughing, but my laughter stops abruptly when I realize she’s no longer smiling.

“I met my fiancé online,” she says icily, raising her chin a tad.

Whoops. Once again, I’ve managed to offend a more sensitive soul by putting my foot in my mouth. I’m pretty used to it by this point in my life.

I give Cora a small apologetic shrug. “Well, I’m obviously not saying you or your boyfriend are whack jobs. Just that—”

“There’s no wait at this time. Would you like to be seated now or when your date arrives?” She cuts me off, her voice and demeanor aloof.

“I’ll wait,” I say, doing my best to stifle a grin. I can’t help but find it funny that she’s so offended. Chloe’s online dating statistics alone are proof that one in three matches are loony tunes, but I was mostly just trying to be funny. *Chill out, lady.*

I step aside to make way for the group of people behind me, and head to the end of the bar next to the window displaying the neon martini glass sign. No sooner do I lean against a wall when a noticeably tall man ducks through the entryway. I can’t see his face clearly due to the distance and the dim lighting, but what are the odds of another guy as tall as Kyle showing up at Tiki Time tonight? He looks around as the group in front of him starts following a server to their table and a path to the hostess clears.

“Coordinates Kyle?” I say, peeking over at Cora to see if she’s watching us. She is, of course, as she rapidly taps the cap of the pen she’s holding against the podium in front of her.

Kyle is all smiles when he looks down at me and extends a hand. “Jess. Awesome to meet you. Oh, and you can just call me Kyle.”

“Are you sure? I think Coordinates Kyle has a nice ring to it.”

I loosen my grip on his hand, expecting to pull back, but he maintains a light hold and says, “Yeah? Then by all means, feel free to keep calling me that." His bright toothy grin returns, and he finally releases my hand.

I wonder if his teeth are really as white as they look or if it's because of the dim lighting or his dark hair and olive complexion. Maybe a combination of the two?

"Are you ready to be seated?" Cora interrupts. I glance at Coordinates Kyle to see if he notices the glare she's giving me. Judging by the way his smile has migrated over to her, I'm guessing he hasn't.

"That would be great. Thanks," he responds.

"So. You two met online," Cora says. It's a statement not a question.

"How'd you guess?" Kyle glances at me with a look of surprise.

Cora shrugs. "Oh, you know. A lot of couples come here on first dates. And lately, a lot of them have met through dating sites."

"So, any guess as to whether this date will go smoothly or not? You know, since you witness couples like us so often?" He grins at me sideways. I grin back before both of our gazes migrate to Cora.

She stares at me, blinking a few times, before returning her attention to Kyle. "I'd limit my alcohol intake if I was you. She has quite the whack job vibe going on."

Kyle laughs until he notices Cora's deadpan expression. "Wait, are you serious?"

Cora ignores him as she hands two menus to the server who's just arrived at her side. "Right this way," the petite brunette says loudly above the voices of the people who've arrived behind us. Resisting the urge to even look at Cora, I follow the server, tugging gently on Coordinates Kyle's sleeve to make sure he follows too.

Seconds later, Kyle and I are scooting into a cozy arc-shaped booth next to the bathrooms. Our server places menus on the table in front of us. "I'll give you a few minutes to decide," she says as she retrieves a pen and order pad from her apron before scurrying off to a table across the room.

"I can't believe the hostess said that!" Kyle's expression is two parts concerned and one part amused. I like the combination. It tells me he's probably a compassionate, non-confrontational guy.

"Actually, I *might* have unintentionally offended her before you arrived," I say raising an eyebrow.

He nods slowly and smirks. "Okay, let's hear it."

So I tell Coordinates Kyle about the ridiculous reason for the hostess' rude comment, and we have a good laugh over it. Then we discuss how it wasn't the least bit rude of me to call *most* online daters whack jobs, yet it was definitely rude of her to call me the exact same thing. The discussion makes me feel a certain sense of camaraderie with him.

Every time someone goes in or out of the bathroom, our faces are illuminated by the glow of fluorescent lighting. This allows me to get a good look at Kyle, and I like what I see. He's the perfect example of tall, dark and handsome. Plus, he has the sexiest dimple on his left cheek, and a laid back demeanor that complements my own.

By the time our drinks arrive, we've moved on to discussing details about his job as a cartographer and mine as a flight attendant. Then when our next drink (a fish bowl drink for two) arrives, we move on to talking about old TV shows we used to watch when we were kids. I have no idea what led us to the topic, but to me, it's evidence that the date is going well. After all, "Different Strokes" was a favorite of his too, and his Arnold impression is spot-on. *Whatchoo talkin' 'bout Willis?*

By the time we're about halfway through our fishbowl, our conversation takes a more serious turn. Kyle begins telling me about his most recent relationship, which ended a few months ago when he decided to move to Milwaukee for his current job. Apparently, he was blindsided by the abrupt breakup.

"So you dated exclusively for a year, and she broke up with you just like that?" I ask.

"Just like that," Kyle responds with a nod as he rolls up a sleeve of his navy and lime green checkered button down shirt. I can't remember the body type he listed on his profile, but his forearm is nice and toned. It makes me wonder what the rest of his body looks like.

"She didn't even entertain the thought of getting a teaching job in Milwaukee and moving with you?"

He shakes his head and begins rolling up his other sleeve. "Nope."

"No mention of trying the long distance thing or waiting to see if you could eventually find a job closer to Homewood? Homewood isn't even that far from here." I'm being more nosey than usual, but something seems off about this break up. Not with Kyle, but with this ex of his. I can't help but wonder if she was looking for a reason to end things with him.

Kyle finishes the sip he's taking from our rum-laden fishbowl and shakes his head again. "She just said it was the perfect opportunity for us to take a break." I sigh with a heavy heart over the glint of sadness in his eyes. "Anyway," he continues, "Enough about me. What about you? When did your last relationship end?"

"It's complicated," I say as I automatically reach for the emerald gemstone dangling between my cleavage.

"Try me." He props his elbows on the table and rests his chin on his laced fingers. The pose makes me think of the therapist I used to see after my parents got divorced, and suddenly I'm overcome by an urge to spill my guts.

So I give him the Cliffs Notes of my on-again-off-again relationship with my ex, Ned.

"Wow, that guy sounds like a total douchebag." Kyle says.

On one hand, I feel a sense of retribution upon hearing his assessment of Ned. But on the other, I feel a sliver of guilt. After all, I did leave out certain details that might not have painted me in the best light, including the fact that I *just* broke down and slept with Ned a few days ago.

Oh well, no need to tell him everything. "I'm certainly no saint," I respond. "But yeah, he's a rather large douche."

Sighing sympathetically, he grabs his straw from our nearly empty fishbowl and holds it up, prompting me to do the same with mine. "Here's to forgetting about our asshole exes and to all the whack jobs that are going to help us do it."

"Amen," I say as we tap straws. Then we proceed to polish off the rest of our drink, which now consists mostly of rum and melted ice.

~

"This is me," I say to Kyle, stopping next to my car.

He turns to face me and says, "I had a lot of fun tonight."

"Me too," I say, nodding and smiling. In fact, I had such a great time that I wouldn't mind continuing the date back at my place. But I'm trying not to steer things in that direction for a change.

He stares at me intently, giving off the vibe that the contemplative wheels in his mind are turning. Should he kiss me or not? "Would you —" *Hiccup.* "Excuse me. Would you like to—" *Hiccup.* "Shit. This is embarrass—" *Hiccup.* "—ing."

Poor Kyle takes a deep breath and holds it in as an attempt to rid himself of this sudden bout of hiccups. Me? I'm laughing so hard I can barely breathe, but I'm also wondering what he was going to ask.

He exhales slowly and then waits a moment before attempting to speak. "Okay, I think they're gone. So, would you like to—" *Hiccup.* "Damn it. I can't—" *Hiccup.* "—believe this!" He rolls his eyes. Then he hiccups again.

"I'm so sorry for laughing," I say as I clutch my belly.

"Don't be. People always—" *Hiccup.* "—laugh when this happens to me."

"Always? How often does this happen to you?"

He slowly exhales another breath he'd been holding. Then, looking embarrassed, he rubs his brow before answering. "I guess it's—" *Hiccup.* "—not always, but sometimes when—" *Hiccup.* "—I'm nervous."

This tidbit sends me into another fit of laughter. Except now I'm not just laughing at his hiccups. I'm also laughing because I'd almost forgotten how I met Kyle, aka Coordinates Kyle. It figures that he suffers from this bizarre hiccupping condition.

"So-can-I-see-you-again?" He quickly slurs the words together just to get them all out before another . . . *Hiccup.*

There's an uncomfortable silence as I imagine what it would be like to make out with Kyle. Would he become nervous and hiccup in my mouth? Would we ever even make it to first base? Or would he be too busy trying to cure a hiccup attack? Then my mind shifts to how much I enjoyed his company—tonight and earlier when we were messaging back and forth. I think about the sad look on his face when he told me about his ex dumping him on the day he accepted his job here in Milwaukee. I think about how attentively he listened as I revealed choice tidbits about my relationship with Ned. I think about the adorable dimple in his left cheek and his overall attractiveness. I also have a lot of questions about this hiccup issue of his.

Shifting his weight awkwardly from one foot to the other, Kyle waits for my response.

"Sure, sounds good," I say as I stand on my tippy toes and lean in for a goodbye hug.

Hiccup.

chapter two

It's three forty-five on a Friday afternoon, so I don't even bother checking the caller ID before answering my cell phone. Unless she has bus duty, Chloe is typically alone in her classroom by now, calling me.

"Hey, how was your day?"

"Terrible. There *has* to be a full moon tonight." Chloe teaches first grade and she swears the behavior of her students coincides with the phases of the moon. Sort of like how women suffer from PMS every month.

"That bad, huh?" I ask as I finish slathering freesia-scented lotion on my arms.

She doesn't respond right away, but I hear typing, so I assume she's finishing up an email or grade book entry. "Yep, full moon tonight. I knew it . . . " she mumbles. "Anyway, forget about *my* day. Let's talk about your date tonight!" She's suddenly enthusiastic, almost like looking forward to this particular conversation has been what got her through the work day.

"Okay, but first let me tell you about the date I went on last night." I grab the phone from the crook of my neck and move to my closet to sift through my wardrobe.

"Ohhhh, so *that's* why you didn't call me back last night. Who'd you go out with? Wait, please tell me it wasn't—"

"No, it wasn't Ned. It was someone I met online."

"Someone different from the guy you're meeting tonight?"

"Yep."

"How'd that happen? And why didn't you tell me about it yesterday? *Before* you met up with a perfect stranger?" The alarm in Chloe's voice doesn't surprise me because she's ridiculously paranoid about stranger danger. I suspect it has something to do with the fact that her mom is always calling her to discuss the latest episodes of *Dateline* and *48 Hours*.

"Calm down, Chloe," I say in a singsong voice. "We met at Tiki Time, so we were surrounded by people. And he was perfectly harmless."

"Perfectly harmless? Really? He could have drugged you, carried you to his car, and taken you who knows where. Or he could have followed you home and forced his way into your apartment."

"Well, he *was* pretty cute, so . . ." Chloe sighs and I laugh. "Seriously, though," I continue, "you're right. I should be more careful. I'll be sure to tell you where and when I go on future dates."

"Thank you. Now, tell me all about the date. Do you like the guy?"

I lay a few prospective outfits out on my bed as I fill Chloe in on everything about Kyle, from all the messages we sent to each other yesterday afternoon to the toast he made in the spirit of forgetting about our asshole exes. She decides Kyle definitely deserves a second date when I tell her what he does for a living, not because he makes maps but because of his clever screen name. When I finally get to the end of the date, explaining how Kyle and I were standing next to my car and he was gazing at me lustfully, she interrupts.

"See? It was only your first date and you had a great time! I told you online dating would be—"

"Hang on a second." I take a seat at my makeup table. "I haven't told you how the date ended."

"Let me guess . . . You invited him into your car or back to your place for a quickie, and he has a small dick."

"Whatever," I say with a grin as Chloe snickers. "I told you, I'm going to hold off on anything sexual, at least until I've gone on a few dates with someone. New leaf, remember? Besides, the guy is like six and a half feet tall. You know what that probably means . . ."

"He wears big shoes?"

"Exactly! Ha, ha! Anyway, even if I did invite him over, I'm pretty sure nothing would have happened."

"Why's that?"

"Because he developed a bad case of hiccups." I say, grinning at the memory of Kyle holding his breath.

"Yeah, so? Do you have something against hiccups? Daran gets them all the time," Chloe says.

"No, of course not. But . . . okay, here's the thing . . . he said he gets them whenever he's nervous."

"Really? Huh, interesting. Maybe that's why his ex broke up with him."

"They dated for a while so probably not. I'm assuming once he's comfortable with someone, his nerves are probably fine. Who knows, though?" I shrug into the unseeing phone. "Can you imagine making out with someone who can't stop hiccupping? I don't think I'd be able to stop laughing."

"Well, you still had a good time with him, so maybe give it another date or two and see how it goes. You might end up liking him enough that you don't notice the hiccupping. And like you said, maybe he won't hiccup anymore once he's more familiar with you."

"I already agreed to see him again, mainly to find out more about this hiccupping issue of his."

"Ha! If hiccups are his only oddity, you got really lucky for your first date. Now, which guy are you meeting tonight?"

"Uhhhh . . ." I say, holding the phone with one hand and curling my eyelashes with the other. "I can't remember his name off the top of my head, but I know he sells something for a living. Insurance, I think?" I blink my hazel eyes a few times to separate my curled lashes and examine the results.

"What do you mean you can't remember his name? You told me about this date a couple days ago. How do you not remember his name?"

"Well, I've been messaging back and forth with a lot of guys for the last two weeks. It's kind of hard to keep track with all the screen names and real names, you know?" I say nonchalantly as I toss the eyelash curler onto my makeup table, deciding I'm happy with the results. My eyes are bit more olive green today than seaweed brown, which is a good sign in my book. "Guess I should check, huh?" I grab my laptop off my bed.

"Or you *could* go in blind. God knows knowing his name won't affect your attraction to him. Or lack thereof. If he turns out to be the love of your life, you can always sneak a peek at his I.D. when he's in the shower!" We both giggle as I plug my laptop into the printer on the desk I never use and press the power button.

"Please tell me again why you thought an online dating subscription was better than a spa certificate? I swear I thought it was an April Fool's Day joke, not a birthday gift. Do you even know me?" I joke as I examine myself in the full-length mirror hanging on the back of my bedroom door.

"What makes you think a spa certificate could help you find the love of your life?" Chloe's tone is ripe with sarcasm.

"Who says I'm looking for the love of my life? That sounds like an awful lot of commitment. Anyway, even if I were, I'd probably have a better chance of meeting him at a spa than online. You should see some of the male masseuses at the spa my mom goes to over on Lake Drive. Mmm . . . the last one I had . . ." I lean into my closet and grab a pair of black strappy sandals from the multi-tiered shoe rack on the floor.

"Just keep giving it a fair chance, okay?" Chloe is back to being serious. "I mean, hiccup guy was nice, right? Hopefully you'll meet a few more nice guys, and then you'll finally be able to steer clear of . . . your bad habits."

Her reference to "bad habits" makes me cringe. I know exactly what, or rather *who*, she means, and it puts me on the defensive. "Look, I really appreciate the gift, but your personal fairytale ending and my one okay date haven't changed my mind about online dating. I still think it's weird." I move back in front of the mirror to see how the sandals look with my outfit.

"Tell that to eHarmony's four million subscribers. *And* I just saw an article that said they're expecting that number to double by the first half of 2005," Chloe says with pride, as if her own experiences with online dating had something to do with its growing success. She didn't even meet Daran on eHarmony.

"So eHarmony is booming, yet you got me a subscription to Yahoo! Personals?" I ask as I take a few steps backward and fall into a sitting position on my bed.

"Eh, I'm sure Yahoo! Personals is booming too. Besides, eHarmony is overpriced . . ."

"Well, regardless of the site or cost, we both know I can just as easily meet guys in a bar or while I'm working. Not only are those methods *normal,* but they're also *much* less exhausting than thinking up things to type to so many guys. Good thing I finally wised up last weekend and started copying and pasting messages." I smile proudly at my ingenuity and Chloe laughs. It's a halfhearted laugh that morphs into a sigh, and I expect another reminder about my New Year's resolution.

But the line stays quiet instead, and I suspect she has that look on her face. The look she's been giving me lately whenever my "dating life" comes up. The look that tells me she's doing her damnedest to not get on my case for continuing to hook up with one of the "bad habits" she mentioned earlier: my lingering ex, Ned, or Brant, a pilot with the airline I work for. Although, he wasn't exactly a habit, more like a mistake that went too far too many times. Fortunately, we haven't worked on any of the same flights or run into each other in the crew lounge since I cut ties with him cold turkey about a month ago.

"Look, I know I made a pact with myself to get my love life in order. Yet here I am. It's been three and a half months since I made that New Year's resolution, and things haven't changed much." I pause, giving Chloe a chance to interject with some words of encouragement, the way she usually does. Maybe praise me for only seeing Ned once this week.

Wait, who am I kidding? It's Friday. The week isn't over yet.

"Well, it's never too late to make a change, right?" There it is. Chloe's encouraging teacher voice. "I mean, it's only April. A lot can happen over the next eight months. Heck, a lot can happen in three months. Look at me and Daran."

"Darn skippy," I say, switching the black sandals on my feet out for a silver pair.

Despite my mock enthusiasm, Chloe makes a good point about how quickly things can change. After months of online dating, she finally met someone who was worth all the hassle. And now, Daran and her are talking about moving in together. That's close enough to a fairytale ending in my book. Except, now Chloe insists that just because it worked for her, it'll work for me too. I'm not so sure, though. Even the surprisingly good date I had with Kyle hasn't shaken my feeling that Chloe might have wasted her hard-earned money on a Yahoo! Personals subscription for me when I would have been happy with a bottle of cheap vodka for my twenty-sixth birthday.

"And who really cares about a stupid New Year's resolution, anyway?" Chloe continues in a supportive tone.

Me. That's who. But every time I've slept with Ned over the last few months, I tell myself it's okay to fall off the resolution bandwagon once in a while. People do it all the time when they ring in the New Year with a vow to go to the gym more regularly or stick to a new diet. It should be fine if I cheat a little too, right?

Or maybe I should just save this resolution for next year. After all, I'm only in my twenties. (Okay, LATE twenties.) Does it really matter if it takes me an extra year to get shit straight with my love life? Besides, I don't actually have any love to get in order at the moment. It's more like comfort zone chaos that needs to be tamed—my habitual attraction to Ned being the root of all evil.

"Hey, are you still there?" Chloe interrupts my contemplating.

"Yeah, I'm here . . ." I sigh, kicking a pair of Ned's boxers up from under my bed and tossing them into the trash can next to my nightstand. "Hey, can you hang on a sec?"

"Sure."

I place the phone on my makeup table and stare at myself in the mirror, focusing on the emerald necklace around my neck. It takes me back to my birthday last year when Ned showed up from work too late for us to keep our dinner reservation. As a result, we ended up at his favorite dive bar eating mozzarella sticks instead. Again. He charmed me back into a good mood with this damn piece of beautiful jewelry.

Without taking my eyes off the shimmery green nugget, I reach back, lift my hair out of the way, and unclasp the silver chain around my neck. Then I open the jewelry box in front of me—a musical one from when I was a kid, complete with a miniature ballet dancer inside. The expensive gift from Ned falls with a clank before I gently close the pink floral lid and pick up the phone.

"Hey, I'm back."

"Where'd you go? It's not Ned, is it? *Please* tell me he's not at your door." She whispers the last bit, as if he'd be able to hear her if it was him.

I can't help but laugh. "No, of course not. You and I both know it's much too early for Ned to be showing up at my door," I say jokingly, even though it's the truth.

"Good point. But seriously, have you thought about what you'll do if he shows up tonight and you're with . . . whoever you're going out with?"

"No, because my date isn't going to end up at my place," I say before smacking my plump freshly glossed lips together and sitting down in front of my laptop. "How many times do I have to remind you? I want to get to know the next guy I sleep with."

"Oh yeah? What if he's super hot and even nicer than the hiccup guy . . . but without the hiccups. What if you can't resist?"

"Gee, thanks for the vote of confidence. I *am* capable of controlling myself you know. Even if I find him or anyone else I meet online irresistible, my plan is to hold off on sex until at least date three. That's standard, right?" I pause long enough for Chloe to mutter in agreement. "But let's get real here, after your experience with online dating, odds aren't too high that I'll meet another semi-normal guy tonight. Two in a row? Probably not happening."

"What do you mean after *my* experiences? It ended up working out just fine for me. I mean, you like Daran, right?"

Oh, great.

"Yes! For the billionth time, yes! Sheesh, I thought you were done worrying about what everyone else thinks."

"You're right . . . I am." Chloe pauses long enough to make me question her certainty. "Anyway, back to you. Where are you meeting this guy?"

"Free Bird," I say, as I click to print his profile.

"What?"

"That's his screen name. Free Bird." I note that I have three new icebreakers, four pokes, and two new messages (one of which is from Coordinates Kyle) before I log out of my account.

"Oh boy." Chloe stifles a laugh.

"Eh, kinda lame I guess. But it's just a screen name." I smile to myself and glance at the digital alarm clock on my nightstand. "Crap. I need to get going."

"Wait, are you worried about being late? You're not nervous are you?"

"Pfft. Again, do you even know me? You know I hate to keep people waiting for me. And we both know I'm not the nervous one," I tease.

"Yeah, yeah. Where're you guys meeting? You never said."

"Molly McGinn's. I figure there's a better chance I'll get lucky in an Irish bar."

"You're kidding."

"Me kid? No way," I say with a grin. "Seriously though, my co-worker friend, Anne, works there, remember? She says working there a couple of nights a week more than makes up for when she doesn't get enough flight hours. I figure I can cross two things off my to-do list tonight. Check out Molly's—maybe even fill out an application—and meet..." I glance down at the profile again. "Free Bird."

"You do that. Just promise me you'll wait until he leaves before you fill out the application."

"Sorry. I can't make any promises. I'm a free bird too."

A last onceover in the mirror confirms that all the stationary biking and jogging—if you could call it that, my pace was more of a speedy waddle—I did with Chloe at the gym over the winter hasn't changed my figure one damn bit. Not that there's anything wrong with my figure, but . . .

"Stop it. Plenty of guys think a little extra hippage is sexy," I say to myself for possibly the hundredth time. Then I place my hands on my hips and smile as I turn slowly to check myself out from different angles. Content with my appearance, I grab my purse off my bed.

Ready or not, here I come, Free Bird.

chapter three

The sight of my barely worn sneakers jogs my brain back to thoughts of exercise the second I climb into my car. Ned never exercises, unless you consider golf exercise. And he never encouraged me to exercise either. I used to think it was because he loved my body just the way it is, but during our last argument (the one that occurred the day I called our relationship off for good), he said some really hurtful things that made me think otherwise.

Wait. I need to quit allowing Ned to invade my thoughts. We are *not* together, not for anything other than sex anyway. And that's definitely a good thing—that we're not together. As for the sex? Unfortunately, it's the only thing about our relationship that was never lacking. But a healthy relationship cannot be based on great sex alone. That's what the mature, responsible part of my brain keeps telling me anyway. Mental and emotional chemistry are important too.

Besides, if we'd stayed together, we'd have ended up an old, haggard couple hanging out at dingy dive bars every weekend. Maybe even every night. And we'd never have said more than a few words to each other in between rounds of screwing our brains out. That's what I keep telling myself anyway—whenever I catch myself missing the sameness of being in a relationship with Ned.

"Feel Like Making Love" by Bad Company starts to play on the radio as I pull out of my apartment's parking lot. I can't help but roll my eyes and laugh. I should have ended things with Ned early on in our relationship when he blasted the raunchy tune while we sat on his couch drinking bottles of Pabst. I'd told him I wasn't really a beer drinker, but that was all he had. The dim lighting and "mood music" (as he'd called it) was the only time I can recall him attempting to be romantic throughout our entire relationship.

I stab the power button in a futile attempt to extinguish my thoughts of Ned before I arrive at Molly McGinn's. But even in the silence of my car, the song continues to play in my head, along with more thoughts I'd rather not be having.

To be fair, Ned did offer plenty of surface niceties. The expensive dinners. The constant gifts he appeased me with when I was feeling ignored or unappreciated. The clothes he'd buy for me when I tagged along to "help" him with suit shopping. The funny thing is he never ended up purchasing the shirts and ties I chose to go with his new suits. He always went with what the sales associate suggested. This trend often left me wondering if I was really just there so he could buy me the outfits he wanted to see me in.

Eventually, our relationship started to feel like some sort of arrangement or show he put on, as if it was something he thought he had to maintain, just another image he had to keep up in the mirage of his perfect life. We usually ended up meeting up with his buddies after our dinner dates, and that's when the show would end. I often sat by myself sipping a cocktail until we went home and Ned was ready to get his rocks off.

The sad thing is I got used to the whole setup. I had a boyfriend who made a lot of money being the number one salesman at his dealership. He took me to expensive restaurants, and there was no need for me to keep him occupied with affection or deep conversation. It was easy. I ate good food, received nice gifts and had mind-blowing sex on a regular basis. The only problem was I was craving some real attention and emotional affection, which meant any guy who looked at me with interest sparked something in me. That's why things ended up going too far with my co-worker Brant, and that's how I justified messing around behind Ned's back. But for some reason, even though it was all a big façade, I was addicted to the consistency of our relationship and the safety of low expectations.

Last December when Chloe finally called me out on my constant cheating, I realized it was time to let go of the illusion of Ned and I. For his sake and mine. He might not have been the most attentive or caring boyfriend, but that certainly didn't mean he deserved to have me cheating on him every chance I got.

And that's how my New Year's resolution for 2004 was born.

So maybe I am a bit nervous about tonight. Nervous because I want to stick with my resolution. Nervous because I really could use a distraction to keep me away from the bad habit that Ned has become. And most of all, nervous because part of me really does hope online dating works for me like it did for Chloe.

Beeeep! Beeeep!

I peer into my rearview mirror to find the guy behind me flailing his arms. "Okay, okay. Calm the fuck down," I say under my breath.

I slowly apply my foot to the gas and wave politely. He flips me off in response. Nothing pisses a guy like this off more than getting a pleasant response to his assholishness. *Two seconds, buddy.* I continue eyeing him in the rearview mirror, but even with sunglasses, I can't see him too well because the sun is suddenly shining directly into my rearview mirror. *You'll get to where you're going a whole two seconds later than you would have if I'd noticed right away when the light turned green.* The second my urge to slam on the breaks of my shitty Toyota Corolla dissipates, Mr. Jackass revs the engine of his shiny black SUV and pulls up next to me, even though I'm now going five over the speed limit. *I will not look at you. I will not look at you. I will not—*

"Hey! Hey, Ginger!"

What did he just call me? I glance right long enough to gather that this lunatic is not going to leave me alone. His window is down and he's looking back and forth from me to the road while driving and screaming at the top of his lungs, waving one arm like a windmill gone askew.

Debating whether I should speed up to attempt losing him, I check my surroundings. With the exception of a mid-sized sedan approaching from behind, there aren't any other moving cars in sight. Fearing it could be a cop behind me, and considering the assortment of accidents I've been in, I tap the brakes lightly to shave off some speed instead.

"Hey! Who the hell taught you to drive, lady? Your granny?"

I gasp. How dare he insult my grandmother! Rolling my window up, I do my best to ignore him even though I'd love to ram my car into his. *Hmm. My car is a piece of crap. Maybe if I just give him a little . . .*

"Hey! I know you can still hear me!"

Ignoring the voice inside my head screaming at me not to, I glance over at the lunatic just as he speeds up, cuts me off and zooms through a yellow light, tires squealing. Slamming on my breaks to avoid running the red, I glance in the rearview mirror, hoping the sedan behind me is in fact a cop cruiser and that it's going to speed after the jackass. No such luck.

Asshole!

chapter four

After Mr. Black SUV sped by, I actually drove the speed limit for once, mostly to avoid getting stuck at another red light with that jerk. As a result, I pull into the Molly McGinn's parking lot later than I had planned. But I still have time to spare, so instead of getting out of the car right away, I pull Free Bird's profile out of my purse.

Looking at it, I laugh to myself as I think about how Chloe would freak if she knew my online dating strategies. Strategy number one consists of saying yes to anyone who asks me out. Free Bird happened to be the first. Strategy number two is to ignore every single piece of advice Chloe gave me the night we set up my profile.

"Set parameters," she said. Kind of ironic coming from a woman who spent hours creating her online dating profile and setting said parameters, only to end up meeting a barrage of guys she never would have agreed to go out with had she met them face to face in the first place. There was the psycho stalker with a girlfriend, the guy who wore green and gold Zubaz and just might be the Green Bay Packers biggest fan (and Chloe doesn't even watch football), and the guy who told Chloe he knew she had "chinky" ethnic origins. But my personal favorite was the guy who used his senior picture as a profile photo and whose snot ended up in her hair when she hugged him goodbye just to be polite.

"If you don't specify the type of guy you're looking for," she continued, "Your list of matches is going to be full of people you won't be interested in. And it's going to be huge. Too huge to manage."

"Fine," I said with a shrug. I started ticking boxes.

No preference.

No preference.

No preference.

"Wait. What are you doing?" Chloe angled my laptop to get a better look at the screen.

"Setting parameters."

"But all you're doing is ticking off the *no preference* box for everything. That's not really a parameter. And how can you not have a preference for someone's relationship status?"

"Oops. I didn't realize what that one was for," I lied and proceeded to uncheck the *married* box.

"Jess, do you want to do this or not? You're not even reading the choices . . . wait, you're okay with a widower?"

"My God, Chloe. I honestly don't care about any of these parameters. Because none of it is going to determine the kind of chemistry I'm going to have with someone. Maybe the love of my life is a chain-smoking Jewish porn star whose wife has been in a coma for the last twenty years. How will I find him if I set too many *parameters*?"

"Twenty years? That would make him kinda old for you. Don't you think?" She responded, ignoring my sarcasm.

I rolled my eyes. "That's not the point."

"Come on, you know what I mean," Chloe continued. "You have to narrow down your matches somehow. Otherwise you'll have hundreds to sift through, maybe even thousands."

I downed my glass of wine and then closed my eyes with a sigh. "Fine. How about if you do it for me?"

"Seriously?" Her voice became giddy.

"Sure," I said, getting up from the floor to open a fresh bottle of wine. "What the hell."

And so it began. The creation of Chloe's new online dating profile.

"You don't care what color a guy's hair is, right? I'll just pick no preference. Oh wait, but you don't want a guy with white or gray . . . Social drinking is fine. Definitely not daily . . . Now you need to upload a few profile pictures. How about this one? You look so professional in your uniform . . ."

By the time Chloe was done, the second bottle of wine I'd opened was gone. And I had no clue what type of guy Yahoo! Personals had been programmed to set me up with.

A week later, I deleted the three pictures of me with forced smiles Chloe had uploaded and replaced them with one of me holding a glass of wine. The smile in that one was definitely real. Then I changed all of Chloe's preferences to my own, which means no preferences at all. At least not when it comes to the options offered on the dating site.

Now, if there were a box for *kind,* I'd check that. And I'd be all about checking an *open-minded* box. And a *doesn't take himself too seriously* box. But I don't give a shit about someone's religion or which salary range they fall into. I'd just like to hang out with a good person, and if I happen to find him attractive, that's a bonus.

As I look down at Free Bird's profile picture, it occurs to me that, just like Coordinates Kyle, he's the physical opposite of Ned. Dark hair and eyes compared to Ned's blue eyes and thinning red hair, which he keeps shaved. A clean-shaven, angular jawbone versus Ned's scruffy, rounded facial features. The juxtaposition causes a small wave of anticipation in me, making me suddenly eager to meet Free Bird, even though I had been indifferent before. Finding someone who's nothing like Ned would probably be good for me. Too bad there isn't a *Nothing like Ned* box to tick.

I begin reading Free Bird's stats.

~

Free Bird – 29
Location: Milwaukee
Brunettes Only Please

Relationship Status: Divorced
Kids: No
Want Kids: Maybe
Ethnicity: Mixed
Body type: Fit
Height: 6' 0"
Religion: Catholic
Politics: Conservative
Smoke: No
Drink: Yes

Pets: No

Education: Bachelor's

Employment: Professional

Income: 80,000-100,000

~

Wait a second. He's conservative? And he calls himself Free Bird? Perhaps he had an eagle in mind? Not that there's anything wrong with being conservative. But I don't have a conservative bone in my body . . . So I'm guessing he's not going to love me.

Huh. I guess I do have at least one preference after all. Oh well, should make for lively conversation. Besides, what really matters is the two polite and grammatically adept emails he sent. I remember them now that I know his screen name and have seen his picture. I also vaguely recall him saying his real name is Louis, but I could be wrong.

Crumpling the profile into a ball before tossing it on the floor, I snort at his request for *Brunettes Only* and shrug off the ridiculous tagline. If Chloe's experiences taught me anything about online dating, it's that profiles are useless.

I pull down the visor mirror to give my makeup and freshly dyed hair one last inspection. The thought of that asshole driver calling me Ginger makes me love my crimson locks even more. I look down at the solid black A-line dress draped over my knees—perfect for hiding my hips, but probably a bit too much for Molly McGinn's. Ned liked me to get all dolled up whenever we went out, even if it was just to a dive bar. I guess that's why I opted for overdressed despite all the other outfits I'd considered. "Damn you, Ned," I whisper as I reach into the backseat for the cropped jean jacket that's been living in my car for several weeks. Hopefully it will tone down my dress. I shove the jacket into my oversized purse, which could fit a hoagie sandwich, according to Ned's friends. What a bunch of dicks.

As I make my way toward the entrance, a black SUV catches my eye, summoning an image of the jackass who harassed me on my way here and causing me to stop dead in my tracks in the middle of the parking lot. I can still hear his jeering voice. *"Who the hell taught you to drive, lady? Your granny?"* Suddenly I have an overwhelming urge to key the shiny new vehicle despite the fact that it couldn't possibly be his.

Or could it?

I laugh off my paranoia as I spin to head inside.

"Hey, heads up." The warning is followed by an excessive honk, causing me to drop my keys. I quickly snatch them off the ground and stumble a few steps backward to make way for a carload of people.

A guy in a white chef's jacket and navy blue bandana is seated on one of the wrought iron benches flanking the entrance. He exhales a wave of smoke. "Sorry, didn't mean to startle you," he calls out. An infectious smile spreads across his face when we make eye contact.

"No worries." Free Bird is most likely waiting for me inside, but I can't help but check this guy out as I approach. "Second time I got honked at today." I say, pointing a thumb over my shoulder.

He holds out a pack of cigarettes. "Sounds like you could use one."

I check my watch. Then I nibble my lower lip, willing myself to resist the temptation. "What the hell. I still have a few minutes," I say, grabbing one. Temptation has been my number one weakness since my freshman year in high school when I discovered all the fun there was to be had with alcohol, nicotine, pot and sex—anything for a rush.

We lean toward each other—me bending a bit with the cigarette poised between my lips, ready for a light, and him reaching out, lighter in hand. He scoots over and glances at the empty spot he's made for me. I lean against a light pole instead.

"No offense or anything. It's just. . ." I gesture to my dress.

He chuckles, and a puff of smoke escapes into the air. "None taken. Your dress is very nice, by the way. Er . . . pretty, or whatever."

Now it's my turn to chuckle. Either this guy is totally clueless or he's just really bad at flirting. Suddenly, I hear Ned chastising me. *"Why do you think every guy you meet is flirting with you? Sometimes guys are just being nice."* Or maybe he's just a nice guy.

"Sorry about that," he says, interrupting my thoughts.

"About what?"

"The 'whatever.'" His eyes migrate to the ground.

"What do you mean?" I ask with a quizzical expression.

"I have an ex who always hated when I said 'whatever.' Said it was rude. I hardly ever mean whatever, though." He raises his ice blue eyes and they lock with mine. "You know?" He brings the cigarette to his lips again, and it's my turn to look away. *Those eyes. Those lips.* "It's just an expression," he continues. "Your dress is pretty." Tilting his head up, he releases the next puff of smoke more slowly than the last.

"Well . . . thanks for the compliment," I say, eyeing his immaculately trimmed goatee.

"Didn't you say you only had three minutes?" He takes another drag, and I imagine rushing over to suck the smoke out of his mouth just so I can lock lips with this complete stranger whose name I don't even know.

"Oh . . . yeah, I have to get going." I quickly stub out my cigarette and toss it into a garbage can. "Thanks for the smoke."

He nods as he takes a final drag from his cigarette before flicking it into the trash.

"And for saving my life," I say with smile.

"Any time."

I turn to walk away and kick myself for not getting his name or telling him mine, but I'm already late so I keep moving.

Molly McGinn's is a typical Irish pub. The interior is covered with dark wood paneling and decorated with vintage knickknacks. Everything is illuminated by neon green clovers and muted amber lighting, and there are Guinness, Jameson and other Irish liquor signs scattered about. I've heard that McGinn's has an impressive selection of Irish ales, stouts and lagers on tap. But I'm not exactly a beer connoisseur.

"Just you?" The petite bubbly hostess with short, curly, Jennifer-Grey-in-*Dirty-Dancing* hair asks. She has this adorable smile, one that makes me want to pinch her rosy cheeks. And her teeth are big, the kind that are always exposed, whether she's trying to show them or not.

"No, I'm meeting someone," I say as I browse the dining tables in the main bar area. There are also a few couches and loveseats situated along the perimeter of the room. I don't see Free Bird, though. Maybe he asked for a table in the larger dining area, where there isn't as much hustle and bustle. "I think his name is Louis."

Still smiling, she gives me a knowing look and whispers, "You must be Jess." Her head jerks back over her left shoulder several times, reminding me of a turkey. "He's sitting at the high top next to the bar."

I glance in the direction of her spasms, leaning a tad so I can see behind her. There's a guy sitting with his back to the crowd.

"He said he was waiting for a Jess and then asked to be seated where he had a view of the TV . . . Oh, and his name *is* Louis," Miss perma-grin continues.

"Great," I mumble.

"What was that, hon? You *are* Jess, right?"

I smile and nod, but an alarm is going off in my head. Why you'd want to sit with your back to the entrance when you're expecting a (basically) blind date is beyond me. "Yep, that's me. Thank you."

As I make my way over to Free Bird, I have flashbacks of the way Ned used to pay more attention to sports on TV no matter where we were—at home, at his mom's house, when we were out to dinner. Reluctantly, I reach out and tap Louis's shoulder a few times. "Hey you," I say in an upbeat tone. No sense letting my sudden apprehension about this date ruin our first face-to-face.

His expression goes from expectant to irritated when he turns to look at me. "You."

Ignoring his rudeness, I extend a hand. "Louis, right?"

"Oh. My. God. I can't believe *you're* my date." Now he's laughing and shaking his head.

What's up with this asshole?

"If you mean me, as in Jess from Yahoo! Personals, then yeah, it's me. Not so sure why that's funny. I mean—"

"Are you serious?"

Then it hits me . . . Black SUV. I think back to his profile picture and imagine him wearing sunglasses.

"Hey, what were you doin' at that light anyway? Twiddlin' your thumbs?" He hops off his stool and obnoxiously waves for the waitress who's finishing up at a table across the room. Then he puts out a hand. "Good to meet you."

Now it's my turn to stare as I debate telling this guy to go blow himself, but I decide to give Louis the benefit of the doubt. Not soon enough, though, because as I reach for his hand, he snatches it away and smoothes his hair. He snickers as he sits back down and turns his attention to the approaching waitress, leaving me standing there shocked as I slowly lower my arm.

"Hey, sweetheart. Can I trouble you for another Kettle One on the rocks and whatever she's having," he says as he cranes his neck to look at the TV.

The waitress turns to me. "What can I get for you?"

I debate whether to continue the date, and my growling stomach and need for a part time job win out. "I'll go with the same. Oh, and is it possible for you to bring over a couple of menus and an application?"

"Sure thing."

"An application?" Louis turns away from the TV just long enough to glance in my direction. "I thought you were a flight attendant."

Instead of answering him right away, I sigh and wonder if there's any chance I could be on a practical joke show. Did my date really try to run me off the road earlier? Did he really snatch his hand away from me? Is he *really* watching TV while I stand next to him? I glance over at the door, again debating whether I should just leave. But then he speaks, pulling me from my thoughts.

"Are you going to sit?" He briefly points at the seat across from him.

"I guess so," I mumble as I move past him. I do my best to avoid contact, but our arms brush against each other causing tingles to course through my veins. I can't help it. Despite all the strikes he's already accumulated, Louis is one good looking guy. Too bad he has the personality of a spoiled frat boy and a bad case of road rage to boot.

"To answer your question," I say, hopping onto the stool opposite him, "I am a flight attendant, but I don't always get as many hours as I need. Gotta pay the rent." I barely finish my sentence before he cuts me off.

"So," he reaches across the table and tugs on a lock of my hair, "what's with the red? You have dark hair in your profile picture."

His ostentatious SUV appears in my mind. Then I hear him yell, *"Hey, Ginger!"* and my blood boils. "Ever hear of hair dye?"

"Feisty! I like feisty. Not a huge fan of the red, but since it's only temporary . . ." Eyeing me playfully, he shrugs. "I suppose I can live with it."

"Well, based on the way this date is going—" I start to say with narrowed eyes.

"Here you go!" The waitress arrives, a serving tray balanced on one palm and two menus in her free hand. She places the menus in the middle of our table and then a drink in front of each of us. "Two Kettle Ones on the rocks. And I'll be back in a sec to take your orders."

The words *thank you* are barely out of my mouth before Louis is interrupting me again.

"You were saying?" He asks with a cocky grin that remains even as he takes a swig of his drink.

He's right, I can be feisty, but it's not my style to pick a fight. And even though I already have a feeling this first date will be our last, I figure I might as well make the most of it before ditching him. So I soften my tone and continue with what I was about to say before our drinks arrived. "I was saying . . . based on how this date is going so far, there probably won't be a need for you to *live* with my hair color. Which I happen to like, by the way." Out of habit, I run my fingers through my hair, allowing the long layered locks to fall in cascades over my shoulder. Louis's cocky grin fades and he sits up a little straighter.

Oh great. Does he think I'm flirting?

"Look," he says, glancing at my cleavage, "when it comes to red hair, that shade actually doesn't look too terrible on you. It's just . . . like I said, I've never been a fan. We all have our parameters, right?" He checks out my chest again as he hands me a menu. Then he opens the other one up for his own perusal.

Parameters. There's that word again. Chloe couldn't accept my reasoning when it comes to parameters (or lack thereof), so I'm not even going there with this guy.

"You know what? You're right."

He looks up from his menu and nods, seemingly pleased with my false admission. Then his eyes pause on my cleavage again before ending up back on the menu.

"So how long have you been online dating?" I ask, hoping to steer our conversation onto another topic right away.

"How about we decide what we want to order first? Then we can talk."

"Fine by me." I shrug.

But it really isn't fine by me, so why did I say it was? Ned always made decisions for us. Sometimes he even doled out orders. And that's how it feels for Louis to suggest we decide what we want before he answers my question.

As I stare down at my menu, I decide the Ned vibe Louis is giving off definitely trumps his good looks. Plus, he's the SUV asshole!

"You two ready to order?"

"Sure toots, we'll start off with—"

"Claire," I say loudly.

"Excuse me?" This is the most polite thing to come out of Free Bird's mouth yet.

"I was just telling you her name is *Claire*, not toots. See?" I point to the waitress's name tag. "It's right there in black and white. Claire. You can read, right?"

It feels good to give this guy what's coming to him, but the smirk on his face makes it clear that he isn't going down without a fight—or a vengeful comeback anyway. He's about to say something when the intro to "Gin and Juice" starts blaring obnoxiously from his crotch, prompting him to bob his head while digging the phone out of his pocket. The fact that he seems to think his gangster rap ringtone is impressive serves as the highlight of the date. My funny bone is always triggered by dipshits who think they're cool. But it's definitely not amusing enough for me to continue with the date any longer.

"Claire?"

She raises her eyebrows at me. "Yeah?"

"I'll have the blue cheese bacon burger medium-well with sweet potato fries and a side salad with ranch on the side, please. And I'd appreciate if you delivered it to me at the bar." I hop off my stool and toss the menu onto the table.

"Sure thing!" Claire replies cheerily.

Looking at Louis, who has his phone to his ear, I say, "It was nice meeting you, but I think I'd rather eat at the bar. Have a good night." He acknowledges with a slight nod as I turn and attempt to move as far away from him as possible, wrapping up my first official bad online date.

Or so I think . . .

chapter five

I bypass two open spots at the end of the bar, hoping I can get more than four feet away from Free Bird. But as I make my way through the crowd, it becomes clear that the bar is full. "Crap," I whisper as I turn to head back to the empty spots I just passed up. Instead of gluing my eyes to the floor, I hold my head high, doing my best to avoid Louis's gaze. I don't need to see him to know it's his obnoxious voice coming from across the room.

"Hey, yeah you, Claire!" He blares, as if being told off on a first date hasn't phased him at all—just a normal everyday occurrence for him.

I climb onto the furthest empty stool and sneak a quick peek just in time to see him snapping his fingers in the air and Claire making her way to him from a few tables over.

This oughtta be good.

"Another drink?" she asks innocently.

"No, I think I'm good with the nearly full one I have here." He holds it up.

Asshole.

"Oh, right! So, how can I help?" Somehow Claire manages to sound pleasant, but I'd be willing to bet a hundred bucks she's going to spit in his next drink. I know I would, anyway. And I'd do it with a smile on my face.

"Just letting you know you can go ahead and bring me some Reuben rolls and Irish stew. And bring it to the bar. I'm moving too."

"Um, okaaay, but I don't think there are any . . ."

Claire's voice trails off into the growing noise of the crowd. *Wait, he's not thinking about . . .* I glance over at the empty seat next to me. Then I quickly begin removing my purse and coat from the back of my chair to transfer them over to make the spot look taken. Is it possible he didn't get the hint? Does he think I'm playing hard to get or that I want him to follow me? Could he possibly think our date was going well?

Just as I'm about to drop my things onto the seat next to me, someone pulls it out.

No no no no no no no!

"Look, Louis . . ." I reluctantly raise my eyes, and relief washes over me when I realize it isn't him.

The guy in the chef's coat I met earlier climbs onto the stool. He captivates me with his smile and those brilliant blue eyes of his. His bandana is gone, revealing a head full of salt and pepper hair. I can't help but stare with surprise. With just a light sprinkling of gray facial hair, wrinkle-free skin and a boyish twinkle in his eyes, I never would have guessed him old enough to have so much gray on his head. For Chloe, the color would be an instant deal breaker, but I happen to think salt and pepper is sexy, especially when it's a bit shaggy.

"We never properly introduced ourselves," he says holding out a hand. "I'm Sawyer. As you can probably tell, I'm a cook here." He waves his other hand toward his uniform.

I'm about to place my hand in his when Free Bird shows up.

"Hey, Buddy! That seat's taken!"

Sawyer and I swivel our stools at the same time causing our knees to brush. You-know-who is standing behind us holding his drink, looking like he's ready to brawl.

"Yep, it is now," Sawyer says before he takes a drag from a cigarette.

I stifle a laugh.

Louis laughs too, making me wonder if he knows the cook or if this little scene could be some kind of joke. But then his laughter becomes alarmingly obnoxious before it stops abruptly. He glares and says calmly, "No, that seat was already taken before you sat down. You see, this lovely lady and I are on a date." He looks at me as if he thinks he's rescuing me or doing me a favor. "Right, hon?" He winks, causing me to burst into laughter.

"Is this a joke? Do you two know each other?" I look from a grinning Sawyer to a confused Free Bird.

"No, we definitely don't know each other," Sawyer says, still grinning. Then he shakes his head and swivels back around to face the bar, giving me a wink when our knees make contact again.

"Looks like this asshole isn't going to give up the seat," Louis says gruffly, squeezing my shoulder. "How about we go on back to our table?" He doesn't even wait for my response before he's snapping and calling for Claire.

"Hey!" It's the snapping that sets me off. "Get a clue. I moved over here because *this* . . ." I motion to the space that separates us. ". . . isn't going to happen. Was I not clear enough when I said *Have a good night*? Thank you for meeting me here, but I'm not interested."

"Well, why didn't you just say so?" He shakes his head, a disgusted look on his face. "Damn redheads." With that, he shoves some cash into a startled Claire's apron pocket and zigzags through the crowd toward the door. I shrug at her as she reaches into her pocket. Her eyes become wide as she unfolds a couple of twenties. Well, whadaya know? Maybe Louis isn't as big of an asshole as he led us to believe.

"At least he left enough to cover your meal too," she says with a wink.

"Nah, I doubt that's what it's for. You keep it. I don't want that guy buying me anything. Besides, you deserve every penny after putting up with him."

She laughs. "Yeah, okay. What's your name?"

"Jess."

"Nice to meet you, Jess." She reaches into the large center pocket of her apron, and pulls out a mangled application and a pen and holds them out to me.

"Thanks," I smile and accept the items.

She nods. "I'll be back with your food."

I swivel back toward the bar and find a drink waiting for me. Sawyer eyes me sideways as he takes a sip of his beer. "What's this?" I ask.

"Vodka gimlet. On the house . . . er, on me anyway." He holds up his Miller Lite. "Here's to getting rid of that loudmouth asshole, *Jess*." The way he says my name gives me goosebumps. But I'm pretty sure he's not trying to be sexy, especially when he doesn't even wait for our drinks to clink before downing half his beer.

"Thanks. I'll drink to that," I say, secretly impressed that he just happened to order me one of my favorite cocktails. Could it be fate?

Sawyer slips another cigarette between his lips. Most women are turned on by a guy's ass or abs or arms or tattoos. Me? I'm a lip girl. He holds the pack out to me, and I ogle those lips of his as I grab a cigarette that's sticking out a hair. Then he lights my cigarette before lighting his own.

We both take a few puffs before he asks, "What were you doing with that guy anyway? Blind date?"

"Good guess. Kinda . . . I met him online."

"You're kidding." Sawyer nearly chokes on his drink. A grin spreads across his face.

"No, why?"

He shakes his head, still grinning. "No reason. It's just . . . bizarre."

"What? Online dating or *me* online dating?"

He considers my question for a couple seconds. "Both."

"Okaaay?"

He takes a drag and tilts his head. "This whole finding *love* online thing?" He makes air quotes when he says love. "It's weird. I mean, people are trusting computers to decide who they're going to be compatible with? It's a step down from that show Love Connection. You know? The one where a dude would hear facts about three women without seeing what they look like and then he had to pick one?"

I nod, a wave of nostalgia hitting me. "Yep. I remember watching it when I was in grade school."

"No shit. Grade school, huh?"

"Yeah, why?"

He shakes his lowered head and continues, leaving me wondering what grade he was in back when Love Connection was popular. "Anyway, that show confused the hell out of me. I didn't understand why someone would agree to go on a date with a person they never had a real conversation with, and I always got the feeling the contestant chose wrong."

He pauses to take a drag, and I nod in agreement even though I never took the time to analyze the contestants' choices. At eight years old, the most entertaining thing about the show was when Chuck

Woolery would say, "We'll be back in two and two," right before a commercial break.

"Of course, I knew it was all just for entertainment, but I remember thinking it was sad. Finding someone you're compatible with—someone you could love—is a lot more complicated than asking a few questions. Hell, sometimes it takes thousands of questions and conversations. And sometimes, even after you think you've found what you're looking for, you might still change your mind at any time it seems."

I stare at him, mouth agape, unable to decide if I'm turned on or repelled by his depth. Where the hell did that come from? We stare at each other for a few moments, neither of us moving. It's weird. Not that we're staring at each other, but the fact that it doesn't feel the least bit awkward. Still, this conversation is too heavy for my liking. After all, I don't even know this guy.

"Wow. I guess you won't be heading up any campaigns to bring the show back then, huh?" I playfully nudge his shoulder.

He responds with a chuckle and then takes a long swig of beer before speaking again. "Seriously, though, you look too smart to waste your time letting a few stats guide your love life." He shrugs and holds up his beer. "Here's to bizarre."

I clink my glass against his bottle and say, "Too bizarre." But I don't mean it the way he thinks I do. I mean it really is *too* bizarre. My second date with someone through online dating—something I've always thought was a waste of time—and I end up sitting here with this guy, someone I feel more chemistry with than I have with anyone in a long time.

At this point, I expect Sawyer to ask why I'm online dating. That's what I'd ask, anyway. Instead, he says, "My break is over in a few minutes, but I get off at nine if you want to hang out later."

"Sure," I say with a shrug, trying not to appear as pleased as I really am about the invitation. "I don't have anywhere else to be tonight."

"Great," he says, swiveling toward me, his knees brushing against mine.

We lock eyes for a few seconds, causing the loveliest ache between my thighs, and then those enticing lips disappear into the kitchen.

chapter six

My first thought when I wake up to a face full of hair is *please be in your own bed.* I swipe the thick red locks out of my eyes and am relieved to see familiar surroundings. *Phew.*

The clock on my nightstand reads seven twenty. It's definitely too early to drag myself out of bed on a day off, so I close my eyes and try to piece together what happened after Free Bird stormed out of Molly McGinn's. After Sawyer's shift ended, we talked and played a couple of rounds of bar dice with the bartender. At some point, there was a political conversation between Sawyer and a few of the regulars. Politics ranks right up there with golf and bowel movements on the list of things I'd rather not discuss, so I kept my mouth shut and observed the crowd. It was then that a rowdy group of bachelor party goers popped in to do a shot. They invited me to join them and I didn't want to be rude, so I accepted. The last thing I remember is dancing with Sawyer to some Steve Miller Band songs on the jukebox and promising myself that I would not sleep with him. The memory brings a smile to my face, and I give myself a mental pat on the back for sticking to my guns. After the dance, I have no idea what happened. I can only assume Sawyer brought me home, so I'll have to remember to thank him the next time I see him.

I begin to roll from my right side onto my back, but a low rumbling sound causes me to freeze. *Was that a snore?* I slowly continue rolling all the way to my left, dreading who it might be . . .

Please don't let it be Ned. Please don't let it be Ned.

It's Sawyer. He's on his back, and if he moved as little as half an inch to the left, he'd fall off the bed. That's how far away from me he is. His hands are folded across his chest, and his mouth is slightly ajar. Another low rumble emanates from his throat, causing me to giggle. But then I remember the promise I made to myself to *not* sleep with him, and my grin fades. So much for sticking to my guns.

I slowly slip out of bed, surprised to find myself wearing a t-shirt and workout capris in lieu of my birthday suit. Then I follow the clothes and shoes that trail out of my bedroom and into the hallway. My cats are curled up on separate articles of clothing. When I bend to pick up Sawyer's cat-free Molly McGinn's t-shirt, I'm hit with a memory of him talking in an Irish accent and me laughing hysterically. It makes me feel a little better about sleeping with him. At least I know he can make me laugh. I shrug and toss the t-shirt over the arm of a chair in my living room before tiptoeing into the bathroom.

A few minutes later, I'm off to my usual morning routine. Toothbrush hard at work, I use my free hand to start a pot of coffee and feed the cats. I notice the answering machine light flashing so I press play and continue brushing as I listen. The first message is from my mom.

"Hi Sweetie. Just me. I believe you have a hot date tonight, but I wanted to let you know that I seem to have come down with something, so I had to cancel my dinner plans with Rod. Thought maybe if you got home early enough you might want to swing by for some girl time. If not, I'll see you next Friday for lunch. Restaurant Hama, two o'clock. Bye, sweetie. Love you."

Rod is my mom's flavor of the month. I'm pretty sure he's my age, just like all the others. After my stepfather's midlife crisis, during which he took a sabbatical from his marriage vows to have sex with an office intern, my mom's midlife crisis began. Although, I think midlife crises are supposed to end at some point. When my stepfather's ended, he came crawling back to my mom, but she'd already vowed to never do the commitment thing again. Hence Rod, one of the dozen boy toys she's had in the last two years. There have been times when I've considered having a talk with her, but the thought of discussing my mom's sex life always makes me chicken out. Besides, I'm not exactly qualified to dissuade someone from having a lot of casual sex.

I'm done brushing but there's still one more message, so I hold my toothbrush and crouch down to pet Mags, the half-Persian who's circling my legs, as I listen.

"Hey, babe."

My heart stops.

"I haven't seen you in a few days, so I was wondering if we could get together. Not tonight though . . . I've got this . . . thing. But I am free tomorrow after six. I'll give you a buzz. It would be nice to catch up . . . I miss you, woman."

By *thing*, I'm sure he must have been referring to something either golf- or alcohol-related. Why do I allow this to continue? My mom and stepfather's issues were hidden. No one knew. But my issues with Ned have never been a secret. Everyone knows he's a selfish, borderline alcoholic who's more inclined to get off on a hole-in-one than sex and who never intends to make an honest woman out of anyone.

Out of nowhere, I feel a familiar twinge of emotion. It's the same twinge I always seem to get with Ned, like when you know you shouldn't have one last drink but it's right there in front of you, tempting you. You love the flavor at the beginning of the night. It goes down smooth and tastes so good. But as the night goes on, it becomes flavorless. And your brain has lost all control of sound decision-making. So instead of saying *nope, that's it for me,* you take another sip. And another. It's just a reflex, a habit. Sure, you wake up the next morning feeling like shit, but for a while things feel good. Funny how things that you know are bad for you sometimes have a way of making you feel content. For a split second, I consider the possibility of returning his call. But then I hear the telltale signs of Ned heading back into the shithole bar where he likes to hang out with his coke-dealing bartender buddy, and I'm snapped out of the state of sentimentality I've fallen into.

Turn that leaf, Jess! I think to myself as I delete the message. When I turn to head back toward the bathroom to rinse my mouth, I hear a clank from the kitchen.

Sawyer is at the stove. He's wearing a tight fitting faded black t-shirt that accentuates his athletic physique. The McGinn's t-shirt and loose-fitting chef's jacket he was wearing over it last night made him look stocky. I never would have guessed he looked like *that* underneath.

I wonder if he heard the messages, Ned's in particular. If Chloe was in my position right now, she'd ask and immediately go into damage-control mode. Me? I said I wonder, not that I care all that much.

"How about some eggs?" He asks, already whisking them and without looking my way.

"Mm-hmm," I garble. *And go right ahead, make yourself at home.*

Sawyer peeks curiously over his shoulder just in time to catch me scurrying off to ditch my toothbrush in the bathroom. I pause at the mirror and consider brushing my hair and dousing myself with a splash of daylily body spray before deciding not to waste my time. We've already had sex, so what difference does it make if I look or smell decent now?

"So . . ." I say, sauntering into the kitchen and leaning against the counter next to the stove. Sawyer shifts his gaze away from the eggs he's in the process of scrambling to look at me for a second, an inscrutable grin on his lips. "How did we end up . . . you know . . ."

"You warned me you wouldn't remember anything after we left the bar," he chuckles, turning the burner to low and moving to the fridge.

"Well," I shrug, "at least I was being honest."

He chuckles again as he deposits a few things from the fridge onto the counter. Then he opens and closes a few cabinets and drawers, retrieving coffee mugs, plates, forks and a cheese grater. His movements are fluid and precise, as if he's been in my kitchen before. "How admirable of you." Smiling, he fills the mugs with coffee and hands one to me before turning to grate cheese onto the eggs.

I add a spoonful of sugar and a splash of milk to my coffee as I admire his backside and wonder what he thinks of our little tryst. This isn't the first time I've brought a guy home and not remembered the sex. Some guys are offended by it. Some act like they're fine with it at first but then end up confessing they're actually a little hurt. And then there are the ones who can relate. The ones who sometimes don't even remember my name. I wonder where Sawyer falls on the spectrum.

"So how was last night, anyway?" I ask playfully.

He turns with a dead serious expression and moves closer to me so that we're only about a foot apart. Then he reaches out and slowly runs his fingers through my hair and down my cheek to my chin as he whispers, "Wouldn't you like to know?"

The way he's looking at me, I expect him to kiss me and carry me back to the bedroom, or tear off my robe and take me right here on the kitchen counter. I certainly wouldn't raise any objections at this point.

Instead, a sly grin spreads across his face as he spins back toward the stove and begins plating our breakfast, causing my jaw to drop.

I close my mouth and exhale after what seems like minutes even though it couldn't have been more than a few seconds. For some reason, the sudden thought that he could be a total player pisses me off, so I say the first thing that pops into my head.

"Look, Sawyer, you're not the first guy I've come home with and not remembered a thing about . . . It's nothing against your abilities or anything."

I immediately feel like an idiot for saying something so stupid, but to my surprise, he laughs as he turns to face me again. He's holding plates filled with toast, cheesy scrambled eggs, sliced green onions, and dollops of salsa and sour cream.

"Relax, Freckles. Despite what you might think, I'm not the kind of guy who takes advantage of a drunk woman. But trust me, my *abilities* are just fine. Better than fine, in fact." He waggles his eyebrows at me. Then without missing a beat, he asks, "Ready to eat?" before heading out of my cozy kitchen and into the dining room.

"You're full of it," I say as I follow, wondering if he's telling the truth about last night and pretending to not be the slightest bit affected by what he's just said about his abilities. In reality, his confidence gives me tingles.

I take a seat in front of an exquisitely plated meal and look to Sawyer for a response to my skepticism.

He shrugs. "I'm telling you, we didn't have sex."

He hungrily digs into his eggs.

"Then why is there a trail of clothes in the hallway?"

Chewing, he shakes his head and grins. "Let's just say you made it hard for me to resist." He glances down at my plate. "Food's getting cold."

I still don't know if I believe him but decide to shelf the conversation for now.

A comfortable silence settles in while we devour our Tex-Mex-style breakfast. The kind of silence that's usually only possible after you've known someone for a while. It reminds me of the easy feeling I had when we discussed the concept of online dating and Love Connection.

When we're both done polishing off our food, we settle into a discussion about cats versus dogs. Unlike most guys I know who prefer dogs, Sawyer is a fan of both. He tells me all about the cats he had as a kid and asks questions about mine, including how long they've been with me and where I got them from. I'm floored when he picks up Mags and holds her like a baby, and I'm shocked that she doesn't wiggle her way out of his arms. She just lies there staring up at him as he rubs her tummy. I wonder if maybe it's a sign, but then roll my eyes at the absurdity of the thought.

I've just finished refilling our mugs with fresh coffee when the phone rings. My first reaction is to let the answering machine get it, but then I realize it could be Ned. He gets up early sometimes on Saturdays and Sundays to hit the golf course. So by the third ring, I jump to my feet and dive for the handset.

"Hello?"

"How did it go with Free Bird?" Chloe chirps.

"Why are you calling so early?"

"I don't know. I went to bed early last night so now I'm up early. How was the date?"

"Eh," I say as I head back to the dining room for my coffee. Sawyer is already busy clearing our empty plates off the table."

"What do you mean? Eh, as in, *he-was-okay-so-we-might-go-on-another-date* eh? Or eh, as in, *he-was-no-good-in-bed* eh?"

"Eh, as in, *remind-me-why-you-thought-it-was-a-good-idea-to-sign-me-up-for-online-dating* eh."

"That sucks. But don't forget, you promised you wouldn't throw in the towel until you've gone on three consecutive *bad* dates in a row."

"Right," I say, nodding in gratitude to Sawyer who's just added a splash of milk to my coffee. "How could I forget?"

"You can't. Not with me around, anyway," she says proudly. "So, do you have another date already lined up? Or do you need me to—"

"Hey, Chloe, I'm actually kind of in the middle of something right now. Can I give you a call in an hour or so?" Sawyer is busy cleaning up my kitchen like he owns the place, which is sort of starting to bug me. Or maybe it's the fact that all of a sudden I think I might be a little hung over. Either way, I need to wrap things up with this guy before I can get into this with Chloe.

"Waaaait a second. What do you mean you're in the middle of something? Who's over?"

Most of the time I love how close Chloe and I are, the way we're able to read into what the other says for hidden meaning. Not this time, though.

"One of the cooks from McGinn's," I whisper, walking down the hall to the bathroom. I snatch my clothes from the night before off the ground along the way. "But I'm about to shoo him out of here." I close the door as I toss the clothes into a corner.

"But, I thought you said you weren't going to—"

"I know, I know, okay? But he says nothing happened."

"What do you mean *he says*? You don't remember?"

"No, and trust me, I know how bad that sounds. I'm sure I was all over him, though, so why would he lie about us not doing it?

"Well, maybe—"

"Wait, hold that thought. I should really get going. Are you free for lunch in a few hours? I'm sure I'll be ready to scarf down some greasy food after I get some more sleep. Then we can finish talking about this too."

"Works for me. I *do* have some Daran stuff I need to talk to you about. What do you feel like? Beans and Barley? Ma Fischer's?"

Hmm, Daran stuff. Probably means she's thought up another miniscule reason to question their relationship. It's only been three months since they met online, and the guy has already successfully weathered a few of Chloe's attempts to push him away. I'm hoping this means good things to come for them in the future. "I don't know. How about you pick me up around noon, and then we'll decide?"

"Sounds good. See you then."

I return the phone to its base, and then note the spic-and-span condition of the kitchen. It occurs to me that Chloe would appreciate this guy, since tidiness ranks high on her list of desirable qualities in a mate. Me? I'm satisfied if a guy can manage to hit the inside of the toilet on a regular basis. Though, if he can put the toilet seat down, bonus points.

"Sawyer?" I peek around the corner into the living room. No sign of him or the t-shirt I threw over the arm of the chair earlier, so I head to the only other possible place he could be, wondering along the way if there's a chance he took off without saying goodbye. It wouldn't be the first time, but a bit unusual considering the whole five-star breakfast service he just pulled. "Sawyer?"

"Oh, hey," He looks up from the chest at the foot of my bed where he's putting on his boots. "I'll be out of your hair in a sec."

"Oh, no worries. Don't rush," I lie. "Thanks for the breakfast," I say, flopping sideways onto my bed and propping my head up to look at him.

He stands and takes a few steps toward the door as he turns to face me, grinning. "So, how'd Chloe take the news?" He gestures with a thumb in the general direction of the hallway.

"What news? Wait . . . how'd you know who I was talking to?"

"Wow. You really don't remember, do you?" I respond with two raised eyebrows and a shrug. He laughs and explains, "You told me she'd be calling this morning. And you mentioned she might be disappointed with you for ditching that guy you met online for me."

"Oh, pfft. She's fine. As gung-ho as she is about me making the most of my subscription, she definitely doesn't want me suffering through any bad dates."

"Well, that's a relief." He grins and seems undecided about leaving. I suspect he's debating whether to kiss me goodbye. But he turns with a wave instead. "See ya around, Jesstine."

Jesstine? No one calls me that. In fact, most people don't even know Jess is just a nickname. I wonder what prompted me to tell Sawyer. But by the time it occurs to me to ask, my apartment door closes. "See ya, Sawyer," I whisper, rolling onto my back and closing my eyes so I can try to remember something from after we got to my apartment . . . anything.

Nothing concrete comes to me.

I hop out of bed and get busy changing my sheets like I always do after an encounter such as last night's. I toss the final piece of used bedding toward my wicker hamper, but it falls into the garbage can next to my desk instead. As I transfer the pillowcase to its intended destination, I notice a balled up heap of unwrapped condoms and condom wrappers in the trash.

My lips form into a sheepish grin, and I wonder why Sawyer would lie about last night. Then I shrug off my confusion because it really doesn't matter. Too bad I screwed up. He probably would have been a good one to spend more time getting to know before hopping into bed with him.

I sure do suck at turning over new leafs.

chapter seven

"So, tell me what's going on with Dar—"

"Hold that thought." Chloe's hand goes up as she interrupts me. "Who am I?" She begins obnoxiously snapping overhead and calling out "Hey, toots, yeah you. That's right..." in the direction of a cluster of Ma Fischer's wait staff. Then she laughs so hard she emits a snort.

I roll my eyes and take a sip of water, not interested in playing along. Sharing details about my short-lived date with Free Bird was torture enough. I'm certainly not up for Chloe's jokes right now.

"Oh shit. Our waitress thinks . . ." Chloe half stands and waves her off. "No, no. I wasn't . . . It was just a joke . . ." The waitress half smiles and turns back to her post next to the order window, probably cursing about the idiot with the ponytail. Chloe cozies back into her seat, a grin forming on her face again. "Sorry, I couldn't resist. Not after the way you and Ned made fun of my first online date. Remember that Scott guy?"

"You mean snot guy?" Now I'm the one smiling. "He had that really cool Members Only jacket and—"

"Alright, alright, enough. I think we're even," she says, throwing a balled up napkin at me. "So what's up with the cook?

I shrug. "Nothing's up." And normally that's where conversation about a one-nighter would end for me. But this time, Sawyer's gorgeous eyes pop into my head, and I hear his gruff voice—*see ya around, Jesstine*—and I can't help but look forward to seeing him again. Too bad I messed up by sleeping with him already.

I glance up at Chloe and grab my water, suddenly feeling warm. This guilt over having sex on a first date—which technically wasn't even a date—is all new to me.

"Alright." She shrugs and unwraps her silverware as she continues.

"I'm only asking because you said you may or may not have gotten it on."

"Yeah, about that. I found a bunch of condoms and wrappers in the garbage. So I guess I'm not the only one whose memory of last night is spotty."

"Maybe he couldn't get it up and the condoms were never used?" Chloe suggests.

I shrug. "I doubt it, but whatever. I fucked up. So much for getting to know the next guy I sleep with."

"Oh stop! So you slipped up. If you think you might like him, you can still get to know him."

I smile at Chloe in appreciation for her support. "True, but if I get the job at McGinn's, I might need to reexamine the lessons I've learned about dating guys I work with."

"I think what you mean is the lessons you've learned about dating *married* guys you work with." She raises an eyebrow at me, and I toss the balled up napkin back at her. "Hey, it's true though, right? I'm not trying to be an ass. There's nothing wrong with dating a co-worker."

Our food arrives and we focus on eating for a good five minutes before it occurs to me we haven't talked about Daran yet.

"So? How's Daran?"

Chloe puts a finger up and starts chewing faster, so I take another bite of my BLT. After her chewing tapers off, she takes a sip of water, dabs her mouth with a napkin, and scans our surroundings. Then she leans in as far as possible without climbing onto the table.

"He shaved me last night," she whispers with cupped hands circling her mouth.

"Really? Where?"

Her eyes get real big and glance downward.

"Ooooooh . . . straight-laced Daran has an alter ego in the bedroom? I never would have guessed."

She nods and then whispers, "I feel so . . . naked. And itchy. And it was so *messy*."

I wave her off. "Who cares if he shaved your cooch? You've never shaved it before?"

"No way!" She sits upright and looks around again. "Why? Have you?"

I'm chewing, so I affirm with raised eyebrows and a shrug.

"Really? Wait, who shaved it? You or someone else?"

"Both," I say, still chewing.

"Oh." Chloe wrinkles her nose. "Well, that's not all."

I grin devilishly and rub my palms together. "Let's hear it. Spit it out!"

"Before he shaved me . . ." *For the love of Pete! Stop looking around and say it.* ". . . he tied my wrists to his headboard."

My grin melts into a look of boredom as I shake my head and pop the last bit of my sandwich into my mouth.

"What? You don't think that's kinky? I mean, all this time I thought he was a clean-cut momma's boy, and now this." She cups her cheeks and props her elbows on the table.

"Nope. Doesn't rate too high on my personal kink-o-meter. Now, if there was a camera involved, that could be kinky!"

Chloe's eyes become real big and her head zips left then right in one swift arc. "Shhhh!"

"Alright, enough of the paranoid schoolteacher crap. What's wrong with the word kinky? Kinky, kinky, kinky!" I say, increasing my volume with each repetition of the word. "It's not a big deal, Chloe. No one is even listening to us." Except for the four guys in the adjacent booth. One waves and the others laugh. I wave back.

"Thanks a lot, Jess," Chloe says, crossing her arms over her chest.

"For what? Who cares what they think? Back to Mr. Kinky. You guys have been dating for a while now. Live a little, Chloe." I hold my hands up, palms clamped together with fingertips touching. "Try something other than missionary." My devilish grin returns as I slide-turn my palms so that my fingertips are to my wrists.

"Oh, you mean like . . ." A look of recognition spreads across her face. "Gross."

"Hey, don't knock it 'til you try it. Especially now that you're all nice and clean down there."

"That's disgusting. How are we even friends?" she says, looking around with a hint of a grin on her lips. "And for the record, I have done *non-missionary* things before."

"Not gross. Adventurous. The way you two have been going at it, he must be itching to experiment a little. I mean, how can you not be? I'm not saying you should do something you're uncomfortable with, but you said yourself that you feel more at ease around Daran than any guy you've ever been with. So why not let go of some of your inhibitions in the bedroom? It'll be good for you, good for your relationship."

She pokes at the ice in her water and shakes her head. "I don't know. Considering all the stuff we did last night, I wonder what else he's done. I mean, he's been all over the world, and he's admitted to sleeping with at least a dozen women. The thought kinda intimidates me if I think about it too much."

"Then don't think about it. Who cares what or *who* he's done in the past? He's doing you now. Right?"

"I guess. But Shelly thinks—"

"Stop right there," I warn, covering my ears long enough to make a point. Hearing Shelly's name pisses me off. "I don't want to hear what she thinks because: A, I'm not interested, and B, she doesn't know what she's talking about. And if that isn't enough for you, I'll remind you what C stands for when it comes to that—"

"Okay! I get it. Sheesh. When are you going to get over it? That tiff we had didn't even have anything to do with you."

I open my mouth, ready to protest, but the waitress arrives to leave the bill and offers to refill our waters. I settle for a disappointed shake of the head over Chloe's last statement. Any time someone disrespects my best friend, it has to do with me.

Shelly is Chloe's friend from college and ex-roommate. Although, "friend" is putting it generously. Chloe is an intelligent woman. I mean, she's a teacher. Teachers have to be intelligent, right? And she's generally not a pushover. But the way she keeps up her friendship with Shelly after how that bitch treated her is baffling.

Back when Chloe started online dating, Shelly was supportive about her dating multiple people and encouraged her to ditch her habit of moving too quickly into something exclusive. But when Shelly became serious with her current boyfriend, Craig, she started belittling Chloe for enjoying the freedom of dating around. Then Shelly's brother Tom showed an interest in Chloe, but Shelly insinuated that Chloe could not date her brother because she's not "relationship material." Chloe walked away that night feeling as though she'd been called a slut by someone she considered to be a close friend. So they stopped talking, and Chloe even avoided the Home Bar where they typically hung out every Wednesday for ladies' night. Unfortunately, two months later a mutual friend invited Chloe and Shelly to a party where they were reunited. To make matters worse, Shelly was all excited to find out that Chloe and Daran were dating exclusively. That meant Shelly and Craig had a couple to go on double dates with.

I can't believe I still have to put up with that judgmental bitch. In my opinion, Chloe should have told Shelly to fuck off when she saw her at the surprise party. But she's just too forgiving of a friend to do something like that. Me, on the other hand . . . let's just say Chloe is the yin to my yang.

"*Anyway* . . . I assume you still plan to go out with Kyle again?" Chloe asks.

"Hang on. First, promise me you're not going to flake out on Daran just yet."

"Nope. I'm good . . . *we're* good. I just need to figure out some stuff, I guess."

Not exactly a promise but probably all I'm going to get out of her right now. "Alright, but no over-thinking anything. Okay?"

"Got it. Now, back to you. What about Kyle?"

"Yeah," I say with a shrug. "I mean, I haven't heard from him yet, but I'm pretty sure we'll go out again."

"Good," she says, nodding. "What else? Any other dates lined up?"

"I actually have one on Thursday and another on Friday," I say before taking a quick sip of water.

"Oooh. Two in one week. That'll keep your mind off of Ned."

Not really, but I know better than to open that can of worms, so I nod. "I guess. But it's not like my mind is *always* on Ned."

She ignores that. "Where are you meeting them?"

"I'm meeting the first guy at some bar near Miller Park for Thursday night karaoke. Then on Fri—"

"Karaoke? Really?"

Chloe loves watching people do karaoke almost as much as she loves cleaning her apartment, so I sense a double date in my near future.

"Yep. Why? Do you and Daran want to—"

"Join you? Damn right, we do! That is, if you don't mind. And maybe you should check with your date first. What's his name?" She asks, handing the waitress an empty plate.

"Well, I don't know his real name yet, but his screen name is . . . Karaoke . . ." A chuckle starts in my stomach and works its way upward as I picture this guy's ridiculous moniker.

"Karaoke? What's so funny about that?"

"No, no . . . it's Karaoke Wayward Son."

A smile spreads across Chloe's face. "Actually that is kinda funny. Clever funny. A clever karaoke fan. You might have found yourself a winner here."

Nodding her head, she gives me a wide smile, and having her vote of approval suddenly has me second-guessing agreeing to go out with a guy because of a ridiculous screen name that made me laugh.

After all, I really can't stand karaoke.

chapter eight

It's five o'clock when I finally return home. Somehow I let Chloe persuade me to see *Dawn of the Dead* at Budget Theaters after we had lunch. Ugh. I don't blame Daran for not wanting to see it with her. I spent half the movie rolling my eyes at her extreme reactions, and now my head hurts.

The first thing I do when I enter my apartment is pop a couple of Tylenol. Then I preheat the oven to make a frozen pizza and pour myself a glass of cheap red wine.

I mosey into the living room and find my furry roommates congregated together in a shrinking sunny spot on the carpet. "What do you say, kitties? Shall we take a peek at my Personals account?" After the movie I just saw, I could use some quality entertainment. I take a sip of wine and plop myself down on the living room floor. I hardly use my desk or table, so my laptop is usually stationed on the large storage ottoman in my living room, or on my lap in bed.

My dashboard is full of red notifications when I log in. Yahoo! Personals has sent me dozens of new matches, and now there are five messages, six pokes and four icebreakers. Earlier today, I brushed off Chloe's suggestion that I should be checking my account daily. I don't even check my email every day. But now that I see what two days' worth of Personals notifications looks like, maybe she's right.

It doesn't take me long to decide what to do with the pokes and icebreakers. Any guy who resorts to a poke has got to have self-esteem issues. I mean, you're already hiding behind a computer screen and you can't muster the courage to type *Hey, how's it going*? or even a simple *Hello*? And then there's the icebreaker guy. Please *grow a pair.*

I have a good click/delete rhythm going, but the final icebreaker makes me pause. It's from a woman. I'm tempted for half a second to check out her profile but decide it would be a waste of time. I'm already pretty sure I'm not into women. As I click delete, the oven beeps, prompting me to put the pizza in. Then I set the timer, top off my wine, and resume my position in front of my laptop screen.

Now for the messages.

I start with the oldest one, which was received from Coordinates Kyle yesterday at eight a.m.

Hey Jess,

I know we exchanged numbers, but I was poking around on here so I figured I'd drop you a line. Plus I can't imagine asking you what I'm about to ask you over the phone so…

As you know, I haven't been back in the dating world for very long since my breakup with Amy, so I'm kind of rusty at reading women. (Plus those damn hiccups were distracting me!) I'll just come out and ask instead of dragging this on…. When you said you'd like to go out with me again, did you really mean it? Or were you just being polite? Because I'm not that guy whose feelings will be hurt if you say you're not interested. Besides, I'm not looking for anything serious. Just a friend who's fun and easy to talk to. (But anything more would be a bonus.) And you seem to fit that bill.

Anyway, if you're really interested in getting together again, how about tonight?

Kyle

At first, I don't feel bad for not responding to Kyle yesterday. After all, I haven't been active online since Thursday evening, right before I left to meet up with him at Tiki Time. But then I remember that the dating site shows when people last logged on to the site (talk about enabling stalkers), and my profile would have indicated that I had logged in yesterday afternoon before my date with Free Bird. I feel a twinge of guilt in the pit of my stomach because I don't like the thought of making a nice guy like Kyle feel ignored. Ned's phone used to magically erase my messages quite often, so I know exactly how it feels.

Kyle had been active two hours earlier, but now he's logged out. I click to respond.

Hey Coordinates Kyle,

Online dating tip #1: Check your messages on a daily basis.

Sorry I didn't read your message until now! I promise I wasn't avoiding you. I just suck at checking messages. I logged in yesterday to view a profile and then logged right back out. Had I read your message then, I would have definitely been open to meeting up. Anyway, I hope you had a productive day of mapmaking yesterday, and I hope you're doing something equally as fun this weekend.

I won't be around for the next few days because I'm heading out of town for work. Maybe we can hang out when I get back!!

Jess

I hesitate before sending the message because I have no idea why I told him I would have been open to meeting up. I guess I have a soft spot for Kyle after seeing the despair in his eyes when he told me his breakup story the other night, and the thought of making him feel paranoid over an unanswered invitation just makes me feel bad. So what harm is there in a little white lie to boost his ego? I hit send and move on to the next message, which was delivered last night around ten.

BossMan411 is a cat lover. He's one of the less memorable guys I've met so far. In my last message to him, I sent a few answers to some basic questions he'd asked. I also sent my email address because the Personals site doesn't allow photos to be attached to messages, and he wanted to share a few pictures of his cats.

Jess,

Thanks for the answers. Turns out we have more in common than just our love for Skittles and cats. My favorite type of music is country too! I've been to at least a dozen concerts. Garth Brooks, John Michael Montgomery, Rascal Flatts, Brad Paisley, etc. Lots of the big namers. Do you like concerts? Maybe we can go to one sometime, but first we should probably ease our way into talking on the phone. What do you think? Also, do you have any questions for me?

I'll email you those pics of my cats I promised right after I send this message. I'd love if you responded with some pics of yours in return…

Until next time,
BossMan411

Yeah, I have a question. What the hell is your name? The fact that he closed with his screen name for a third time now is irritating for some reason. If he can't reveal his real name he must be hiding something. But what? As I continue pondering why BossMan411 has never offered his name, I open a new window so I can check my email. I want to see the guy's cats, and I'm hoping to get a better look at him since he's wearing a hat in his profile picture.

I wince when I log in and find fifty-eight unread emails and fourteen messages in my spam folder. BossMan411's message is the fifth one down in my inbox. The subject is MEOWWW, which strikes me as weird. But then again, who am I to say what's normal? I click expecting to see photos of the furry creatures he described in his first message to me, and that's exactly what I find, except that's not all I find. Mouth open, I examine the images, not really sure where to focus my attention. Sure, I love a cute cat as much as the next girl, but I'm also not one to pass up a sneak peek of a dick. Wow, this is really something.

The first photo is of a large, fluffy black and white cat lying on a light gray comforter. Lying on his side behind the cat is BossMan411. I'm guessing it's him, anyway, because his head has been cropped out of the picture. He appears to be nude, but the cat is concealing his midsection, so maybe not. The second photo is of an orange tabby cat sitting on the floor in front of a full-length mirror. Standing behind the cat is the same person from the first picture, evidence by the distinctive tattoo around his bicep. BossMan411's physique isn't bad, I'll give him that. But nude pics with cats? That's downright creepy, so I don't plan on sending him any pics in return or a return message for that matter. He'll get the hint. Sorry BossMan411. You've definitely made yourself memorable, just not for the right reasons.

Before deleting the photos, I forward them to Chloe along with a quick message: *This guy wants to know if I think his cats are cute. What do you think?*

I delete all the messages in my spam folder, still trying to shake off BossMan411's creepy cat pics. Then I quickly scroll through my inbox, checking all the junk for deletion and saving everything else for tomorrow. I have plenty of time for checking and responding to emails when I'm overnight for work. I close the window and get back to the remaining Yahoo! Personals messages.

The next one was sent late last night and is from the guy I'm meeting on Thursday. We already established what and where but never discussed when.

Hi there Jess,

I hope you had a pleasant Friday evening. In case you were wondering, mine was spectacular... Took second place in the American Legion Club of Muskego's third annual karaoke competition! Did I mention I'm a karaoke fanatic? Like you couldn't figure it out from my screen name!

Anyway... I'm looking forward to meeting you on Thursday night. But just to warn you, I usually take the stage at least five times on a good night. Maybe we can sing one together? It would definitely be a great way to test our compatibility! So get your vocal cords ready!

So 7:00 on Thursday at Ron & Roy's on 34th and Greenfield.

See you then!
Brandon

Gnawing on my thumbnail, I count the number of exclamation points in Karaoke Wayward Son's message. Five seems ridiculously excessive. I click to reply. Then my fingers hover over the keyboard for a second.

Brandon,

Wow, second place in a karaoke competition. That's . . .

Hmm. How exactly do I feel about that? Impressed? Surprised? Interested? No. Nope. And Uh-uh. But it does tickle my funny bone.

Brandon,

So, I hate to do this, but . . .

Instead of finishing the message, I click on his profile. And for the third time I'm impressed by how attractive he is . . . in his profile picture, anyway. But that's not even what made me accept his invitation to meet up this week. It was his screen name that sold me. I couldn't stop giggling about it. Although, all the wine I drank that night might have had a little something to do with my amusement.

Karaoke Wayward Son – 31
Location: Muskego
Looking for a lady with love in her heart and rhythm in her bones.

Relationship Status: Never Married

Kids: No
Want Kids: Yes
Ethnicity: White
Body type: Slim
Height: 5' 10"
Religion: Non-Denominational
Politics: Middle of the Road
Smoke: No Way
Drink: Socially
Pets: Yes
Education: Associate's
Employment: Facilities Maintenance
Income: 40,000-60,000

~

Sure enough, it makes me giggle again. I need to meet this guy, even if it ends up only being for a good laugh. So I delete my second attempt at a response, and start over.

Brandon,

Wow, second place! What an accomplishment! I look forward to hearing you sing.
See you Thursday at 7!

Jess

I click send and move on to the next message from my date for Friday night, JustJustin77. It was sent a few hours ago. Justin and I have been messaging back and forth since the night I set up my profile. He's the one who opened communication with a dumb knock-knock joke. Our exchange went something like this:

JustJustin77: Knock knock.

Me: Okay, I'll play along. Who's there?

JustJustin77: Cheese.

Me: Cheese who?

JustJustin77: Cheese you're pretty!

Of course I laughed because the joke was so stupid it was funny. And then I actually spent some time reading his stats, when all I'd previously done with anyone else's profile was scan.

~

JustJustin77 – 28
Location: Pewaukee
A Bottle of Red, A Bottle of White

Relationship Status: Divorced
Kids: Yes
Want More Kids: Yes
Ethnicity: Tell you later
Body type: Athletic
Height: 5' 9"
Religion: Christian
Politics: Middle of the Road
Smoke: No
Drink: Socially
Pets: No
Education: Master's degree
Employment: Operations Management
Income: 80,000-100,000

~

The fact that he was divorced and has at least one child stood out and made me reconsider continuing our correspondence at first. So I went back and reread our exchange. I thought about all the lame pickup lines I've heard while out at bars over the years and wracked my brain trying to remember if anyone had ever used a joke to break the ice with me before. Justin was the first, and that was when I decided I didn't care that he was divorced or that he's a dad. That was also when I admitted to myself for the first time that online dating might not be so bad. But admitting that to anyone, especially Chloe, would be like betraying the pessimistic little girl inside my head who thinks the whole concept is just plain dumb. So I've kept it to myself. I'm not sure why I feel I owe that little girl anything. I just do.

To be honest, besides the fact that I've begun to wonder why Ned hasn't called, Justin is a big reason why I logged on tonight. All of his messages are so pleasant and normal. I don't get the sense at all that he's trying to be something he's not, which is something I've sensed from a lot of the guys I've come across online. Or could I just be paranoid after having a front-row seat to Chloe's Circus of online dating experiences?

No, probably not. People definitely stretch the truth when they're hiding behind a computer.

Hi Jess,

How goes it? Max's party last night was a riot. Paintball, pizza and then a bonfire. Ahhh, to be six again and have an unlimited supply of energy! Tonight will be more laid back. We plan to grill some steaks, shoot some hoops and watch a movie. Action/adventure. Your favorite! Kidding, kidding.

Well, just wanted to touch base and see how your weekend is treating you. I know you fly out early tomorrow morning so no worries if you don't get back to me right away. But hopefully we can "chat" a few more times before our date next Friday night. Looking forward to it.

All the best!
Justin

After typing out a quick reply, I mean to move on to the final message from someone with the screen name 'Scotty' but accidentally click to view my new matches instead. When I see his face, my heart rate increases tenfold and the nachos I had at the movie theater threaten to evacuate my stomach.

It's Ryan Cross.

chapter nine

Ryan looks the same as he did when we were in grade school, but with whiskers and sans the baby fat. He still has a pursed-lip grin and the horizontal scar above his left eyebrow from when he got hit in the face with a baseball in fifth grade. The deep dimple on his left cheek can be found on every single school picture he's ever taken. Then there's his light blond hair, of course. I recall overhearing our third grade teacher, Mrs. Suthers, telling him it would probably darken by the time he reached middle school to match the coloring of his two older siblings. She was wrong.

I never thought Ryan was cute back then. He was just another boy whose class I ended up in every year of grade school and who blended in with the crowd. The kind of boy I considered a good friend but never thought of as boyfriend material until it was too late.

I want to click through to see his profile, but I'm hesitant after our last encounter as adults. The little arrow on my computer screen hovers over his face as memories creep from my brain and make their way to my heart. The unexpected surge of emotion causes me to lower the lid of my laptop. Maybe I can just pretend I never saw his picture pop up . . .

Then again, maybe not.

I quickly reopen my laptop, heart racing. I'm in such a hurry to get back to his profile that I incorrectly enter the password on my home screen two times. When I finally get it right and Ryan's face reappears, I click on it immediately without considering the fact that he'll see I've viewed his profile.

Damn . . . Oh well, what's done is done.

~

HistoryBuff – 26
Location: Waukesha
Seeking a Beautiful Mind

Relationship Status: Single
Kids: No
Want Kids: Yes
Ethnicity: Caucasian
Body type: Fit
Height: 5' 11"
Religion: Catholic
Politics: Liberal
Smoke: No
Drink: Socially
Pets: No
Education: Bachelor's Degree
Employment: Education
Income: 30,000-40,000

~

Ryan got good grades and used to tutor people in high school, so the fact that he works in the education field doesn't surprise me. Nothing else surprises me either, except maybe his political stance, given his parents were hardcore Republicans.

We lived down the block from the Cross's before we moved to Mukwonago. Their professionally manicured lawn always displayed multiple political signs for whatever elections were going on. I only knew the signs were in support of the most conservative candidates because my stepdad often made snide comments when we would drive by, calling Ryan's parents immature names like "republiturds" or "repuppetcons." In addition to the signs, Ryan's mom always tried to strike up political conversations with other parents when she'd pick him up from school. I'll never forget how red his face turned when we were in second grade and his mom dropped off cupcakes adorned with mini flags endorsing Ronald Reagan for president. I wonder what made him reject his parents' political leanings?

As soon as I'm done scanning Ryan's stats, I click to view three additional photos he uploaded. Who knew he'd turn into such a fine specimen? After ogling his photos for a few minutes, I return to his tagline. *Seeking a Beautiful Mind*. I can't help but wonder if he's been burned by someone whose beautiful exterior deceived him.

The last time I saw him was at a popular bar in downtown Milwaukee. He'd been approached by several drop-dead gorgeous women—the kind that looked like they belonged in a Victoria's Secret commercial. Not surprising either. He'd gone from an underdeveloped, homely looking mama's boy to a muscular, designer-thread-wearing Adonis with a perfect smile. I remember when his pearly whites were hidden behind braces and his skin was dotted with blackheads.

I catch myself smiling at Ryan's main profile picture when the oven timer starts beeping. The scent wafting from the kitchen should have been enough to alert me the pizza was done, but I didn't even notice because I was so wrapped up in Ryan's profile. For a second, I contemplate leaving his profile up so I can message him. Instead I steal one last look at his handsome face and log out of Yahoo! Personals for the night. I highly doubt he wants to hear from me.

As I stand at the kitchen counter eating pizza, I mentally prepare myself to ignore Ned if he calls or comes over tonight. He mentioned in his message from yesterday that he didn't have plans tonight and wanted to see me, but that doesn't necessarily mean I'll hear from him. That's one of the most frustrating things about Ned, you can't trust anything he says. For example, he *says* he's accepted that our relationship is over, yet he's ended up in my bed after bar close almost every Saturday night for the past three months. It's definitely time to break him of that habit.

Who am I kidding? It's time to break myself of that habit and let Ned worry about himself.

I wrap up the leftover pizza, and pour myself another glass of wine, leaving about a quarter of the bottle. Then I make my way to the bathroom for my hot date: a tub full of bubbles.

As the tub fills, I light a few candles and grab a book just in case I decide to read for a while. Then I slide into the steamy water and lie back against the inflatable plastic pillow suctioned to the tub. The fluffy sheath of bubbles covering my body reminds me of when I was a kid. I always put way too much bubble bath in the water, so much that sometimes I could hide within the fluffy mass that formed.

I use my index finger to flick the surface, causing a spray of bubbles to hit the wall. I smile at a memory it elicits of my dad and me competing once to see who could flick bubbles farther. We had so much fun until my stepmom barged in and had a cow over all the water that had splashed outside the tub. After my half-sister Ashley was born, my dad didn't have as much time to hang out with me while I got ready for bed. Instead he had to take care of Ashley while my stepmom cleaned up the dinner dishes or made lunches for the following day. The resentment I felt toward both my stepmom and Ashley still lingers to this day, even though I've always known how selfish my feelings were.

Enough. What's gotten into you? Why the sad thoughts all of a sudden? Maybe it's an aftereffect from watching that stupid zombie movie with Chloe. Too much death or something. Next time I'm going to insist on an unrealistic rom-com.

Lying on my back as flat as possible, I submerge my ears and close my eyes. Usually this relaxes me, but at the moment all I see in the darkness behind my eyelids are flashes of screen names, stats, Ryan Cross, Ned, and BossMan411's happy trail. I quickly slide out of the water and when my eyes flutter open, I'm scared shitless by two green eyes and whiskers grazing my cheek. My cat Savannah freaks out too, yowling as she slips and her back paw enters the water. She falls to the floor with a thud and skitters away, the sound of her back claws clacking against the tile floor.

"Serves you right, you nosy little shit," I quietly laugh as I crawl out of the tub and reach for my towel. So much for a relaxing bath. Oh well. I need to pack for the work trip ahead of me anyway. Six a.m. to Columbus will be here before I know it.

After I dry off, I wrap up my hair in a towel and throw on the least sexy thing I own—a puffy yellow terry cloth robe. I haven't worn the thing in over a year because it had been shoved into the back of my linen closet one night when Ned showed up unannounced. After securing the robe around my waist, I stand in front of the bathroom mirror and smile. I've missed the comfort of this ratty old robe.

It's ten forty-five and still no call from Ned. I remind myself that it's a blessing in disguise and fight the urge to check again if he texted, despite the fact that I would ignore him anyway. Bad habits die hard I guess.

I've been in bed for nearly an hour, but my cats aren't snuggled up to me like usual because I keep tossing and turning. It isn't all about Ned either.

I can't stop thinking about Ryan Cross. If one of my girlfriends confessed to having obsessive thoughts similar to the ones I'm having tonight, I would tell her to just knock it off and move on. Why is it always so much easier to give relationship advice than it is to take it?

I watch the red digital numbers illuminating my nightstand as the time changes from ten fifty to ten fifty-one. What is wrong with me? My stomach is in knots over a guy who pined over me when we were kids. A guy I snubbed time after time. And look at me now. I'm addicted to a guy who's all talk and no action, and the talk is usually about *him* and what he wants instead of *me* or *us*. What's even more disturbing is I broke up with him three months ago, yet here I am wondering if he's going to try to see me tonight.

I hop out of bed, settle on the floor next to my closet, and remove the heart-decorated Keds box from the lower left compartment of a shoe rack. I remove the cover, and there's a Molly McGinn's coaster right on top where I knew it would be. (Even when I'm drunk, I somehow always manage to grab a coaster.) Sawyer's name is scrawled in my chicken scratch handwriting in the upper right corner of the large four-leaf clover in the bar's logo.

The box dates back to a sixth grade Valentine's Day party. I spent hours decorating it, hoping Toby Johnson—with the cool rattail, spiky hair and skateboard—would slip me a Valentine that professed his love for me. Well, Toby never came through, but sweet Ryan Cross—with the Polo shirts, khaki shorts and mountain bike—gave me one that all the girls were jealous of. It was a homemade red heart, complete with silver glitter and a doily fringe border. It read: *My heart beats only for you.* A tiny heart with the initials *RC* appeared just below the sweet message. On the playground after school, while all the girls were giggling, oohing and ahhing over Ryan's Valentine, I was busy watching Toby do tricks on his skateboard with the other skaters. Later that night, when I went through all of the Valentines, candy, tattoos and other junk, my mom examined Ryan's work of art and let out a big *awwwww*. But her expression slowly went from lighthearted to sad. She sighed heavily.

What's wrong? I asked.

Well, Jess, this here is a boy who has the potential to make someone a sweet husband someday. It's just a shame that by the time he's old enough, that innocent little heart of his will likely have been broken many times over, and he'll end up like so many others.

I shrugged because I had no idea what she meant at the time and I didn't care because I wasn't interested in sweet Ryan. I liked the troublemakers. The ones who made fart noises in class, the ones who snapped girls' bras, the ones who would stand around at recess making fun of people instead of playing kickball.

That summer, we moved to Mukwonago and I only saw Ryan a few times throughout middle school and high school when I would visit Chloe or other people in the Milwaukee area. Once, at the swimming pool when we were in eighth grade, Ryan and a couple of his friends invited Chloe and me to play a friendly game of basketball. Chloe accepted enthusiastically while I was busy scanning the crowd for hot guys. At the end of the afternoon, I ended up giving my number to Ryan's friend Mike who kept dunking me, oblivious to the fact that Ryan was upset. Because even when he was upset he managed to smile. (Hindsight is such a bitch.)

I ended up making out with Mike at the Budget Theater in New

Berlin several times that summer. And then he took me to his school's homecoming dance freshmen year and pretty much ignored me the whole time. Luckily, I knew people at the dance so it didn't bother me much. Plus, Chloe was there with a junior, so I was a bit distracted by her date's friends. Ryan was there too, but I'm guessing his date was just a friend because he still asked me to dance. And I would have, except that ended up being the one time Mike decided he wanted to dance. Go figure. So Ryan quietly backed off while Mike proceeded to feel me up on the dance floor.

It wasn't until years later when Chloe and I were in college and hanging out at a bar on Water Street that I saw Ryan again. At the time, I was a few months out from having my heart broken into pieces for the first time and was beginning to wonder if it was time for me to start actively pursuing nice guys. So when I saw Ryan waiting for drinks at the end of the bar, my heart fluttered a bit at all the memories of him pining over me. It seemed like fate. But when my confident open-armed approach was met with a standoffish *Oh, hey Jess. What's up?* I knew I'd missed my chance. Besides the fact that he'd grown nearly a foot and bulked up, he'd changed. His eyes no longer twinkled with care, compassion and friendliness. Instead, his expression was closed-off, unreadable. And instead of being attracted to his aloofness (which usually worked for me with other guys) I was crushed.

Later that night, as I watched Ryan glance with disinterest at all the gorgeous women who were clearly eyeing him, I remembered the way my mom had stared sadly at the Valentine he'd made me, and my heart broke as I thought about the sweet boy he used to be.

That night, I drank too much (as usual) and ended up going home with some random guy. I know his name was Lou, because I wrote it on a coaster—the first coaster I ever placed in my old Valentine's Day box. The one-night stands started out as some pathetic form of self-punishment for passing up Ryan for so many years, for not being able to recognize a nice guy when he was right in front of my face just waiting for me to notice how great he was. Then I met Ned and thought he was the answer. Somehow, he helped fill the empty hole in my heart. Little did I know that being with him would exacerbate the loneliness inside of me and bring all of my abandonment issues and the sense of unworthiness that is rooted so deep within me to the surface once again.

Now, six years later, the box is filled with coasters, and the homemade Valentine that Ryan made for me back in the sixth grade—the Valentine I didn't appreciate until that night when I was actually ready for a guy like him—lives at the bottom. He will never be the same sweet Ryan I knew when we were kids. If only . . .

Leaving the contents of the box splayed out on my bedroom floor, I crawl into bed and close my eyes with a heavy sigh. I continue to toss and turn for a while but eventually doze off with visions of Ryan, as a kid and as an adult, lingering in the blackness behind my eyelids.

When my alarm jolts me awake, I sit up and immediately look at the floor next to my closet. It's still dark outside but the hall light illuminates the dozens of coasters I've collected over the years. Without much thought and absent of the emotions I was feeling last night, I climb out of bed and crouch down to clean up the mess. I glance down at the Valentine Ryan made for me nearly fifteen years ago for a moment before stacking the piles of coasters back on top of it. Then I replace the cover, and put the box back in its place at the bottom of my shoe rack.

Putting on my happy mask, I'm ready for the new day to begin and to concentrate on work for the next four days.

chapter ten

As I approach Concourse E, the Midwest Express terminal, I sip coffee from my *It's too early for you to say things...* travel mug. Not that I really need the mug to deter friendly passengers or TSA guards from trying to chat with me. People are usually pretty comatose at five a.m. on Sundays. However, I can't help but groan when I get to the TSA checkpoint. No snarky saying in the world would deter Stan Boyd from trying to strike up a conversation with me.

"Morning, Jess," Stan says, the right half of his mouth curving up into a perverted grin. "Long time no see."

"Hey, Stan. New shift?" I say politely to the tall, chiseled guard as I scan my ID.

"Mm-hmm . . . covering for Al for a few weeks." He scans me from head to toe a few times without even trying to hide it. Then he nods approvingly. "Looking good. Still working out with that Chinese friend of yours?"

"No, not lately . . . Chloe's Taiwanese, not Chinese," I say, pausing for him to acknowledge the error.

Chloe has always taken issue with people mistaking Asian ethnicities. Even back in grade school when the boys used to chant *Chinese. Japanese. Dirty knees. Look at these!* and then pull their shirts out as if they had pointy tits, she usually responded by rolling her eyes and telling them how dumb they sounded because she isn't Chinese or Japanese. I wanted to kick those jerks in the nuts, or tape KICK ME signs on their backs at the very least, but Chloe always said their stupidity wasn't worth it.

"Oh yeah, I do remember her saying that," he mumbles, eyeing the ceiling as he scratches at his short, thick beard. His eyes find mine again and he shrugs. "Pretty much the same thing, though, right?"

Fast-forward sixteen years, and now I kind of want to kick Stan in the nuts. "Actually, Taiwan is an entirely different country," I respond, admonishing myself for the millionth time for making out with him back in January at the Airport Lounge two weeks after I decided to break up with Ned.

The only good thing about that near hookup with Stan is it went no further than the back room of the bar. The downside is that Brant (the pilot I'd been sleeping with for about a year, mostly when Ned and I were on the outs) was the one who broke up our make-out session by shoving Stan against a wall and choking him with an elbow to the neck. What followed was an even more embarrassing scene: Brant begging me to believe he was going to leave his wife for me right in front of a wide-eyed Stan, and Chloe and Daran dragging my drunk ass out of the bar. Stan never mentioned anything about that night, but his advances have been less aggressive ever since.

He shrugs and opens his mouth to speak, but I cut him off. "Look, it was nice seeing you Stan, but I need to get moving," I say, making a move to be on my way.

He sidesteps, blocking my path. "Hang on a sec. Are you seeing anyone? Still hooking up with that pilot?"

I inhale sharply and instinctively look around, paranoid that one of my Midwest Express colleagues might suddenly be within earshot. After all, my relationship with Brant was never supposed to be exposed to anyone, but Brant's jealous nature got the best of him. As luck would have it, my coworker Val is a few feet away. She's newer, though, so I'm not too worried she'd be able to connect the dots even if she did hear Stan's mention of me hooking up with a pilot.

"Good morning!" Val says in a sing-songy tone a little too chipper for my liking. She smiles as she scans her ID, her flat-ironed hair looking freshly highlighted and shimmering radiantly even under the unflattering airport lights. Who flatirons their hair for a five a.m. show time anyway?

Stan shuffles over to Val. Then he focuses all of his googly-eyed attention on her.

"Hey, Val," I say with a wave.

"Good morning, Val. You're looking lovely as ever," Stan says in a gentlemanly voice.

I'm awed by his quick change in demeanor. Why does she get the nice guy act?

"Thank you, Stan! I just had my hair done yesterday." She reaches up and smoothes her silky locks as she smiles flirtatiously. "You're looking pretty good yourself."

Knowing what a pervert Stan can be, I wait for him to capitalize on the attention she's giving him. Instead, he holds out her IDs and says, "You have a good flight, Val. Chat with you later?"

She nods and gives his bulging bicep a squeeze as she walks past him. Stan can't help but follow her with his eyes, but she doesn't seem to mind. Then her friendly gaze falls on me.

"Isn't he hot?" she whispers as we fall into step next to each other.

"Yeah, he's alright," I say, watching for her reaction.

Her eyes widen. "Just alright? Are you blind? The man looks like a Greek god."

"Okay, fine. He's hot. But I'm guessing you might not find him quite so attractive if you heard the way he usually talks to women. The way he just interacted with you," I point a thumb back toward the TSA podium, "that's not what he's really like." Val just started working for Midwest a couple of months ago so I don't know her too well. But I still want to make sure she's privy to the real Stan.

"Oh, trust me, I know. He used to behave like a scumbag with me too, always making crude comments and touching me inappropriately. I figured since I was new, I'd wait to see if ignoring him would make him stop."

"What gives then? Because I've known him for years, and he hasn't changed much. Yet he was super polite with you just now."

She shrugs. "I'm not really sure. But I did run into him a few weeks ago while I was out with my girlfriends. He put the moves on me, and crossed the line by grabbing my butt. So I slapped him across the face. Then I told him if he ever wanted to have a chance with someone like me he'd have to learn how to treat a woman. Ever since then, he's been on his best behavior when I see him. And to tell you the truth, he's growing on me. Now I can appreciate his good looks."

"Wow, Val! Way to take control of the situation. Any chance you can whip him into shape for the rest of womankind?"

"Baby steps, girl, baby steps. Flipping the script on a player takes time," she says with a giggle.

I laugh too and hope Val and I get assigned to the same service. She seems like someone I could get along with.

Val and I retrieve our identical trip schedules only to learn that our first assigned leg from Milwaukee to Columbus has been delayed due to mechanical issues. This leaves us waiting for reassignment along with Mindy, another member of our cabin crew.

While we wait, I log onto one of the computers in the crew lounge to check my Personals account. When my dashboard finishes loading, several notifications pop up, but the sight of one in particular takes my breath away. It's a message from Ryan Cross. I inhale sharply and stare at the little envelope icon with his name next to it.

"You okay?" Val asks from a lounge chair where she's reading a novel she pulled out of her purse. Based on her pristine makeup, manicured nails, and freshly dyed hair, I would have pegged her as a Cosmopolitan reader instead. As they say, never judge a book . . .

"Oh, yeah . . . I'm fine. Accidentally clicked on something. You know how annoying that is."

She nods and goes back to her book, but James, another flight attendant waiting for an assignment, wanders over from the Nescafe machine where Mindy is still waiting for her watered-down latte. I want to click on Ryan's message something fierce but not with James peering over my shoulder, so I click to view my new matches instead.

"Yahoo! Personals, huh?"

"Yep." I quickly remove several matches from my feed.

"My aunt met her second husband through a personal ad in the

Milwaukee Journal Sentinel." James says matter-of-factly and then takes a sip from his flimsy paper coffee cup.

"That's great, James, but online dating is completely different than placing an ad in the Personals section of the Sunday newspaper. My cousin met her boyfriend on Match.com," Mindy adds as she stands next to him to snoop over my shoulder. "Jess, click on that guy. He looks cute!" She reaches over my head and taps the clean-cut face of a guy with longish blond hair who's dubbed himself as Wildman.

Still distracted by the notification about Ryan's message, I oblige.

"What happens if you do this?" James asks as he grabs the mouse and clicks on the *Poke* option.

I nearly snap my neck turning to look at him. "Seriously, James? It virtually *pokes* the person. Now he's going to think I'm into him when I haven't even read his profile yet!"

"Oops." He shrugs. "Can you take it back?"

"No, you can't take it back!" Mindy scolds. "It's like sending an email. Once you click send, there's no stopping it." She rubs my shoulder reassuringly. "Don't worry about it, Jess. He looks like a nice guy."

I sigh and roll my eyes. I guess online dating in the crew lounge was a bad idea.

"Please don't take this the wrong way, but are you sure online dating is such a good idea? I've heard some horror stories." We all turn to look at Val who's now getting up to join us at the computer.

I snort. "No, I'm not sure, but a friend of mine got me this subscription for my birthday, and I promised I'd give it a shot. She met her boyfriend online, and as skeptical as I am about the whole concept, he's actually a nice guy."

"Or so you think . . ." James pipes in.

"What do you mean? I thought you said your aunt met her husband through a personal ad," Mindy says.

"Yeah, well, he's a total asshole."

Before any of us can respond, the red phone rings. Val is closest so she picks it up. We all know it's someone from Crew Scheduling calling to dole out an assignment. I glance down at the message notification from Ryan one last time, itching to take a quick peek.

"Gate D9," Val repeats. Then she drops the receiver back into place and announces, "We're going to Boston."

Mindy and Val move briskly toward the door, rolling their suitcases behind them the way flight crew stereotypically do.

"You coming?" Val asks over her shoulder.

As much as I wish I didn't have to, I log out of my Personals account. Then I grab my suitcase and race off after Val. "Yep. Let's do this."

"Have a great day, ladies!" James calls after us. "Let me know how that date with Wildman goes, Jess."

I smile sweetly at him and flip him off before exiting the crew lounge.

After the three of us board the plane, we get right to work with our preflight tasks. I take care of making sure all the seats are in upright positions, stock the seat pockets with Sky Magazines and puke bags and then do safety checks on all the equipment. Val and Mindy work on stocking the galley, the bathrooms, and the overheads with pillows and blankets. When I finish the cabin safety checks, I head to the cockpit to say hello to the pilots and introduce myself if I haven't worked with them before. But after three years, I don't often run into many unfamiliar pilots.

Mindy is already standing just inside the cockpit, chatting and laughing. I'm about to squeeze in beside her when I hear a familiar hearty chuckle, causing me to stop dead in my tracks.

"What's wrong? Did you forget something?" Val asks.

Mindy turns and smiles at me, leaning against the cockpit doorway so the pilots can get a full view of Val and I standing outside. And there he is.

I haven't been on a flight with Brant for four weeks and two days, and I haven't received a drunken message from him lately either. But I knew it was just a matter of time before we crossed paths again. He gives me a subtle, cocky grin as everyone greets each other. His handsome, rugged look, and memories of all the passionate moments we've shared make my chest (as well as other parts of my body) ache instantly. But then, just as quickly, I'm overcome with a sense of shame. Given everything I now know about him, I shouldn't be having such a libidinous reaction to his presence.

"All set," I say, standing a little taller and clasping my hands tightly. My smile makes its way from Mindy to Val to the co-pilot Evan and then finally to Brant. I could win an Emmy for the nonchalant way I fleetingly glance at him, as if he never fingered me in the back row of a DC-9 when we rode as passengers on a return flight from Grand Rapids to Milwaukee. In my defense, that was before I knew he'd lied about being separated from his wife. (Not that that makes me any less of a home wrecker or a cheater.)

We all spend a few minutes conversing—the standard how's this or how's that, and then two different conversations begin. Evan, a wholesome family man in his forties who always displays pictures of his wife and kids in the cockpit, recalls the few times we've flown together. He spends the bulk of his stroll down memory lane on the trip we spent stranded in Virginia during Hurricane Isabel. His wife, who was his high school sweetheart, had been on the verge of giving birth to their fourth child. I do a lot of smiling and nodding while only half-listening because one of my ears is honed in on Brant as he flirts with Mindy and Val.

Maybe he's not really flirting. Maybe he's just trying to get under my skin by shamelessly saying things he once said to me when I was a fairly new flight attendant. *Pretty young women like you must be having the time of your lives jet setting around the country . . . Trust me, I know what it's like. I was young and single once too, back when I first started this gig . . . Just make sure you watch yourselves out there. We shuttle around a lot of businessmen with wandering eyes and hands . . . Let me know if you ever need help warding off any creeps.*

He comes across as a father figure, someone you can confide in. The kind of guy a girl like me with daddy abandonment issues might find herself lusting after if she isn't careful. I cringe when he laughs his friendly, good guy laugh, but on the outside I'm still nodding at Evan. I hate myself for feeling jealous. Such a waste of an emotion, especially at the expense of a narcissistic liar like Brant.

As soon as we wrap up our respective conversations, Mindy and Val take care of some last-minute cabin preps.

We repeat the same process two more times when we re-board the plane in Boston to head back to Milwaukee and vice versa. All three flights go smoothly, despite the guy in the Polo shirt who kept getting up to use the bathroom on our second trip to Boston. The annoying thing wasn't the fact that he kept using the bathrooms but that he kept trying to make idle chitchat with me in the aft galley instead of returning to his seat. Politely asking this guy to return to his seat a dozen times so I could read my magazine in peace was really nothing, though, compared to some of the weirdos and assholes I've had to deal with over the years. So all in all, a good day, especially since I managed to avoid any one-on-one interaction with Brant.

It's nearly five o'clock on the east coast when we finally arrive at our hotel. Evan and Val are checking in while the rest of us wait in line. Mindy and Brant are both on their phones, and I'm engrossed in composing a lengthy text to my mom. I might not even send it, but I want to look busy in case Brant gets off his phone before Mindy and tries to talk to me.

"Yes, with Evan . . ." Brant mumbles into his phone. "Probably just order room service and rent a movie . . ." His hunched shoulders coupled with his hushed tone can only mean one thing: He's talking to his wife. I sigh heavily and make a conscious effort to stop listening in on his conversation.

Instead, I eavesdrop on Mindy's call.

" . . . at six o' clock? Great, see you then," Mindy says just before ending the call and looking up at me. "We have a reservation at Sea to Shore at six."

I glance up from my phone and nod, wondering who she means by "we." If she plans to invite Brant, I may need to fake a headache, even though it is my favorite seafood restaurant in the area.

~

I played it cool when I found out that Brant was, in fact, included in that "we." Then as soon as I got to my room, I'd texted Mindy and Val to let them know I wasn't feeling up for dinner. Unfortunately, Mindy showed up at my door begging me to join them right when I was about to open Ryan Cross's message.

"Ohhhh, so *that's* why you don't want to go to dinner with us," she'd said, peering at my personals dashboard. Then, as she closed my laptop, she proclaimed, "You have five minutes to put on some real clothes and brush your hair. History Buff can wait."

So now, thanks to Mindy, I'm stuck sitting at a large round table directly across from the man who used to hide in a closet in the entryway of his home whispering sweet nothings to me while his wife was busy getting their kids ready for bed. *I've never done anything like this before . . . I feel terrible for betraying my kids, but my wife, she's horrible to the kids and me. We haven't been happy for years . . . Please don't throw away what we have just because the timing isn't right. I'm so in love with you . . . You're all I think about . . . I printed out the divorce paperwork today. I'm going to leave her for you . . . I've never felt so in love with another woman before.* All lies. But lies or not, I was just as big a villain as he was the way I was cheating on Ned and the way I was knowingly involved with a married father of two, regardless of whether their marriage was really in ruins or not. I really did hate myself for it. Still do.

"How's your head?" Val asks, lowering her menu a tad to make eye contact with me.

"Oh, it's—" I begin, but Mindy cuts me off.

"She's fine! You know why she really didn't want to come out tonight?" Mindy asks with a giggle.

Val raises her eyebrows, looking from Mindy to me and back to Mindy while Evan continues browsing the menu and Brant waits, curiosity written all over his face, to hear what Mindy has to say. I imagine shoving a balled up napkin in her mouth so she'll keep her trap shut.

"She wanted to spend time with all the guys she's been dating through Yahoo! Personals instead." Mindy thinks she's being cute when she's really being an annoying busybody.

Val rolls her eyes and goes back to looking at her menu. Brant shifts uncomfortably, and takes a drink of water. He's probably wondering if Ned and I are done for good or if I'm still seeing him while online dating on the side.

"Interesting," Evan says. "I read an article in *Investment Guru* a few weeks ago about the projected growth of the online dating industry."

I nod, pleased with the direction Evan is steering the conversation. "My friend read something about that recently too."

"So what do you think? Have you had any luck?"

I hesitate, cursing Mindy for bringing up the topic and wondering how much I should share. On one hand, I don't want Brant knowing anything about my personal life, but on the other, I don't really care because we're done. "Well, I just set up my profile a couple weeks ago, and I've only been on two dates. So . . . it's still too early for me to decide."

That's when the waitress arrives to take our orders. After I place mine, I thank her as I hand her my menu. But I'm not just thanking her for doing her job. I'm also thankful that her arrival put a stop to the conversation about my online dating endeavors. Or so I hoped . . .

"So how was the first date and how many guys are you talking to?" Brant reignites the topic immediately. "Don't get me wrong. My dating days are behind me, but I still think this whole Internet dating business is pretty interesting," he says, looking around the table.

Interesting my ass. When I told him Chloe was online dating, he made fun of the concept, saying it was for desperate losers.

"Um, one was good. The other not so good," I say with a shrug, not wanting to elaborate. "And like I said, I just started, so I haven't really had a chance to connect with too many people yet."

Mindy's eyebrows scrunch together in confusion. "Really? It looked like you had a bunch of messages in your mailbox. And what about History Buff?" She gives me a stupid grin, which I return in lieu of telling her to keep her nose out of my business.

"Well—" I begin only to be cut off by Val. Thank God.

"Drinks are here! Time for a toast."

Mindy, Val, and I hold up our one allotted drink for the evening while Evan holds up his iced tea. Brant isn't supposed to have alcohol within twelve hours of flying, but he's holding up a whiskey sour.

"To a safe day of flying. Today *and* tomorrow," Evan says, eyeing Brant.

We clink our glasses, and Evan and Brant immediately settle into a quiet discussion among themselves. So we girls proceed to taste each other's specialty drinks and share a few laughs over certain passengers from earlier that day. In between our bouts of laughter, bits and pieces of Evan and Brant's conversation can be heard.

Evan is voicing his concern over Brant having a drink, and Brant responds by explaining that things at home have been rough. Then he stares at his drink, poking lazily at the ice cubes. "I'm pretty sure a separation is inevitable," he says loud enough for all of us to hear. Our table goes silent, and my blood boils because they're all buying his act. If I've learned anything about Brant, it's that he uses half-truths and lies to manipulate others. Sure, he might actually be getting separated from his wife now, but why is he presenting it as a sob story? According to him, he's wanted a divorce for years. And why tell Evan and announce his "failing" marriage loud enough for Mindy and Val to hear? So he can have his drink without being looked down on? It's pathetic.

Evan is the first person to speak. "I'm so sorry to hear that, brother," he says, placing a hairy hand on Brant's shoulder.

Still staring down at his glass, Brant nods somberly. Then he raises the tumbler to his lips and polishes off the contents. And that ends the discussion about Brant's supposed impending separation.

When our waitress arrives with appetizers and Brant orders another drink, no one bats an eyelash. No one seems to notice his third or fourth drinks during dinner either, despite the way he was struggling to crack open his crab legs and his flirtations toward Mindy, who's sitting to his left. It isn't until the waitress asks if we'd like to see dessert menus and he tries to order a fifth that Evan steps in.

"Brant, I don't think that's a good idea. We'll just take the check, please," Evan says to the waitress.

"No problem," she says, leaning in between Brant and Mindy to place the bill folder on the table.

"No no no no no," Brant slurs as he grabs the folder and tries to hand it back to her. "Just one more drink," he says, grinning like an idiot.

The waitress holds the bill folder limply and glances around the table at each of us, waiting for direction.

"Evan is right, Brant—" I begin, hoping to snap him out of the destructive state of mind he's in. But he interrupts.

"You know what, forget it," he says, shaking his head and pulling his wallet out of his pocket. "Here." He hands a credit card to the waitress. "Put the whole thing on this." Evan, Val and I protest and try to stop her before she disappears to run the card, but she's too fast, probably itching for us to drag Brant's drunk ass out of her section.

"Awwww, that's so sweet of you, Brant," Mindy coos as she drapes an arm around him and leans her head on his shoulder for a few seconds.

"Sure, no problem." He grins at her and pats her on the thigh the way he did several times during dinner.

Mindy grins back.

chapter eleven

Evan, Val and I ride the hotel elevator to the third floor in silence. I don't know about them, but I'm still processing the spectacle Brant made of himself at the restaurant and in the lobby just moments ago. When the doors open, Evan exits with a wave. "Good night ladies. See you in the morning."

"Good night, Evan," Val and I say in unison. He already has his phone to his ear when the doors close, probably calling to say goodnight to his wife and kids. Brant, on the other hand, is at the hotel bar, probably inching his fingers up Mindy's thigh.

Val pushes the button for the fourth floor and then looks to me for a floor number.

"I'm on four too."

She nods and the elevator begins to rise. "So, what the hell was that all about?" she asks.

"What? Brant's drinking? Or the way he was all over Mindy on the way home and in the hotel lobby?"

"Both. But also the way he got all weird when Mindy mentioned you were online dating." She says as we exit the elevator, eyeing me as if she's waiting for me to confess something to her.

"Let's just say Brant can be . . . flirty when he drinks. As for Mindy? I've heard she can be more than just flirty," I say, taking a seat on one of two floral chairs flanking a decorative mahogany table with a courtesy phone on it. Val sits in the other. Surprisingly, I'm not dying to escape to the solitude of my room the way I normally would be in the presence of most other women I work with. Maybe it's because I like the way Val appears to be above Brant's and Mindy's behavior, yet she isn't giving off the vibe that she's judging them either. A girl can always use a mature, open-minded friend, right?

"Thanks for the warning," she laughs. "That asshole tried to grab my ass when we were leaving the restaurant. Right before he hopped into the back of the cab and pulled Mindy onto his lap." Her smile morphs into a concerned look and she produces a lengthy sigh. "I hope Mindy is okay with him."

I have to admit I do feel slight concern for Mindy. It wasn't that long ago that I was in the exact same position she's in. Except Brant was much more discreet in his pursuit of me, and there was no one to warn me to stay away from him. "Come on," I say, hopping to my feet and heading back to the elevator, "Let's go back down and get her."

We exit the elevator into the lobby and march straight to the hotel bar where we said goodnight to Brant and Mindy less than ten minutes earlier. But now they're gone.

Val and I both look at each other, but don't say anything. I can't help but think we let Mindy down.

As soon as I enter my room, I set my phone on the bedside table and plug it in. Then I power on my laptop. While I wait for it to boot up, I change back into the sweats and t-shirt I was wearing before Mindy dragged me out to dinner. My computer still isn't ready when I hop into bed and plop it onto my lap, so I grab my phone off the nightstand. I have one text from my mom and a voicemail.

Mom: Just wanted you to know that Ashley called again. You really should give her a call. Life is too short. XO

I reread the text twice and then the last sentence a third time. She's right, life is too short. And I really should call my half-sister. After all, she's been trying to get ahold of me for weeks.

Finally, the home screen of my laptop appears. I open the Web browser, navigate to Yahoo! Personals, and log in as I listen to the voicemail.

"Hey, babe. Sorry I didn't get in touch last night. I know you're working, so

you might not be able to get back to me right away. Just wanted you to know . . ."

My Personals dashboard opens as Ned's voice becomes background noise. The screen is filled with even more red notifications, but there's only one that I'm truly interested in. I'm about to click on Ryan Cross's message but freeze when I hear what Ned says next.

"I miss you. Not just being intimate with you either. I miss YOU . . ."

Never before has he made the distinction between missing *me* versus our physical relationship. Maybe I'll call him back.

"And I've been thinking . . . this off again on again shit isn't working for me. It's time for us to figure out where our relationship is headed once and for all. Either we're going to be together or we're not. And by together, I mean no more fucking around with other guys whenever you—"

I press seven to delete the message. True to form, Ned couldn't help but display the hostile, domineering beast inside of him, which rears its ugly head when he loses control over a situation or when things don't go his way. Yes, I know how shitty it was of me to cheat on him. We've discussed my betrayals he knows about dozens of times, and I've apologized ad nauseam. However, we've also discussed my discontent over never being a priority to him above things like golf or watching sports with his friends or making calls to his bookie. But all of that's water under the bridge at this point because I'm done. Now I just need him to get on board with us going our separate ways.

I turn the volume on my phone all the way down and slide it facedown onto the nightstand. It's already a little after nine thirty, and I certainly don't feel like being woken up in the middle of the night by another call from Ned. Then I pick up the phone in the room and press zero to request a five a.m. wake-up call.

After that's taken care of, I turn my attention back to my computer and Yahoo! Personals.

Ryan Cross's message is my first priority before I read the one from Scotty (the guy whose message I never got around to checking yesterday) and BossMan411 (the gross cat/dick pic guy). There's also a fourth message from Wildman (the guy James poked this morning). I take a deep breath and exhale slowly as I click on Ryan's message.

Jess? Is it really you?

When I saw that you viewed my profile but didn't send a message, I thought maybe there was a chance you didn't recognize me?? Either way, I figured I'd drop you a line. Hopefully it's not weird. If so, keep in mind I just started online dating. Like anything else, I'm sure there are a few rules to be learned.

So, how have things been? And what brings you to Yahoo! Personals? Surely you aren't hard up for a date. (I mean that as a compliment.) Me? I'm tired of the bar scene.

Anyway, if you're interested getting together to catch up, let me know where and when. I'd love to hear how things are going.

Take care,
Ryan

I read his message a few times, analyzing it for hidden meaning that isn't there. Well, he's obviously not mad at me anymore. In fact, his message ranged from neutral to friendly. No, he's not asking me on a date, but he wants to catch up. *And no, he isn't excited that you checked out his profile. He's just saying hi to an old friend.* He's obviously more mature than me, as usual. Otherwise, I would have messaged him to say hello first.

I click to respond.

Hi Ryan,

Yep, it's me! Nope, not weird at all that you messaged me. Honestly, I've been thinking I should have messaged you last night when I viewed your profile. It's just that I was so shocked to run into you on here. Well, that, and seeing your photos really took me back. (You look amazing by the way.) As for why I'm on here, remember Chloe Thompson? Well, Little-Miss-Fix-It is now Big-Miss-Fix-It, and she thought online dating might be my ticket to finding the love of my life. So here I am . . .

I'd really like to catch up sometime, too, so how about if you let me know when you're available and we can go from there?

I look forward to hearing from you!
Jess

I click send without rereading my response and immediately feel a slight twinge of anticipation in my belly. Is it possible that online dating could result in me dating Ryan Cross after all these years?

I move on to the message from Scotty, which is short and sweet.

Dear Jess,

You seem like an amazing woman, and I'd like to get to know you better if you're interested. If not, I understand and no hard feelings!

Sincerely,
Scotty

I can barely see what this Scotty guy looks like because his profile picture is unfocused, but my brain is still jumbled with thoughts of Ryan Cross, so I don't even bother checking his stats. I'll just send him a quick message now and look at his full profile another time.

Hey there Scotty,

Sounds good! Why don't you start by telling me something about yourself that isn't already in your profile? I'll start . . . I have a degree in psychology from UW-Milwaukee. I don't know if I'll ever make a penny because of it, but it sure does come in handy sometimes!

Have a great night,

Jess

The next message is from BossMan411. Ugh. Do I even want to look at it? My heart says no, but my brain is too curious to delete it without taking a peek.

Have you had a chance to check out the pics I emailed you??

That's it? That's all he has to say? The least he could do is say hi, or better yet, he could just come right out and ask what I think of his junk. We both know that's what he's really phishing for anyway. Part of me wants to respond just to see if I can get him to send more pics of his "cats," for Chloe, of course. Instead, I end up deleting the message and then promptly block him from communicating with me again.

Moving on.

Hey there lovely lady!

Thanks for the poke. To be honest, I don't usually respond to pokes, but your profile looks great, and based on your photo, you look like the kind of girl I'd love to get to know better. Hope to hear from you again soon! (Unless that poke was just an accident. In that case…oops!)

Brock Wildman

I look like the kind of girl he'd like to get to know better? What the hell does that mean? Is it because I'm holding a glass of wine? Maybe he likes wine too. Or is it because I'm laughing hysterically in my profile photo? Wait. Why am I analyzing this? It makes no difference what this guy's message says (or any guy's message); the only thing that matters in the end is how I feel when I'm standing face-to-face with someone. That was my whole philosophy going into this, right?

I decide to respond, mainly because any guy who calls himself

Wildman is a guy I *need* to have a live conversation with. If he turns out to be a total ass, I'll blame James and move on.

Before I respond, though, I click to actually view his profile. His main photo is a close up of his forehead and eyes, which are wide as saucers. The other photo attached to his profile is the zoomed out version of the main photo. It shows his whole face (mouth wide open just like his eyes), torso and the bottle of beer he's holding like it's some sort of trophy. Oh boy.

~

Wildman – 26
Location: Greenfield
Let's do this!

Relationship Status: Never Married
Kids: No
Want Kids: Yes
Ethnicity: Mixed
Body type: Average
Height: 5' 11"
Religion: Catholic
Politics: Moderate
Smoke: No
Drink: Socially
Pets: No
Education: Tell you later
Employment: Self
Income: 100,000+

~

His tagline makes me snort. Okay, Wildman, let's.

Hey Brock,

To be perfectly honest, the poke actually was an accident. (Oops.) I've learned my lesson, though: Never online date in the presence of meddling co-workers! But now that we're acquainted, what the heck . . . let's do this.

So how long have you been online dating? I'm a newbie and went on my first two dates this week. One went okay and the other was pretty painful. What about you? Have you been on any worthwhile dates yet?

Jess

Before logging out, I delete all the pokes and icebreakers without even looking at any of the screen names. Why bother when I don't plan to respond to any of those people anyway? Besides, I have enough online dating action just from people messaging me. With the exception of the accidental poking of Wildman, I haven't reached out to anyone first. It's probably for the best since I have a proven track record of choosing assholes. Take Ned and Brant, for example.

I turn off the light and hop back into bed, my body ready to shut down for the night but my brain still running at full throttle. Will I get the job at Molly McGinn's? Is Sawyer working right now? Why did he lie about us sleeping together? Has Free Bird ever been in a relationship? *Probably not. He's such an ass, I doubt he even has friends.* Is it possible that Ryan Cross still has feelings for me? *No, that's a ridiculous thought. You guys were kids when he had a crush on you. And he barely acknowledged you the last time you saw him.* But what if us running into each other on Yahoo! Personals happened for a reason? Could it be fate bringing us back together? *Oh great. Now you sound like Chloe with all of her fortune teller Angel Lady bullshit. Stop thinking about Ryan Cross! Go to sleep!*

I have one final thought before drifting off into unconsciousness.

I wonder if Chloe still has the Angel Lady's number . . .

The wakeup call I requested is delivered at five a.m. on the dot. Surprisingly, I feel rested despite my brain refusing to shut down until well after midnight last night.

I hop out of bed and start a pot of coffee. Then I stretch my arms high in the air as I yawn and make my way to the bathroom to brush my teeth. As I'm brushing, I think about Brant and Mindy. I have a bad feeling that things might have gone too far between them, but I resolve to stay out of it. It's not my business who either of them sleep with, and I'm selfishly relieved that their hookup kept Brant away from my door. Not that I would have let him in, but I have no doubt he would have caused a scene.

I actually feel kind of bad for him, the way he seems to be coming apart at the seams. If he continues screwing co-workers and getting drunk on overnights, I imagine his job will end up at risk just like his marriage.

It takes less than fifteen minutes for me to finish getting ready for the day. I fill my travel mug with coffee, then grab my phone and charger from the night stand. The sight of multiple text notifications makes me cringe, considering they were all delivered in the middle of the night, and I don't recognize any of the numbers.

I open the first one, and my stomach turns as soon as I realize it's from Ned.

414-555-2100: HEY, SORRY I FREAKED OUT IN THE MESSAGE I LEFT EARLIER. GIVE ME A CALL WHEN YOU GET HOME.

I roll my eyes as I delete the message, and the screen shifts back to the list of new texts. The next one in line is from another unfamiliar number. Turns out it's actually a thread of texts.

414-958-2370: JUST GOT DONE FUCKING YOUR FRIEND MINDY.

Gross.

414-958-2370: It wasn't the first time either.

What the hell?

414-958-2370: She's a much better lay than you. Her ass is so much tighter than yours and her tits are so much bigger. Have fun online dating.

I laugh at Brant's desperate attempt to get a response out of me and almost delete the thread before realizing it will be good for a few laughs the next time I see Chloe. It will also serve as a good reminder of one of the biggest mistakes I've ever made.

Hesitantly, I click on the final text from yet another unfamiliar number.

414-959-2222: Hi Jesstine. Bobby and I just did a shot in your honor. You'll find out why soon enough... Sawyer McCoy (Got your # from Molly)

I smile at the sight of his name. Then I laugh at the absurdity of him signing off with his full name. Sawyer McCoy. I don't remember him telling me what his last name was, but I'm pretty sure we should be on a first name basis with each other. I wonder for a second how my name came up and why they did shots in my honor. The only thing I can come up with is that I may have gotten the job. The prospect brightens my mood, and I tap out a quick response.

Me: I hope it was a good one! :)

Before heading down to the lobby to meet up with my co-workers, I store my new friend's number in my phone. First name only.

chapter twelve

"Hey you two," I say, climbing into the back seat of Daran's teal Honda Accord with its sporty spoiler and subwoofers hidden in the trunk. I snicker, wondering if any woman has ever been impressed by it. "Thanks again for picking me up."

"Hi, Jess. No problem." Daran gives me a friendly nod before checking his mirrors and pulling away from the curb.

"Hey, you." Chloe turns sideways to face me. "How was work? Where'd you go?"

"Boston, Baltimore, Grand Rapids."

"Did you go to that crab shack in Boston you always rave about?"

"Actually, we did . . . Guess who else went?"

"Who?" She asks, turning down the radio.

"Brant."

"Oh, crap! Seriously? Do you think he switched with someone to work with you?"

"Uh-uh," I say shaking my head. "There's no way he had anything to do with it. It was a last-minute schedule change due to a mechanical issue. Just a stroke of bad luck."

"Who are you guys talking about?" Daran asks, hands at eleven and two on the steering wheel and eyes glued to the road. Chloe sometimes refers to him as Mr. Cautious.

"The married pilot." Chloe waits for him to acknowledge that he knows who we're talking about but he offers a shrug instead so she elaborates. He sighs as if he regrets asking.

While Chloe covers every nauseating detail about Brant's relentless pursuit of me, despite having a wife and kids, I check the spotless floor and laugh to myself about how this car was cause for Chloe and Daran's first argument. The first time she rode in it, it had been spotless, but as weeks went by, the floor became more and more littered with trash.

Same with his apartment. But Chloe didn't go to Daran's place nearly as much as she rode in his car during the first month after they met. Finally one night she came rushing into Home Bar, bypassing me and heading straight to the bathroom. I'd looked to Daran for an explanation but all he had for me was an exasperated headshake. I immediately took Chloe's side, assuming Daran must have done something pretty lousy, and rushed into the bathroom where she was lathering up her hands.

"What's going on?" I'd asked.

"I don't know if things are going to work out with Daran and me."

"Why? What happened?"

"His car is a total pigsty!"

When my uproarious laughter failed to snap her out of the funk she was in, I realized she was either more of a germophobe than I knew, or she was still struggling with a fear of commitment. "His car?"

"Yes. And his apartment is starting to look pretty shabby too," she said with urgency, as if she was running out of breath.

I turned off the water and squeezed her hands dry with some paper towels. "Chloe."

"It was all so clean when I first met him . . ."

"Chloe."

"His profile said he was a neat freak . . ."

"Chloe."

"And then it was a few wrappers here and a few wrappers there . . . and now the garbage in his kitchen trash can has been growing higher and higher . . . and there are clothes all over his bedroom floor . . . and—"

"Chloe! Breathe!"

Finally, she looked at me, chest heaving.

"All of that can be cleaned up. Is everything else okay?"

"Well, yeah, but . . ."

"Then calm down and let's put things into perspective here. It's just clutter and garbage. Talk to him about clearing up the clutter and throwing away the garbage before you throw away the relationship."

"But he lied." Finally she looked me in the eyes, and hers didn't look like the eyes of a crazed lunatic. She just looked . . . scared.

"About what?"

"I told you. When we first started dating, he led me to believe he liked to keep things tidy."

"Chloe," I said as compassionately as possible. "So maybe he fibbed a little. Or maybe he has a different idea of tidy than you do. At least he doesn't have a girlfriend on the side and he's not boring or rude. And who knows, maybe he's just too busy thinking about you to remember to take out the trash."

"One little fib might mean there are more to come. Bigger ones."

"Maybe, but why not give him the benefit of the doubt? And remember, he is a dude. Dudes are dirty. Ya know?"

"What are you looking at? Is there garbage back there?" Chloe asks, bringing me back to Daran's now spotless car. She cranes her neck to look at the floor of the back seat.

I catch an eye roll from Daran in the rearview mirror and chuckle. "No, I was actually just admiring how clean it is back here."

Chloe rubs Daran's arm affectionately before turning her attention back to me. "So, back to Brant. You seriously don't think he had anything to do with your schedule change? I could totally see him screwing up a plane to get you reassigned. That guy's crazy."

Even though her hypothesis is completely unrealistic, I can't help but wonder if there's any possible way Brant could have caused mechanical issues with an aircraft. He did work as a mechanic when he was in the Navy . . .

"Gimme a break," Daran says to Chloe, "There's no way a pilot, let alone anyone, could tinker with a commercial aircraft without someone noticing. Besides, do you really think he'd risk his job just to fly with Jess?"

"Daran, I *just* got done telling you about some of the crazy shit this guy did when Jess stopped seeing him. If anyone could figure out how to tamper with an airplane so he could get what he wanted, it would be him." Daran shrugs as Chloe turns quickly to look at me. "How long has it been since he last harassed you? Five weeks? I told you it wouldn't last."

"Chloe, seriously, it was a coincidence that we ended up working together. And it was only one overnight."

"So what happened?"

"Well, things were fine when we were working. You know, with him being confined to the cockpit and all. But then my attempt to avoid dinner by feigning a headache was botched by my co-worker Mindy. She pretty much dragged me out of my hotel room and then announced to everyone that I tried to ditch out on dinner to peruse Yahoo! Personals instead."

"Oh boy," Chloe says, her eyes wide and twinkling with curiosity, "I bet that got Brant's attention."

Nodding, I continue. "The questions he peppered me with in front of everyone made me pretty uncomfortable, but I did my best not to react. Thankfully the other pilot shifted conversation away from me, and Brant proceeded to get wasted."

"Aren't pilots restricted from drinking a certain number of hours before flying?" Daran asks. I didn't even think he was listening.

"Yes, but I think Brant is too narcissistic to think the rules apply to him."

Keeping his eyes on the road, Daran responds with a few slow nods while Chloe shakes her head in disbelief.

"Anyway," I continue, "when he was a couple of drinks in, he started flirting with Mindy who flirted back. By the time we arrived back at the hotel, it was pretty apparent they were headed toward way more than just flirting."

"He wasn't even trying to hide it?" Somehow Chloe's eyes have gotten even bigger.

"Nope," I say as I pull up the string of texts Brant sent in the middle of the night. "And look at this." I hand Chloe my phone, and then glance out the window to see how close we are to our destination.

She gasps and then yells, "Oh my GOD!" causing Daran to swerve a little.

"What is it?" Daran asks, eyeing me in the rearview mirror for a second.

Chloe glances back at me, her expression asking for permission to share the texts with Daran.

I shrug and say, "I don't mind if you read them to him."

"Well, it says . . ." Chloe pauses to clear her throat, "*Just got done fucking your friend Mindy. It wasn't the first time either.*" She reads Brant's words robotically, as if to make them sound less angry and insulting. Daran glances sideways at her and she continues. "*She's a much better lay than you . . .*" She clears her throat again. "*Her ass is so much tighter than yours and her tits are so much bigger. Have fun online dating.*"

"Wow. He sounds like a real winner," Daran says sarcastically.

"Yep, a real winner," I mumble as Chloe hands my phone back.

"So what happened when you saw him the next day? And what about Mindy?"

"Nothing," I say, shaking my head. "Neither one of them said anything other than 'good morning' to all of us, and they didn't talk to each other either. We went about our flight back to Milwaukee as if nothing happened. Then I was reassigned to a flight out of Baltimore with a whole new crew, and I didn't see Brant or Mindy again for the rest of the week.

The car comes to a stop, prompting Chloe and I to look over at Daran, who's now turned sideways. "Guy sounds like nothing but trouble. Why don't you report him? Then I guarantee you'll never have to work with him again."

"No, I can't do that to him. He has a family to take care of."

"Interesting."

"What? What's interesting?" My eyes shift to Chloe for a second. She looks just as curious as I am about what Daran has to say.

"It's just that . . ."

"What?" Daran usually doesn't weigh in on my conversations with Chloe, so I'm dying to know his opinion.

"Well, you weren't all that worried about his family back when you decided to start sleeping with him. I mean, you knew about his wife and kids before it all started, right?"

"Not at first, but yeah, near the end I knew. But that's different. Sleeping with him didn't put him in danger of losing his job. And, I actually thought they were separ—"

"Oh, well, okay then." He raises his hands only to let them fall, surrendering to my obvious logic. "Whatever you think is best. Not my place." He purses his lips before breaking eye contact with me and then looks at Chloe. "You ready?"

~

"Do you see him?" Chloe asks.

I scan the crowd again. "Nope."

Daran looks at me as he steps up to the bar. "What can I get for you, Jess?"

I'm still a bit miffed at him for cutting me off in the car and for calling me out about not wanting to report Brant, but I've never been one to turn down a drink. "Vodka cranberry . . . thanks."

Chloe stabs an elbow into my ribcage before moving off toward an empty table.

"Ouch. What was that for?"

"Don't take it personally. I told you he's a goody-goody."

"Yeah, a goody-goody who tied you up and took a razor to you," I snort.

"Wait a second. You didn't think anything of it on Friday. What happened to 'live a little, Chloe?' Don't get all pissy just because he doesn't agree with you protecting Brant."

"Oh, please. Daran is entitled to his opinion, and I'm fine with it." I try to act casual, like I'm not guilty of exactly what Chloe just accused me of. But deep down I know she's right. And maybe Daran is too. "It's just . . . I don't know . . . I'd like to just put the whole thing with Brant behind me. You know? Besides, he's the last married guy I'll ever touch. I swear."

"Right, but what about his wife? Don't you think she deserves to know what's going on?"

Before I can respond, Daran arrives with our drinks. "No Wayward Son yet?" He grins at Chloe when he says it.

"No," I say, checking my phone. "But he should be here by now. The only personal tidbit he shared with me is that he prides himself on always being early. I'll give him a call if he doesn't show up within the next five minutes."

"Just like you, Daran!" Chloe's elbow nudge is met with a smirk that goes unacknowledged before turning back to me. "So, all you really know is what he looks like?"

"Yep. Oh, and his name is Brandon. But keep in mind that looks aren't *my* top priority," I say with an elevated eyebrow, unfolding Karaoke Wayward Son's profile and sliding it toward Chloe. "It's not like I'm searching for an imaginary Adonis like you were." I'm joking, of course, just to mess with Chloe. But my chuckles are met with an eye roll from her and a slight smirk from Daran. "What? I'm just kidding. He's pretty good looking, don't you think? And Daran, you're totally an Adonis. Seriously. How else do you think you ended up with Chloe?"

To my surprise, he laughs.

"Okay, okay. Very funny. Maybe looks were a high priority to me when I first started online dating, but I learned from that mistake, didn't I?" Chloe says, pulling the profile from under my fingers. Within seconds, she's laughing right along with Daran. Except they're both laughing at the profile.

"What's so funny?" I ask. But before Chloe and Daran can answer, the iconic first line of "Carry On Wayward Son" fills the bar. "Wait. Is that . . . ?"

We grab our drinks and I shove the profile back into my purse before scurrying off to the back where a makeshift stage is set up. Sure enough, Karaoke Wayward Son is up in front of the crowd, mic-less hand outstretched in a theatrical manner as he loses himself in the Kansas classic. The crowd goes wild and sings along when he gets to the chorus. Even Chloe hoots and hollers as Daran bobs his head. I sway a little, but I've never been the type to bust a move or wave my arms in the air like some of the people in the crowd, which I'm guessing is full of regulars based on the way they whistle and yell out things like *Sing it B!*

and *Branduuuun!* Don't get me wrong, I sing. Just not in front of people. My shower, my car, and church on Christmas are pretty much the only places I express myself through song.

On the final note, Brandon points directly at me, causing dozens of eyes to look our way. Serious as a heart attack, he holds his gaze a tad too long for dramatic effect. Then he grins with pride, hops off the stage and heads in our direction, high fiving people along the way. A group of middle-aged women—no doubt belonging to the group of regulars who were going bonkers over Brandon's performance—glare at me and begin whispering.

Chloe is too busy applauding to notice, but Daran regards the estrogen cluster with amusement and then gives my shoulder a couple of pats. "Looks like your date has groupies." I have a feeling the sarcastic chuckle that follows is intended to get under my skin. Little does he know it takes far more jeering than that to rattle me. Chloe's a much easier target.

"Yeah well, if it wasn't for his age, he'd definitely be American Idol material," I match his sarcasm and we both start laughing.

"What's so funny?" Chloe asks just as Brandon arrives. Eyes trained on me, he bypasses Chloe and Daran.

"Jess, right?" His handshake is firm. Three businesslike pumps. "Sorry I wasn't up front when you arrived. I didn't mean to go up there yet, but Dizzy . . ." He nods stage right at the big burly guy with a voice like butter who's introducing the next performer. The sign draped across the front of his equipment says Dizzy Dan's Karaoke. "As soon as he spotted me, he dragged me back here to show me some new equipment, and then he forced me up there. Did you enjoy the show?" He eyes me expectantly.

"Oh, yeah . . ." I say, "Nice job. I'm just . . . still getting over the shock of how good you are. Really good. You really killed it up there." I wonder if that was a bit too much.

In response, Karaoke Wayward Son, aka Brandon, stands a little taller and pulls on the hem of his shirt. "Well, thank you, thank you very much." His faux Elvis Presley accent makes me groan internally, but I plaster a smile on my face and will Chloe to stop talking to Daran and look at me. *Bad date number two has begun.* I try to deliver my thoughts telepathically. Well, through a laser beam stare anyway.

"Brandon, remember how I said I might bring a couple of friends?" I ask, steering his elbow so that we are both facing Chloe and Daran. "This is Chloe and her boyfriend, Daran."

He dips a shoulder, leaning a tad to the right and targets Chloe with both of his index fingers. "I saw you rocking out while I was up there. You must be a fan," he says, smiling broadly. *Of him or of karaoke?* I'm not sure what he means, and judging by Chloe's slow nod and unenthusiastic wave, I'm pretty sure she has no clue either. Then, extending a hand to Daran, Brandon says, "Thanks for coming out, man."

Daran mirrors Brandon's robust handshake. "Yeah, yeah, of course. You were great up there, man. How long have you been performing?" And that's all it takes. That one little question turns into an excruciatingly long conversation about the origins of Brandon's interest in karaoke. It all started back in 1984 with the debut of a popular television lip-sync show…

"So, anyway, to make a long story short, despite the musical ability I inherited from my great-grandpapa, if it weren't for *Puttin' on the Hits*, I'd never have answered the stage's calling." Brandon takes a deep, nostalgic breath, his gaze migrating to the guy up front who's singing the worst rendition I've ever heard of "When Doves Cry."

Daran chuckles quietly as he observes Brandon watching the Prince imitator, and Chloe's glazed eyes widen as she takes a long guzzle of her drink. Part of me is tempted to laugh out loud and give Brandon a good-natured slug in the shoulder, calling his bluff. Because he has to be joking. No one is this serious about karaoke. No one. But as the seconds tick by, Brandon continues to stare longingly toward the stage despite the excruciating sound coming from it. And when he starts singing along with the rest of the crowd, I decide to bite my tongue instead and enjoy the rest of my vodka cranberry with a twist of lime. After two more of these, I might be a little more receptive to Brandon's enthusiasm for karaoke.

"Do you guys want more drinks?" Daran leans in over the small circular table, raising his voice over the music. Chloe and I both nod. "What about him?" Daran nods toward my date.

"Hey, Brandon," I say to his back. He doesn't respond, probably because Dizzy Dan has just finished encouraging everyone to applaud the last performer. As I reach out to get his attention with a tap on the shoulder, his name is called and he disappears into the crowd in the direction of the stage. I shake my head at Daran who disappears toward the bar for three more drinks.

"Okay, so, you know I love karaoke, right?" Propping her elbows onto the table, Chloe drops her chin onto upturned palms.

"Yeah?"

"Well, this dude more than loves it. I think he's obsessed."

"You don't say," I respond with a heavy sigh.

"It's one thing to—" Chloe stops mid-sentence when the crowd goes bonkers over Brandon's spot-on approach to "Born to be Wild" by Steppenwolf. "You know what, though?" She yells over the noise, jumping to her feet. "He's really good!" She pulls me to my feet too and we proceed to enjoy the show.

When Daran returns with our drinks, Chloe gives him no choice other than to deposit them on the table and dance with us. His stiff, uncoordinated movements cause a good giggle from Chloe and me, but he doesn't seem to care. In fact, our laughter appears to egg him on as he throws in some moves reminiscent of Pee-wee Herman. The sight of his uncoordinated arm swings and jerking hips warm my heart. Chloe, who can be a bit of a stick-in-the-mud, needs a guy who isn't afraid to make a fool of himself from time to time.

After singing two more songs, Brandon hops off the stage and slaps meet his back and arms from all directions until he arrives at our table. He's smiling from ear to ear. "Looks like you guys enjoyed the show!" He reaches out and gives my back a few rubs. His attention (or maybe it's a side effect of the alcohol in my system) makes me warm and tingly, and out of habit I imagine what it would be like to kiss him. So I pull him down onto the stool next to me, suddenly open to the possibility of getting to know him better and maybe even going on another date with him.

Over the next hour or so, conversation winds here and there and everywhere. The four of us share some laughs over things like Saturday morning cartoons that used to be on when we were kids, funny old commercials, and 80s fashion disasters. Hearing Brandon talk about things other than his love for karaoke is nice, and it enhances the attractiveness of his messy dark hair and goatee. I cozy up to him, and he cozies back.

"Sing a song with me, Daran. Pleeeease," Chloe whines.

"Yeah, get up there with her," I interject with a smirk. "Show us you have the voice to go with those awesome moves of yours."

"Tell you what," Daran says to Chloe, "I'll go up there with you *after* you go up and sing one on your own."

"Really? Okay."

Daran's unexpected terms divert my attention from Brandon. "Wait, you're going up there to sing . . . by yourself?" Chloe might love watching karaoke, but getting up in front of large crowds isn't exactly her forte, especially when she's alone.

"Well, sure, if that's the only way I can get him up there with me, then why not?"

Daran has a shit-eating grin on his face, but he looks perfectly sober, which makes my blood boil. Does he want her to go up there and make a fool of herself?

"Why? Because you normally won't do karaoke by yourself. How many drinks have you had anyway?" I force a laugh as I count the number of empty glasses piled up on our table.

Chloe responds with a shrug and a muffled string of words that tells me two things. One, she has no idea how many drinks she's had, and two, she has no idea what she's just agreed to do. Maybe I'll just shut my trap and see where this goes. It could actually turn out to be more entertaining than anything we've seen so far tonight. And she's not likely to remember her performance anyway.

Chloe rubs her hands together as she hops off her stool. "What should I sing?" Her gaze sweeps quickly from Daran to Brandon and finally lands on me.

"Wait a sec. One more thing." Daran grins the same stupid grin, but still, I'm curious to hear what he has to say. "You have to let me pick the song."

I shrug at Chloe. Seems harmless enough.

"Okay. What song?" she asks.

"Wait here," Daran says as he rushes off to submit a request.

Shielding her eyes from the bright lights, Chloe grins and squints out at the crowd. She's holding the microphone limply. Dizzy Dan bends over to say something in her ear. She nods in response and sways a little, causing me to consider yanking her off the stage.

"Hey, Daran—"

"Up next, we have Chloe! Let's give her a warm welcome, folks!"

A brief applause ensues accompanied by a drawn out whistle from Brandon. I cover my right ear to mute the piercing sound and stare at him out of the corner of my eye. Jesus, I've never heard a guy whistle like that before. Back in high school, the Wrestlette cheer squad used to do it all the time. It was almost as annoying to hear Brandon do it now as it was back then.

I don't recognize the song when the music starts, but others must because there are a few hoots and a couple of gasps. Wait, why would anyone gasp? The muted sound of the lyrics begins, but Chloe isn't singing so I still can't make out what song it is. I squint, trying to determine if she's even trying to read the teleprompter. Oh shit. Judging by her wide eyes and the O-shape of her lips, Daran must have chosen a doozy. Then I hear it. Above the people who are screaming for Chloe to sing, I hear a few belting out the chorus to "I Touch Myself" by the Divinyls.

Daran is hunched over with laughter. He might even be crying he's laughing so hard. Chloe sort of starts mumbling the lyrics as I make my way to the stage to rescue her. My initial plan is to drag her down and save her from further humiliation, but when I pass Dizzy Dan, he shoves a mic in my hand. I try to give it back but he refuses and a few audience members start egging me on. But I don't care what they want or what they think. Until I spot Brandon's cluster of groupies and the snide looks on their faces. That's when I decide it's time for some karaoke.

Chloe is barely whispering the second chorus when I shimmy next to her, thrust my hip into hers, and belt out the masturbatory lyrics as loud as I can. Whoa. That was unexpected. She looks over at me, a startled, wide grin on her face and her voice becomes a little louder.

By the time the final chorus rolls around, Chloe is singing like nobody's watching. In other words, she sounds like a Tomcat in heat. But the crowd is loving it, which proves that a little confidence goes long way. So I decide to have a little fun. Instead of singing along with her, I park myself right in front of Brandon's groupies and accompany Chloe with, "I touch myself . . . I do . . . I really, really do . . . No really, I seriously touch myself." My fun is met with eye rolls and troll-like expressions from the groupies I'm delivering my lines to. In fact, these five chicks seem to be the only members of the audience who aren't going nuts with applause and laughter as Chloe and I make our way off the stage.

"You're such an asshole!" Chloe teases as she hip checks Daran, who's laughing too hard to talk. "You're lucky Jess saved me up there." She grins appreciatively at me, but the look on her face morphs into concern when her eyes migrate over to Brandon.

Tap tap tap tap tap. His right hand is balled up and his knuckles nervously tap against the table.

"Hey, let's get some water for everyone," Daran says, eyeing Brandon but still chuckling lightly. He takes her hand and guides her through the crowd.

Brandon's tapping and pouty posture are interesting but also annoying enough that I almost wish I'd escaped with Chloe and Daran. Since they're already halfway there, I decide to weather whatever storm Brandon's brewing up inside that head of his.

"So? How'd we do? I mean, in your expert opinion, of course." I wink and place my hand on top of his. It has nothing to do with the fact that he's attractive. I really just want the incessant tapping to stop. And what can I say? I'm just a touchy kinda gal. Especially after I've had a few.

"I don't think making fun of the art of karaoke is something to be proud of."

I laugh so hard, my spiked tonic sprays the table, a few drops landing on his hand as he swiftly pulls it from under mine.

"Wait, you're serious." I stare at him wide-eyed as I use a napkin to mop up the mess I made.

"And that friend of yours . . . that Daran . . . requesting a song for his girlfriend that she doesn't even know?" He shakes his head, disappointment affecting his entire demeanor.

"Well, it's not that she didn't know the song. It was more of a joke. You know? So she was just—"

"Look, Jess, it's been nice meeting you. But I made a pact with myself to be honest throughout this whole . . ." He makes air circles in the space that separates us. ". . . process."

"Okay. And?"

"And I'm going to have to cut our date short." He stands, raising both hands in a parting gesture, as if to say "See ya, losers." Then he turns and struts over to his pod of groupies. They take turns welcoming him with open arms and shooting me dirty looks.

I shrug. People are so weird.

"What happened to your guy?" Daran hands me another drink.

Chloe answers for me with a loud gasp. "What the hell? Why is he grinding on those chicks?"

"He didn't appreciate our performance."

"So he ended your date? He's not coming back?" Chloe is beside herself.

"Nope," I say, before taking a long guzzle.

"What a dick! Are you okay? Do you want to leave?"

I can't help but chuckle at Chloe's concern. She should know I couldn't give two shits. "I'm fine! His loss. Besides, do you really think I want to spend my Thursday nights watching people do karaoke? You gotta give the guy credit though. At least he knows what he's looking for and isn't about to waste anyone's time. I can respect that."

Daran nods. But Chloe looks away, grabbing her drink. I think I see a bit of red in her cheeks. Darn it. After all of her uncertainty before she met Daran, my comment must have seemed like an insult.

"Oh, Chloe, wait . . . I wasn't talking about—"

"No. No, no, no." She shakes her head vigorously and glances nervously at Daran, but he's paying more attention to the guy on stage singing "You Give Love a Bad Name". "You're right. I give him credit for having such big balls, too." She slowly grins. "But as far as him being over there flirting with all those women when you're still here? What a jerk!"

We laugh and clink glasses. Then we down our drinks.

Chloe nudges Daran and says, "I guess you get a pass tonight on singing with me."

"Thank God, for Brandon's sake anyway!" I say, slapping Daran on the back. "Poor guy would *really* be pissed if you stole the limelight from him."

Bad date number two down. Only one to go.

chapter thirteen

My mom's brand new red Lexus is not among the dozen or so cars in Restaurant Hamma's parking lot. Instead of heading in without her, I opt to hang out in my junky Corolla, which stands out like a sore thumb in these upscale surroundings.

During my grade school years, we lived in a blue-collar community where Chloe and I used to ride our bikes all over town. When it was winter or when the weather was shitty, we'd hop on a city bus. Summers were for hanging out at one of the community pools, playing softball or kickball at our school's playground or wandering around the State Fairgrounds, whether it was up and running or not. During the school year, we spent a lot of time at the mall. But then when my stepdad decided to move us to Mukwonago, my mom was randomly leery about me visiting Chloe in our old neighborhood. Suddenly my old stomping ground wasn't safe or good enough.

Nowadays, my mom still prefers to confine herself to certain areas, the North Shore being one of them. So here I sit in my car, staring out at a display full of Persian rugs that cost several thousand dollars or more apiece. I can't imagine why anyone would pay that much for a rug. Do people who own these rugs even walk on them? Or are they just for show?

I jump when my mom raps on the window. "Ready to eat, sweetheart? Oh . . ." She laughs her subtle sophisticated laugh. "I didn't mean to startle you, Jesstine!"

"Hi, Mom," I say, climbing out of my car and slamming the squeaky door shut. Then I lean in for a customary peck on each cheek.

"You look beautiful, honey. That red hair really suits your spunky personality," she says, winking and draping an arm over my shoulder as we make our way to the restaurant entrance.

"Thanks! With all my new dating prospects and being on the hunt for another job, I figured a new look was in order." I laugh to myself as I remember the expression on Free Bird's face when he saw my hair. *Brunettes only.* Puh-lease!

Upon entering, we're met with broad smiles from several striking Asian women standing behind the hostess station. My mom comes here for lunch at least once a week, so they proceed to fuss over her arrival like she's a celebrity, coming out from behind the counter to hug her and drawing the attention of a waiter and the bartender, who both come over for a little gushing themselves. Then the tallest of the beautiful trio—no more than five foot—grabs two menus and escorts us to my mom's usual table. "Enjoy," she says with a slight accent before bowing and disappearing back to the front.

"So with all the new dating prospects . . . does this mean *the golfer* is out of the picture?" My mom smiles sweetly and tucks a long auburn bang behind her ear before briefly fixing her gaze on something behind me. Then she looks down at her menu.

At forty-three, my mom is beautiful and looks like she could be my older sister. Why my dad and stepdad ever strayed will always be a mystery to me. Although, besides gorgeous, sweet, smart, and supportive, she can also be a bit passive aggressive. I mean, I appreciate the way she's never come right out and said she doesn't like Ned, but she's only used his name when he's been present. Otherwise, it's "the golfer" or "Mr. Polo Shirt." And one time, when I showed up at her house in tears because he neglected to invite me to his sister's wedding, it was "that car peddler."

Sometimes I wish she'd come right out and tell me when she thinks I'm making a bad decision or being an idiotic doormat. Sometimes I want my mom to just tell me what to do. But I suppose Pavlovian conditioning and emotional coercion are par for the course when you grow up with a psychology professor for a mom.

"Yes, *the golfer* is definitely out of the picture." She peeks over the top of her menu with a raised eyebrow and piteous grin, telling me with just one look that she thinks I'm full of shit. "Seriously, I'm done with his nonsense. I don't have a clue why I put up with his indifference for so long." That's not exactly true, though, because I've contemplated my dysfunctional relationship with Ned since the beginning. It started with fun, late-night booty calls which slowly morphed into dinner first followed by obligatory sex which somehow morphed into a vicious cycle of me being at Ned's beck-and-call and eventually cheating on him every chance I got because I felt resentful of his indifference toward our "relationship," which was clearly never going anywhere. But I never wanted my mom to know just how weak I was with him, that I allowed myself to fall into such a dead end. Luckily, I decided early into the relationship that there would be things she'd never hear about.

"Well . . . good for you, Jess," she says, closing the menu and placing it on the table to signal that she's ready to order and that I'm off the hook. Then, folding her hands and leaning in, she says with a cheery grin, "So then, tell me all about online dating. And without making it look obvious, have a look at the handsome young men sitting behind you in the corner."

A not-so-stealthy glance over my shoulder reveals a couple of nice-looking guys in suits. They both make eye contact with me and one waves, prompting me to smile and nod. I have to admit, they're hot, and I'd be all about approaching them in the right setting. But their appeal is lost on me due to the fact that my mother is scoping them out.

"Seriously, Mom? Can we just have lunch? Besides, you're still dating Rod, right?"

"Of course I am, honey, but that doesn't stop me from looking. It's okay to look, you know. And I wasn't looking for myself. Keep in mind I have a beautiful, smart, funny, sweet daughter who happens to be single," she says with a sly smile.

"No." I shake my head vigorously. "Uh-uh. Please halt that thought right there. I don't want you on the lookout for me. I'm online dating, remember? Plenty of guys to choose from."

She laughs. "Well, if you don't mind, I just have to continue admiring for my own pleasure." Again, she glances at their table and gets a look on her face that tells me they're returning the attention.

I don't embarrass easily, but my mother flirting with guys who are my age is enough to make me want to crawl into a hole and hide. If it was any other older woman, it wouldn't phase me one bit. It's just . . . she's my mom.

"So," I say loudly, bringing her attention back to me, "about online dating. My experiences so far have been . . . interesting." I proceed to give her a rundown of my dates with Coordinates Kyle, Free Bird and Karaoke Wayward Son, only pausing when we place our orders. Even my mom laughs at the absurdity of Kyle's hiccups, Louis's ghetto ringtone and rude behavior, and Brandon's obsession with karaoke. When I disclose a few tidbits about Sawyer, she smiles broadly with a little twinkle in her eyes. That's the best thing about my mom; I can tell her just about anything because she doesn't judge.

"You know, Jess, I understand that you're still skeptical of this whole process and hoping your date tonight ends up being strike three so you can say you tried and call it quits, but honestly, I think it's great that you're finally ready to give the golfer the boot and go back to playing the field a little."

Um, yeah. Totally with you on giving the golfer the boot, mom. Except, here's the thing, I never completely left the field for Ned.

". . . The various mental and emotional connections humans are capable of making with each other is astounding," she continues, "and the more connections you make, the more you learn about yourself. And like I've been telling you ever since you were a teenager, knowing yourself is the key to being truly happy. So keep learning, honey." She pats my hand and then prepares her wasabi and soy sauce for dipping.

"I will," I say with a smile and an appreciative nod.

"Now," she continues, "tell me about Chloe and that fine young man she met online. Daran, right?"

I can't help but chuckle at her description of Daran. She only met him once when we were out for Chloe's twenty-sixth birthday, and he was on his best behavior, of course. That was also the first time Chloe's mom and stepdad met Daran. What a treat it was for everyone to witness Chloe's mom request to see Daran's military I.D., just to be sure he wasn't lying about having been a captain in the Army. As usual, my mom laughed thinking Jan was just being funny, but Chloe and I knew better. Her mom is leery of every guy on the planet and would probably ask the President of the United States for I.D. if he showed up at her door accompanied by his security detail. When Jan wondered aloud in an accusatory tone why the I.D. was expired, everyone laughed so she was forced to go without an answer to her dead-serious question. Daran handled Chloe's mom like a champ, though, making himself look like quite the catch. Then later that night, he made fun of the interaction, revealing his sarcastic side. Even though she didn't say anything, I knew it pissed Chloe off.

"That's right. Daran." I snicker to myself before continuing. "They're doing alright. I mean, except for the times when Chloe can't help but nitpick. Other than that, he seems to be a good fit for her. He appears to be a smart, hard-working guy, and he has a laid-back, humorous side, which is something Chloe really needs. I guess he also stays in daily contact with his parents and sister, so that's a good sign, right? A family man?"

"That's wonderful. Chloe's a smart girl. And like I've always said to you girls, it's up to you to make the decision to be happy. I'm glad Chloe is working toward that decision. It seems online dating was a success for her, yeah?"

I shrug. "So far, I guess. But I think it'll be a while before she figures out if Daran is "the one."

"Oh, Jesstine, don't be silly. There isn't just one person for each of us. And remember, even if Chloe doesn't end up with Daran, she's learning. Don't forget: Make the connections and learn about yourself. That's all part of the decision-making experiment we call life. You're a smart girl too, you know."

Seeds. My mom is always planting seeds. Seeds of the mystery variety. The kind that I'm forced to sow on my own, not knowing what they might turn into. I think the subtle way she tends to share her perspective is one of the reasons I can be so blunt about voicing mine. The bigger issue here is that I barely heard a word after she said there isn't just one person for everyone. That's not what she used to say.

There was a time when my stepdad was it for her. Does she really believe the claim she's just made? Is her belief in soulmates broken?

"But, what happened to—"

The arrival of our sushi boat interrupts my thoughts, forcing me to wait until the waitress retreats to the kitchen. The second we're alone again, I open my mouth to remind her about our jigsaw puzzle nights when we used to discuss things like dating and love and finding the one. But before I can utter a sound, she excuses herself to use the restroom. Does she know what I'm going to say? Is she trying to permanently divert the conversation? I check my phone for the time. My mom still has thirty minutes before she needs to head back to campus. That leaves plenty of time for us to further discuss why she no longer believes in something she used to encourage me to believe in too.

While I wait for her to return, I separate my cheap wooden chopsticks and roll them against each other to eliminate slivers. Then I rotate between adding small amounts of soy sauce and wasabi to my little ceramic condiment dish, sampling until the ratio is just right.

When she finally returns, I don't waste any time. "Remember our jigsaw puzzle nights?"

"Hmm?" She gives me a curious look as she pops a tiger roll into her mouth. I know my mom well enough to know she's trying to skirt the topic.

"Our jigsaw puzzle nights. When you used to tell me there was one special person in this world for everyone and that you were lucky enough to have found that person and that I would too someday." I take a deep breath, wondering why this is such a big deal to me anyway. Why does it really matter that my mom has changed her stance on the existence of soulmates?

She avoids eye contact with me as she takes a sip of her warm green tea. Then she slowly sets down her cup and pats and smoothes her hair with both hands, something she's always done when she feels uncomfortable. I remember her doing it in my high school principal's office after I got caught smoking in the bathroom during fifth period, when she told me about my stepdad's infidelity, and right before she informed me of my biological father's death. She pats and smoothes as if to ensure that at least something is as it should be, even if it is just her hair.

"Jesstine . . ." She finally looks up at me but immediately starts shaking her head and looks off into the distance behind me. I hear the two men she was checking out earlier getting up to leave, but her gaze isn't on them. She's not really looking at anything. Her eyes are just . . . sad, making me wish I'd just let it go. Despite all of our heart-to-hearts on jigsaw puzzle nights, I'm not even sure I believe in soulmates anyway. So why put her through the pain of remembering a time when she was certain my stepdad was hers?

"Never mind," I say, pinching another sushi roll between my chopsticks. "It's not a big deal. How are things with Rod?"

Like magic, her stoicism returns, and she's back to smiling her confident smile by the time I swallow the roll.

"Oh, honey," she laughs, "Things with Rod are wonderful. You know, I've been having some of the best sex I've ever had in my life." With a look of pure bliss on her face, she devours another piece of sushi.

The thought of my mom having the time of her life because of Rod's . . . well, rod, causes me to choke on a delicious piece of yellowtail.

"Honey? What's wrong? Too much wasabi? Here, wash it down with some tea." She quickly refills my cup, never taking her concerned eyes off me.

Raising a hand, I shake my head to let her know the coughing fit was not wasabi-induced. But she proceeds to add more soy sauce to my dipping dish anyway, diluting the perfectly blended mixture I'd concocted.

"There you go. That's better." And with a smile she goes back to her meal.

"No, Mom, it's not."

"Well, you know as well as I do the burning sensation will wear off as soon as you sip some tea. Anyway, what were we talking about? Oh, yeah . . . Rod. Jess, you wouldn't believe the size of his—"

"Mom! No, I mean it wasn't the wasabi! I can't . . ." I put a hand over each ear and shake my head as if I'm avoiding a gnat. "I can't listen to you talk about sex."

She lets out a laid-back, flippant sort of laugh. "Oooh, really? Since when? We've been talking about sex since your thirteenth birthday. Besides, how do you know I was going to disclose the size of Rod's penis anyway?"

I shudder at the sound of the P-word coming from my mom's lips. Not that I haven't heard her say it before, but all the other times it was for educational purposes. "No, Mom . . . I guess I should clarify. I can't listen to you talk about YOU having sex."

She tilts her head, a confused look on her face. "Well, that's a bit one-sided. Don't you think?"

"No. It's not."

"Fine, fine, fine," she says with a shrug, an airiness to her voice. "Moving on, then. You know . . . I ran into Ashley at the Target in Delafield yesterday. She said you still haven't called."

I nod, my body otherwise frozen at the mention of my half-sister.

"Jess, you know me, I don't usually stick my nose where it doesn't belong, but I really think it would be good for you and Ashley to get reacquainted. You know, move past what happened the last time you visited them in North Dakota."

"Yeah, I know. I'm just not sure it'll be as simple as *moving* past anything."

"Well, she's tried to make contact . . . What? At least half a dozen times since she moved back? So she must be ready to bury whatever went on. And Jess, it's not her fault Gwen is such a . . . well, we both know Ashley is a much nicer person than her mother."

I nod, a lump forming in my throat as memories of my last visit with Gwen and Ashley dance around in my brain.

I'm trying to figure out what to say when my mom glances at her watch. "Oh, honey. I hate when it's time to say goodbye, but I must be off," she says, gathering her purse, sunglasses and keys from the chair next to her. "I have a lecture that starts at one. You wouldn't believe all the attractive young men I have this year. Ah, to be a college student again."

I stand to follow her up front to pay. As usual, I offer to pitch in half or to at least pay the tip, but she tells me I can pay next time.

"Thanks, Mom. Love you."

"Of course, honey. Love you, too," She says as she hugs me tightly on the walkway in front of my car before we part ways.

I hop into my car and as I watch her walk away, I hope to be as put together as she is someday. Not just on the outside but on the inside too.

chapter fourteen

As I drive home, I can't stop thinking about the last time I saw Ashley and my bitch of a stepmother.

It was four years ago (when I was twenty-two) that Gwen decided to sell their house in North Dakota. My dad's job had relocated them there from Milwaukee when I was nine and Ashley was five. Only two years later, he died in a tragic car accident.

Fortunately for Gwen, she grew up in North Dakota, and the bulk of her family still lived there. So even though Ashley was moved away from her grandpa (our dad's father) and me, she barely noticed because she had both of Gwen's parents, several sets of aunts and uncles, and dozens of cousins to dote over and distract her. Unfortunately, for me, their move marked the second time I felt abandoned by my dad—the first time being when he married Gwen.

I didn't care much about being so far away from Ashley because we never really bonded due to our four-year age difference and the fact that I resented her for taking my dad's attention away from me. I cared even less about Gwen. But having my dad so far away . . . that was hard. At least for the first few years after he died, as convoluted as this might sound, I was comforted by the fact I had already gotten used to him being gone when the accident happened and he was gone for good.

After my dad died, my mom never received another child support payment and never saw a penny from his life insurance policy. So when Gwen invited me to North Dakota, I thought maybe it was to surprise me by sharing a small part of the proceeds from the sale of their house. After all, my dad had paid for the massive property outright. So I thought maybe she felt bad for convincing him to desert me and wanted to make amends by giving me *something*. Not that I cared about the money, though—my hope was based more on principle, on actually wanting to have some semblance of a relationship with her, as one of my last ties to him.

To my chagrin, Gwen did have something for me, but it wasn't a check. It was a U-Haul box. Packed snugly inside were a few old photo albums containing pictures of me that my mom had given to them over the years, my old blankie (which I'd given to my dad when I was three so he wouldn't forget me when he and Gwen went on their honeymoon), my old soccer ball, two baseball gloves (mine and my dad's from when he was a kid), a chess board, and every single card and gift I'd ever given him for Father's Days and birthdays. Even though I appreciated that it was filled with objects that represented the love I had for my father and the things we enjoyed doing together, I was angry with Gwen for packing it all up into a box and handing it to me as if it was a bunch of clutter she was glad to be rid of. Luckily, Chloe had kept me company during the long road trip from Milwaukee to Williston. If she hadn't been there to place a supportive hand on my shoulder, I would have lost it. All of the resentment I'd had towards Gwen for convincing my dad to move thirteen years ago would have come tumbling out. And I most certainly wouldn't have been able to bite my tongue about the fact that she's gotten remarried within months of his death.

So there I knelt on the floor of my dad's nearly empty house in North Dakota, staring into a box of daddy-daughter memories. I did my best to hold back the tears and thanked Gwen for saving the mementos for me. No need to start a tiff. I was never going to see her again, not by choice anyway. Plus, I didn't want to upset Ashley, who had actually done her best to stay in contact with me over the years after our dad died, writing letters, calling, and asking if I could visit or vice versa. I rarely reciprocated, and neither of us ever ended up visiting the other. Even though part of me wanted to get to know my little sister, I was still too bitter over the fact that she got to spend so much more time with our father than I ever did.

When Gwen and Ashley invited Chloe and I out to a celebratory closing-day dinner that night, I declined, saying we were too tired from the long drive. But we did make plans to have brunch at Gwen and her new husband's new condo the next morning.

As soon as I loaded the U-Haul box into the trunk of my car, Chloe and I headed straight to the nearest bar. The anger I was feeling over that damn box had me on a mission to numb myself with alcohol, and boy did I succeed. Based on spotty memories of body shots, spilled cocktails, taking off my shirt and falling off of a table while dancing, I know I made a fool of myself that night. But Chloe, the amazing friend that she is, stayed sober and watched over me as I purged myself of all the anger and resentment that had built up in me over the years. And she's never breathed a word about that night since. Nor has she breathed a word about the scene that unfolded in Gwen's dining room early the next morning when I was still half in the bag.

I have four hours before I'm supposed to meet JustJustin77 at Potawatomi Casino for dinner. Neither of us are gamblers, but we both love the casino's upscale steak and seafood restaurant, Dream Dance. If things go well, we might catch a comedy show afterward.

Before going on a date, I usually crank up some tunes and give my full body a good grooming. An avocado-cucumber mask, full leg shave (not just up to the knees like most days), deep hair treatment, eyebrow pluck, and sometimes I even soak my feet and treat them to some love from a pumice stone. But right now, I'm just not in the mood for a pre-date spa treatment.

Plopping myself down on the sofa, I punch in the code for the voicemail on my cell phone and then navigate to the first message Ashley left four months ago.

"Hey, Jess. It's me . . . Ashley. I'm sure your mom already told you I called her for your number. I hope you don't mind. And . . . I'm assuming she probably told you that I moved back a few months ago? Or maybe she didn't. Anyway, I got a teaching job. Special Ed. And I'm loving it. Well . . . I was just calling to see if you might want to get together for coffee or dinner or something. It's been a long time and . . . and I miss you. I know that's weird since we hardly saw each other growing up but . . . well, you know I always wished we had. And Jess . . . all that

*stuff I said when . . . well, you know. I was just upset because of all the things you said. And I'm sorry . . . for everything I said. *sigh* God, this has to be the longest, most confusing message ever. Sorry. I just . . . Can you just please give me a call when you get a chance? My number is 414-959-3727. But you can probably see that on your caller ID. Anyway, please give me a call. We don't even have to—"*

She rambled on so long that my voicemail cut her off. I've listened to this message at least a dozen times and every time I wondered what she was going to say next. About half those times I started dialing her back but backed out. I'm not one hundred percent sure why, especially since it's clear she's willing to let bygones be bygones. I just still can't help but feel like the biggest asshole on the planet for all the horrible things I said to her and her mother. I just don't know if I can face her. My baby sister, my dad's other child.

A glutton for punishment, I'm about to replay the message, but my phone rings and Chloe's face pops up on my screen.

"Hey. Why aren't you teaching?"

"My class has gym. Thank God, too. They all have a bad case of spring fever. Is something wrong? You sound weird."

I sigh heavily. "Nah. I'm fine. Just tired from being out late last night. And I got up early to walk a few miles." I have no idea why I just lied about the walk. Maybe because I meant to get up early for a walk? Whatever.

"Nice! The weather was perfect for a morning walk. Wish I could have joined you."

Chloe pauses for me to respond, the polite conversationalist she is. But I don't feel like compounding the pointless fib. So there's just an uncomfortable silence for a few seconds until she picks up the conversation again.

"Anyway, how's your mom? And how was the sushi?"

"The sushi was great. You should take Daran there sometime since he loves sushi so much." I laugh because Daran claimed to have liked sushi when they first started dating, but it turns out the only thing he'd ever tried was a California Roll.

"Hardee har har. You're hysterical. But yeah, I should choose a sushi restaurant every time it's my turn to decide where we go. It would serve him right." She giggles. "Now, what about your mom?"

I consider whether or not to mention our strained conversation, if you could call it that, about soulmates but decide I'm not up for discussing anything that deep right now. "You know her. She's great, as usual. And get this. She was scoping out guys when we first got there."

"What?! Seriously? That's hilarious."

"Yeah, to you maybe. And then she tried talking to me about her sex life and Rod's cock and—"

"Wait, did you say Rod's cock?"

"Yeah, but—"

"Oh, my God! I love your mom!"

"Chloe . . ." I wait for her laughing to die down. "Imagine you're out to lunch with your mom and she starts talking about how much sex she's having with Glen and then she starts raving about the size of his—"

"Okay, okay. Ewwww. Gross! Never mind."

Now it's my turn to chuckle.

"So what are you and Daran up to tonight?"

"Actually, I think we're staying in. Daran wants to watch this series he has on DVD, *Band of Brothers*. Plus, I've been feeling kinda tired lately. I don't know. Daran just got over a cold, so I think I might be coming down with something now."

"That actually sounds appealing to me right about now."

"What? Staying in? You mean you're not looking forward to your date? I thought you've been chatting with this one and he's pretty cool."

"No, I said he *seems* pretty cool. We both know that could change. Do I need to remind you about your psycho stalker? You messaged back and forth and talked on the phone with that weirdo for a month and thought he was perfect."

"Now, hang on a second. That whole situation with Drew," aka Psycho Stalker, "that was different. There were red flags I didn't acknowledge. You know? You and Shelly tried to warn me, but I wouldn't listen. Remember?" The tone of her voice has gone from casual to defensive, causing me to regret bringing up Drew.

Is she kidding? Of course I remember the possessive glint in his eyes as he watched Chloe dance innocently with Shelly's little brother. The guy was a fucking freak.

"Yes, Chloe, I remember," I say with a snort in an attempt to make the conversation light-hearted again. "And, yes, Justin *seems* cool, so I'm looking forward to meeting him. But going out tonight just doesn't appeal to me at this moment. I'm tired."

"Does this have anything to do with Ned?"

"Of course not!" I say a little harsher than I intended. I make a conscious effort to soften my tone when I continue. "Why do you always assume it must have something to do with him if I'm not in the mood to go out?"

"Sorry. I didn't mean anything by it. But let's get real here . . . Ned has had a lot to do with the emotional ups and downs you've experienced over the last few years. And I know it's not always so simple to just cut ties with someone when you've been seeing him that long. If anyone can relate, it's me. C'mon, you know that."

"I know, Chloe, but I honestly haven't seen or spoken to Ned. And I wouldn't hide it if I did." Not anymore, anyway.

There's an awkward pause, and I feel like one of my closest confidants thinks I'm full of shit. Whatever. I'm done with all the Ned drama. Let my mom and Chloe think what they want.

She continues as if Ned had never come up. "So, who are you talking to besides the guy you're going out with tonight? Any other dates lined up?"

"Hmm, let's see . . . Kyle, the hiccups guy, and I chatted on the phone for about an hour when I was overnight in Grand Rapids. I'm supposed to contact him for a second date when I have some time. Then there's this guy named Scotty who I've exchanged several messages with this week. He wants to keep messaging for a while instead of meeting up or talking on the phone and mostly tells me things about his job as an insurance claims adjuster. So while he's nice, he's also kind of boring. I'm not so sure I'll even agree to a date if he ever decides to ask. Other than that, I've been in contact with a few other guys whose screen names I don't even remember off the top of my head. One hasn't responded to my most recent message, and I've decided I'm not interested in the other two. One of the two keeps inserting 'snort snort' in his messages to convey laughter. And you wouldn't believe the stuff he finds funny—a co-worker of his who got fired, a dead fish that he forgot to feed for three days. Laughing at shit like that is deranged." I laugh, and it suddenly occurs to me that I just detailed my online dating action for the week in one fell swoop. Except I did leave out one tidbit; I haven't told Chloe about Ryan Cross yet. No sense mentioning him when he hasn't even returned my last message, making me wonder if he's had second thoughts about reconnecting with me.

"Eh, depends what the guy was fired for. For instance, maybe he got caught making copies of his ass, which plenty of normal people have done. But the goldfish is definitely not funny, so I'm with you on that being a messed up thing to laugh about."

While I'm busy contemplating Chloe's nonjudgmental attitude toward people who make copies of their asses, she continues, bringing me back to the topic at hand. "Wow, I'm impressed." I sense a hint of delight in her voice.

"Why?"

"Because you're actually keeping track of people!"

"Whoooa, don't get all excited over nothing. I promised I'd try it, and I'm just going with the flow. Bad date number three could happen tonight. And if that's the case, I'm sorry, but— "

"Shhhh, don't say that! You'll jinx it!"

"Okay, I won't say it. I'll think it," I jest.

"Very funny."

"Hey, don't you have to pick your class up from gym?" I ask.

"Crap! I'm late! Call me tomorrow."

There's a click and the line goes dead.

Before I start getting ready for my date with JustJustin77, I lie back on my couch and listen to Ashley's message two more times.

chapter fifteen

Potawatomi Casino is only about ten minutes from my place, but I leave thirty minutes early just in case it takes a while to find a parking spot. As I make my way over the Hoan Bridge, my phone vibrates, but I don't recognize the number so I let it go to voicemail. As soon as the message notification pops up, I listen to find out who called. I don't recall giving him my number, but part of me hopes it was my date calling to cancel.

"Hi, Jess. It's Molly McGinn. Calling to chat about you joining our team! If you're still interested, that is. Either way, please give me a call back tonight to let me know. My cell number is 414-555-3815 Or feel free to call the bar and ask for me. That number is 414-950-2257. Oh, and since you indicated every other Saturday would work for you, we'd love for you to stop in tomorrow if possible! Thanks, Jess. Look forward to hearing from you. Bye."

I pull over as soon as I arrive on the other side of the bridge and replay Molly's message so I can jot down her number. Then I return her call and we iron out a few details. I'll be working twelve to twenty hours per week divided among every other Saturday, Thursdays and the occasional Friday. I couldn't ask for better hours to supplement my flight attendant income.

By the time I arrive at Potawatomi, I only have ten minutes to spare before I'm supposed to meet JustJustin77 at the entrance to the main gaming area. Valet parking is free, but I don't have a lot of extra cash for tipping the attendant, so I pull into the parking garage. I'd much rather risk being late than feeling like an ass because I stiffed someone.

To my surprise, someone is pulling out of the spot closest to the skywalk entrance that leads to the casino. *Must be my lucky day.* If Ned were with me, we'd go right in and bet a hundred dollars on black at the roulette table or on a hand of blackjack. I'll just take the spot though, thank you very much.

As I make my way through the double automatic doors leading into the skywalk, a flirtatious whistle rings out from behind me. If it were dark and I was going in the opposite direction, I'd increase my pace, but since it's a little before five and there are people all around, I slow a bit, curious to get a look at the source of the whistle. I won't look over my shoulder just yet, though. Several muffled voices come from the same direction of the whistle and I sense bodies closing in behind me. Another low whistle. I can't help but grin because it feels good to be noticed, even if I don't know who's whistling. But then it occurs to me that it could be some slimy pervert, so I decide to pick up my pace after all. Another whistle, louder than the first two.

"Jesstine? Is that you?"

The familiar voice makes me stop dead in my tracks, and as I turn around I hear a different voice.

"Wait, you know her?"

"Yeah, I think so."

Standing in front of me is the whistler, a tall guy I don't recognize. He's surrounded by guys of all ages and sizes. Most keep walking right on by, but one stays with him.

"Yep, I do. Hi, Jesstine," Sawyer says with a sparkling smile that makes my stomach do somersaults.

"Sawyer, hey. What are you doing here?"

"Ahem," the whistler coughs a little. "Dude. You gonna introduce me?"

Sawyer chuckles and shakes his head, seemingly amused by his buddy's interest in me. "Sure. Jeff, meet Jesstine. Jesstine, this is my cousin Jeff."

Despite Jeff's extreme height, I can see the resemblance. They both have the same icy blue eyes and youthful look, despite their salt and pepper hair. Although, Jeff's hair has a bit more pepper than Sawyer's. But unlike Jeff, there's something about Sawyer that draws me to him—something I can't see. I felt it the first time I met him in the parking lot at McGinn's, and I feel it now.

Jeff extends a hand. "Lovely to meet you, Jesstine."

"Yeah, you too. And . . . it's actually Jess."

Sawyer grins at me, causing more somersaults.

"Damn, Sawyer. You need to at least be able to remember a name if you're going to have any success out here in the dating world." Laughing, Jeff slaps Sawyer on the back.

I can't help but wonder about the story behind Jeff's comment. Has it been awhile since Sawyer has made an appearance in "the dating world"? Perhaps a recent break up?

Sawyer's sexy grin is gone, and he's shaking his head. "It's not like that, Jeff." He briefly makes eye contact with me and then his eyes dart back to his cousin. "Can you give me a sec here? I'll catch up."

So he doesn't want to be in "the dating world"? Is that what he means? Or maybe he isn't interested in me, so he's not interested in advice from Jeff.

"Yeah, sure dude." Jeff eyes Sawyer quizzically. Then he looks to me and says, "I hope you know those whistles were meant as compliments." He follows up with a wink before slapping Sawyer on the back and taking off after the others.

"Bachelor party," Sawyer says, nodding toward the mass of men in the distance ahead of us. Then he rests a hand on my lower back for a split second, guiding me as we start walking toward the I.D. checkpoint. "You?"

"Date."

"Another guy from online?"

"Yep."

"Well, hopefully this one isn't an asshole because I won't be there to rescue you."

"Assuming I'd want to be rescued."

We look at each other sideways, both of us grinning.

"Hi there, ma'am. I.D. please?" The security guard says politely.

"Oh, yeah, of course," I say as I begin frantically digging in my purse for my driver's license. "Maybe you can check his while I get mine."

"Nah, I don't need to see his."

"Hmm, yeah, I suppose not, huh? He does look a lot older than twenty-one. Older than thirty even," I say, smirking at Sawyer as I hand my license over to the guard.

"Thirty!" the laughing guard exclaims. "Try forty!"

"Thanks a lot, Tony," Sawyer says with a grin.

My eyes are still wide with disbelief moments later when Sawyer and I ride the escalator down to the main level of the casino. "You're forty?"

He lets out an airy laugh through his nose. "I just turned forty-one last month. Surprised?"

"Heck yeah. I was totally joking back there. You don't look a day over thirty! How did the guard know? Are you a regular here? A gambling addict?"

"No," he says, shaking his head. "I don't gamble. Mmm, that's not true. I don't gamble in casinos. Tony has lunch at McGinn's at least once a week." Another airy laugh escapes him, giving me the overwhelming urge to feel that very air on my skin. As we step off the escalator it hits me. Maybe I should be going on a date with Sawyer instead of some guy I met online who I might not have an ounce of face-to-face chemistry with. "So, have you figured out why Bobby and I did a shot for you?"

"Yes! I just got the call from Molly herself on my way here. At least, I assume that's what you're talking about, that I got the job."

"Yep. Congrats." He slugs my shoulder as if we're old buddies. "So I guess we'll be seeing a lot more of each other then."

"Guess so," I say with a shrug, trying to play it cool, despite the surge of excitement that just coursed through my veins at the mention of seeing more of each other. I've never been this attracted to a buddy before.

"Well, I have to catch up with the rest of the guys." He says the words, but his hands are in his pockets and he doesn't move to leave.

Maybe he's thinking the same things I'm thinking. I hope so, anyway.

As I open my mouth to speak, I notice Justin on the escalators. He's watching Sawyer and me and waves when I make eye contact. I raise my hand in a half-assed wave. "That's my date."

Sawyer gives me that grin of his, sending my hormones into a frenzy, and he turns and waves at Justin too. Then he starts moving backward onto the casino floor, "Good to see you, Jesstine." He gives a casual salute and disappears into the crowd.

"Bye, Sawyer," I whisper to myself.

I muster the most sincere smile I can and head toward my date for the night, a big part of me wishing it was Sawyer.

~

When I get close enough to Justin to see his face clearly, I'm struck by how much more handsome he is in person. His hair is sandy brown, and his eyes are hazel like mine, which wasn't apparent in his profile pictures. I'm also surprised by how much more bulky he is than I expected, given that he described himself as athletic. It's actually a pleasant discovery because I can't help but feel a bit self-conscious around guys who are really fit. But the initial physical attraction I feel toward him does nothing to ease the butterflies over Sawyer that are still zipping around in my stomach, and I can't help but be a Negative Nelly and think to myself that there's no way Justin's personality will live up to his good looks.

"Hi, Jess," He says with a confident grin that screams *Look out! I'm a charmer!* "It's so good to finally meet you. You look beautiful."

I glance down at my simple jade shift dress and strappy silver sandals then back up at Justin. "Thank you," I say, a real smile spreading across my face this time. "Good to meet you too." He's way too handsome and charming for me to not give him a fair chance. So I resolve to forget about Sawyer. For now, anyway.

When we get to the table, Justin briefly takes over for the maître d' and pulls out a chair for me. Then he makes me feel even more special by requesting a bottle of red wine and a bottle of white when I can't decide which I want. It occurs to me that this just might turn out to be the best first date I've ever been on. Even if the date takes a turn for the worse at some point, this could still go down in history as the best first fifteen minutes of a first date.

"So, Jess, tell me about yourself. I want to hear anything and everything."

"Whoa, talk about pressure," I joke, taking a sip of white wine.

He laughs. It's a friendly, sophisticated laugh, the kind that makes me feel like I really could tell him anything. But I don't, of course, because there are just certain things you don't tell people, especially on a first date. For example, when he asks about Sawyer, it doesn't seem like the best idea for me to disclose that he's a guy I picked up in a bar last week after meeting him for the first time. So, instead, I tell him I work with Sawyer. It's really not a lie because, technically, I have been hired. I just haven't worked my first shift yet. And when he asks why my last relationship ended, I simply tell him marriage wasn't in the cards for us, that we didn't share the same values. That answer is probably received much better than if I'd told him I was basically acting the part of Ned's perfect Stepford girlfriend, and that instead of ending things with him when I knew I wasn't happy playing this role, I decided to cheat on him every chance I got. These things might make for awkward conversation.

I do tell him about the six years I spent partying while I earned an undergraduate degree in psychology (UW-Whitewater for two years and UW-Milwaukee for four) and about my job as a flight attendant. To my surprise, he doesn't laugh or look confused or even ask why I utilized my hard-earned degree to become someone who serves people drinks and cocktail peanuts on airplanes. Instead, he tells me how much he respects flight attendants because being responsible for the safety and happiness of others is an extremely tough job. That sentiment put his brownie points through the roof.

"So you're out of town three to four nights a week for work and as of tomorrow you'll be waitressing at Molly McGinn's a few nights a week? Sounds like you thrive on variety."

Tilting my head and looking up to the ceiling, I contemplate that for a few seconds. "Yeah, I guess I do. For now anyway," I say as I take a bite of my spring green salad with goat cheese and walnuts. It feels good to not have someone tell me I'm wasting my potential or that I'm working a dead end job with no ladder to success—both things Ned used to say.

"Wow," Justin says, dabbing the corners of his mouth. "You have to try these scallops." He holds out a forkful of the appetizer he ordered.

I quickly swallow what's in my mouth. "Um, can I just . . ." I pick up my unused fork and point it toward the dish in the middle of the table.

"Oh, geez," he says pulling his hand back. "Of course you don't want to eat off my fork. Sorry. It's just that I'm feeling surprisingly comfortable with you already . . . Please, help yourself." He pushes the appetizer plate closer to me, then smiles shyly as he takes a tiny sip of wine, barely putting a dent in it.

"No, it's not that," I say stabbing my fork into a bite-sized, bacon-wrapped scallop. "I just feel weird about being fed," I say with a laugh. "I actually wouldn't mind swapping spit with you at all." I shove the scallop into my mouth as my face reddens at the realization of the unintentional insinuation I just made. This surprises me because I've purposely insinuated much worse on many occasions. But as I already suspected, Justin has a good sense of humor to go with his perfect manners and crazy good looks.

"Sounds great. Let's go." He half-stands, pretending he's ready to rush out of the restaurant for a make-out session.

Grinning, I shake my head. "Maybe later. I don't think I know you well enough yet to risk missing the opportunity to eat my steak while it's warm and juicy."

We both reach for our wine glasses as he sits back down. The face-to-face chemistry between us in undeniable as we eye each other coyly and sip our wine.

"You're right, those were amazing," I say, nodding toward his empty appetizer plate and setting my glass back down. The only way I'm going to avoid jumping this guy's bones tonight is if I focus on getting to know him instead of allowing myself to overdo it with the wine. "Your turn. Tell me more about you."

"Well, you already know the basics about my son Max."

I nod and smile. "Yeah, sounds like you two had a great time last weekend, for his birthday. What's your schedule like with him? When will you see him again?"

For the first time tonight, Justin's happy, light-hearted demeanor falters slightly. "Ah . . . I don't get to see him much. Two or three times a month, tops. With my work schedule and the tight extra-curricular activity schedule his mom keeps him on, it can be a challenge. Having him on his actual birthday was such a treat. But . . . I do what I have to do to see him as regularly as possible." His eyes migrate from the table to meet mine. I sense sadness and that he might be in need of a sympathetic ear. "Unfortunately, his mom would like nothing more than to cut me out of the picture completely."

Everyone has baggage. Even if they appear to have their shit together, there's always something. I'm guessing this is Justin's something—a difficult ex and a child in the middle.

"Well, that sucks. What's wrong with her? Why would she not want you to see your son?"

He closes his eyes and slowly shakes his head before reopening them. "Do you really want to know about all this? I feel like I've already said too much for a first date."

"Of course, I do," I say, giving his hand a squeeze.

But at that moment, the waiter arrives with our food and we become distracted by the heavenly aromas. After we've both had a chance to indulge in a few bites, I try to reignite our conversation where it left off, but Justin insists it would be more appropriate some other time—after we've gotten to know each other better. Keeping me in suspense is certainly one way to ensure a second date.

"So where does your son go to school?

"Max goes to Dalton Elementary in Pewaukee. That's where he lives most of the time too. With his mom and stepdad."

"He's in kindergarten?"

"Yep. Hard to believe I have a kindergartener already." He eyes me, as if he's trying to determine whether or not I'm leery about him having a son. I'm not and I'm tempted to just come right out and tell him so, but then I figure maybe it's better if I don't just in case I need an excuse to stop seeing him in the future. It's probably a selfish reason to not say anything, but at this point, everything I do is going to be in my best interest, not his or anyone else I happen to meet through Yahoo! Personals.

So I change the subject.

"Tell me more about your job. You said you're in security at Miller Park?"

"Well, sort of . . . I'm actually the vice president of park operations."

"What? Wow, that's . . . amazing. This might be a dumb question, but what exactly does a VP of operations do?"

He laughs. "Definitely not a dumb question. In fact, I wondered the same thing when a friend of mine suggested I apply for the position two years ago. Before that, I was actually living in Minnesota and working for the Twins."

"Did . . . all of you live there? I mean, your ex-wife and your son too?"

He pauses, staring at his wine glass as he gently swirls its contents. Then he smiles, and I sense the expression is forced. "Yes, my ex and I met in a class at the University of Minnesota, and Max was born there."

"Oh, okay. Now what were you saying about your job?" I ask, letting him off the hook about discussing his ex.

"Right, anyway, the technical description of my job is something like *oversees the day-to-day operations of the facility and all of its events and blah blah blah*. But," He dramatically raises an eyebrow. "I'm basically a glorified supervisor for Miller Park employees—the vendors, the maintenance staff, the security guards, the ushers. Trust me, my title makes the job sound much more exciting than it really is."

"What do you mean? That sounds like an amazing job. And how cool is it to be able to tell people you're the vice president of an entire ballpark?"

"Well, I'm not the only Miller Park employee with a job description that includes VP. But since you're so impressed, feel free to call me Veep," he says with a wink.

"All right then . . . Veep. Say, any chance you can get a girl into a game for free. You know, with all the pull you must have?"

"Actually, I can. All you'd have to do is give me a call at least thirty minutes before a game starts and let me know which gate you're at. I could probably get you and a few others in. But you'd have to do one thing for me."

"Oh yeah? What's that?"

"You have to agree to go out with me again."

"Hmmm . . . I'll need some time to think about that, Veep." I say with a grin. Free ballgame or not, I'd be crazy not to go on another date with this man.

"Okay." He stares at his watch for a few seconds and then looks back up. "Time's up. Do we have a deal?"

I can't help but laugh out loud and say with a dramatic sigh, "Alright, alright. If that's what I have to do to score a free Brewers game, then that's what I have to do."

Now we both laugh and the lighthearted mood of our banter continues throughout the rest of dinner. In fact, we talk so long that the nine o'clock show at the comedy club, also located in the casino, is no longer an option.

"So . . . are you up for another drink? Or maybe a little gambling?" Justin asks, reaching out to brush a misplaced bang away from my eye. Despite nursing my third glass of wine throughout the bulk of our time at the dinner table, the sweet gesture has me ready to shove my tongue down his throat. Instead, I do my best to harness my attraction for him and remind myself of my goal to really get to know him before any serious messing around.

"Well," I check my phone, not because I really want to know the time but because my raging hormones have me feeling flustered. One more drink is likely to turn into one more and then . . . "I have to be to McGinn's tomorrow . . . by ten. And I'm afraid if I don't get a good night's sleep—" Lame. Of all the excuses I could have come up with. It's only ten fifteen. Who needs *that* much sleep? Damn hormones.

But Justin doesn't seem to notice I'm fumbling my words. "Say no more. I completely understand. At least let me walk you to your car." He offers an arm, which I lace mine though, locking elbows with him. "Did you use the valet?"

"Nope. Second floor first spot right outside the doors."

We make our way toward the escalators and for some reason I can't help but look for Sawyer among the crowd surrounding the Blackjack tables. What's wrong with me? Justin just treated me to the best dinner I've had in months, and he was a perfect gentleman, the kind of guy I've been reminding myself I deserve. The kind of guy who makes Ned look like the biggest douchebag on the planet. Yet I'm searching for a guy I barely know.

Turn that leaf, Jess.

We're about to step onto the escalator but instead I pull Justin off to the side.

"What's wrong? Did you forget something at the—"

Shaking my head, I raise myself onto my tippy toes, lean in, and kiss him smack dab on the mouth. Our lips stay locked together for only a few seconds but it seems like minutes. I open my eyes and begin to pull back, but to my surprise, Justin wraps his arms around my waist and pulls me in for more. The second kiss is much longer and more intense. Nothing slobbery though, not the way Ned used to kiss me after he'd been drinking, or the way Brant *always* kissed me. Justin's lips are strong and soft, and he's doing something I don't recall anyone ever doing before while kissing me. He's holding back, and I get the sense it's because he's a gentleman, not because he's playing hard to get.

Even when a group of people pass by to board the escalator, we continue to kiss. But then I hear a couple of low whistles and someone whispers, "Looks like your friend is going to get lucky tonight," causing me to pull back and peek over Justin's shoulder. And there's Sawyer, watching me swap spit with Justin. He's halfway up the escalator and surrounded by fellow bachelor partygoers. His cousin is standing next to him and watching us as well. The sly grin on Jeff's face is in stark contrast to Sawyer's unreadable gaze.

Justin turns to see who I'm looking at, and he immediately raises a hand to acknowledge Sawyer and Jeff. Or maybe he's doing it to give them a hint. Something along the lines of *quit staring, assholes.* However they took it, it works like a charm and they turn away, blending back in with the pack.

When Justin turns back around, his eyes lock on something behind me. It's a guy selling single flowers with the little water tubes attached to the stems. "Wait here," he says, pulling out his wallet as he rushes off.

While he's away, all I can think about is the blank look on Sawyer's face, and it takes every fiber of my being to resist the temptation to look in his direction again. Just when I fear I can't hold out any longer, Justin returns with a single daffodil and holds it out to me.

"Will you accept this . . . daffodil?"

"Oh great, a Bachelor wannabe," I say with a chuckle, taking the yellow flower from him. "Yes, I accept. And for the record, you're much hotter than the guy they have on that show right now."

"Why, thank you." He again offers me an arm, which I accept. "Now, let's get you to your car."

Justin calls my cell so that we have each other's numbers and makes me promise to text him when I get home. Then he kisses me again before I hop in my car, only a peck this time though.

My stomach does somersaults.

chapter sixteen

By the time I finish washing my face and getting into my purple plaid pajamas, it's a little after eleven. I don't feel like crawling into bed just yet, so I wander out into the living room, not really sure what I plan to do. I'm not a TV person, and I don't feel like starting a book because then I'd run the risk of staying up all night. Besides, after three glasses of wine, I won't be able to concentrate on either of those things anyway.

As awesome as Justin was about me declining his offer to have another drink, he had to have thought my excuse was odd. Our date was perfect as far as first dates go. Too bad I suck at providing excuses on the fly. But I had to get my butt home in order to avoid letting myself down. Odds are good that if I'd spent more time with him, especially without a large table in between us and people all around, we would have done much more than kiss.

As if telling me what she thinks I should do, Mags jumps on top of my laptop and meows. I reach a hand out to the Persian, and she aggressively nuzzles my fingertips.

"I don't know, Mags, the guy I went out with tonight is nice. *Really* nice. Maybe I should go out with him a few more times before setting up any more dates." Mags meows. "Fine," I groan dramatically as I move her to the sofa, "I'll see if I have any messages. But I'm *not* sending any."

Opening my laptop, I take a seat on the floor and lean my back against the sofa. Then I wait for the old thing to fire up while Mags nuzzles my hair.

Before logging into Yahoo! Personals, I sort through my email. It doesn't take long because it's mostly filled with spam from online retailers and friends who spend way too much time sending out stupid chain emails and long life-lesson stories that are intended to make people cry. The only thing the stories do is make me do is click *delete*.

My inbox also contains two notifications from Yahoo! Personals. One is my daily list of matches, which is always ridiculously long because I don't have any parameters set. So I guess any guy who signs up is a potential match for me as far as the system is concerned. The other email tells me that I have two new messages and a few pokes. I open this one and click through to the Personals website.

As usual, my first order of business is to ignore the pokes. There are actually five now because the email had been delivered to my inbox several hours ago. I click to ignore the first four, but the last one takes me by surprise. It's from the same woman who poked me a week ago. At least I think it's a woman since the screen name is Woolf Woman. Curious to find out, I click the profile. The little thumbnail enlarges to fill a quarter of the screen, revealing an attractive female with black shoulder-length hair and blunt bangs. Her bright red lipstick makes her skin look ghostly pale, but I only ponder for a second if she ever goes out in the sun because I'm too distracted by how beautiful she is. In fact she's so beautiful that if I was a lesbian . . . Wait, I didn't categorize myself as a lesbian. So why did Woolf Woman poke me? Do I look like a lesbian to her? And what kind of a screen name is Woolf Woman, anyway? If it was a guy who spelled wolf wrong, I'd exit out of his profile immediately. Heck, I'd never have opened the profile in the first place. But this is a fellow female so I assume there must be a reason for the error and continue checking her out.

Woolf Woman – 32
Location: Milwaukee
Seeking Friendship and More

Relationship Status: Never Married
Kids: No
Want Kids: No
Ethnicity: White
Body type: Curvy

Height: 5' 5"
Religion: Spiritual
Politics: Don't Ask
Smoke: Socially
Drink: Socially
Pets: No
Education: Bachelor's+
Employment: Library Media
Income: 30,000-40,000

As with all the others, her profile doesn't offer much insight, in my opinion. What people should do is make a video of themselves doing something from everyday life. For example, I'd love to see Woolf Woman assisting a library patron. Watching someone converse with strangers or doing something they do often would be so much more revealing than these meaningless stats.

I close out of her profile and drag the little pointer on my screen to delete the poke, my finger hovering over the touchpad. But for some reason, I don't click it. Instead I ponder if I could be missing out on the love of my life by ruling out women. On impulse, I poke Woolf Woman back.

Great. Now I'm a pathetic poker too.

On to the messages, of which there are now three instead of two.

The first message is from Scotty, the insurance claims adjuster with the fuzzy profile photo.

Hi Jess,

How was your day? You had sushi with your mom, right? Any plans for tonight? No, I'm not suggesting we meet up. Not yet anyway. Just curious. I've really been enjoying getting to know you through our messages.

Work was craaaaazy today. Most people think being an insurance adjuster is boring, but I beg to differ. You wouldn't believe the case I had today. Picture this: a compact car and a city bus. Let's just say the bus won, and I had a doozy of a time filling out the paperwork. Now, tell me my job is boring. Ha!

In case you're wondering, I'm doing a little bowling tonight. Fingers crossed I get a lot of turkeys!

My favorite type of food is Italian. What's yours?

Talk to you soon,
Scotty

Up until now, the only thing Scotty has told me about is his job and that he's a big fan of Shark Week on Animal Planet. So the fact that he's revealed he bowls and that he likes Italian food is actually a big step. Not necessarily a step that makes me want to meet him any more or any less than I already do, but a step. I sigh and tap out a quick response, despite the fact that I didn't plan on sending any messages tonight. I ask Scotty what superpower he'd choose if he could and how often he bowls and who with.

Message two is from Ryan Cross.

Hey Jess!

Sorry it took a while for me to get back to you. I had a crazy busy week because report cards were due and I help out as assistant coach for the boys golf team. (Did you know I teach world history at Waukesha South?) I also try to avoid this account during the week. I'm not even going to tell you how long I've been going through notifications!

Of course I remember Chloe! I didn't talk to her much in high school because she hung with a different crowd and always dated older guys, but how could I forget her? You two were attached at the hip all through grade school and middle school! What's she up to these days? Do her parents still live in our old neighborhood? Mine moved out to Delafield last year. And what about your parents? Are they still in Mukwonago? I see your profile says you're in Milwaukee. What part?

I could go on and on, but I actually have to head out the door in a few minutes. (I'm meeting up with someone for a second date tonight. Wish me luck!) As for the two of us getting together, I'm booked for the rest of this weekend and then I'll be heading off to Cabo San Lucas next weekend for my cousin's wedding. How about if I give you a call when I get back? That is, if you're okay with sending me your number. Mine is 262-959-9587 if you'd like to just text it to me. No point in us communicating through Yahoo! Personals when we've known each other for over a decade.

I'll be in touch in a couple of weeks.

Take care,
Ryan

A few seconds pass before I realize my brow is creased and I'm frowning at my laptop screen. He has a date and wants me to wish him luck? What the fuck?

I guess Ryan isn't my destiny after all.

I shake my head, suddenly annoyed with myself for even thinking that finding Ryan on Yahoo! Personals was anything more than a coincidence.

I grab my phone and text him.

Me: Hey Cross. Now you have my number. Have fun in Cabo! ~Jess

The final message is from Wildman, the guy my co-worker James poked without my consent. I'd actually forgotten about him until now.

Jess!

Just checking in to say HEY! How's it going? Any chance you're willing to bypass all the online chitchat and just meet up sometime? I assure you your co-worker didn't poke no lunatic. Scout's honor. I work weekends and most Thursdays, but I happen to have this coming Thursday off if you're free. Let me know if you're interested.

Cheers!
Brock

Even though he didn't answer a single question I asked in my message to him, I click to respond. The questions were pointless anyway, and I'm all for diving right in to see if there's any chemistry.

Hey yourself, Brock.

Sure, I'm game for skipping all the messages back and forth. My number is 414-950-1304. Give me a call and we'll figure something out.

Talk to you soon!
Jess

I hit send, log out of Yahoo! Personals and my email, and shut down my laptop. "So much for not sending any messages," I say to Mags as I close the lid. "You happy now?" She meows a few times as if to say *it's about time you put some work into dating*. Or possibly *Good, because I'd hate for The Golfer to start coming around again*.

Ready to hit the sack, I peel myself off the floor with a yawn. I turn off the lamps in the living room and then head to the kitchen for water, Mags trailing behind me. As I'm filling my glass, the phone rings. On the second ring, I pick it up and check the caller ID. Just as I suspected: Mr. Polo Shirt. On the third ring, I almost answer. Almost. By the fourth, I come to my senses and slam the handset back onto the base. Then I unplug the phone to prevent the answering machine from picking up.

When I walk back into the kitchen to finish filling my water glass, the daffodil from Justin catches my eye. It's on the counter in a smooth, turquoise vase with a bulbous base and thin neck only big enough for a couple of flowers. The colors remind me of summer days when Chloe and I used to ride our bikes all over town. And suddenly I feel happy, almost euphoric. I know it's probably a result of the wine, but it still feels good, the feeling and the fact that I'm actually dating for real for the first time in my life.

And like my mom suggested, I'm learning. Learning to give people a chance, myself included.

chapter seventeen

When I arrive at Molly McGinn's for my first day on the job, I'm shocked by all of the cars already in the parking lot. There are at least a dozen, and it's only a little before ten. This would make sense if it was St. Patrick's Day (or even the week of) or if there was a festival going on and people were taking the McGinn's shuttle to the Summerfest grounds, but there's nothing this week. I guess McGinn's is more popular than I thought.

"Hey, Jess!" Claire greets me with a sunny smile the moment I walk through the door. Seeing her gives me a brief flashback of my date with Free Bird. Yikes. Hopefully that doesn't happen again. "All set for your first shift?"

"Hi, Claire," I say with a polite grin. "It's been awhile since the last time I waited tables, but I think so. Molly instructed me to see you, so . . ."

"Yep. You're with me today," she says, beaming. "Come on. I'll show you where to punch in and where the clean aprons are."

We proceed to the right of the bar and walk through a door that leads to the kitchen and a back room. My heart rate increases for a second because I'm wondering if Sawyer is here yet, but the kitchen is empty.

"The kitchen always opens at eleven, but as you just saw, people—mostly regulars who treat this place as a second home—still come in for booze bright and early. The only time you should need to come in here is before and after your shift—to punch in and out, and to get your apron and other stuff." She stops at a little machine that looks like a credit card reader but twice the size, and taps in a four-digit code. "I waited to punch in until you arrived," She says while retrieving a little piece of paper from her apron. "Your employee number is two six six zero. Go ahead and punch in. Then hit enter." I do what she says as she keeps talking. "When you're done, the screen should show your name and the time. Make sure it says IN next to the time when you punch in and OUT when you punch out." I check. "If you forget to punch in and it says IN when your shift is over, that's a pain in the ass for Molly because she has to go in and manually enter your start time. Not that it takes long, it's just annoying. You know?"

"Yep. Totally understandable. Aprons?" I point to an assortment of McGinn's embellished clothing (aprons, chef jackets, T-shirts) arranged in neat stacks on a shelf right next to us.

She nods and grabs two aprons. She hands one to me and begins putting the other one on. "These are always clean. At the end of your shift, just throw your dirty apron in that bin." She points to a corner of the room. "If you ever show up without your T-shirt or need a clean one, that's what these are for." She motions to the stack of tees and then moves a few steps over to a row of cubbies. Pointing at them, she says, "Order pads and pens. Here you go," she says handing me one of each and placing an identical set in her apron pocket. I do the same.

"If you have a bag or purse, you can stick it in one of those lockers, but you have to bring a lock. I don't think anyone here would steal your stuff but you never know, I guess. That Sawyer can be a slippery asshole sometimes." She peers over my shoulder with a grin. I turn to see Sawyer punching in. "Totally kidding. Sawyer's the last person who'd steal anything from anyone."

Sawyer smiles and nods. "Hey, Claire." He makes eye contact with me and winks, and the flirtatious gesture causes a brief flutter in my chest.

"Jess? You still with me?"

I turn quickly to face Claire. "Yeah, of course."

"Great, let's get out there then so we can go over a few procedures and get today's specials on the board."

By the time eleven o'clock rolls around, Claire and I are bombarded with customers, those who arrived well before the kitchen opened as well as a steady stream of newcomers. Fortunately, most people are ordering the specials: homemade Reuben rolls and smoked fish soup with Irish potato bread. Even so, the crowd might be overwhelming if I'd never waitressed before, but the constant movement and need for me to stay focused is doing wonders for my sanity. No down time to think. No wondering if my date with Justin was a total fluke. (Can a guy really be that great?) No wondering if I'll actually hear from Ryan when he returns from his trip to Cabo. No wondering how long it will be before Ned shows up at my apartment unannounced.

Shortly before three, just when I'm beginning to wonder how much longer Claire and I will be able to stay on top of orders, my airline co-worker, Anne, arrives for her shift.

"Anne! How are you?" I ask.

"Super! And happy you're here," she says. "I knew they'd hire you. With all the new specials Sawyer has been whipping up, they really needed more quality help."

Sawyer is the one who comes up with the specials? I might have to stick around after my shift ends to see what all the fuss is about.

"Well, thank you. I owe you big time for referring me. The hours I'll be working fit in perfectly with my flight schedule."

"That's why I love it here too. Molly is so flexible with scheduling, and the shifts are over before you know it. I need to punch in. See you in a bit?"

"Yep, talk to you later."

~

"Are you cool with taking care of the next order on your own while I deliver this one?" Claire's hands are gripping the large serving tray we've just loaded up for table nine.

"Yeah, of course," I say with enthusiasm. Since Anne arrived, things haven't been as hectic, and I've basically been shadowing Claire's every move for the last couple of hours. As a result, bored to death doesn't even begin to describe how I'm starting to feel about training.

"Awesome! I figured you wouldn't mind," She says as she lifts the heavy tray and turns to leave.

According to the big glowing Guinness clock on the wall, it's five fifty-five. Another waitress named Jillian is supposed to take over for Claire and me at six, but Claire says she's always at least five minutes late.

"Here you go, Jesstine." Sawyer says, placing two corned beef sandwiches in the pickup window.

"Thanks." I crease my brow at him for using my full name, but he's already busy reading the next ticket, so I grab the plates and turn to deliver the goods.

"Hey," he calls out when I'm already a few feet away. I return to the window expecting him to ask a question about the next order. Instead, he surprises me by saying, "Are you hanging out for a while after your shift?"

He's been nothing but business with me all day long, so to be honest, my ego is feeling a bit bruised. After spending a night with him, even if it was just a fling, I can't help but wish for a little extra attention beyond the lame wink he gave me earlier.

"Not sure," I say with a shrug. "I was thinking about staying for a bite to eat because I hear the specials are halfway decent. But I may just head up the road to McDonald's to grab something I know I'll like." I try to keep a straight face as I dole out the sarcasm.

"I guarantee whoever is grilling up the frozen burger patties over at Mickey D's isn't going to put his heart into making your meal like the cook here will. And I'm guessing he's not nearly as good looking either. So I think you should stay," he says with a coy grin that causes a flutter in my chest.

"Well, since you put it that way . . . I guess I'd be silly not to stay for Reuben rolls and fish stew." With that, I turn to deliver the food I'm holding. I sense Sawyer's eyes are still on me, causing a smile to spread across my face as I put a little extra sway in my step.

Fifteen minutes later, I'm climbing onto the same barstool I sat on the night I met Sawyer. Claire and her husband have reservations for Comedy Sportz at eight, so she left as quickly as possible after introducing me to Jillian.

"What can I getcha?" The burly bartender, Bobby, leans forward so he can hear over the crowd, his bearded cheek and gauged right earlobe only inches from me. He's a good looking guy with thick dark hair and green eyes, but the strong, syrupy scent of his cologne causes me to lean back a few inches before answering.

"I don't know. Surprise me."

"Yeah?" He stands upright. "You sure?"

I shrug, too tired to decide.

"If you say so," Bobby says with a mischievous grin.

I'm on my feet when I'm serving people on airplanes, but I get to sit down during takeoffs and landings. And during longer flights there's always plenty of time in between to read a little or sit and stare out at the tops of the clouds. Today, there was no down time. What I should really be doing is going home to take a bath because my feet are killing me. But the way Sawyer asked me if I was staying and the pointed glances he gave me when I was punching out has me itching to spend more time with him. Plus, I'd like to ask him about the condom wrappers I found in my garbage can.

Bobby begins pouring assorted ingredients into a shaker. I saw vodka go in, so I'm not worried. Anything with vodka tastes good to me. As I listen to the ice rattling loudly, I catch a glimpse of Anne leaning her elbows on the server counter. Looks like she's flirting with someone. My gut tells me it's Sawyer, but I can't see who she's talking to from this particular angle. Jesus, could she force her tits together any tighter?

"Here you go!" Bobby says as he sets a double highball glass in front of me, careful not to spill the hazy pink liquid.

"What is it?" I ask, grabbing the straw and giving the concoction a stir.

"That bitch," he points at the drink with both index fingers, "is a Mongolian Motherfucker."

"Well then," I say, amused by the dead serious tone of his voice, "it best be tasty with a name like that."

He motions for me to give it a try, so I lean in and take a long hard sip from the straw. The second the liquid hits my tongue, I know it was a mistake to tell Bobby to surprise me because this is *not* the surprise I was hoping for. The drink is so strong, my face involuntarily contorts, and I start gagging and motioning for Bobby to grab a glass. "Water . . . I need water!"

"Oh . . . your face . . . Oh my God . . . Priceless . . ." Bobby can barely talk he's laughing so hard.

"When I said surprise me, I didn't mean by poisoning me! Is that even a real drink?"

"Hell yeah, it's a real drink. Look it up. Mongolian Motherfucker." He grabs the drink from in front of me, and moves to dump it, but I stop him just in time.

"Hey, wait a sec! I'm going to see if a friend of mine wants to join me. She'll drink anything."

Bobby smiles as he places the nasty beverage back on the square McGinn's napkin in front of me and slides it a little to my right. "Now, what can I really get for you?"

"A vodka cranberry please."

He nods and gets right to work making a more palatable drink for me, and I flip open my phone to call Chloe.

"Hey, what are you doing right now?" I ask as soon as she answers.

Bobby delivers my drink and I give him a nod.

"Nothing really," she says with a yawn. "I just woke up from a nap."

"Why? You never nap."

"I told you I haven't been feeling well, didn't I? Or maybe I told my sister. I don't know, I feel like I can't remember anything lately."

"No, that was me. Maybe you should see a doctor if you're not feeling better soon."

"Yeah," she yawns, "I think I will, but it won't be until Thursday. Report cards are due on Monday and we have parent teacher conferences on Tuesday and Wednesday night. Too much stuff going on."

"Any chance your nap has you energized enough to come to McGinn's for dinner? I just finished my shift and—"

"Wait . . . you just got done working eight hours, and you're going to stay there to eat?"

"Yeah, so? I'm hungry," I say pointedly.

"Are you sure that's the only reason?"

"Yeah, why? The specials look amazing and—"

"The specials, huh?" I hear the playful suspicion in her voice. "This wouldn't have anything to do with a certain chef would it?"

"Of course not," I lie, chuckling as I continue. "I told you, I'm hungry. And I told you this morning what a great time I had with Justin. So what makes you think I'm stalking Sawyer?" I lower my voice to a whisper and cup my free hand over my mouth when I say Sawyer's name.

"Well, you did mention that it kind of drove you nuts when you saw him last night and he gave you a buddy vibe."

"Right. But why would I want to hang out with him in a T-shirt that reeks of corned beef and armpit sweat if I wanted to create a different vibe between us? If that were the case, I'd go home and shower first or change my shirt at least." *Hmm, maybe I should change my shirt.*

"Well, I still don't think you'd give his behavior toward you a second thought if you weren't interested in him. And after eight hours on your feet, I know a big part of you—the part that isn't affected by raging hormones—probably wants nothing more than to go home and take a hot bath. So something is keeping you there."

"Well, at least you got something right . . ."

Chloe chuckles. "What? That your hormones are raging for him or that you want a hot bath?" I remain silent causing her to continue laughing as she asks, "So, what are the specials?"

"Does that mean you'll come?"

"Depends. What are the specials?"

"Irish fish soup with some Irish type bread and Reuben rolls. Those are Irish too."

"Well, no shit. You do work in an Irish pub and grill."

"*So*? You coming?"

"I guess so, but I can't stay long. I have to be home by nine at the latest. Daran is coming over after he gets done having drinks with some of his co-workers."

"He didn't invite you?"

"He did. But I didn't feel like driving thirty minutes to where they're meeting."

"Lucky for me McGinn's is only a ten minute drive for you. Do you want me to order something for you?"

"You and I both know I won't be there in ten minutes, so no thanks."

"Well how long do you think you'll be?"

"Maybe thirty . . . forty minutes."

Great. Knowing Chloe, it'll be at least an hour unless I badger her a little. "Come on, Chloe. Throw on some jeans and a T-shirt and hop in your car already. Or just wear whatever you're wearing. It's already after six, so by the time—"

"Alright, Alright. I'll be there in twenty."

"Fine, I guess I can live with thirty minutes."

"I said I'll be there in . . . Ohhh, you're funny."

"I know," I say with a smile on my face.

We both know it'll be closer to forty.

chapter eighteen

"Awwww, that's so sweet," Chloe swoons over the daffodil Justin gave me. Then she goes into analysis mode. "I wonder if he'd have gotten you one if you guys hadn't made out . . ."

I respond with a shrug as I flag down Bobby. Then I change the subject. "I can't believe you drank that mess. You don't want another, do you?"

"Uh-uh. I need to eat. That drink . . ." She hiccups. "Excuse me. That drink was too strong even for me." She swallows hard a few times and rubs her stomach before continuing. "Actually, I'm not even sure I'll be able to eat much. Now my stomach is feeling crappy too."

I order myself another vodka cranberry and both specials. Chloe orders the same thing but with water instead of alcohol.

"So anyway, I'm pretty sure I'll see Justin again sometime next week, but we haven't planned anything yet. He knows I fly out tomorrow and I'll be back on Wednesday evening, and I know the Brewers are in town this weekend, which means he has to work. So that narrows down the days we have to choose from. Either Wednesday night or Thursday when I get done here."

"Why don't you bring him to Home Bar for BAB night?"

"Ugh. I can't believe you still go to that." An image of the Wednesday night crowd at Home Bar pops in my head. People of all different ages and shapes and sizes are all stuffing their faces with big ass burritos the size of sub sandwiches. BABs, as the regulars call them. And by regulars I mean people like Chloe and Shelly.

"Don't forget, Wednesday is also ladies night. Hellooooo, dollar top shelf mixers . . ." The way she announces the discounted drinks makes her sound like a game show host. "Seriously, it'll be fun. And cheap. It's your turn to pay, right? And then Daran and I can meet Justin and give you our opinion of him."

I'm not sure why she thinks I even want Daran's opinion, and I'm really not that interested in finding out. So, moving on . . . "Dollar top shelf drinks *are* a nice incentive, but I'll have to ask Justin what he wants to do before I give you an answer. I don't even know if he likes Mexican food. Speaking of Daran, anything new? Do you have any freshly shaved—"

"Stop! Gross. I told you that shit's not for me, so no. But Daran *has* been wanting me to do something even *less* appealing."

"What is it?" I resituate myself on my stool, sitting straighter and leaning into Chloe so I don't miss a word she says.

She sighs, shaking her head and grabbing a Reuben roll from the double order Bobby just set in front of us. Then before taking a bite she says, "Dirty talk."

"Ooooh. Tell me more!" Chloe stops chewing and frowns at my enthusiasm. Obviously, she'd like me to share her disappointment, but I happen to think a little dirty talk is arousing and fun. I pop a Reuben roll into my own mouth and pause to savor the flavor before motioning with a hand for her to continue.

"What exactly do you wanna hear? The stuff he says or the stuff he tells *me* to say?"

"Both."

"Well, he says all the typical things you'd expect to hear in a porno. You know, lame shit like *you know you want it* or *you're soooo wet, baby*. It all sounds so absurd!" She rolls her eyes and pops another roll into her mouth. She must be tipsy from the Mongolian Motherfucker because she proceeds to talk while she chews. "Wow, these are really good." Nodding in agreement, I pop another roll into my mouth, and we just sit and chew for a bit. Then Chloe goes on, "But the stuff he says is nothing compared to the things he wants *me* to say."

"Yeah, like what?"

With a sigh, she delivers a list of requests that even I'm a little shocked by, not because any of it is too dirty for me, but because I can't picture straight-laced Daran saying these things. ". . . *your cock is magic, fuck me harder, make me your cum bucket,* oh and my favorite, *I'm your dirty little cum whore*. Do you believe this bullshit?"

She flips me off when I burst into laughter. "Sorry, it all sounds so ridiculous coming . . ." I have to pause for another laugh. ". . . *coming* from you. And what's the big deal anyway? If you don't want to talk dirty, then don't."

She balks at my suggestion. "At first it was fine because I thought we'd do it the one time and then maybe only when we've both had too much to drink. But ever since he got me to say a few nasty lines, he wants me to say them every time! Every. Fucking. Time. Last night I told him it does nothing to enhance sex for me and it's actually kind of a turn off, so he agreed to cut it out."

"Well, then that's good, right? I mean, if it's what you want."

"No, no, no. He agreed before we got going but then during, he kept whispering things. *Please, Chloe, please just say it once. Just one time. Tell me you're my dirty little cum whore.*" At that moment, Bobby sets our soup and bread in front of us. His eyes transform into saucers and a sheepish grin spreads across his face at the mention of a dirty little cum whore. He's about to say something, something constructive, I'm sure, but Chloe is so worked up she just keeps right on talking. "It really pissed me off because he agreed we could have sex without all that nonsense." Bobby turns away reluctantly when a customer at the other end of the bar waves him down.

"Maybe he was just caught up in the moment?"

"No, please don't do that," She says shaking her head vigorously. "Don't make excuses for him. We've been having sex for months now and all of a sudden he can't cum without me saying all sorts of brainless filth? I'm dead serious, Jess, brainless. On Tuesday I said everything he wanted me to say in a monotone voice. I mean zero inflection. And he came super fast! This is just my luck. I meet a nice guy who's got everything going for him but all of a sudden he can't cum without dirty talk. Do you think there's something wrong with him?"

"What? No, of course not! He's a man for Pete's sake! All men like a little bit of nasty. All men. Don't flake out over this. Honestly, I don't think it's a big deal."

"Wait! I forgot to tell you. He also wanted me to tell him about a time when I blew someone, *while* we were getting it on! Tell me *that's* not weird. I mean, why would he want to envision me with some other guy's cock in my mouth? Do you think he has homosexual tendencies?"

Apparently that last question was rhetorical, because Chloe freaks out when I pause to ponder my answer.

"Dammit! Just my luck. He's probably bisexual. And things have been going so good."

"Chloe. Do you hear yourself? You went from complaining about filthy talk in the bedroom to thinking Daran is bi in less than five minutes. Daran's not bi or gay or whatever. I'm sure of it . . . So which story did you tell him?"

"I didn't tell him one," she says, shaking her head at me as if it was a stupid question. Then she takes a bite of her soup.

"I bet Daran would love the one about horse cock guy."

Chloe chokes on her soup. Perhaps it's the result of a flashback.

"Hey, ladies," Anne says as she pulls up a stool behind Chloe and me.

"We'll come back to horse cock later," I whisper to Chloe before addressing Anne. "Hey," I say scanning the packed pub. "Don't you have tables?"

Her mouth full of Irish potato bread, Chloe looks over her shoulder and gives Anne a nod and a wave. Then she turns back to finish eating.

"Yeah, but everyone has been served their meals. So I'm taking a short break. Jillian is going to walk around and see how everyone is doing."

I nod once and then ask, "Do you mind?" I use my spoon to point to the bowl of soup in front of me.

"No, not at all. Do you?" She holds up a cigarette.

"Nah, go ahead. Wait, Chloe what about you? Do you mind if Anne has a cigarette while we're eating?"

"Uh-uh. This soup is so good," she mutters, glancing briefly from me to Anne and then back at her bowl.

"Yep, that's Sawyer's magic. He's such a talented cook." Anne lights her cigarette and then cranes her neck as she looks toward the order window. "Hot too."

Chloe's head snaps to face us, her attention finally off of her soup.

"Don't you ladies think so?" Taking in a big drag of her cigarette,

Anne looks from me to Chloe and then back toward the kitchen blowing the smoke behind her to avoid sending the secondhand smoke right in our faces. Chloe cranes her neck, too, curious to check Sawyer out for herself. "I'll be surprised if you don't. A lot of the single ladies who come in here—hell, even some of the married ones—ask if he's seeing anyone. We tell them yes, of course."

I hope that's a lie and they only say it to keep the predators at bay. Or maybe he is in a relationship and that's why he insisted nothing happened between us. Maybe he feels guilty. I think about asking Anne for clarification, but Chloe jumps in.

"So, Anne, you've been working with Sawyer for a while now . . . Anything ever happen between the two of you?" She raises an inquisitive eyebrow.

"Nah . . . it was nothing."

"Wait, what does noth—"

"What do you mean by—"

Chloe and I start talking at the same time, but Anne interrupts. "Oh, no! Nothing like that. I mean, we've hung out a few times after our shifts and talked about some pretty heavy stuff, but that's it."

It was nothing. I only allow her words to bother me for a few seconds before reminding myself it doesn't matter either way. The nature of Sawyer and Anne's relationship is none of my business.

Chloe and I both nod and take bites of our soup while Anne takes another drag. Then she says, "So how's the online dating going?"

"Eh, okay, I guess," I say with a shrug. I go back to my soup, hoping to end the discussion of online dating before it even gets started. I like Anne, but I get a weird vibe from her sometimes, as if her judgment meter is waiting to kick into high gear.

"Oh, come on," Chloe says to me. Then she looks at Anne. "She had a *great* date last night. With a guy who works for the Brewers."

"Oh, yeah?"

The tone of Anne's voice tells me she thinks Chloe is being too optimistic, that maybe she thinks I'm not capable or worthy of a great date. Or maybe it's all in my head. I'll forever be embarrassed that she knows about Brant as a result of one unfortunate night when we shared a couple bottles of wine over fondue at my apartment. Not that Anne's an angel or anything—she did confess to me about cheating on a boyfriend once when they'd had an argument—but I got the feeling she lost respect for me when she found out I messed around with a married man. So I don't exactly feel like sharing the details about my date with her.

"Yeah, it was a good time," I say dismissively.

"So you'll see him again?"

I nod and finish chewing the chunk of fish in my mouth. "That's the plan."

"And she has two more guys lined up to meet her," Chloe says enthusiastically. I look at her with probing eyes, wishing she would stop offering information to Anne so freely. I can't even say for sure that I'll even end up going out with Scotty and Wildman. She raises a confused eyebrow and busies herself stacking her dishes and wiping breadcrumbs off the bar in front of her.

"Well, that doesn't surprise me," Anne says.

Chloe quickly turns to face her. "What is that supposed to mean?" I didn't get the feeling Anne was trying to be condescending, but Chloe obviously did.

"I don't know." Anne's eyes widen and her cheeks redden. "Just . . . I'm not surprised that she's meeting a lot of people. Isn't that the point?" She shifts uncomfortably in her seat, probably because Chloe's glare hasn't eased up one bit. Now I'm not sure whether she's defending me or online dating, but either way, I love her for it.

"Well then," Anne hops off her stool and slides it back in place at the empty table right next to us. "I should get back to work. Maybe I'll see you tomorrow," she says to me, doing her best to ignore the awkwardness in the air.

Chloe gives the counter in front of her one more wipe and then reaches over to stack my dishes too.

"Yeah, maybe we'll both get the Atlanta route," I offer.

"Oh, I love that route!"

"Yeah, me too," I say with a weak grin.

"Nice to see you again, Chloe," Anne says as she turns to leave.

Chloe's expression softens considerably in response to Anne's friendly demeanor, and we both say goodbye to her in unison. Then we flag Bobby down for water refills, and I proceed to tell Chloe about how Kyle and I have been playing phone tag and how I sent Wildman my number. I want to tell her about Ryan Cross, too, but decide to wait and see if he contacts me when he gets back from his trip to Cabo. No sense discussing someone from my past who may very well end up staying there.

She's excited about the prospect of me meeting yet another guy in person and marvels at how much better online dating seems to be going for me than it did for her. I consider bringing up the fact that maybe it had something to do with how hard she tried to whittle down her options by being insanely choosy, but we've already discussed many times that even the slightest change in her strategy could have altered her course. And then she might not have met Daran. So I simply agree with her that things are going well, and I surprise myself by really believing it's true.

When I bring up Woolf Woman, her expression goes from pleased to confused.

"Wait, so did you poke her back just to be polite? Or are you really interested in her?"

"No, I didn't poke her to be polite. The fact that she poked me twice got my attention and triggered an impulse poke from me."

She ponders my spontaneity for a few seconds, and then says, "Well, you did make out with Shelly's friend Cally in the bathroom at Home Bar that one time . . ."

I laugh, remembering that drunken night. She just shrugs and goes back to being excited. After all, it's because of her that I'm putting myself out there. And it's a hell of a lot further out there than she ever ventured with online dating.

"I'm so happy online dating is going well for you, Jess. I just hope you can stay strong with keeping Ned out of the picture. I'd hate for him to ruin the experience for you."

"Well, that shouldn't be too hard because, like I told you—several times—I'm not taking Ned's calls anymore. Besides, you were totally right about using online dating to keep my mind off "old habits." Granted, I've been extra busy lately, but that's not the only reason I have zero desire to see Ned. I'm pretty sure I felt butterflies this week . . . they were good ones too."

"With Justin?" she beams.

I nod because she's right. Justin did give me a few flutters. What she doesn't know is that I also felt flutters because of Sawyer and a few times when I was reminiscing about Ryan Cross. I guess now that I've split from Ned for good, the butterflies inside of me that have been subdued for so long are finally waking up.

"I'm *so* done with Ned." And that's when my phone, which is sitting face-up on the bar, vibrates and displays Ned's picture. *Oh great.*

"You sure about that," she says, looking up from my phone.

As soon as the vibrating stops and the asshole's face disappears, I grab my phone and delete the call log and his number, purposely holding it up so Chloe can see what I'm doing.

"See? I told you. I'm done."

"Alright," She says skeptically. "I believe you."

My phone vibrates to indicate a voicemail notification, but Chloe doesn't notice because she's now focused on something else. Or should I say *someone*? I follow her gaze to where Sawyer is filling a pint glass with something from the soda gun at the opposite end of the bar. He stares in our direction and smiles with his eyes when my gaze meets his.

"Hey!" Chloe taps my arm. "I know that guy!"

"You do?" I ask, looking over at her.

"He bought everyone at Home Bar a round of shots on Wednesday night," she says, turning to face me. "What? Why are you looking at me like that?"

"That's Sawyer," I say with a subtle grin, my eyes migrating back to him. He's about to head our way when Bobby taps him on the shoulder, causing him to turn away from us.

"*That's* Sawyer?"

I turn back to Chloe, meeting her troubled gaze. "Yeah. Why do you look like that?"

"Oh, no reason. I'm just surprised, that's all." She grabs her water and takes a few swigs, averting my gaze.

"Baloney. What's up?"

"Well . . . I talked to him that night. He was sitting at the bar all by himself and I was waiting for drinks. It was after he bought the round of shots for the twenty or so people who were there. I thanked him and asked what the occasion was." She takes another sip of water.

"That was cool of him. What was the occasion? And why are you acting weird?" *Please don't say he hit on you.*

"He said he was celebrating because . . ." She stares at her water glass, slowly running her index finger across its sweaty surface.

"Come on . . . just tell me. What was he celebrating?"

"Signing divorce papers," she mumbles.

"Divorce papers?" I ask, the wheels in my head picking up speed. She nods and picks up her glass for another drink. "On Wednesday?" She nods again, this time while taking a long sip of her water. "So, did he mean he actually got divorced that day? Or . . . "

"No," Chloe says softly, finally looking at me again. "He said the next six months are going to be the longest six months of his life. Because I guess that's how long you have to wait to actually get divorced after you sign the paperwork."

I close my eyes and sigh.

"Hey, at least you didn't know this time." Chloe's voice is filled with compassion.

But I should have known, especially since I felt such an attraction to him. My DNA just doesn't allow me to feel anything for guys who would be good for me. It always has to be the messed up or married ones. I wonder what Justin has hiding in his closet.

"Jess, you didn't know," she says more sternly.

Shaking my head, I say, "It doesn't matter. I still slept with another married man. What the fuck is wrong with me?" My eyes snap open, and I glare in Sawyer's direction. I'm not necessarily glaring at him, but rather at what he represents to me at this moment.

"What do you mean? You *did not* know. You just met him, and he didn't tell you. So don't be so hard on yourself."

"It's not just that he's married. I fucked another guy I *just* met. *What* is wrong with me?"

"Nothing's wrong with you, Jess, nothing's wrong with you," she says as she rubs small circles into my back.

But her words of comfort do nothing to lessen the anger and disgust I feel toward myself.

chapter nineteen

"Ladies," Sawyer says with a nod and a charming smile. He leans over the bar, extending his right hand to Chloe. I eye his arm, which is only inches from me, and have a flashback of staring at the very same arm the morning we sat at my dining room table eating breakfast a week ago. "I'm guessing you're Chloe? I'm Sawyer."

She nods and shakes his hand, a confused look that mirrors my own spreading across her face. He doesn't remember her? I look up, hopeful that Chloe was mistaken about seeing him at Home Bar that night.

Sawyer's smile fades slightly as he draws his hand back, his eyes migrating over to me. "I'm glad you stayed. How did you guys like the food?"

Chloe and I simultaneously tell him how much we enjoyed the specials as he glances back and forth between us. When we finally stop talking, he cocks his head and narrows his eyes at Chloe. "Have we met before? I feel like—"

"Yeah, we have actually. I was at Home Bar on Wednesday when you were out . . . celebrating." Chloe purses her lips and raises her eyebrows. Then she grabs her water glass and looks up at one of the TVs mounted behind the bar as she takes a sip. This is her way of giving us the illusion of privacy, even though I know she'll be listening to every word Sawyer and I are about to exchange.

Sawyer nods, realization spreading across his handsome, whiskered face. "Oh. Yeah, that's right. You were with that group that was playing cards."

Damn. So it was him.

His expression turns apologetic when he meets my gaze. "Judging by the look on your face, I'm guessing Chloe told you what I was celebrating?"

"Yep."

"And I'm guessing you'd like an explanation?"

"That's up to you," I say, shrugging and trying to make it seem like I'm not at all curious about his situation even though I am. How could I not be curious? "You must have your reasons for not mentioning you're married. Either way, no worries. We can still be friends."

He gives me a dubious look. "Tell you what. Dinner service ends at nine." He glances at the Guinness clock on the wall. "So I'll be shutting things down in the kitchen in about fifteen minutes. Then, if you're willing, I'd like to talk some more. What do you say?"

"Sure, but I hope you don't feel like you owe me anything."

"Great, then I'll be back in a bit," he says, ignoring the latter part of what I just said to him. Then he turns to Chloe. "Hey, nice seeing you again."

"Yeah, you too," she says with a wave.

We watch Sawyer walk away, and as he disappears into the kitchen, Chloe says, "I can see why you're attracted to him. Not only is he good looking, but he seems like a really sincere guy. I wonder what his story is."

"Me too," I say, despite giving Sawyer the impression that I'm not at all curious about his relationship status.

Just then, Bobby shows up. "Can I get you two anything else besides water? The kitchen is closing soon so this is your last chance to order from the dinner menu. After that, the only thing available will be pizza and nuts."

"No, thanks I think we're good. Just the bill please," I say with a smile.

"No problem," he says as he heads off to the cash register.

Chloe stands, pushes her stool in and adjusts the red hobo bag hanging across her body. "I need to get going. It's almost nine. And . . . " she yawns, ". . . I'm super tired. How much longer are you planning to stay?"

"Just long enough to chat with Sawyer a bit."

"Okay," she says as she begins to yawn again. "Call later if you need to talk."

"I will."

Bobby plops our bill down on the bar and keeps moving on to the people sitting next to us. Chloe digs around in her bag and then throws some cash on the bar. I do the same, except my bill is a lot less since I get a free meal when I work.

"So I'll see you Wednesday at Home Bar?" Chloe asks as she leans in to give me a hug.

I wrinkle my nose at the mention of the dive bar she loves so much. "I don't know. Depends on if Justin and I make plans for that night. If we do, I'll mention it as an option and let you know."

"Dollar top shelf mixerrrrs . . ." she says as she takes baby steps backwards. I roll my eyes and wave her off, prompting her to turn with a laugh and make her way through the crowd to the door.

I turn in my seat to face the bar and contemplate ordering another drink. But for once, my better judgment prevails, and I resolve to stick with water.

I want to remember everything Sawyer has to say.

~

"This seat taken?" Sawyer asks as he pulls out the stool Chloe had been sitting on minutes earlier.

I peel my eyes from the TV behind the bar and smile at him sideways. "Chloe had to take off, so it's all yours." I look at the TV again, my heart racing because there's no longer a chef's coat covering his fitted gray t-shirt. I can smell the same fresh, manly scent I smelled on him the first time we sat at this bar together. In contrast to cologne, which most men seem to wear too much of, Sawyer's scent is clean and subtle like a body wash or deodorant. He isn't wearing his blue bandana anymore either, exposing his salt-and-pepper hair, which has developed a bit of wave because it's longer than it was a week ago.

Watching the TV is an act, of course. Ever since Chloe left, I've actually been inconspicuously scoping out the kitchen door. I tried people watching a few times, but my eyes kept migrating back to the kitchen. So I settled for the Brewers game instead, but my mind never stopped keeping tabs on that door.

Sawyer slides his keys, phone and a pack of Camel cigarettes onto the bar as he climbs onto the stool. Then he looks from one end of the bar to the other until he spots Bobby and flags him down. "You want something besides water?" He asks, eyeing my glass.

"Thanks, I'm good. I have to get up early tomorrow for work, so . . ." *And the last time we drank together, you ended up in my bed.*

Sawyer orders a bottle of Miller Lite and a water refill for me. We don't exchange any words while we wait for Bobby to grab the beer, but we do stare at each other. It's only for about ten seconds, but it's long enough to make us both crack smiles.

"Here you go." Bobby places the beer in front of Sawyer as he uses the nearest soda gun to refill my water. Then he raps twice on the bar with his knuckles before rushing off to help more customers. "I got that one," he says over his shoulder.

Sawyer raises his bottle in gratitude and takes a swill. Then he sets it on the bar with a sigh before swiveling his seat to face me. Instead of turning my whole body to face him, I turn my head and rest my cheek on my palm.

"So, you're married," I blurt.

"I am, but we've been separated for a little over three months . . ." He looks around. I assume it's to make sure no one is listening in on our conversation. ". . . and as you know, we officially filed for divorce earlier this week."

"Yeah, I'm sorry to hear that."

He cocks his head. "So, you're not upset that I didn't say anything when we met?"

"Pshh. No, of course not." I sit upright and turn my body to face his. I'm not being completely honest, of course.

"Are you sure? Or was I imagining the awkwardness earlier when Chloe mentioned my *celebration* at Home Bar?"

"No, you weren't imagining, but I wasn't upset with you. I was upset with myself."

"Why?" He asks, furrowing his brow. "You're not dating anyone exclusively, so it's not like you cheated. And trust me, there's no reason for you to feel bad about my wife. Our marriage ended months before we decided to separate." He grabs his beer and takes a long pull, polishing it off.

While he's drinking, I'm busy admonishing myself for my experiences related to the issues he mentioned. I may not have cheated on anyone this time, but I've got a long way to go before I can live down all the times I betrayed Ned, even if he is an asshole. Then there's Brant's wife and kids . . . Even though I'm no longer an accomplice to his betrayal of them, I don't think my conscience will ever allow me to forgive myself. Not fully anyway.

"Jesstine?" Sawyer's voice pulls me from my thoughts.

I smile at him. "Why do you keep calling me that?"

"Because it's your name?" He says it like it's a question.

"Right, but only my mom calls me Jesstine. How do you even know that's my full name?"

He clutches his chest with both hands and laughs. "You know, I'm actually a little bit hurt that you've forgotten so much about last Friday night. I thought we really connected."

Shaking my head, I bring my fingers to my eyes. "I know! I'm sorry. It's not something I'm proud of. That's for sure."

"Hey, I'm joking," he says with a throaty chuckle as he gently grips my wrists and pulls my hands from my face. Then we lock eyes. "Not about us connecting—I meant that—but about me being hurt. Who hasn't gotten shitfaced a time or two and woken up with alcohol-induced memory loss?"

We stare at each other long enough that I need to remind myself to breathe. At that point, we both look away, me reaching for my water and Sawyer flagging Bobby down for another beer.

"Okay, so back to my name," I say. "How do you know it?"

Bobby slides another Miller Lite onto the bar, and Sawyer nods a thanks before answering. "First, will you tell me why you were upset with yourself?"

My initial thought is to say no or make something up, but before I know it, the truth comes spilling out of me. "I was involved with a married man, a pilot. Of course, I didn't know he was married at first, but after a while I found out through casual conversation with a fellow co-worker. Not only does he have a wife, but he also has two kids. But . . . I continued to see him anyway because he led me to believe his wife was horrible to him and that they were headed for divorce soon. I know it was wrong, and that's why I cut things off with him for good several months ago and vowed to never do something like that again. I still don't even know if his wife really is horrible to him or not. Doesn't matter though. Whatever the situation is, it just doesn't matter. Sleeping with a married man is wrong." Once it's out, I wait with baited breath for Sawyer to tell me what a rotten person I am or to agree that I should feel bad.

Instead, he says, "Well, that's good. You did the right thing. But you do realize what happened with us is different, right?" He grabs his Camels and taps the pack against his palm until one pops out. He lights it up and takes a drag before looking at me again.

"I guess so, but the bottom line is you're married, and I slept with you without even bothering to ask. What's worse is I was too drunk to ask."

He shakes his head at me and then takes two more drags before responding. "So, like I said, my marriage ended months before my wife and I separated. That's the first thing I hope you can wrap your head around. The second thing is something else I already told you . . ." He leans in close to me so that our noses are inches apart. "We didn't have sex." Then he sits back upright, widening the distance between us, and continues in a more lighthearted tone. "As for you being drunk? I dunno. Drunk schmunk. People get drunk. I can't help you with that one," he says with a laugh.

I have questions about his insistence that we didn't have sex, but instead of asking, I laugh too. I can't help it. "Drunk schmunk?"

He shrugs and his laugh tapers off. "Alright. Back to your name. Do you remember those older guys, Artie and Duke? The regulars we were talking politics with?"

"You must mean the ones *you* were talking politics with? I don't talk politics . . . No, not really."

"Okay, so somehow the fact that you're online dating came up again, and Artie and Duke were asking you all sorts of questions. You know, because the idea of online dating is unfathomable to a couple of old geezers like them?"

"You're an old geezer," I say, grinning.

"Watch it." He grins back and points the neck of his beer at me. "Anyway, you mentioned that Chloe gave you the subscription for your birthday and that you thought it was an April Fool's Day joke at first. Well, Artie's birthday happens to be on April first too, and apparently he's never met another person with the same birthday. He joked about not believing you, so you whipped out your driver's license to prove it. And that's when I noticed your name."

"So you peeked at my license when I showed it to Artie? That's creepy. Did you memorize my address too?"

He laughs as he sets his empty beer bottle down on the bar and checks the time on his phone. "You want to get out of here?"

"Like . . . together?"

"Yeah, I'm having a good time talking to you and it's not even ten yet. We could hang out at my place. What do you say?"

"No," I say shaking my head, "I can't go to your place."

"I'm not hitting on you, Jesstine. I just like hanging out with you."

"Oh, no, I didn't think you were. It's just that I really need to get some sleep since I need to be at the airport by six a.m. tomorrow morning."

"Shoot, that's right. Another time, then."

"Definitely."

Sawyer stands and gathers his things off the bar, and I follow his lead.

"So, I'll walk you to your car then," he says as he tosses a five dollar bill on the counter.

"Thanks, but you don't have to. There are cameras all over the parking lot."

"Yeah, I know. But I'm still walking you."

When we get to my car, I open the driver's side door but don't get in right away. Part of me is tempted to say screw it and go to Sawyer's or invite him to my place so I can spend more time with him, and I almost do. But then Sawyer says, "Hey, I forgot to ask how online dating is going . . . You'll have to update me on your escapades next time I see you."

"Sounds like a plan," I say, trying to sound upbeat even though the last thing I want to discuss with Sawyer is my dating life. "And you'll have to tell me more about what happened when we got back to my place last Friday night. I have questions."

"And I have answers," he says, smiling. "Now go on, get out of here. You need some sleep."

Sawyer waits until I'm in my car with the door closed before he turns to leave. The butterflies in my stomach go nuts as I watch him walk away.

Why does he have to be married?

chapter twenty

As soon as I pull into a parking spot outside my apartment, I dig my cell phone out of my purse. It vibrated a couple of times while I was driving, reminding me that I haven't checked it since I called Chloe earlier. I have one voicemail, which I know is from when Ned called earlier, and the two texts that recently came through.

The first text is from Justin and the second is from the number I recognize as Ned's. I make a mental note to find the owner's manual for my phone one of these days to see if I can block his calls and texts. For now, I'll just delete and ignore. I open Ned's message and immediately press the key to delete without reading a single word. I can't help but notice a few words in all caps, but I couldn't care less what they say. Next, I click on Justin's message.

> **Justin:** I hope your first day on the job went well! Ready to plan our next date?

I'm happy to hear from Justin, but my chest began tightening as I read his message and not in a good way. The feeling confuses me, and I can't help but suspect it's because of the small crush I'm developing on Sawyer, the crush I know I shouldn't have, at least not until his divorce is finalized. But a lot can happen in six months, so allowing my feelings for him to get in the way of other, more imminent dating prospects doesn't make sense. I sigh heavily as I get out of my car without texting Justin back right away.

When I insert my key to unlock the door to my apartment, the resulting muffled thuds and skitters from inside make me chuckle. My cats are big babies when it comes to needing attention so they tend to charge to the door when I return after being gone for extended periods of time. Fortunately, Chloe lives close enough to swing by when I'm overnighting to feed them and give them a little love. The moment I open the door and flip on the hall light, my cats aggressively rub against my legs, nearly causing me to fall on my face as I make my way inside.

"Hey, you two. I know, I know. I'm sorry I was gone so long," I say as I duck into the dark dining/living room to toss my purse on the dining room table. Then I bend down to give each cat a thorough scratch on the head. This appeases Savannah, and she disappears into the kitchen. Mags, on the other hand, follows me into my bedroom where I change into comfy shorts and a t-shirt and then into the bathroom where I wash my face and brush my teeth. When I emerge from the bathroom, I'm tempted to flip off the hall light and take a left back into my bedroom so I can crawl into bed. But then I remember Justin's text so I turn right instead. Mags follows.

The flashing answering machine light catches my attention as I enter the dark living room. I grab my purse as I pass the dining room table on my way to the machine. When I press play, Ned's voice fills my apartment, causing Mags to hightail it into the safety of my bedroom. My index finger inches toward the delete button, but the surprising sound of sobriety in his tone stops me from pressing it.

"Jess, we need to talk. I don't want to be a dick and just show up, so please call me. Look, I get why you're pissed. I was out of line when I left you that voicemail message on Sunday. I have an early tee time tomorrow morning so tonight's going to be an early night for me, but I'll answer if you call . . ."

It's unusual for him to be sober on a Saturday night and even more unusual for him to be home so early, even if he does have an early tee time in the morning.

"I love you, babe . . ."

But the most unusual thing by far is the fact that I still don't give a shit about what he's saying.

"It's time for us to kiss and make—"

I jab the delete button and head to the kitchen for a drink.

I open the fridge and reach inside for a cold bottle of water. Before the door is completely closed, my eyes are drawn to the illuminated turquoise vase that contains the yellow daffodil Justin gave me. This prompts me to flick on the light above the stove and add fresh water to the vase. Then I twist off the cap of the water bottle and take a long guzzle before grabbing my phone and texting Justin back.

> **Me:** Hey, Veep! My first day was a cinch. ;) How do you feel about a double date with my friend Chloe and her boyfriend on Wednesday night? It would involve a dive bar and burritos . . .

I flick off the light above the stove and head to my bedroom. Before I climb into bed, I set my phone on my night stand and double-check that my alarm is set for five a.m. No sooner do I close my eyes when my phone vibrates. I grab it, assuming it's a response from Justin, but I'm wrong.

> **Sawyer:** Thought you might be interested to know Love Connection is on. I'm taking notes for you. Sweet dreams, Freckles.

Sighing heavily, I reread Sawyer's text once before shutting down my phone and putting it back on the night stand. Then I close my eyes and do my best to clear my mind so I can fall asleep.

chapter twenty-one

I'm greeted by a grinning Stan Boyd when I arrive at the TSA checkpoint. Even though he told me he'd be working Sunday mornings for a few weeks, I still can't help but sigh.

"Good morning, sunshine," he says.

I glance up at him as I scan my badge. "Hi, Stan. How's it going?" I regret asking the question the second it's out of my mouth. Most people respond to such a nicety with something like *fine* or *okay, how about you?* but not Stan. To him, the question is an invitation to engage in conversation. When will I learn?

"Can't complain. Life is good," he responds cheerily.

I expect him to tell me about his most recent conquest or about the wild Friday night he had, or to say something inappropriate bordering on sexual assault, but he just stands there smiling at me.

Stan slaps his forehead. "Shoot. Where are my manners? How are you doing, Jess?" He asks with genuine interest.

I wait a beat before responding. "Um, fine. Thanks." I continue to eye him suspiciously.

"Well, have a great day," he says with a polite nod that sends me on my way.

When I'm a few feet away, he calls out, "Hey, Jess!"

I knew it.

"Yeah?" I ask, turning.

"If Val ever asks about me, would you mind putting in a good word?" The sincerity in his tone both shocks me and warms my heart.

"Yeah, of course. No problem."

And with that, I head off to find out which gate I'm departing from for the day, feeling an unexpected sense of camaraderie with Stan. After all, it seems we're both trying to turn new leafs.

After a long day filled with delays and angry passengers, Anne (who ended up getting the same route as me after all), Lisa (a pleasant, more senior flight attendant) and I are more exhausted than usual. So Anne and I decide to skip going out to dinner with the pilots and have dinner at the Cleveland Marriott restaurant instead. Lisa, who is known for keeping to herself outside of required work duties, opts to order room service. My plan is to have a quick dinner and then retire to my room for some privacy. Kyle left a message earlier saying he needed an ear, which surprised me because we still haven't managed to go on a second date yet. Even though I don't know him that well, I'm curious to find out why he sounded so down. I'd also like to check my Personals account.

I make it halfway through my chicken parmesan before Anne brings up the topic of doom. "Have you worked with Mindy lately?" Anne asks as she cuts the remaining steak on her plate into bite-size pieces.

Mouth full, I nod and clean the corners of my mouth with a napkin. When I finish chewing, I say, "Last week actually. Why?"

"Oh," she says, her eyes widening, "So . . . were you on the overnight with Brant too?"

I feel my temperature rising, uncomfortable with where I think this conversation might be headed, but I do my best to act cool. "Yeah, but surprisingly it was fine. I mean, except for the part where Mindy forced me out to dinner with the whole crew, but . . . nothing happened between Brant and I . . . in case you're wondering." *So much for acting cool.* I reach for my ice water as I curse myself for letting Anne get to me. Besides, she hasn't accused me of anything. And even if she had, I wasn't lying when I said nothing happened between Brant and me, so who cares what she thinks?

"No! I wasn't wondering that at all. Not about you and Brant anyway," she mumbles the last part and pauses before continuing. "I did hear something about Brant and Mindy, though."

Anne gives me a pointed look, clearly waiting for a response despite the fact that she hasn't actually asked a question. So we stare at each other for a few moments as I contemplate what to say next, or if I even need to say anything at all. I opt to play dumb.

"Really? What?" I take a bite of my food.

She gives me a skeptical look, but accepts my charade. "Apparently—and you didn't hear this from me—something went on between them. Like, over dinner and after drinks and *in* Mindy's room. Now Mindy seems to think whatever happened with them is something special. You seriously haven't heard a *thing* about this?"

Sighing, I shake my head. I actually do feel upset for Mindy. The poor girl has no idea what she's gotten herself into.

"I was thinking maybe you should say something to her?"

"Like what? This has nothing to do with me. Brant is out of my life, thank God."

"Jess, Mindy is younger than you, and from what I know about her, she has the mentality of a teenager. Don't you want to help the girl out? Save her from a lot of ridicule and embarrassment? Possibly even heartache?"

"It's not my place," I say, shoving the last bite of chicken from my plate into my mouth. I'm so frazzled, I don't even bother chewing and swallowing before I continue. "Besides, you're the only person at work who knows what happened between Brant and me. I certainly don't want anyone else to find out." Okay, so Stan knows, and I have a feeling Val might suspect something too, but Anne doesn't need to know this.

"Then how do you feel about anonymously reporting him to his superiors? I've heard he's hit on a lot of flight attendants, especially the newer, younger ones. Maybe if enough people complain, they'll put him on notice or something."

"I'm sorry, Anne, but why do you even care? Has he ever hit on you?"

"Because I think women should stick together when it comes to scumbags like Brant Mathis," she snaps, causing me to flinch. Not just because of her tone but also because of the truth in her words. Apparently, Anne is even shocked by her tone because she sighs heavily and softens her expression before continuing. "To answer your second question, no he's never hit on me. But that doesn't mean I haven't been hit on—grabbed even—by guys like him. I've been a flight attendant for eight years and before that I worked in a nightclub for five, so I've been subjected to his type more times than I care to remember."

We sit in silence for a few moments, Anne staring at her food as she shoves it around on her plate with a fork, and me staring at Anne. Something about the look in her eyes makes me wonder if she's ever been in a taboo relationship. Could this be why she's so emotional about Brant's devious ways? Or could she finally be snapping over all the sleazebags she's come across in our profession? Whatever the reason, she's getting to me. Maybe it *is* time for me to do something about Brant, but he's been working for Midwest Express longer than me or Anne, and I know he has friends in high places. If I report him, I could be risking more than just my reputation at work; I could be risking my job. Suddenly an idea comes to my mind, but I dismiss it because at that same moment Anne mumbles, "Maybe I'll just report him myself."

I nod, agreeing that this would be a much better solution.

By the time I get back to my room, it's nearly nine o'clock. The thought of getting up at five a.m. makes me want to hop right into bed, but then I think about Kyle's somber tone. For some reason, I feel like he really needs a friend. I can skip checking my personals account tonight, but calling Kyle back seems like the right thing to do.

I quickly change into flannel PJ bottoms and a t-shirt, wash my face, and brush my teeth. Then I request a wakeup call before crawling into bed with my phone. I dial Kyle's number, and he answers on the second ring.

"Hey, Jess. How's it going?" His voice is still somber.

"Good. Just got done with a long day of flying and now I'm overnight in Cleveland. How are things with you?"

He sighs heavily twice, making me feel like I'm about to be broken up with. Except, that's impossible, isn't it? Kyle might be new to online dating, but he has to know that all he needs to do if he's not interested in someone is stop communicating with them. Especially after only one date.

"Kyle? You okay?"

He sighs again. "So, I went home this past weekend, and I saw Amy at a bar. She was out for a bachelorette party and . . ."

Kyle goes on and on about every single person his ex was with and every single move she made, from doing a shot to dancing to "Cotton Eye Joe." He also talks about how his friends encouraged him to talk to her and how he'd made up his mind to just get out of there. But then as he got up to leave, Amy's eyes locked with his from across the crowded bar.

"It was like she knew I was there and was waiting for me to make a move . . ."

I consider interjecting several times as he recaps that night for me—twice to ask why he's telling me all this and once to ask if he developed hiccups at any point—but Kyle doesn't pause, except to ask if I'm still there, so I end up not asking anything.

While he's on the part about them debating whether or not they should sleep together, I get up to retrieve my laptop. Then I bring it back to bed with me and fire it up. At this point, I'm barely listening to Kyle. I mean, good for you buddy, you got laid. I don't need to hear all the details. As soon as my Personals dashboard opens, Kyle goes silent.

"Hello?" I say.

"Yeah, so what do you think? Did I make a mistake?"

"Wait, you're asking me for advice?"

"Look," he sighs, "I'm sorry if I've made you uncomfortable. It's just that you're the only impartial person who knows about my situation with Amy. Everyone else—all of my friends and family—they're just too close to Amy and me. So I know they'd all tell me to take her back. Plus, after everything you went through with your ex—Ned, right?—I feel like you might be able to understand how confused I am."

"Oh my gosh . . ." I know this is no time for laughing, but I can't help it. "I thought you were telling me all of this as an excuse to not see me again."

"What? Uh, no," he chuckles. "Wait, is that considered proper online dating etiquette? To provide ridiculously long and detailed explanations as to why you aren't interested in seeing someone again?"

"I have no idea, but I'm pretty sure the same rules of etiquette that apply to dating someone in person also apply to when you do it online. And I don't know about you, but after one date, I certainly don't need an explanation."

"Agreed." I can hear the smile in his voice. "So what do you think? Can you give me your honest opinion?"

"Sure, but who cares what I think or what anyone else thinks for that matter? This is really up to you and what your heart wants, at least it should be."

He sighs again.

"Do you still want to know what I think?" I ask.

"Yeah, I do."

"Okay, well, people make mistakes and it sounds like Amy believes it was a mistake to break up with you. If you still love her, why not give the relationship another chance?"

"I'm just afraid the long distance thing won't work out for us."

"Then it doesn't work out and you break up again. At least you won't wonder what could have happened ten years down the road." It's odd how I'm able to give others such solid advice when it comes to relationships, yet when it comes to my own matters of the heart, my brain turns to mush. Good thing I'm working on that.

Kyle is silent for a few seconds and then he says, "I have a lot to think about. Thanks for the advice."

"No problem at all. Any time."

"Hey, the first day we chatted online, you mentioned you've never seen *The Lord of the Rings* movies. Interested in watching the first two this weekend? I grabbed the DVDs from my parents' house—the third doesn't come out until May."

The first thing I wonder is if Kyle might be asking me to watch *Lord of the Rings* when he really just wants to make out (my mind always goes straight to the gutter), but I dismiss the thought almost as quickly as it pops into my head. Of course Kyle doesn't have an ulterior motive; he just got done spilling his heart out to me about his ex. "Yeah, I could go for a movie marathon. Can I let you know which night works for me later this week?"

"Sure, just shoot me a text when you know."

"Sounds like a plan," I say enthusiastically.

"Great, then I'll see you soon."

"Okay, bye Kyle."

"Have a good night . . . oh, and Jess?"

"Yeah?"

"Thanks again."

"You're welcome."

After Kyle and I hang up, I unlock my laptop and turn my attention back to my Personals dashboard. It takes seconds for me to eliminate the pokes and icebreakers, then I open a message from someone with the screen name Bowhunter Beau. Could I be the only person who uses my real name?

Hey there pretty little lady. I'm thinkin you and me need to get to know eachother. I like my women with just a few extra curves, so looks like your just my type. I can see you like to have yourself a drink and I make a helluva moonshine. How would you like to try some?

The least he could have done is opened with a greeting and ended with a closing, but it's not fair for me to judge Bowhunter Beau on his letter writing skills. He could also use a lesson on homophones. Just for fun, I read the message a few more times before clicking on his profile.

~

Bowhunter Beau – 35
Location: Vernon
Up for a Fling?

Relationship Status: Married
Kids: Yes ...

~

Did I just see what I think I saw? I go back one line and sure enough, his profile says he's married. I was willing to give him a chance despite his letter writing and spelling abilities, but the fact that he's married? Where does this guy get off being so cocky? I exit out of his profile, return to his message, and click to respond.

Bowhunter Beau,

Sorry, but I'm not a fan of moonshine, and I don't date married men.

Good luck to you and your wife,
Jess

I hesitate before clicking send because I feel torn about saying I don't date married men. But then I remind myself I've never dated married *men*. It was one man, and I've learned my lesson. I send the message and move on after updating my preferences to only receive matches who are single. Message two is from Woolf Woman.

Hi, Jess!

You must be wondering why I poked you when you don't appear to be shopping around in my category. To put it bluntly, I think you're beautiful, and I'd love to meet you in person.

In case you're wondering, I don't make it a point to shop profiles based on pictures alone; I've also read about you. Historical fiction happens to be my favorite genre too, and believe it or not, I can't stand popcorn either! Match made in heaven, you and me.

I almost didn't go through with poking you again, but I figured sometimes the second time can be a charm too. So what do you think? Would you be willing to meet up sometime?

Pamela

After reading Bowhunter Beau's message, Woolf Woman actually sounds appealing. At least she can form a proper sentence and knows how to spell. (Except for Woolf, but there has to be a reason for that.) I begin typing a response to her but then delete everything. I'm not sure if I want to go out with a woman, so I'd hate to lead her on. Then again, I already poked her, so what the hell. I quickly tap out a response and hit send before I have a chance to reconsider.

Hi Pamela,

You're right, I haven't done any shopping around in your "category," but I do appreciate you noticing me. Thank you for the compliment!

I have to be honest, I deleted your first poke without a second glance (same with every poke and icebreaker), but for some reason, the second one caught my attention. I don't know why. Maybe because I like when people don't give up or maybe I just happened to see it at the right moment. Whatever the reason, I poked you back without giving it much thought. And here's another bit of honesty for you... I've never gone out with a woman before. I did kiss one once, though . . .

To answer your question, yes, I'm willing to meet up. I don't want to give you the wrong idea though. Remember that kiss I mentioned? I'm pretty sure it helped me figure out that I'm not as attracted to women as I thought I was that night.

So if you're cool with just a friendly meet-up—with no expectations—let me know.

Take care,
Jess

There. Now I don't feel like I've led her on in any way, and I doubt she'll take me up on meeting up. Why would she when she probably has access to hundreds of women who are seeking other women?

I still have a message from Scotty and one from Wildman, but my laptop clock confirms it's almost ten, which makes me yawn. I stare at the screen, my eyelids heavy and begging for me to close them. Scotty isn't in any hurry to meet me, so his message can definitely wait, and I thought I gave Wildman my number, so if he wanted to talk to me badly enough he could have called. Both messages will have to wait.

I log out of Yahoo! Personals, lower the lid on my laptop and set it on the nightstand. As I flip off the bedside lamp, my phone vibrates and the screen lights up. I smile at the sight of Justin's name as another yawn escapes me.

> **Justin:** I happen to love burritos and dive bars. So I guess we have plans for our second date. Send me your address and tell me what time to pick you up. Nighty night, Jess.

Anne and I work together on Monday, too. Thankfully, we're back to our usual friendly way of conversing, and she doesn't breathe a word about Mindy or Brant. When we get to dinner, we talk about working at McGinn's, which leads to a conversation about Sawyer.

"So, when I left work on Saturday, I noticed Sawyer at the bar talking to you and your friend Chloe," Anne says as she stirs sweetener into her iced tea.

"Mm-hm," I muster through a mouthful of chips and salsa.

"Just curious, how did he end up chatting with you guys? I've never seen him behind the bar before, and he usually stays in the kitchen during his entire shift."

I immediately think back to the night I met him when he sat down next to me at the bar. "Really? I thought you two have had *deep conversations* in the past. How did you manage that if he rarely comes out of the kitchen?" I might as well get some answers for myself, since she's the one who brought up Sawyer.

She finishes taking a sip of her iced tea before responding. "He hangs out afterward once in awhile, but even then, he pretty much just talks to Bobby and a few of the regulars. So what were you guys talking about?"

Part of me is feeling self conscious about Anne's question because of my past with Brant. After all, I have no idea what the circumstances are surrounding Sawyer's pending divorce. For all I know they could still get back together. What would Anne think if she knew we hooked up? Then there's the other part of me who doesn't give a rat's ass what Anne thinks because I've done nothing wrong this time, except maybe let myself down by breaking a promise I made to myself.

"He was asking me to wait for him to get off of work so we could talk."

"Why?" Her tone is incredulous.

"Because we hung out last week when we first met. I had a date at McGinn's, it didn't go so well, and Sawyer sort of rescued me. That was also the night I applied for a job."

"Interesting. How did he rescue you?"

Suddenly I'm having flashbacks of our conversation about Mindy and Brant. I also feel like I'm being interrogated, which doesn't sit well with me. "No offense, Anne, but why do you care? Is there something going on between you and Sawyer?"

"No, not at all! I was just curious." She polishes off a chip and then grabs for another right away, apparently done with the conversation.

I still have questions, though. So I tell her the gist of what happened with Sawyer and me, hoping to get some info about him out of her. I know I can easily ask Sawyer myself, but who knows when we'll hang out again, or if we ever will.

"My date was a real loudmouth, so I decided to say goodbye before we got the food we ordered. For some reason, he didn't understand that I was cutting the date short and he attempted to follow me to the bar. That's when Sawyer stepped in. I assumed he sat in the empty seat next to me that night by chance, but now I don't know . . ."

Anne listens and eats chips the entire time I'm talking. Now she's shaking her head. "It wasn't chance."

I shrug. "Chance or not, I'm glad he intervened. That guy was such an ass."

"He must have been for Sawyer to take notice," she says laughing. "So what happened after the asshole finally got the hint?"

"Sawyer and I chatted until his break was over, and then we chatted some more after his shift ended. Lots of chatting." I leave out the part where we continued "chatting" back at my apartment.

Anne responds with a nod, and the waitress shows up with our food —shrimp tacos for Anne and chicken fajitas for me. We're both famished, so we eat for a good five minutes before conversation resumes.

"Have you ever met Sawyer's wife?" I ask.

She gives me a funny look. "No. From what I hear, she's never stepped foot in the place. Not even way back when Sawyer worked at McGinn's the first time around."

"Way back? Wait . . . Sawyer worked at McGinn's a first time?"

"Yeah, I guess he grew up with Molly and worked there during high school and on and off during college, when her dad owned it."

"So he met his wife in college?"

"I think so. I mean, I don't think they knew each other before that."

As I polish off a fajita, I think about my next question, but Anne speaks up first.

"Why do you want to know about Sawyer's wife? Are *you* interested in him?"

"Eh, he's an awesome guy but he's not even divorced yet. So I think I'll just stick with online dating."

Anne seems pleased with my response. "Speaking of online dating . . . what's going on with that? Are you still talking to that guy who works for the Brewers?"

And with that, the door is closed on the rest of my questions about Sawyer. Instead, Anne and I move into a lengthy conversation about my online dating progress. We share some laughs over Coordinates Kyle's hiccups, Karaoke Wayward Son, BossMan411, Bowhunter Beau and even a few of the guys Chloe met online back before she met Daran. By the end of dinner, Anne has talked me into showing her my Personals dashboard and how everything works in person. Thirty minutes later, we're both in our lounge clothes and sitting in my hotel room in front of my laptop.

"Wow, looks like you're getting a lot of virtual action." Anne gives me a sideways glance and waggles her eyebrows.

"Not really, it just looks that way because I haven't logged on for two days. Besides, most of these notifications will disappear within seconds. Watch."

I click to display the six icebreaker notifications. Then I promptly delete them all. As I do the same thing with the four pokes, Anne asks, "What's the difference between a poke and an icebreaker?"

I pause to consider her question. "You know what? I have no idea. Does it really matter though? If a guy can't take the time to say something—anything—then he's not worthy of my time. I picture guys who send pokes and icebreakers as the ones who give women creepy stares from across a bar. The guys who make you want to stand up and ask, *"What? What do you want?!"*

We laugh as I delete the final two pokes. Then I'm about to give her a rundown of the anatomy of a profile, when a text from Justin comes through. This is the fourth text he's sent me today, but I don't mind. It's kind of nice to know I'm on his mind.

"Here," I say, getting up and offering the spot directly in front of my laptop to Anne. "Do you want to check out my new matches? Just click on their profile pic if you want to see all of their stats. I have to check my phone real quick."

"Another text? Wow, someone likes you," Anne says with a grin, but her eyes remain plastered to the array of matches on the screen.

"I'm not so sure jokes and movie lines are indicative of his feelings for me, but he does seem impressed by my cinematic knowledge," I say as I grab my phone off the nightstand. Then I pace a four foot square into the floor next to the bed as I read Justin's text and respond.

Justin: Dong? Dong?! Where is my automobile?

Me: Easy! Sixteen Candles. When are these going to get

HARDER? ANNE IS HANGING IN MY ROOM RIGHT NOW. SO I'M SIGNING OFF FOR THE DAY. TALK TO YOU TOMORROW.

JUSTIN: LUCKY ANNE. NIGHTY NIGHT, JESS...

I silence my phone and set it face down on the nightstand before returning to peruse the personals site with Anne. I sit crisscross on the bed beside her. "Any good ones?"

"Meh. Not anyone I could see you with."

I shrug because I really don't care. I rarely peruse my matches and if I do, I only stop if someone's picture really catches my eye, like the guy who was wearing a big orange sombrero and a poncho with palm trees on it. I would have contacted him but he was forty-eight, and I decided based on some of the more senior matches I've been getting that forty-five is my max age. I even updated my preferences. Look at me setting parameters!

"That guy is kind of handsome," she says, pausing on an attractive black man and eyeing me for a reaction.

I nod and say, "Click on his picture so we can see his profile." She clicks and right away I realize I need to set another parameter. "Nope. He lives in Appleton. Too far."

"Well," Anne says as she yawns and stretches her arms above her head, "I'm beat. I'll leave you alone with your matches."

"Alrighty, sounds good." I grab my laptop and scoot to the head of the bed so I can lean against the headboard. With a wave, Anne opens the door to leave. "See you bright and early," I call out as she heads out into the hallway.

Surprisingly, the only messages I have are the ones from Scotty and Wildman from the day before. This is a relief because it won't take me long to respond, but at the same time I can't help but feel a bit disappointed that no one else has tried to reach out to me.

I click on Scotty's message first.

Hi Jess,

You're not going to believe this . . . I got three turkeys last night! (In case you didn't know, a turkey is three strikes in a row.) That's a personal best for me, but I hope to break that record soon because I signed up for a bowling league. So starting in two weeks I'll be bowling every Friday night up at the Classic Lanes on Oklahoma Avenue. Up until now, my buddies and I tried to go once a month. Do you like to bowl?

I've been thinking about your superpower question nonstop because I want to give you the most honest answer I can. So here it is: I'd want to be able to read people's minds. Then I'd know how bad you want me to ask you out. That was a joke. In all seriousness, though, imagine the power you'd have over people if you could read their minds.

So, how about we go bowling on our first date?

Scotty

For the first time since I started talking to Scotty, I'm feeling irked by him, and it isn't because of this terrible joke. It's because of his mention of wanting to have power over people. *Creeepyyy*. I might have to reconsider whether I want to continue messaging this guy. Moving on . . .

Howdy Jess!

How's it going? Any chance you're willing to bypass all the online chitchat and just meet up sometime? I work weekends and most Thursdays, but I happen to have this coming Thursday off if you're free. Let me know if you're interested.

Cheers!
Brock Wildman

Something about Wildman's message seems oddly familiar, so I scroll back to his first message from the other day. Sure enough, it's virtually word for word the same. The only difference is he addressed the confession I'd made about James poking him by accident. I should be mad that this guy has no idea we've already exchanged messages *and* that I already gave him my number. Instead I laugh remembering how I copied and pasted quite a few messages during my first week of online dating. It sure did beat trying to come up with original things to say over and over to person after person.

Brock,

You sent me a message nearly identical to this one last Friday. No worries, though. I totally get it. Way too many people to keep track of. Anyway, in response to your message from Friday, I sent you my phone number. Are you still able to access that message? If not, maybe you can just share yours with me and I can give you a call.

Have a good night!
Jess

chapter twenty-two

After a long few days at work, I'm frantically brushing my teeth at Home Wednesday night when there's a knock on my apartment door. I rush out of the bathroom, still brushing and doing my best not to drip foam onto the lacy black top I just changed into, and peer through the peep hole. After confirming it's Justin, I throw open the door and motion for him to enter. He chuckles when I point at my toothbrush and then toward the bathroom before rushing off to rinse my mouth out. I hear him close the door and then the sounds of him removing his shoes.

"I have the same dining room table," he calls out.

"Colder's Furniture?" I call back just before I slurp a little more water into my mouth from a cupped hand.

"Yep, except mine is black . . . and it's all scuffed up from arts and crafts with Max." His voice trails off when he says Max's name and then I hear him walking around.

I spritz myself with a few pumps of freesia body spray and return to the main living area of my apartment. Justin is standing in front of the entryway to the kitchen, his gaze is fixed on the flower he'd given me on Friday night, which is now wilted. He turns to me with a bright smile, and holds out an identical replacement.

"I figured you might need a new one," he says softly with a look in his eyes that tickles my insides.

"That's so sweet of you. Thank you." Beaming, I reach out to grab it.

When I have the flower in my hand, Justin surprises me by pulling me close for a long, tight hug. We stand there, our bodies molded together, and he rubs my lower back in slow circles, making me feel like I could hold the embrace all night long.

"We should probably go . . . right?" he whispers into my hair, causing my skin to explode with goose bumps. The question is laced with innuendo, as if he's feeling me out to see if just maybe I'd prefer seeing what this hug could evolve into in lieu of eating burritos at a dive bar.

A lustful sigh escapes me as I do the opposite of what pre-New-Year's-resolution Jess would do. I give his back a few swift, neutral rubs and then gently break away from the hug. Now it's his turn to sigh, a sheepish grin spreading across his face.

"I'm going to put this in some water," I say holding up the yellow daffodil, "and then we really should go."

"Okay," he says with a warm smile. "Can I use your bathroom real quick?"

"Yeah, go ahead." I nod toward the hallway as we sidestep each other, and head in opposite directions. I smile when Justin reaches back and gives my ass a tap.

The night has just begun and temptation is killing me already.

Tapping my thumbs impatiently against the steering wheel, I wait for a little white car to pull out of a curb spot two blocks down from Home Bar. The driver inches forward for a third time, then backs up on the same exact angle he did moments earlier. The maneuver doesn't give him enough room this time either. Even Chloe, who's terrible at parallel parking and failed her first driver's test because of it, could probably get this guy's car out of the spot. "I don't get it. It's like the size of a go-cart," I mumble under my breath.

Justin laughs. "Even though I'm glad I get to see how cute you are when you're frustrated, you should have let me drive."

"No way. This piece of shit fits in much better around here than that pretty new car of yours would have," I say as I give my dashboard a few taps.

Justin insisted on driving but I didn't feel good about him having to park his brand new Nissan Maxima on the road. I've seen way too many scratches and dings appear on cars parked in front of Home Bar over the years.

Convinced the person attempting to park must be drunk, I throw my car into park and open the door, intending to get out and intervene.

"Wait, what are you doing? You're not going to wig out on him are you?" There's a hint of concern in Justin's voice.

"No," I snort. "I'm highly skilled at keeping my road rage behind closed car doors. If this guy is drunk, I'm going to offer to call him a cab."

"You're something else, you know that?" Justin says with a slight grin. As I crinkle my nose trying to decide if he meant *something else* in a good way or a bad way, he gives my thigh a friendly rub, retrieves his phone from his pocket, and opens his car door. "You stay here. I'll talk to him."

Justin gets out of my car and cautiously approaches the white one. His initiative makes me smile. Ned would have advised me to stay in the car and mind my own business, and he never would have offered to go in my place. As Justin is about to lean over and knock on the window, the car peels out of the spot, narrowly missing his feet. I throw open my door and get out of the car.

"Holy shit! Are you okay?"

"Yeah, yeah, I'm fine," he says as he makes his way back to the passenger side and gets in. I get back in too, a little worried that he's pissed about almost getting plowed over because of my bright idea. Instead, he looks at me with a playful grin and says, "But you might owe me a little more than a kiss for that."

"Welcome Home!" Chris the bartender hollers when we enter. "Hey, Jess, it's been a while."

"Hey, how are you?" I ask.

"Couldn't be better. Vodka cranberry and a burrito with cheese, tomatoes and lettuce?"

"You know it," I say, waving to Chloe who's flagging me down from a table at the back of the bar. She knows we won't head back there until we get our food, but that won't stop her from continuing to wave off and on.

He reaches a hand out to Justin and introduces himself. "Chris."

"Justin. Nice to meet you."

"What can I get you?" Chris asks.

"Blue Moon?" Justin points to the beer taps. "And a burrito. Go ahead and load it with whatever you have."

"Coming right up."

Chris returns with our drinks in less than a minute. As we wait for our food, we chat about our jobs, and Justin tells me about his plans to take his son Max to an indoor water park in Wisconsin Dells this weekend. While we're talking, I steal a few peeks at the group of people with Chloe. A glimpse of Chloe's college friend, Shelly, gives me the urge to leave, but we've already ordered, and I don't feel like explaining a quick exit to Justin, so we'll stay. As much as I dislike Shelly, Chloe continues to defend that she's a loyal friend. I see right through her, though. In my opinion, the girl is a selfish, judgmental opportunist who would stab Chloe in the back if the reward was great enough. And she's a whiny bitch if someone has something she wants. For example, Chloe's job. Shelly's a teacher, too, but she works at a school in a rough part of Milwaukee. Chloe, on the other hand, works in a nicer part of town. According to Shelly, it was pure luck that Chloe got assigned to the school where she works. What she neglects to acknowledge is that Chloe student taught at her school, and if she hadn't made such a good impression, they never would have hired her. So, no, it wasn't luck. It was the fact that she worked her ass off as a student teacher, often staying two to three hours late every night just to make sure she was ready for the next day. And she still stays late even though, according to Shelly, it's luck that results in great opportunities, not hard work. No point in harping to Chloe about what a wolf in sheep's clothing Shelly is, though. She'll figure it out someday.

"Here you go, folks," Chris says as he sets two huge, foil-wrapped burritos in front of us. Justin hands him thirty bucks and tells him to keep the change. "Hey, thanks, man. Enjoy."

"Um, you know those burritos were only eight dollars apiece and my drink was only a buck, right?" I ask as soon as Chris is out of earshot. Not that he doesn't deserve a big tip. He's a good bartender and an all-around good guy. He has to be to remain calm in the face of all the drunken shenanigans that go on in this place. Never once have I seen him treat a drunk asshole with disrespect, and if he wasn't always showing people pictures of his wife and kids, I most likely would have hit on him long ago. It's appealing the way he always keeps an eye on the single ladies, even the ones who are clearly looking for someone—anyone—to go home with at the end of the night. I know because I've been that lady a time or two. *Okay, maybe three.* Chris never judges though; he always makes sure to have a few words with any woman before she leaves the bar with just anyone.

"That's okay. He seems like a nice guy. Should we head back to where your friends are?"

"Friend."

"What?"

"I said friend, but I guess I consider Daran a friend now, too. The rest of the people are Chloe's friends."

I must sound more agitated than I mean to because Justin raises an eyebrow. "Is there going to be drama tonight? Because I'll carry you out of here if I have to."

"Whatever," I say rolling my eyes and laughing.

Just then, Chris returns. "Hey, you two. You better get back there before Chloe throws a shoulder out of socket trying to flag you down," he says with a chuckle.

Justin and I grab our drinks and burritos and make our way through the crowd to the back.

"You made it!" Chloe throws her arms around me as soon as I set my drink and burrito down. Justin follows my lead.

"We did!" I wave to a large group of people consisting of Shelly, Shelly's sister and brother-in-law, a few co-workers of Chloe's (who I vaguely recall meeting at a PartyLite candle party or something boring like that), and several other people I don't recognize. Some are eating burritos, and some are chatting. Everyone acknowledges with a smile or quick wave. Then I look back to Chloe who's already moving toward Justin for a hug and say, "This is Justin."

That's Chloe for you. Always bubbly and friendly after she's had a few drinks. It makes me laugh because most people would never guess that such a serious and obsessively organized person could turn into such a social butterfly. Two of her past boyfriends used to become irritated with her when they'd drink out in public. Not because she flirted or annoyed people, but because she didn't focus all of her attention on them. And then there was Cliff, her most recent ex prior to online dating, who was usually stoned, so her over-the-top alcohol-induced highs never seemed to phase him. He'd just sit there and smile, not talking to anyone. Daran handles her differently, staring at her like she's an adorable puppy, not caring the least bit when she floats about chatting with everyone and anyone within a ten-foot radius.

Chloe releases Justin and starts giggling as she focuses her gaze on something behind him.

Justin and I turn and get a glimpse of Daran launching a wobbly dart, which hits the wall about half a foot away from the board. A roar of laughter erupts around him.

"Oh great. Are you and Daran both drunk?" I ask.

"Naaaaah, I've only had three drinks, and I've switched to water," she says, waving me off and giving Justin a pointed grin, "and Daran just sucks at darts."

"Yeah, well, seems like he'd probably suck at driving a car right now too. Who drove?"

As though she hasn't heard a word I've said, Chloe envelops me in another hug. Did I mention she's also like a dog distracted by a squirrel when she's been drinking? I glance over at Justin and he's grinning from ear to ear, obviously amused by my best friend.

"Well, that's a switch." Shelly pipes in, followed by an annoying, ditzy laugh that makes me want to cover her mouth with duct tape. She smiles at Justin, then reaches out to shake his hand and they exchange names.

I gently loosen the death grip Chloe has around my neck as Shelly comes in for a hug. I hug her back, but only for Chloe. She likes to see Shelly and I getting along.

"What's a switch?" I ask as Shelly and I part, daring her to confirm what I suspect she's getting at.

"You wondering who the designated driver is." She smiles sweetly as if what she just said isn't bordering on insult.

"Well, excuse me for being a *good* friend and wanting to make sure they get home safely." I glance at Justin just in time to see his eyes return to normal from a wide-as-saucers state as he takes a sip of his Blue Moon and begins unwrapping his burrito. I wonder if he'd really carry me out of here if I started throwing punches.

"Whoa, whoa, whoa," Chloe flutters her hands slowly between Shelly and me. "This is supposed to be a friendly social gathering, not an episode of *GLOW*."

"What the hell is *GLOW*?" I ask.

Chloe and Shelly look at each other and then at me, stunned. "You didn't watch the Gorgeous Ladies of Wrestling when you were a kid?" Chloe asks, both her and Shelly shaking their heads in disbelief.

"No," I say, bewildered. Justin gives me a shrug.

And just like that, Chloe and Shelly dive into an animated discussion about their favorite lady wrestlers from back in the day. I feel like I'm in *The Twilight Zone* when strangers around us join in, and it occurs to me that maybe this is what Chloe gets out of her friendship with Shelly that she could never get from ours—brainless conversation about meaningless shit. I guess everyone needs to unwind somehow, and Chloe does tend to need a lot of unwinding. In her defense, she has been drinking, but still. She's going to be so embarrassed when she's completely sober and I give her crap about this *GLOW* business.

Instead of staying and listening to a conversation I can't contribute to, I signal to Justin with a neck jerk that it's time for a location change. We wander over to Daran and the group of guys he's shooting darts with, drinks and burritos in hand. Shelly's boyfriend Craig is up, and Daran is leaning against a table half-full of empty shot glasses. He's holding a full one unsteadily, and Shelly's brother Tom and three guys I don't recognize are razzing him to down it.

"Mmmmm. Don't mind if I do," I say, grabbing the shot from Daran's hand and downing it myself. An eruption of moans follows.

"Dude. He lost a bet," Tom whines. Justin laughs a real guy's guy type of laugh, and I roll my eyes.

Immediately after introductions are made with everyone, Justin gets roped into taking Daran's place at the dart board. He takes his drink and burrito (which I wonder if he'll ever get a chance to finish) over to a table closer to the board they're playing on, and Daran takes a seat next to me at the cluttered table.

"Hey, Daran. Nice shooting," I tease.

"Very funny." He gives me a lazy smile, his eyelids droopy.

I unwrap my burrito and devour a third of it as I split my attention between watching Daran fight to keep his eyes open and watching the other guys shoot darts.

"Do you want some water? Or do you want some of my burrito?"

"No, I'm good," he mumbles.

Good my ass. "No offense, but you don't look good. You look wasted. How much have you had to drink?"

He swallows hard, eyelids fluttering slowly—open, closed, open, closed. "I'm not drunk. I'm sick, and I don't want to be here anymore. Chloe said it would only be for a couple of hours. We've been here for three."

"Then tell her you're ready to leave."

"Easier said than done. We drove with Craig and Shelly."

"Dude." Craig arrives, giving me a hello nod and dangling Shelly's keys in front of Daran. I know they're her keys because of the Key West keychain with her name on it. What kind of grown woman has a keychain with her name on it? "Are you still moaning about going home? You can take her car. Seriously. Someone can drop us off at Chloe's to get the car."

"Hey, Craig," I say before turning my attention to Justin, who's shown up too. "Hey you," I say to him, smiling and giving him a playful nudge.

"I don't know. I hate to leave you guys stranded." Daran takes a napkin out of his pocket and blows his nose several times.

"I told you, we can get a ride . . . Let me know if you need the keys," Craig says and then returns to the dart board.

Daran nods and goes back to struggling to keep his eyes open.

"What's up?" Justin whispers in my ear. The sweet, hoppy scent of his warm breath combined with the smell of the subtle woodsy cologne he's wearing reminds me that tonight is going to be a real test of my willpower.

"Daran's actually not drunk he's sick, and they drove with Craig and Shelly." Justin is so close I can see the little copper flecks surrounding his pupils and the circular scar on his earlobe where I assume there was once an earring. I'd really like to kiss him but not here in front of Chloe's and Shelly's friends. Plus, I have burrito breath.

Justin glances at Daran. "He doesn't look so good. Maybe we should just—"

"So how long have you two been dating?" Shelly interrupts as she slides onto the stool next to me. This causes Justin to stand upright and me to turn my body to face the table, widening the physical distance between us. At the same time, Chloe sets a half empty drink on the table as she shimmies in between Daran and Justin. She leans her head against Daran's shoulder and rubs his back.

"This is our second date," Justin offers before downing the last of his beer.

"Huh. So how many other people—" Shelly begins, but she's interrupted by Craig summoning Justin back to the dart board.

"Excuse me, ladies," he says, winking at me before he leaves.

"What were you about to say?" I ask Shelly suspiciously. She lacks a social filter, so I assume it must be something tactless.

"I'm just curious how many other people each of you are *dating*." She uses air quotes when she says *dating*. "Because judging by your body language, and based on *your* dating habits, it seems like the two of you have already been intimate. Am I right?"

"Come *on*, Shelly . . ." Chloe mumbles as she shakes her head and squeezes the bridge of her nose. Now I know for certain she's tipsy. Otherwise, she'd have done more to stop this topic of conversation before it even begins.

I huff through my nose in lieu of saying something I might regret. "Not that it's any of your business, but yes, we've kissed. And if I feel like doing more with him despite the fact that we aren't dating each other exclusively, that's my prerogative."

"Geez, you don't have to be so stabby about it. I wasn't judging you. I was just curious."

Right. Because Miss-Goody-Two-Shoes would never think of judging my "dating habits."

"Yeah, okay, whatever."

Shelly and Chloe sip their drinks, and Daran leans a cheek against one of his palms and finally gives in to his heavy eyelids. I go back to my burrito and wonder why Chloe continues inviting me places when Shelly is going to be there. It's obvious we're not compatible.

"He needs water," I say to no one in particular.

"You're probably right. I'll be back," Chloe says. "You two need anything?"

I shake my head no, but Shelly asks for another mixer. No surprise there. Chloe is only gone for a few seconds before Shelly asks another question.

"So are you at least being careful about who you're meeting up with and where? Chloe mentioned you met up with someone a couple weeks ago and didn't even tell anyone where you were going. That seems dangerous." Her demeanor is as genuine as it gets, lessening my irritation with her.

"Yes, of course I am," I say with a sigh. I'm a little annoyed that Chloe shared my poor decision with Shelly. It makes me wonder what else she's told her. But that's something for me to address with her if it bothers me, not Shelly, so I don't ask. Shelly nods and sips her drink, and I look to see how the darts competition is progressing.

Moments later, Chloe returns with Daran's water, which he gladly accepts. Then out of nowhere, she asks, "So, whatever happened with you and Sawyer on Saturday night?"

I stare at her shocked that she'd bring him up in front of Shelly.

"Who's Sawyer?" Shelly asks immediately.

"A sexy older guy who rescued Jess from a horrible date and who she now works with at McGinn's."

"And you went out with him on Saturday night?" Shelly asks.

Ignoring Shelly, I say to Chloe, "Seriously? I'm out on a date with Justin. Can we talk about this another time?"

"She has a point," Daran mumbles keeping his eyes closed.

"Fine, but you have to promise to fill me in on what's going on with him soon," Chloe says.

I hold up my right hand. "I promise . . . He should really go to bed," I say nodding toward Daran. "We can drive you home if you want. As soon as Justin gets done with darts."

"Yeah, we should go," she says as she places a hand on Daran's forehead. "How long are you staying, Shelly?"

Shelly shrugs as she sips her vodka tonic.

"I said I can take you home," I insist.

"Noo," Chloe moans, "I don't want to ruin your date with Justin."

"Ruin my date?" I snort. "That's hilarious. Do you really think Home Bar is my idea of a great date? We came here because you begged me, remember? Ha, ruin my date!"

"Again, she has a point." This time Daran has his arms folded on the table, and his head is down on them, so his voice is muffled.

"Okay, fine. Thank you . . . but only if you're sure."

After ten minutes of listening to teacher talk between Chloe, Shelly, and their teacher friends who've migrated over to our table, Craig and Justin return. They laugh and engage in some sort of elaborate handshake before parting ways to stand next to Shelly and me.

"Hey," Craig says to Shelly, "Justin works for the Brewers and says he might be able to get us into a game for free some time." He reaches a fist over the table to Justin who does the same. They meet in the middle and bump fists. It's the first time I question Justin's attractiveness.

"Seriously? That's so awesome!" Shelly exclaims. I smile at Justin as I mimic her in my head.

"Yep, I got his number," Craig says, patting his pocket.

"Alrighty then," I say standing. "Chloe? Daran? Are you guys ready to go?"

While they say their goodbyes, I whisper in Justin's ear, "I'm sorry this date sucked."

"Why do you say that? I had fun playing darts, the burrito was tasty, and I gained a couple of new groupies." He grins. "Plus, I got to be near you. I wouldn't say that sucks."

I really want to believe he doesn't think this was the worst date ever, but I don't. We barely got to talk to each other, Daran is so sick he isn't talking to anyone, Craig and Shelly are expecting him to get them into Miller Park for a Brewers game, and I almost got him hit by a car. This guy definitely deserves an award for being a good sport. "You're a really nice guy. You know that?"

"Thanks. You're not so bad yourself." He grins and continues. "By the way, our date doesn't have to end after we drop off your friends. I was hoping we could go some place quieter to talk a little. Oh, and don't forget, you still owe me for getting my feet almost run over."

"We'll see. I have to work tomorrow."

"So do I."

"Yeah, well, either way, you might have to settle for a kiss."

"A kiss from you would definitely not be settling."

We get all the way to Chloe's apartment before she realizes she left her keys in Shelly's car, so we have to drive back to Home Bar.

When Chloe emerges with Craig in tow to unlock Shelly's car, it's a little after eleven. Poor Daran is passed out in the back, and poor Justin most likely isn't going to get more than a kiss tonight. There is a silver lining though. We've had plenty of time to talk and get to know each other better with all the driving back and forth. We already went through a whole list of favorites (Chloe included), and then talked about our extended families, places we've traveled, and places we'd like to travel to.

By the time we get back to my apartment, it's nearly midnight, and there's no way I can invite Justin in. Not if I want to avoid sleeping with him on our second date anyway. I break the news to him as soon as we pull into a parking spot outside my apartment building, and he's a perfect gentleman about it.

Instead of going right to his car like I encourage him to do, he insists on walking me to my door where we share several kisses that are even more intoxicating than the ones we shared after our first date. Maybe it has something to do with the fact that we added groping.

Finally, after what feels like hours but in actuality must be only about five minutes, I whisper, "Thanks for a great night, but I need to go inside."

He sighs and says, "You have no idea how much I want to continue this inside." Then he holds me close, allowing me to grasp just how much he wants it. Now it's my turn to sigh.

And with that, he releases me and watches me enter my apartment building. I wave through the window on the door, and watch as he backs away, not turning until he's reached the end of the walkway that abuts the parking lot.

Jess = 1. Temptation = 0.

chapter twenty-three

My first thought when I wake up is of Justin and the crush I'm developing on him. I lie there for about twenty minutes going over all the things we've learned about each other over the last few weeks and about how incredibly attractive I find him, not just for his appearance but also for his personality. This is new territory for me because Ned and I were mostly into each other for the sex and the convenience of having someone. It was never about Ned being a total package or even a companion I could count on.

And then there were all the guys I hooked up with during my off times with Ned—all the one-nighters and guys who served as distractions from my rocky relationship that was going nowhere from the start. Brant. (Ick. The thought of him makes me nauseous.)

None of my poor decisions when it comes to dating and sexual encounters are Ned's fault, though. It's all on me and the fact that, up until now, I've never really had any serious expectations or been in the right frame of mind to build a relationship with someone. I guess Chloe was right after all, darn it; online dating was just the jumpstart I needed to grow up and start thinking about what I'm actually looking for. Not that I'm one-hundred percent sure I'll find it this way, but it's a start at least. Even if I don't end up in a long-term relationship with Justin, knowing that guys like him exist is a good enough takeaway for me.

By the time I finally crawl out of bed, it's close to eight, leaving me three hours before I have to show up for my second official shift at McGinn's. I decide to make coffee and chores top priority, followed by checking my Personals account. The fact that I'm going to fire up my computer before going to work makes me laugh. It wasn't too long ago that I only went online a few times a week. Now I'm on it daily to do something that I used to think was a huge waste of time.

As I lean against the counter waiting for the coffee to brew, I check my phone and find that I have two texts: one from Justin and one from Kyle. Kyle! I forgot to get back to him about which night works best for me to watch those *Lord of the Rings* movies he's so into. I click on his message first.

Kyle: Hey. Are you still up for watching LOTR sometime this week?

Me: Yes! Sorry I didn't get back to you until now! How about tonight?

After I send the message, I immediately feel a tinge of regret because I wonder if Justin might want to see me tonight. I can't remember what day he's taking his son to the Dells, so tonight could be the last night we could potentially see each other before next week Thursday. I should have checked his message first.

No, don't do that. I shake my head briskly and rub my fists into my eyes as I remind myself not to get in too deep emotionally at this point. It would be silly for me to move forward with online dating and scheduling dates with Justin in mind. I wouldn't be giving this whole process a real chance if I did. Although, I'm pretty sure Kyle isn't interested in me *that way* anymore, in light of the developments with his ex. I guess we shall see.

Just to prove to myself that I'm capable of controlling my emotions, I clean my cats' litter boxes and drink half a cup of coffee before viewing Justin's message.

Justin: I seriously had a great time last night. Can I see you tonight?

My heart stops beating only for a few seconds. Then I regroup. Since turning new leaves is a theme for me lately, I decide to move forward with a tactic I've never used before. Complete honesty.

Me: I had a great time too, all because of you. About

TONIGHT...POSSIBLY. I MIGHT HAVE A DATE. CAN I GET BACK TO YOU?

After I hit send, I tuck my phone away in my purse, vowing not to look at it again until later in the afternoon. Then I turn on an Eagles CD, eat a bowl of cereal, throw in a load of laundry, and get busy with my weekly apartment cleaning. By ten, everything is done, and I'm showered and ready for work with forty minutes to spare before I have to head out the door. I change out the Eagles for the Black Crowes, and boot up my computer.

I don't have as many notifications as usual today. Maybe it's because I popped on and checked my account yesterday during a short layover in Indianapolis, or it could be because I've started to set preferences. Ever since I set a maximum distance I'm willing to travel to meet people and changed the age range I'm interested in from *no preference* to 23 to 45, the number of matches Yahoo! Personals has been sending has been cut by at least a third. Now that the number of matches doesn't seem so daunting, I actually take some time to scroll through the first few pages. I still haven't messaged anyone yet, though, because up until today I've always had new people contact me. Could it be that my preference changes have also reduced the number of people Yahoo! Personals shows *my* profile to?

After deleting two pokes and one icebreaker, I click on the message Scotty sent on Monday. I haven't responded yet because his mention of how cool he thinks it would be to control people didn't sit right with me. But now that I've thought about it further, I know I sometimes do and say things that turn people off. So I suppose the polite thing to do would be to respond, especially considering all the time I've put into messaging back and forth with him.

Hey Scotty,

How's your week going? Mine has been good. I tried a new Italian restaurant in Newark on Tuesday night. (I think you said Italian was your favorite?) Anyway, the lasagna was amazing. If you're ever out in New Jersey, I highly recommend you check out Zucchero Ristorante.

Congrats on your turkey, by the way. I'm not much of a bowler. Pretty sure I achieved my personal high score of 89 back when I was 10. I still think it sounds like a fun date idea though. I'm game whenever you are...

Jess

Next I move on to a message from Wildman. This should be interesting considering the last two messages he sent me were nearly identical.

Howdy Jess!

Arrrrgh! I feel like a total assmunch for those last two messages I sent! So here's the deal, I pop on and off of this site every few days and don't really spend a ton of time on details. To be honest, I'm kind of a scatterbrain. So while those probably aren't the best excuses for not realizing we already connected when I sent that last message, it's the truth. Your forgiveness would be the bee's knees. I found your last message and have your number programmed into my phone. I'll give you a call soon so we can make plans to meet up! I've got a couple dates lined up over the next week and my work schedule is pretty busy this time of year. Did I mention I own a party bus? (Good times I tell you!) So anyway, like I said, I'll give you a call one of these days but it won't be for at least a week.

Cheers!
Brock Wildman

Just like with Wildman's first message, this one gives me a good laugh too. I love his honesty and for some odd reason, I like that he used the word *assmunch*. No, it's not classy, but anyone who can use it in a semi-apology must have a great sense of humor. I'm intrigued by Wildman and look forward to his call.

As I'm cleaning out my email inbox, I remember the laundry I have in the dryer so I shut down my computer and use my last ten minutes of free time to take care of that fun. Then it's off to McGinn's.

I've just finished punching in and am shoving my purse into a locker when I hear someone enter the backroom. Remembering Sawyer's scent, I know it's him before I turn around.

A huge smile involuntarily spreads across my face when we make eye contact. Maybe it's because of what he says or maybe it's just because he makes me smile. I can't say for sure.

"Hey there, Freckles."

"Why do you call me that? I don't even have freckles."

He sighs dramatically. "So you don't like Freckles and you don't want me to call you by your real name. I guess I need to think of something else."

"I didn't say I didn't like Freckles. I said I don't have them," I say laughing. "And what's wrong with calling me Jess? Everyone else does."

"Nothing really. It just seems too common for you. That's all," he says with a shrug. Then he disappears into the kitchen, leaving me to stare after him with a slight grin on my face.

McGinn's is swamped during the peak lunch hours, so the first half of my eleven to five shift flies by. With the exception of my encounter with Sawyer in the backroom earlier, we've hardly had time to talk, only exchanging grins, pleases, and thank yous. Claire arrives at two to join Jillian and me, so I'm able to take a short break. Instead of going outside for some fresh air and to see if Kyle and Justin have texted me back, I hang out in back, hoping to chat with Sawyer since there seems to be a bit of a lull in the dining room.

"Hey guys," I say peeking my head around the corner into the kitchen.

Sawyer looks over from the stove where he's adding ingredients into a large soup pot. He smiles when he sees me. "Stu? Jimmy? Have you had the pleasure of meeting Jess yet?"

Hearing him call me Jess makes me realize I actually like when he calls me Jesstine, or Freckles even.

Stu is a cook who I haven't met yet. He's tall and gangly and his dark shoulder-length hair is pulled back into a ponytail. He briefly looks up from a prep station where he's putting together what looks like homemade Reuben rolls for tonight's dinner service. "Nice to meet you." His tone doesn't sound too friendly. Hopefully he's just concentrating on perfecting those Reuben rolls, but just in case, I make a mental note to work extra hard not to mess up any orders when he's in charge of the window.

Jimmy's blond, buzz-cut hair, bright smile, and short stature make him the polar opposite of Stu. He rushes over to shake my hand for the second time today and says, "Yeah, yeah, yeah, of course I've met her. You're doing great." After addressing me, he goes right back to his job, which consists of clearing the tables, running the dishwasher and keeping everything in the kitchen nice and clean. His movements are swift and energizer-bunny-like. No wonder why everything in the kitchen and dining room is usually spotless.

"You on break?" Sawyer asks.

I fold my arms across my chest and nod. "Don't really need it, but Claire just got here and it's kind of quiet out there right now."

"Yeah, that seems to happen during weekdays around this time. Good thing, too. Gives us a chance to get everything prepped for dinner service."

I nod and watch as Sawyer plates a Reuben sandwich. Then he begins ladling Irish stew into an over-sized bowl.

"Well, looks like you guys are pretty busy, so I'll just—"

"Give me a sec to put this order up. Meet you in back?" Sawyer says.

"Sure. I just have to get back out there in about ten minutes."

He gives me a nod, and I head to the back to wait. I retrieve my phone from my locker and take a seat at a black foldout card table that reminds me of the ones Gwen used to set out for the kids during holiday dinners. The memory elicits a feeling of sadness, which I shake off immediately. No sense feeling sad about a past mistake I can't change.

When I unlock my phone, the first notification is for a text from Kyle.

Kyle: Yep, tonight works! Not sure if I told you this, but I live in a two-room efficiency on Prospect. In other words, shitty parking. Okay if we watch at your place? I'll bring licorice ...

Me: Sounds good. 2946 S Delaware #4. How about 7 and Cherry Nibs?

The next notification has me bummed for two reasons. One, it's not from Justin, and two, it's from Ned. Based on the preview which says *Hey babe, how are you doing? I miss . . .* I know it's more of the same old same old. Ned just doesn't get it!

"Grrr," I say, pressing down on the message to delete it without even opening it.

"You okay?" Sawyer asks as he pulls out the chair across from me and sits down.

"Just . . ." I hold up my phone for a second and then flip it closed. "An annoying ex."

"Oh, you have one of those too?"

"Don't we all?"

He flashes his bright, twinkle-eyed smile at me, and even though I'm beginning to like Justin more, I still want to jump Sawyer's bones. I know it's irrational and an effect of the social norm that leads people to believe we should only date one person at a time, but I can't help but feel a little guilty. I chase away the negative feeling by reminding myself that Justin and I aren't exclusive. Plus, I'm not even dating Sawyer. I'm simply fantasizing about what it would be like to have sex with him perfectly sober. It's only human.

"Wanna talk about it? Or anything else? You seem off." He creases his brow and cocks his head. Then he reaches out and runs his index finger across the top of my hand a few times as he says, "Cooome on. What's bothering you, Jesstine?"

My insides melt.

"Let me guess. You were a psychology major so you have a habit of fishing around for people to psychoanalyze." I give him a wiseass grin.

He chuckles. "Wrong. I actually double majored in math and computer science at UW-Madison, but I still fish around for people to psychoanalyze. The psychoanalysis is more of a hobby though." He winks and gives a small shrug.

I stare at him wide-eyed. "Math and computer science?"

"Yeah. What? I don't look geeky enough to be a math major?"

"No," I say, shaking my head, "You definitely look geeky enough." I try to keep a straight face but fail miserably and we both start laughing. "So, if you have math and computer science degrees—and I don't mean *anything* by this—then why are you working here?"

He sighs but continues to grin at me. "*That,* Freckles, is a story I'll tell you some other time."

"Yeah, okay," I say, nodding. I can see in his eyes that he really means it when he says he'll tell me another time, and for some reason, this makes me want to share something with him. Half of something, anyway. "You wanted to know what else was bothering me, besides the fact that my idiot ex won't stop calling and texting me?"

He nods, sits up straighter, and folds his hands on the table.

"Very nice. That's exactly how my psychologist sits at his desk during my sessions," I tease.

He rolls his eyes and laughs as he loosens his posture. "Better?"

I nod and get to my half-truth. "I kind of like someone I met online." I pause, expecting him to say something, but he simply nods. "And I'm torn about what to do next because I don't want to get all serious with one person right away. I mean, I do have two more months left of my subscription so I should use it, right? But I also don't want to miss out on something that could be good. You know?" The part I don't tell him is that I also kind of like him, and it's confusing the hell out of me.

Smiling thoughtfully, he leans his cheek against his palm. "So don't get serious. Just date him, and date other people if you want. But if you like him, you should tell him because he could be thinking the same thing." He slides his chair back, stands and continues, never breaking eye contact with me. "And if you want to quit online dating before your subscription is up, then quit. Because what's the point of doing something if you're only doing it because you feel obligated? Capiche?"

"Capiche," I say as I stand too.

"Good. My job is done here," he says as he turns to leave, mockingly wiping his hands in the air. And right before he disappears into the kitchen, he looks over his shoulder and says, "Expect a bill in the mail."

"Smart ass," I whisper under my breath. The funny thing is I mean it. The advice he just gave me *was* really smart. But for some reason, I feel like it wasn't meant as advice for how I should deal with Justin. As ridiculous as it sounds, it feels more like Sawyer was telling me how I should deal with him.

chapter twenty-four

If me changing into gray fleece pants and a tee that says *This is My Party Shirt* is any indication that I'm not romantically interested in Kyle, I don't know what is. If I wanted to impress him, I would have worn my black yoga pants instead which accentuate my best asset, or so I've been told.

An hour before Kyle is scheduled to arrive, I preheat the oven for pizza, pop open a bottle of wine, and chop up some fresh veggies. I also brought home some Reuben rolls for us to snack on. I'm pretty sure Sawyer gave me extra because there's enough for a family of four.

My home phone rings just as I put the pizza in the oven. It's Chloe.

"Hel-loooo!"

"Hey, whatcha' doing?"

"Getting ready for a movie marathon with Kyle."

"Hiccups?"

"Yes," I say, laughing. "Not sure how much hiccupping he'll be doing tonight though. I think his mindset has changed when it comes to me."

"What do you mean?"

"Well, his ex wants him back, and I'm pretty sure he wants her back too."

"Then why are you guys hanging out tonight?"

"I don't know. Because he asked. And he's a nice guy. Plus, I'm probably the only person he knows around here who'd agree to watch the first two *Lord of the Rings* movies back to back."

"Huh. Let me know what you think. I heard those movies were good."

"Yeah, okay, but I doubt I'll be able to stay awake for both. So, how's Daran doing?"

"Not so good. He went to the doctor today and was given a

prescription for amoxicillin. I'm actually going to be heading over there in a bit to take him some soup."

"Poor guy. You said neither of you were feeling good last week either. Probably should have gone to the doctor sooner. Are you feeling okay?"

"Eh, I still feel like I could be coming down with something. It's just lingering, you know? But I don't have any of the same symptoms Daran does. Probably a combination of germs I picked up from kids at school. Anyway, let's talk about *Justin*." She says his name like she's talking about Brad Pitt. "What a cutie. And he's nice too!"

"Yeah, I know," I say, smiling as I picture him. "He really has that boy band look going on, doesn't he?"

"Yes! That's exactly what he looks like. A member of a boy band! Except, a little manlier. And to think, you thought he was going to be bad date number three. I think it's a sign."

"I think it is what it is."

"Uh-uh. I think it's fate waltzing into your life to show you who's boss. Although . . ."

"Although what?"

"Never mind. I don't want to influence your thinking."

"Really? You sure about that? Because I think you just insinuated that fate brought Justin and me together," I say, chuckling.

"Yeah, okay, you got me."

"So?"

"I was just thinking about how Sawyer could be a possibility too. You sure seem to have a lot of chemistry with him"

"Right, but he's married, remember?"

Chloe completely ignores me and asks, "Speaking of Sawyer what happened with you two the other night?"

"Nothing much. He apologized for not telling me he was married, and I told him I was more mad at myself than I was at him. You know, for sleeping with another married man."

"You did? I mean, you told him about Brant?" Chloe sounds shocked. I guess I don't blame her. Very few people know about what happened between me and Brant.

"Mm-hmm. Then he reminded me that we didn't have sex and gave me some sort of pep talk. It was very sweet."

"Hmmm. I'm not sure who I like better, Justin or Sawyer . . ."

"Give me a break. I'm not even dating Sawyer, so you definitely don't need to decide."

"Uh-huh. Okay. Whatever you say. But I just want you to know, I don't care if you decide not to finish out the three months of online dating. I'd say you've gotten my money's worth with Justin alone. I told you setting preferences would pay off. Besides, I never expected you to last an entire month and now look at you. You're a pro." If I know Chloe, she's beaming with pride.

"A pro? I haven't even slept with anyone yet," I joke.

"Stop. You know what I mean." We share a giggle.

"Alright, well, Kyle is going to be here soon so I need to get going. Tell Daran I hope he feels better."

"I will. Tell hiccups I said hi."

"Whatever," I say with a snort. "Goodbye."

"Bye."

As soon as I place the handset back on the charging station, there's a knock at my door.

"Come in!" Regret sets in as soon as I say it. *What if it's not Kyle? What if it's Ned?*

But my panic attack dissipates as quickly as it began when Kyle appears, loaded with goodies. He has a bag of Doritos tucked under one arm, a bag of Cherry Nibs under the other, and he's holding a four-pack of Sprecher Root Reer and the movies in his hands. His smile fades when he sees my face.

"Are you okay? I brought the Nibs." He glances down at the bag hesitantly and I burst into laughter.

"Yes, I'm fine. It's just that I yelled for you to come in without even considering it could be Ned."

"Oh." He nods and turns to kick his shoes off by the door. "That's probably a good sign, right?" He walks past me on his way to the coffee table where he unloads everything except for the Nibs. He tosses those to me.

"What do you mean?" I ask, catching the bag of licorice.

I wait for him to respond as he pulls open the bag of Doritos and eats one. "If it didn't even cross your mind at first that it might have been your ex at the door, then you must be getting used to him not being around. Don't you think?"

I nod slowly, my mouth curving up into a grin because I think he's on to something. Then I spread my arms out wide. "Welcome to my apartment."

"Why thank you. And thanks for agreeing to hang out here. My place feels a little claustrophobic sometimes so I'm actually thinking about moving."

"Oh yeah? Where?" He offers me a root beer. "Oh, no thanks. I have a glass of wine in—"

"Nooooo." He interrupts my sentence with a groan. "You can't drink wine while you're watching *Lord of the Rings*. That's sacrilege."

Unsure if he's joking or not, I stand there, staring at Kyle with my mouth open. The oven timer starts beeping in the background.

"Just sayin'." He shrugs, twists the cap off his root beer and takes a long guzzle. That's when I realize he's wearing black sweats and a ratty sweatshirt that says *Disc Golf Association*.

"Oh my gosh," I say, as I crack up and rush into the kitchen.

"What's so funny?" Kyle calls after me.

I quickly take the pizza out of the oven and scurry back into the living room, still chuckling. "I just think it's funny how neither of us is out to impress the other. You're not even hiccupping!"

A grin forms on his lips. "Well, the pressure's off now . . ." He shrugs. "Since I've decided to give my relationship with Amy another chance, my mind isn't set on starting over with someone else. I hope that doesn't make things odd between us."

"No, of course not," I say shaking my head. "I sincerely hope things work out for you two."

"Well, thank you. I really appreciate you being so awesome. And thanks again for the advice. I knew when I first met you we'd make great friends, maybe even more, hence the nervous hiccup outbreak." He closes his eyes as if remembering something. "Man, my hiccups have been such a pain in the ass over the years." He opens his eyes and laughs.

"Nah, they prevented us from doing something you'd probably regret now. And for the record, I think your hiccups are kinda cute." Kyle blushes a little and then swallows hard, suppressing a little hiccup.

Laughing, I head into the kitchen to cut the pizza. Then, before I return to the living room I load up a large bamboo serving tray with paper plates, napkins, and the Tupperware of cut up veggies. Before I return to the living room with the pizza and tray of items, I pour the wine from my glass back into the bottle. There's no reason I shouldn't be able to enjoy dinner and a movie with my buddy Kyle without getting liquored up. Drinking less alcohol wasn't originally a goal for me, but it could be now. Why not? It'll be good for me.

Kyle already has the first movie ready to go when I plop the pizza and tray down on the coffee table.

"Pizza. Nice." He says as he grabs a slice. I do the same, and then I take a seat next to him on the couch. "You know, you're the only person from the dating site who I had any interest in meeting up with in person?"

I shrug and take a second bite from my slice of pizza. "That's because I'm awesome."

"Agreed. Except you have one serious flaw."

"What's that?"

"You've never seen this movie." Remote in hand, he elbows me and then presses play.

Around ten, I get a text from Justin.

JUSTIN: SO I ASSUME YOU'RE ON A DATE?

I respond right away.

ME: NOT REALLY A DATE, BUT YES, WATCHING A MOVIE WITH SOMEONE.

I hold my phone expecting him to get back to me just as quickly as I got back to him. After about ten minutes, my phone vibrates, but it's not a text from Justin.

Sawyer: How's the movie, Freckles?

Me: Good. Only about halfway through. But safe to say I'd recommend it if you haven't seen it.

Before I left McGinn's, I mentioned to Sawyer what movies Kyle and I intended to watch, but he didn't say anything to make me think he's seen them before. He simply handed me my Reuben rolls (which I forgot to take out of the microwave and will make a great midnight snack) and told me to have a good night.

Sawyer: All we have to decide is what to do with the time that is given us.

I stare at the message long enough for Kyle to take notice. "Hey, you watching?"

I nod and turn my phone facedown on the cushion next to me. But I can't concentrate on the movie because I can't stop wondering why Sawyer said what he just said. Is he hitting on me? Then my phone buzzes again and Kyle sighs. "Sorry," I whisper. "I promise I won't look at it again after this."

Sawyer: That's one of my favorite lines from the book. Enjoy the rest of the film.

Justin never texts me back.

chapter twenty-five

My alarm goes off at eight a.m., but after being up watching *The Fellowship of the Ring* with Kyle until three, I'm unable to drag my butt out of bed before hitting snooze several times. When I finally have a cup of coffee in my hand, the first thing I do is check to see if Justin texted me back.

Nothing.

My first inclination is to be bummed about not hearing back from him, but then I remind myself that I *was* with another guy so why would he want to text me back? Even though my relationship with Kyle is totally platonic, Justin doesn't know that. If roles were reversed, I probably wouldn't have texted him back either.

The rest of my morning before leaving for McGinn's passes by in a haze. I clean up everything from the night before, make my bed, shower and get dressed. The extra cup of coffee doesn't wake me up the way I thought it would. Instead, I'm jittery but still feel like I need a three-hour nap. How I'm going to make it through the next seven hours is beyond me.

The first person I see when I walk in is Molly. She tells me what great things she's heard about me from other staff members and some of the regulars, which is so nice to hear. Then she disappears into her office to do payroll. When Sawyer gets in, he looks about as ragged as I imagine I do. But I do perk up a little when I see him. I try to make eye contact with him, only for some reason he keeps his eyes forward and heads straight to Molly's office. By the time he finally emerges, Stu has already grumbled at me several times for not picking up orders from the window fast enough. Apparently, he thinks us waitresses have nothing else to do other than take the orders, enter the orders and then stand next to the window waiting to pick up the orders.

"Hi, Sawyer," I say to him cheerily as I enter an order at the computer. "Geez Louise. Do you ever get a day off?"

He glances at me and smiles, but it isn't the way he usually smiles. There's no twinkle in his eyes today. "Sundays and Mondays are my off days," he says plainly. Then he goes back to cooking.

I want to ask why he seems down, but there just isn't time. We're too busy for small talk so it'll have to wait.

By the time five o'clock rolls around, I feel like I might collapse from exhaustion. But I volunteer to stay anyway when Anne calls and says she's going to be late because I heard Sawyer tell Stu he was leaving at six today. I'd really like to know what's going on with him.

When Anne arrives at five forty, instead of leaving after I punch out, I refold and restack the McGinn's t-shirts and aprons in back. Then I reorganize the supplies. Yes, it feels stalkerish, but I want to be back here when Sawyer punches out.

"Hey, I thought you left."

I jump a little, pretending to be startled, before turning to face Sawyer. A girl's gotta do what a girl's gotta do.

"I did . . . I mean, I punched out, but then I noticed the supplies were kind of disorganized and these stacks looked messy so . . ." I wave a hand in front of the now nice, neat stacks of clothing.

The corners of his mouth turn up into an amused half-grin. Suddenly I feel foolish because I'm pretty sure he knows I stayed for him. So I ramble.

"But I'm done now, and I'm pretty tired because, *damn*, those were the longest movies I've ever seen. Anyway, you have a good night and I'll—"

"You hungry?" I get a whiff of his subtle fresh scent as he removes his white jacket, and my insides tingle.

Say something! "Yeah. I could eat."

"Good, let's get out of here."

"Where to?"

"It's a surprise. How about if I follow you to your place so you can drop off your car? It's on the way."

"Works for me."

Twenty minutes later, we pull up in front of a place called The Soup Otzie's.

I look over at him and smile. "I love this place."

He grins, obviously proud with his restaurant selection.

"Chloe doesn't work far from here," I explain, "so I meet her sometimes for lunch. Best cream of chicken soup I've ever had."

"Agreed," he says, smiling. "And I make a mean cream of chicken soup, too, ya know."

"Do you want the good news or the bad news first?"

He raises an inquisitive eyebrow at me. "Bad. Always the bad first so the good can overshadow it."

"I like that," I say, losing myself in his handsomeness. He waves a hand in front of my face and laughs. "So the bad news is . . ." I say, adjusting in my seat. "They close at three on Fridays."

He slumps back in his seat and sighs heavily through his mouth. "Shoot. That's right."

"But there's good news, too. Remember?"

He turns to face me and leans a little closer. "Hit me."

"I happen to have *two* containers of their soup in my freezer." I flash two fingers at him to emphasize just how much soup I have.

"And you're willing to share?"

"Gladly."

We sit there smiling at each other for a few seconds, and when he turns away I wish I could hit rewind a few times just to stare into his bright blue eyes a bit longer. Instead, he pulls out of the curb spot we're parked in and we go forward.

While the soup is thawing in the microwave, I give into Sawyer's request to see my online dating dashboard. I'm actually fine with showing him, but there's a small part of me that doesn't want him getting any ideas. I know it's highly unlikely he would ever try online dating, but it was also highly unlikely that I would ever try it.

When I finally log in, he reads my profile and then scrolls through my matches. I sit beside him at the dining room table opening my mail and peeking at the screen every few seconds. His expression is neutral for the most part with a slight grin and chuckle thrown in here and there. After a couple of minutes, he slides my laptop over to me.

"So? What do you think?" I ask.

"It's actually a great concept and really not all that different from dating offline. I wish I'd thought of it because it's going to be a huge money maker for years to come."

"What do you mean it's not much different from meeting people offline? When you meet people online, there's no way to know if you'll have face-to-face chemistry with someone. So it's kind of a guessing game. At least when you meet someone in person, you get a sense right away as to whether or not you're attracted to them.

"Right, but immediate chemistry can be just as deceiving as profile stats and words in a message. You can be extremely attracted to someone only to find out days, weeks, even months down the road that they aren't who you think they are. So online, in person," he raises one hand, then the other, "it's a crapshoot either way. People who think they can find a perfect match by setting a dozen preferences online and live happily ever after are fooling themselves if they think it won't take just as much work to really get to know that person . . . You have a message, by the way." He shuffles the deck of cards I'd gotten out so we could play Speed later. I'm still pondering his thoughts about traditional and online dating both being crapshoots as I slide my finger around on the touchpad to wake up my laptop. When the screen lights up, he grins devilishly at me and says, "It's from *Pamela*." The way he says Pam's name is a question in and of itself.

Embarrassed, I immediately raise my hands to cover my eyes.

"What? Are you embarrassed?"

I spread my fingers and peek through them at him. "Maybe."

"Don't be. So are you bi then?"

I lower my hands. "No . . . I don't think so anyway. I've never gone out with a woman before so . . ." I shrug as I stand to toss the junk mail in the trash and place the bills that need to be paid in my purse. "I have kissed one though."

"Oh yeah?" He says in a saucy voice. "And? What'd you think?"

"Eh, I was drunk, so I don't really remember what it felt like. I just know I definitely didn't feel like kissing her the next time I saw her when I was sober." I laugh softly, remembering how angry Shelly was that I'd "led her friend on," as she put it, when it was her friend who came on to me. If I hadn't kissed the woman back, she probably would have said I was being rude.

Grinning, Sawyer starts setting up the cards for Speed. "So how did you end up talking to *Pam*?"

"She poked me a couple of times and I was curious so I poked her back. But then I told her it was just an impulse poke and I'm really not interested in women. So I'm guessing her message is just to say have a nice life and good luck finding a man, or something like that." I straighten out the stack of cards in front of me and pick up five.

"Well, now you can't leave me in suspense. See what she said," Sawyer says, laying down the cards in his hands and placing a finger on the touchpad of my laptop to wake it up.

I stare at him for a second, unsure if I want him to see what Pamela's message says. Then I lay my cards down with a shrug and click on her message and read it out loud, ready to censor it if I have to.

Jess,

Thanks for you honesty. I'd still love to meet you anyway, if you're still up for it, of course. How about tomorrow night? We could play mini golf at that new family fun center over on Layton. A girls' night. No strings.

I hope to hear from you soon!

Pamela

I look up at Sawyer, and he's leaning back in his chair with his arms folded across his chest. "What do you think? Are you going to go out with her?"

I shrug.

"You should. The worst thing that could happen is you'll make a new friend."

"Yeah, you're right. What the hell," I say tapping out a quick response. The idea of making a new female friend is actually appealing to me because I don't have many.

Pamela,

Okay, let's meet. I know exactly where that mini golf course is. Meet you there at six tomorrow?

Jess

"Done," I say, closing the lid of my laptop and picking up my cards.

The microwave beeps while we're playing our first round of Speed. In the end, I kick Sawyer's butt.

"Too slow, old man!" I say, as I slam my final card down on one of the center stacks. I immediately feel bad for saying it, but Sawyer laughs at my smack talk. I love that he can take a joke.

"Hey, I haven't played this game in years, so that was just a warm-up round. You're giving me a rematch after we eat."

"Glutton for punishment, huh?" I jab my elbow into his shoulder as I walk past him on my way to the kitchen. He follows and helps out by pouring two glasses of ice water while I ladle soup into bowls.

We both concentrate on our soup for a few minutes before I decide to ask why he seemed so down earlier at work.

"So what was wrong earlier? You seemed down or distracted."

He freezes, spoon in his mouth, and his eyes meet mine. I take a sip of water, wondering if he thinks it's rude of me to pry. But before I can tell him to forget I asked, he places the spoon in his nearly empty bowl, wipes his mouth with a napkin, and says, "Remember how I told you I have a degree in math and computer science?"

"Yes."

"Well, my wife—you know what? Her name is Beth. I'm tired of calling her my wife. Anyway, she was a computer science major too. That's how we met and started dating. And the guy she cheated on me with—Corey—also went to college with us." He pauses and takes a drink of water as I wait quietly. "So, the three of us are equal partners in a company we started back in 2000, and yesterday, Corey contacted me to find out if or when I plan to return. They basically want to know if I'm going to be able to work with them and pretend things are a-okay between us. And frankly, even though we spent years conceiving the ideas our company is built on, I just don't know if I can do it."

I let out a breath I didn't know I was holding, and we sit in silence for a while, Sawyer fidgeting with his napkin and me staring at him. Questions are swirling through my mind, but none of them seem appropriate to ask at the moment. I'm about to reach out to touch his hand, just to provide some sort of comfort, when he continues.

"You know, it's not like I even care anymore about them getting together. Beth and I started drifting apart about a year after we started the company anyway, when we started reaping the fruits of our labor. I'm angrier that they weren't honest about what was brewing between them."

"What made you drift apart? I mean, you said you met in college, so you've been together for what, like fifteen years?"

"More like twenty—off and on in the beginning though. I really am an old man, aren't I?" He finally glances up at me with a slightly defeated look.

"You are not," I say softly.

He lets out a heavy sigh before answering my question. "When business started booming—and I mean *booming*—Beth started to change. Instead of going home after a long day of work to cook dinner and watch a little TV, she started wanting to go out for happy hours and expensive dinners. And on weekends, instead of stopping at a corner bar for a beer and a game of darts or pool, she wanted to fly to Vegas or go shopping in Chicago. She started spending money on her hair, spa treatments and fancy new clothes. I figured she'd get over it after the novelty of no longer living paycheck to paycheck wore off, but she didn't. And she also seemed to have forgotten about our plans to start trying for a baby after seeing what happened with the company." Sawyer swipes away a tear from the corner of his left eye just as it begins to fall, causing me to tear up.

"Hey, don't do that," he says, getting up and grabbing a tissue for me from the box on the end table next to my couch. "All of this happened for a reason, and I'm over Beth. So please don't feel bad for me. I just get a little choked up when I think I might never be a father. I am an old man now, you know?"

He wiggles his thick eyebrows at me, making me laugh.

"So how did she and Corey end up . . ." I let the unfinished question hang in the air but Sawyer answers anyway.

"Corey was just as into living the highlife as Beth was, which is hilarious because the guy was never into things like clothes or liquor before all the money. In fact, he used to wear sweats or this one pair of ugly painter overalls to parties. People would give him so much shit about his lack of fashion sense. And the guy always drank the cheapest beer possible, even if it tasted like shit." Sawyer catches himself smiling and quickly clears his throat. "Anyway, the money changed them both, but I just wanted to keep living the simple life Beth and I had been living for over a decade. And that's how they bonded. I guess money sometimes does more harm than good."

"So, I totally understand you needing time away from them and taking a break from work, but why do you work at McGinn's?" I ask gently.

"Molly and I used to work there together when we were teenagers, back when her mom and dad ran the place, and Molly and I have kept in touch over the years. She happened to need a cook when the shit hit the fan with Beth and Corey, so I told her I'd help her out. That's actually why I had to talk to her yesterday. I told her she should start looking for someone because it's time for me to get back to business."

My stomach drops when he reveals he won't be at McGinn's much longer, making me realize how much I really like him. I don't let on though, because I'm glad he's ready to return to his real job so he can show those two assholes they didn't break him. "That's great. I'm really happy for you." I smile even though it's definitely going to take me some time to get used to the idea of not getting to see him at McGinn's. "Hey, not that it matters, but what type of company do you own?"

"We're a mobile entertainment and personalization company."

"And . . . what do you do exactly?"

He laughs and says, "We make ringtones, graphics, and games for cell phones."

"Wow. You're a total tech nerd."

"Watch it, Freckles."

My laugh turns into a yawn, prompting me to check the wall clock in the living room.

"Are you pooping out on me already? It's only eight." Sawyer stands and carries our bowls into the kitchen.

"No, but soon. Don't forget I was up until three last night," I call to him as I grab the cards and start shuffling.

Sawyer beats me in our second game of Speed. We play a tiebreaker, and he wins again. So I force him to play another game, which I win. By then, it's almost nine, and I can feel fatigue setting in.

"I should go and let you get to bed. We'll play a tiebreaker some other time."

I sigh, wishing he could crawl into bed with me. Now that I know the story about his wife, it doesn't seem so wrong for me to like him. "You know, now that I know the situation with Beth, I don't feel so terrible about what happened between us the night we met."

"Good, but I wish you hadn't been so hard on yourself before I vented everything to you tonight. It was just some harmless kissing."

I shake my head as I stand to put the cards away.

"What?" he asks.

"You do know there were used condoms in my garbage can the next morning, right?"

"Yes, I'm aware, but I already told you, we didn't have sex. Why don't you believe me?"

"Because that's not me. And this," I gesture between us, "hanging out with you tonight without jumping your bones . . . isn't really me either. Not the person I've been for the last six years anyway."

"What do you mean?" He tilts his head.

"What I mean is that I've never been someone who has to go on three dates before having sex with someone. In fact, I've been a willing participant on first dates more than I care to admit."

I expect my honesty might change his opinion of me, that he might decide I'm not the type of woman who deserves his attention. Instead, he grabs my hand and leads me back into my bedroom. The whole way there, I'm wondering if my confession has caused him to think I'm propositioning him. But instead of leading me to my bed, he stops in front of the closet.

"Is it okay if I . . ." He says, motioning to the closet.

I shrug, without a clue what he's up to. My jaw drops when he slides it open and bends down to retrieve the heart-decorated box from Ryan Cross. After dating him for three years, Ned doesn't even know about the box.

"How do you know about that? What are you doing?" I move to grab it from him, but he jerks it off to the side out of my reach.

"Look, clearly you don't remember anything about that night we first met, so why are you so certain that we had sex?"

"Because that's what I do . . . did. You were my last mistake." I say quietly.

"You wanna know why all of those condoms were in the garbage?"

I widen my eyes at him, palms outstretched toward the ceiling, making it obvious I'm all ears.

"Do I come across as the type of guy who would have sex with someone who was as drunk as you were that night? Someone I just met? Sure, we were obviously attracted to each other from the moment we met in the parking lot, but—"

"Wait, you were attracted to me in the parking lot?"

"That's not the point . . . the point is even though it was pretty clear that night that we were into each other, you were way too drunk to consent to sex. But if you'd been sober?" He raises his eyebrows at me, letting the insinuation linger.

"That doesn't explain the condoms," I say plainly, hoping he doesn't notice that my breathing has increased and I'm blushing over what he just said.

"I'm getting there . . . So we made out, and it was awesome. You wanted to do more, and so did I. But I told you I wouldn't. You didn't ask why, but if you had, I would have told you because you were too drunk. I would have told you about my wife too. But, again, you didn't ask. You just kept working me and eventually things went a bit further than I'd planned. Put it this way, I've seen you naked." He smiles as if he's remembering something specific.

"And?" I cross my arms. "The condoms?"

"Well, that's where the really fun part of our night started. You were blowing them up and seeing how far you could get them to fly across the room." He pauses to laugh at the memory. "I've never seen a woman do that before. Come to think of it, I've never seen anyone do that before."

I take a seat on the bed. "Oh, my God," I say, horrified that I acted like such an idiot.

"And you know what happened after the condom antics?"

"What?" I whisper, staring at the box resting under his arm at his side.

"We talked until the sunlight started filtering through your blinds." He brings the box in front of him, gripping it with both hands. "So, would you like to remove the Molly McGinn's coaster with my name on it or would you like me to do it?"

I look up at him and I feel like I'm going to cry. I don't remember anything about that night after we left the bar until I woke up and found him next to me snoring, but in this moment, I feel more connected to him than ever. Did I feel this way about him that night? Is that why I told him about my box? Or was the connection made *when* I told him about the box? I want to ask if he knows about Ryan, but I don't because I'm pretty sure I already know the answer.

Respecting my silence, he holds the box out to me. But instead of taking it from him, I let him hold it while I remove the lid and retrieve the coaster with his name scrawled on it in my messy drunken handwriting. I replace the lid and hold up the coaster, wracking my brain to come up with some sort of smart aleck comment to take the attention off my stupid box full of coasters. Instead, Sawyer snatches the coaster from me and hands me the box. Then he tears the coaster to shreds and tosses it into the trashcan next to my nightstand.

"That's what you should do with all of them," he says, taking the box from me and turning to put it back in my closet.

After that, we lie in my bed, fully clothed, talking. I'm exhausted and running on fumes, but a break in the conversation long enough for one of us to fall asleep never happens. We talk about his mom and dad who now live in Sun Prairie, about his dog Boscoe (who his ex insisted on keeping), about his memories of playing baseball in high school, about his odd collection of McDonald's Happy Meal toys (which he swears is worth a fortune), about Ned, about my dad's death, my rocky relationship with Gwen, and my estranged relationship with Ashley, about my stepdad's infidelity, about my mom and Rod, about our shared love for roller coasters, and even about my online dating prospects. The strange thing is it doesn't even feel weird telling him about all the dates I've been on or about the ones I have lined up. It just feel like we're old friends catching up.

When the phone rings just before three, I jump up, ready to race into the living room to prevent a drunken message from Ned, but Sawyer stops me. Then we lie there laughing as Ned slurs a message full of *I miss you's* and *I need you's* and repeated pleas for me to pick up the phone and return his calls. After that, our conversation dies down, but Sawyer says one last thing to me as I drift off.

"I like who you are Jesstine, mistakes and all . . . Sweet dreams, Freckles."

The next morning, I awaken to the sounds of drawers opening and closing, clanking silverware, and the scraping of a spatula against a frying pan. My eyes remain closed, until I smell bacon and coffee. That's when they flutter open and my first consequence for staying up until four after only getting five hours of sleep the night before is delivered. I have the worst headache, but I push through the pain and crawl out of bed anyway.

"Hey there, Freckles." Sawyer says with a smile as he peers up at me from in front of the stove.

I moan and elbow him in the side, making my way to the cabinet where I keep the acetaminophen. After I swallow several tablets, and fill a mug full of coffee, I lean against the counter and blow on the black liquid before taking a sip. I usually add milk to my coffee, but a headache like the one I have requires desperate measures.

"Well, this is the second time you've spent the night, and here you are again, making us breakfast. Aren't you tired?"

He turns to face me, holding two plates filled with fried eggs, bacon and English muffins. "Nope." And with a wink he nods for me to follow him to the table.

We shovel food into our mouths until I break the silence, "Sawyer?"

"Hm?" He pops one last bit of English muffin into his mouth.

"Thank you. For breakfast and for last night."

He puts up a finger, chews faster, and then swallows. "You're welcome for breakfast, but why are you thanking me for last night?"

"I don't know. Just because." I shake my head, pondering why myself. I just felt the need to say it.

"Well, you're welcome . . . just because." Then he peers over my head at the daffodil from Justin. "Where'd you get the flower?"

I glance at it and then turn back to Sawyer. "Justin gave it to me."

To my surprise, he laughs.

"Why is that funny?"

"Yeah, he looked like the sort of guy who would give a woman one daffodil."

"Hey, I happen to love daffodils." I don't know where he's going with this, but I'm feeling a bit defensive since Justin has been nothing but a perfect gentleman when we're together or chatting on the phone. Why is Sawyer laughing about the fact that he gave me a flower?

"Do you know what one daffodil symbolizes?"

"Nooo . . . what?"

"One means misfortune or bad luck. So I guess Justin hopes a lot of bad juju is in store for you." He continues to chuckle.

"That's a load of baloney. Everyone knows daffodils are the flower of spring. They represent new growth or new beginnings," I say, scoffing at him.

"Nah, that's only if they're in a bunch, not when there's just one. So if he'd have gotten you more than one . . . well, maybe there'd be hope for the two of you." He grins and takes a sip of coffee.

I roll my eyes. "For your information, he did give me two. Just not at the same time. I bet you're just not the flower-giving type, and that's why you're picking on poor Justin."

"Not true. I give flowers, just not ones that are rumored to bring the recipient bad fortune."

"Give me a break."

"No, seriously, if I was that guy, I'd have bought all the daffodils in the flower store for you. Every last one. Then we'd be sitting here right now staring at a bundle of good things to come."

"Whatever you say, oh wise one."

"Hey, just passing along what I know," he says with a shrug.

chapter twenty-six

Sawyer had to be to work at eleven, so he headed out around nine. I walked him to the door, not really sure what to expect. A hug? A kiss? A simple *see ya, Jesstine*? I still don't know what would have happened had Mags not bolted out the door the second Sawyer opened it to leave, something she hasn't done since she was a kitten. As I stood there in the hallway outside my apartment, holding the fur ball, all I got was a wave. Damn cat.

Now I'm cleaning and thinking about Justin. It's Sawyer's fault really, with that whole conversation he started about daffodils. I'm fine with Justin not texting me back on Thursday night, but he never even bothered to contact me yesterday, which is annoying and makes me wonder if he's playing some sort of head game. Ned and Brant played enough games with me over the last few years. I'm done with games.

After I finish vacuuming, I grab my phone out of my purse. It's dead so I plug it in next to the couch and power it on. Then I take a seat on the floor next to the outlet and a sunny spot where my cats are lounging. I have a missed call from my mom and a missed call from Justin that came through just after midnight the night before, when Sawyer and I would have been lying in my bed talking. I also have two voicemail messages, so I press one to listen.

"Hi, Jesstine. How are you sweetie? I know you're extremely busy with your jobs, but I'm hoping we can make plans to meet for lunch again soon . . . I know you're not fond of stopping over when Rod is here, but he's my boyfriend, honey. I'd like for the two of you to get to know each other." She sighs. *"Anyway, Rod and I are driving to Door County next weekend, so if you already have plans for today, I suppose we'll have to get together in two weeks. Love you. Bye."*

I press seven to delete my mom's message, and the next message begins playing right away.

"Hey, Jess, it's Justin. I'm so sorry for not responding to your text last night, and what's worse is I'm just now contacting you for the first time today . . . actually it's tomorrow already . . . So, here's the deal. I feel like an explanation is in order, but I'd rather not leave it in a message. I'm sure you're fast asleep by now, but as soon as you get this, please give me a call. By the way, I'm no longer taking Max to the Dells, and yes, it has something to do with what happened. Talk to you soon, Jess. Bye."

The skeptic in me wonders if there really is an explanation as to why Justin never contacted me yesterday, but the side of me that likes to give people the benefit of the doubt is wondering what happened. His mention of the cancellation of their trip to the Wisconsin Dells makes me worried that something might have happened to his son.

I know my mom is most likely either doing yoga or speed walking around her subdivision right now. Or maybe she's . . . I cringe at the thought of what else she could be doing if Rod is there. Regardless of what she's doing, I'm sure I'd end up leaving a message if I tried to call her now, so I dial Justin's number instead. He answers after the first ring.

"Hello?" He clears his throat. "Jess?"

"Hi. I just listened to your message. Is everything okay?"

He sighs. "Everything's fine now, but Max had to be rushed to the emergency room on Thursday night because he couldn't breathe."

"Oh no." I bring my free hand to my mouth. "What happened?"

"Well, he's had asthma since he was a toddler, and sometimes when he's sick it flares up. Laura took him in when his coughs started to sound like high-pitched barks. When she called to let me know, I left for the hospital right away. I was in the middle of texting you back."

"Oh my gosh. Your son had to go the emergency room and you're worried about me?" His concern is sweet, but what about his son? "So how is he?"

"He's good now. They ended up admitting and treating him for viral croup. Then they held him for observation until around two yesterday afternoon when he was discharged."

"Thank God. I'm so sorry you had to go through that."

"I'm just glad it's over and he's okay. And again, I'm sorry."

"Well, don't be," I say, thinking that will be the end of it.

"No, I should have at least called you yesterday, but there's a good reason why I didn't. You see, when I left the hospital, I realized I'd left my phone there, and I didn't have time to go back to get it before work. Luckily Laura grabbed it for me so I didn't have to make the extra trip to the hospital before going back to see Max last night. I called you as soon as I left their house."

"So now what? Is he on medication?"

"No, nothing other than acetaminophen, but Laura has him rotating between the steamy bathroom and breathing in cold air from a humidifier. It seems to alleviate the coughing fits. Plus it's a lot cheaper than the steam therapy they were treating him with at the hospital." He sighs, sounding exhausted.

"Well I'm glad he's feeling better, but sad that he doesn't get to go to the water park. Poor kiddo!"

"Already taken care of. We have plans to go in two weeks."

"Perfect. Just enough time for Max to make a full recovery."

"You know, there is one silver lining here."

"Yeah, what's that?"

"Now I'm free to spend time with you tonight." Based on his tone, I can tell he's smiling and probably expects me to jump at the chance. But I already have plans with Pamela. The line stays quiet as I haggle with myself over whether or not to tell him I'm going out with a woman.

"Jess? You still there?"

"Yeah, I just wish I'd known . . . I have plans tonight."

"Oh, okay . . . How about lunch then?"

"Sounds perfect. Name the place and time," I say, relieved that he didn't ask about my plans.

As Justin and I are wrapping up our call, there's a knock on my door.

I rush to the door and have my hand wrapped around the knob when I hear mumbled expletives.

Ned.

I jerk my hand away from the knob and take a step backward as Ned knocks again.

"Jess! I know you're in there!" His knocks continue with increasing force and speed.

"I'm not opening the door, Ned, so you should just leave," I call out as I lock the deadbolt.

The knocks stop and he says, "I just want to talk . . . I miss you." His tone is soft now, and it sounds as if he has his face right up to the door.

"There's nothing to talk about, so just leave." I turn and storm over to my stereo to crank up some music because I know he won't leave, not right away anyway.

"Is it because of that guy who was just here? Are you with him now?" He sounds pathetic. I press play on the CD player and Train starts blaring through the speakers, making whatever Ned is saying now muffled. I increase the volume until the music is loud enough to mute him out completely.

By the time the CD ends, I've finished straightening things up around my apartment, showered and gotten dressed. I know Ned has to be gone by now, but I go to the door anyway and put my ear to it. Silence never sounded so good.

I open my laptop and press the power button. I know it hasn't been long since I last checked my Personals account, but I don't have anything else to do until I need to leave to meet Justin at noon. While my computer is warming up, I grab my phone off of the end table and feel like I'm going to be sick when I see the text that came through about thirty minutes ago. It's a picture of a back view of Sawyer's car. Following the photo is three more texts from Ned.

414-555-2100: It sure would suck if your new guy got pulled over for some reason.

414-555-2100: Maybe for a busted out taillight?

414-555-2100: Or you could just call me...

What the fuck? Now he's threatening Sawyer to get to me? Never in the three years that I've known Ned has he acted like such a psycho. I press his number, intending to put an end to this bullshit once and for all.

"Hello?" he says calmly, pulling a Dr. Jekyll and Mr. Hyde.

"Fuck you, Ned. What do you want to talk about?"

"Us, obviously." I can picture the arrogant smirk on his face.

"See, that's the thing. We aren't dating anymore, and we're *never* going to sleep together again. So there *is* no US!"

"You don't mean that."

"But I do. In fact, I've never felt so strongly about a decision before. Why do you want to fight so hard to stay with me anyway? You hardly ever wanted to spend time with me, unless it was in a bar or in bed, and I've cheated on you more times than I can remember." By the time I finish talking, my voice has gone from frantic and desperate to sullen and defeated. I just can't do this with him anymore.

He doesn't answer right away, and the silence speaks volumes. Could this really be it?

"So, who's the guy?"

"If I tell you, do you promise to stop? Stop calling me, stop texting me, stop coming over to my apartment?"

"Mm-hmm." His response is barely audible.

"His name is Sawyer, and I work with him."

"What is he? A pilot, a mechanic . . . a gay flight attendant?"

That last comment of his almost pushes me to hang up on him—I never could stand his judgmental ways—but I don't because I fear hanging up might thwart any progress we might be making here. Instead, I clear my throat and say, "Actually, he doesn't work for Midwest. I got a second job, and I work with him there."

"Yeah, where's that?"

"That's none of your business, Ned," I mutter.

He stifles a laugh. "Knowing you, I'm sure it's another job that puts your psychology degree to good use." I ignore the condescending comment and he continues. "Are you dating this guy?"

"No, we're just friends."

"So you miss me then . . ." Suddenly alarms are going off in my brain because Ned has used this line on me before. It has always been his go-to line when we've taken extended breaks in the past. I can't let him think there's a chance the tactic could work this time. This has to END.

"No, I don't. In fact, I'm online dating. Have been for about a month now."

"Good one," he says, chuckling.

"I'm serious. I'm online dating. And I've met some really nice guys."

"You can't be serious," he says, still laughing. "After all the clowns Chloe met and all the times you and I laughed about how ridiculous online dating is, you expect me to believe that's how you're meeting guys now?"

"I don't care what you believe as long as you accept the fact that we're done." Ned goes silent, so I take that as my cue to wrap things up. "Look, I have to be somewhere soon, so I need to get going. Are we good?" I hold my breath as I wait for his response.

"Yeah, we're good."

"Bye, Ned."

"Bye."

After I hang up, I sit there on my couch for a second to examine how I feel. Before long, a smile spreads across my face, because I feel nothing but the calming sense of freedom.

The first thing I see when I pull into the parking lot of the Blue Heron Café is Justin standing near the entrance looking like an athletic pretty boy. He's wearing a gray, baseball t-shirt with navy blue sleeves and jeans with aviator sunglasses. When he spots me getting out of my car, he heads toward me right away, and we greet each other with a hug.

"Great to see you," he whispers in my ear

"You too," I say, smiling up at him as we separate.

We hold hands as we walk into the restaurant, and Justin doesn't let go until we're being led to our table.

Until our food arrives, Justin tells me about a few situations he had to deal with at work this week, and I'm happy to listen. From people trying to sneak onto the field and into restricted areas to objects being thrown on the field and drunken brawls, he certainly has his hands full. I've been to a lot of ballgames and it never occurred to me the problems hardcore fans and drunk people sometimes cause behind the scenes. Although, I'm the type of fan who goes to games mostly for the ballpark ambiance, beer, and peanuts, not to watch what other spectators are doing.

I'm about to bite into my burger when he asks how my date with Kyle went on Thursday night. I explain to him that it wasn't really a date because Kyle and I have decided to just be friends.

"How many dates did the two of you go on before you decided that?"

"Only one, but now he's decided to get back together with his ex-girlfriend. So, you know," I shrug, "having a girlfriend makes it kinda hard to date someone you met online." I grin and take a bite of my burger.

Justin laughs and polishes off a few fries before asking, "So what did the two of you do?"

"We watched the first two *Lord of the Rings* movies, which were amazing, by the way. And I don't usually watch those types of movies. Have you seen them?" I pick up the ketchup and tap a small puddle of it onto my plate.

Justin shakes his head as he motions for me to hand him the ketchup. "I wanted to see them, but the only movies I've seen for the past few years have been for kids. Do you think they'd be appropriate for Max?"

"Eh," I waver, recalling all of the battle scenes. "I guess if he was my kid, I'd wait until he was . . . umm, maybe ten?"

Justin nods and takes a bite of his chicken Caesar wrap. I follow his lead, and we both spend a few minutes concentrating on our food. He's the first to speak again.

"Is there anyone besides Kyle and I who you've been out with more than once?"

Sawyer, I think to myself, but that isn't what he means, so why share?

"Nope. What about you?"

"Yes, but not more than twice." He waits for a few seconds, I assume for me to respond, but all I do is nod and take another bite of my burger. "What would you say if I told you I'm more interested in you than any of the other women I've met?"

I stare at him and hold up a finger to indicate that I need to finish chewing. As soon as I swallow what's in my mouth, I tell him, "I'd say I don't blame you . . . I'm awesome." With a grin, I shrug and take the last bite of my burger.

"See, that's one of the things I love about you. Your modesty." He laughs, and we make eyes at each other as he polishes off the last bit of his wrap. Then he asks another question. This one throws me for a loop. "What would you say if I told you my subscription is up in a couple weeks, and you might end up being the only woman I want to continue to date?"

"Seriously? After three months, I'm your best match?" I laugh, trying to make light of the fact that his feelings for me might be ahead of mine for him at this point. I'm hoping he'll laugh too, but instead he half smiles and takes a sip of his Diet Coke.

"Yes, I'm serious. I don't know about you, but I've met a lot of overly eager women. Some of them bombarded me with questions about my ex on the first date and some made reference to meeting Max right away. On the flipside, there've been quite a few who didn't seem interested in knowing anything about Max. You make it so easy for me to share organically, and I really appreciate that. Of course, that's not the only reason I feel like we have a good connection, but it's a big one." He smiles, reaching out to put his hand on mine.

"Well, thank you. I find you easy to talk to as well. I should be honest though . . ." He cocks his head and his brows begin to creep inward. "I have been wondering what happened with Max's mom."

"Phew," he says, sitting up straighter and leaning his elbows on the table. "I thought for a second there that you were going to tell me we should go the friend route like you and Kyle."

I honestly don't know what route I want to go with Justin yet, partly because I don't know anything about why he got divorced and why his ex doesn't let him see Max very often. "No, but it would be nice to know a little bit about what happened with Laura. I certainly don't need or want to know everything, but hearing the gist of things would be nice. Just being honest," I say with a shrug.

He's about to say something when the waitress shows up to ask if we'd like refills. Justin and I both decline, and he asks for the check. As soon as the waitress steps away to print our bill, he shocks me by saying, "I'm the one who ruined my marriage." Then he pauses and I follow his gaze over to our waitress who's already on her way back to our table. He hands her a credit card right away, and she disappears again.

"I can give you cash," I say unzipping my purse, but he puts a hand up to stop me.

"No, I got it."

"Thanks," I say with a weak smile.

We sip what's left of our watered-down drinks and make fleeting eye contact while we wait for the waitress to return. Scenarios to explain how Justin ruined his marriage run through my mind. Did he cheat? Was he abusive? Was he neglectful like Ned? By the time the waitress finally drops off the receipt and credit slip for Justin to sign, the silence has become somewhat awkward. When she leaves, Justin sighs heavily and tells me everything.

"So, I used to have a bit of a drinking problem. No . . . that's a lie. I had a huge drinking problem. I told you that I worked for the Twins when we lived in Minnesota, right?" I nod. "Well, I was young and a bit starstruck by the famous athletes I worked with day in and day out. So I got into the bad habit of wanting to hang out with some of them outside of work too. That resulted in a lot of late-night partying, and it was fun for Laura too at first, but then she got pregnant, and things obviously had to change. Except, she did all the changing, and I barely did any." He shakes his head sadly and slurps the last of the watery coke at the bottom of his glass.

"So you just kept partying?" He nods. "All through her pregnancy?" He nods again. "And what about after Max was born?"

"I helped with him as much as I could when I was home, but by then she was so resentful of how much I neglected her while she was pregnant that we hardly spoke. And most of the time when we did speak, it would turn into an argument, which would lead me to go out and get drunk. It was a vicious cycle."

"So how did you both end up here?"

"One day, I got home, and they were gone. Most of their stuff was gone too, and Laura didn't even leave a note. So I started calling around and eventually got her sister on the phone. She told me Laura was staying with their parents, in Waukesha, and was filing for divorce."

"Was that even legal? For her to take Max across state lines?"

"No," he says, shaking his head, "but I knew I'd fucked up so that was the furthest thing from my mind." He flags our waitress down and asks her for a glass of water. He also asks if she needs the table or if it's okay for us to stay and chat a while longer. It's both amazing and a bit curious the way he goes from the sad demeanor he displayed while he was telling me about the demise of his marriage to charming and light-hearted with the waitress. I guess some people are just good at hiding their emotions. The waitress tells us to stay as long as we like, and brings two glasses of water within minutes.

"So any second thoughts about dating me now?" He asks.

"Not yet. I need to hear the whole story first, silly," I joke, causing Justin to crack a smile.

"There really isn't much more to tell. After a couple of months, it was clear that she wasn't coming back, and I had to be where my son was, so I quit my job and moved here. All of Laura's relatives were led to believe that I cheated on her, so I had a hell of a time whenever I wanted to see Max. We battled it out for about a year, and finally I just gave in to everything she wanted because Max was almost three by then and I didn't want all of his earliest memories to be of his mom and me arguing."

"Laura called you—the other night when Max was taken to the emergency room. Does that mean things are better between the two of you?"

"We're getting there, slowly but surely," he says with a slight nod.

"Well, thank you for sharing," I say, thinking that his skeletons don't seem nearly as despicable as mine.

"Thank you for listening." Justin reaches out and gives my forearm a rub and then checks his watch. "I told Max I'd take him to a movie this afternoon, since he was so bummed about the Dells. Any chance you'd like to go with us?" The shock I'm feeling must be written all over my face because he follows up immediately with, "I'm sorry. I don't know what I was thinking. It's too soon for that isn't it?"

"Maaaybe just a little," I say, smiling and holding up my thumb and pointer finger just a pinch apart.

"Okay, so when can I see you again? You have a date tonight and then you're flying tomorrow through . . . ?"

"I'll be home Thursday, but Chloe is supposed to come over for dinner and Scrabble that night, so how about Friday after I get done working at McGinn's?"

"That'll work. Dinner and a movie or maybe some bowling?"

"Yes to dinner, but how about if we text some ideas back and forth until then?"

"Deal."

Our date ends next to my car where we give each other a discreet peck on the lips. Then Justin gives me a tight squeeze and we stand there for a few seconds with our arms around each other. My cheek is against his chest, and I can hear his rapid heartbeats. The closeness feels so nice. But I'm not sure if it's because of the cozy, secure feeling or Justin himself that I'm craving.

chapter twenty-seven

The last time I went miniature golfing was with Ned. Tonight, I'm hoping to replace that memory with something a little less excruciating. I clearly remember the look on his face when I suggested we go to Putt Putt Adventure Golf. It was one of horrification and smugness. Ned Rasmussen is a serious golfer, not some wacky putter who does it for exercise or, God forbid, for fun. The idea of going miniature golfing was above him. But after some gentle coercion from yours truly, he agreed to go, and it goes down in history as one of the worst dates I've ever been on. Yet another sign I should have broken things off with him much sooner. When you've been with someone for almost three years, doing things you typically enjoy should not be unbearable.

To start things off, I somehow got a gob of bird poop on the back of my hand as I was removing my ball from the first hole. It wouldn't have been that big of a deal, except I didn't realize it was there until I ran my fingers through my hair. Ned laughed hysterically at the gooey streaks. Unfortunately, he was laughing at me instead of with me, and for some reason, it lightened his mood enough that he actually wanted to play. But getting stinky white shit in my hair isn't even what ruined the date. From that point forward, it was game on. Every hole became a fierce competition. For him anyway. He had to analyze each hole, laying his club down on the ground a few times to calculate the distance his ball had to travel. That part was amusing, but when he got into a screaming match with a guy from one of the three groups that got backed up behind us, that's when I thought it was time to call it quits. But Ned refused to quit until he conquered the entire course, and the asshole wouldn't let anyone pass, resulting in a Putt Putt employee asking us to either step aside until there was no longer a line behind us or golf a little faster. Ned had a problem with the teenager's attitude and ended up getting us kicked out. Now he's banned for life. But I'm not. So here I am at Putt Putt Adventure Golf for my first date with Woolf Woman tonight.

As I pull into the parking lot of the mini-golf course, my nerves are firing like crazy at the thought of what I'm about to do. Sure, I've kissed a woman before, but that was on impulse and after several cocktails. This time, I've put a lot of thought into going out with Woolf Woman aka Pamela, and I intend to treat her like any other first date. But still, I can't get certain thoughts out of my head. Will she flirt with me? Will I be attracted to her? Will I flirt back? Will people wonder if we're on a date?

My brain is about to explode when my phone vibrates, alerting me to a new text and distracting me from my rapid-fire thoughts. I glance down at the screen, and the sight of Sawyer's name makes my chest feel tight and tingly. The moment I pull into a spot, I open his message.

SAWYER: PAMELA TONIGHT, RIGHT? HAVE FUN!

My heart drops. Have fun? The message is something I'd expect from Chloe, not someone I've made out with and been naked in front of. Although, if last night proved anything, it's that Sawyer and I make great friends. I just wish I could get the idea of jumping his bones out of my mind. I type out a quick thanks and make my way into the Putt Putt Club.

For six o'clock on a Friday night, this place is hopping. There's already a fair amount of people scattered about playing the outdoor course, and there's a good number inside the Club as well. The crowd is filled mostly with pods of teenagers, but there are also a few families with little kids and one couple playing air hockey. I'm supposed to meet Woolf Woman somewhere between the snack bar and the arcade, so I lean against an old Jurassic Park pinball machine and watch the couple smacking the puck back and forth. *Clink clank. Clink clank clank.* The sound puts me in a trance, causing me to jump when a silky smooth hand touches my arm.

I gasp and jump a little as I turn to meet Woolf Woman's black eyes.

"Sorry! I didn't mean to scare you." She covers her mouth, masking giggles.

My shocked expression softens quickly and my heart rate normalizes as I take her in. She's not much taller than me, and her hair is raven black, an exotic match to her dark eyes. I thought my skin was fair, but hers is like porcelain. Or maybe it just looks pale because of her dark features. I don't usually judge anything about a woman's appearance other than the type of shoes she wears, but I have to admit, Woolf Woman is stunning. It's proof that an online photo isn't to be trusted, only in this case, the real thing is much more appealing.

"It's fine. I was just so focused on their heated game of air hockey," I say, laughing at myself. "I'm Jess."

She reaches for my hand for what I think is going to be a simple shake, but instead she raises it to her lips. As she kisses the sensitive flesh on the back of my hand, I can't help but scan the room to see if anyone is watching. The air hockey couple has finished their game, and based on the way they're looking at us with big grins plastered to their faces as they walk to the service counter, I'm willing to bet they saw. A few teens sitting at a table eating hot dogs are staring and whispering as well. It was only a kiss on the hand, but for some reason it still feels weird that people witnessed it. Maybe this date was a bad idea.

"I'm Pamela. Your pictures don't do you justice. You're absolutely gorgeous," she says as she lowers my hand and continues to hold it. I glance down, itching to pull it free, but I don't want to be rude.

"Thank you," I say with a nervous grin. "What do you think? Should we go up and get our clubs?" I use this as an opportunity to slip my hand out of hers and point toward the counter.

"Yep. Let's do it," she beams. "It's a beautiful night, don't you think? The sky is so clear we should be able to see a lot of stars when the sun goes down."

Well, yes, but hopefully we won't still be golfing by the time the stars come out. The moment the thought pops into my head, I feel guilty. This woman took the time to poke me twice, and she drove all the way here just to meet me. The least I can do is stop thinking such bitchy thoughts, get to know her, and try to have fun.

"It is," I say, smiling.

We retrieve our clubs and balls—she picks purple and I choose green. When the woman at the register says she likes the barely noticeable tattoo under Pamela's left earlobe, my date reaches over the counter and squeezes her arm for a few seconds and thanks her for noticing. The woman who I'm guessing to be a college student judging by the thick book about ecofeminism she's reading, smiles shyly at Pamela. Then she offers us a small discount for no apparent reason, prompting Pamela to place her hand on top of the woman's hand and tell her how much we appreciate it. Considering the touchy-feely display that's happening before my eyes, it occurs to me that Pamela is either a big flirt or she just has a natural proclivity for touching others. Either way, the kiss she planted on my hand doesn't seem like that big of a deal anymore.

"So, tell me about your tattoo," I say as we exit the Club. I lean in to get a better look at the tiny design, no bigger than a nickel, of two fairy-like images leaning into each other, foreheads touching, as if they are one. "It's beautiful."

"Thank you. It's a symbol of the bond between my twin sister and me."

"You have a twin? How cool! I used to think it would be fun to have a twin, but I ended up with an annoying little half-sister."

"Actually, I *had* a twin. She passed away when we were kids . . . She had leukemia."

I stop walking and bring my ball and club to my chest. "Oh, God. I'm so sorry. I shouldn't have—"

"No, don't worry about it," she says, shaking her head and nudging me to keep walking. "It was a long time ago. Besides, she's still with me. Here . . ." Out of the corner of my eye, I see her touch the tattoo beneath her earlobe. ". . . and here." She brings a fist to her heart.

I nod as we take a seat on a bench next to the first hole to wait for the group in front of us.

"So tell me about your job. Your profile says you're a library media specialist. That means you're a librarian, right?"

"Yes, that's exactly what it means. I'm a good old-fashioned librarian.

I even carry around a wooden ruler just in case I spot someone talking or putting a book back in the wrong section." She squeezes my left forearm as she laughs a loud sophisticated laugh.

Smiling, I point to the sign for the first hole with my club. "Would you like to go first? Or should we decide with Rock-Paper-Scissors?"

Her head tilts, an amused look on her face. Then she places her purple ball in her ample cleavage and holds a fist in the air. My fist follows. For our first bout, we both throw paper. Then we both throw rock. Then back to paper. When we both throw scissors on our fourth try, we begin laughing hysterically.

"You go, you go," She says breathlessly, removing the ball from the dip between her breasts, which are hard to miss and make me green with envy.

"You like?" She bends forward a little, squeezing them closer together with her biceps.

"Oh, I wasn't . . ." I lie, shaking my head. "I mean, I was, but not because . . . they're just . . . nice." There. I said it. And I'd say it to her even if we weren't on a date with each other.

With a light chuckle, she stands tall and says, "For a second, I thought you were going to say they're big. I get both responses all the time." A Cheshire grin spreads across her face. "They're real you know. And I'd be happy to let you take a closer look later if you like."

Her invitation causes heat to rush into my cheeks, and a warm tingling between my legs leaves me speechless. Instead of reciprocating her flirtation, I ready myself to start our mini-golf match. I swing my club as hard as possible, hitting my ball over a little creek and onto the green of hole number five.

"Impressive! But wrong direction," she says with a wink, dropping her ball and taking a nice even swing at it.

While golfing through the maze of obstacles, Pamela's flirtations continue. And as I slowly become less focused on the fact that I'm on a date with an attractive woman and more on getting to know her, I begin to cozy up to the idea of flirting a little myself.

We're at the ninth hole when she asks, "Which part of a woman do you find most attractive?"

I lick my lips slowly as I eye her chest, even though I usually don't pay a second glance to anyone's chest. The gesture is mostly for fun, but I do get a kick out of seeing her nipples harden into peaks below her low-cut white tunic. Then I reach out and run my thumb across her lips as I say, "This part," but I don't tell her it's actually the part of the body I find most attractive on men. I've never made a point of checking out a woman's lips before. Not until this very moment, anyway.

Around hole number fourteen, Pamela and I discuss our favorite books and authors. Just like our preferences for music, foods, movies and our ideal vacation destinations, we have similar tastes in books. When she mentions her two favorite authors, the origin of her screen name hits me.

"Wait, your screen name, Woolf Woman . . . it's referring to Virginia Woolf."

"Took you long enough." She grins and takes her final shot at hole sixteen, sinking her ball after four tries on a par three.

"Up until right now, I thought you might have misspelled wolf!" I say laughing and locking my arm with hers as we march off to the seventeenth hole.

After successfully maneuvering our balls between the blades of a windmill and returning our equipment, we take a seat on a bench outside the Putt Putt Club. We lean our heads back and gaze up at the starry sky.

"So, you mentioned a half-sister before. Do you see her often?" Pamela asks.

"No, not really. She actually grew up in North Dakota with my stepmom."

"Just your stepmom?"

"Well, my dad died when I was eleven and she was seven, so yeah."

"Oh, I'm so sorry, Jess. Did I mention I was eleven when my twin died?"

I shake my head.

"God," she sighs, "I'd give anything to be able to talk to her just one more time. You know? You never know when it'll be your last chance to talk to someone you love. Or anyone for that matter."

"Yeah, you're absolutely right," I say quietly as I place my hand on her knee as a show of sympathy.

"It's okay. It's been a long time and I'm good." She places her hand on top of mine and gives a little squeeze. "Do me a favor and make sure you give that little sister of yours a call whenever you get the chance. Okay?"

"Okay," I say with a nod.

I'm about to point out a constellation when without warning, Pamela shocks the hell out of me and leans over to kiss me on the lips. We sit there, very still for a moment, her eyes closed and mine open wide. Do I want this? Was all the flirting real? Could I really date her or is this just a one-time deal for me? As these questions and more run through my brain, she reaches across the front of my body to grip my shoulder and turn me toward her, our lips still together. Then she parts her lips and slowly inserts her tongue into my mouth, the aching sensation between my thighs registers, but my tongue remains frozen due to indecision. Part of me wants to let loose and kiss her with wild abandon, but it occurs to me that I wouldn't even be considering it if it weren't dark outside. So I pull back a little, but Pamela leans closer and places her right hand on the back of my head, making it so that I'll have to pull away with some force if I want to end this public display of affection. When I feel Pamela's left hand touch my breast, I pull away from her, a string of male faces flashing through my mind. Suddenly I feel ill. I'll never want a relationship with Pamela or any woman for that matter. So *what* am I doing?

Her eyes snap open, and she tries to pull me back in.

"Pamela, I'm sorry, but I'm just not into this." I give her a weak smile.

"Would it help if we went somewhere more private?" she whispers.

"No, I'm sorry. That's not it." Wishing I never let things get this far, I sigh and shake my head.

That's when she understands what's going on. "So, there's no chance we'll have sex tonight."

That's certainly not the response I was expecting. "Um, no. Not even a little."

"Damn," she mumbles. "You can't blame a girl for trying." We both laugh, and she checks her watch before continuing. "Listen, it was nice meeting you and all, but I've got to get going. I think I might still be able to get laid tonight," she says matter-of-factly, making me wonder if this whole date was some sort of prerequisite for an obligatory night of sex.

"Oh . . . Okay, well—"

"Unless, you think you might change your mind about trying something new tonight?" She widens her eyes at me.

"Nope," I say, laughing, "I'm definitely into dicks only."

"Oh," she shakes her head dismissively. "Trust me, Jess, if we had sex, odds are you'd never want another dick in you again."

"Tempting," I say with an amused smirk, "but I still have to pass."

When we get to the parking lot, Pamela hugs me in a friendly, non-sexual way. "It was nice meeting you, Jess."

"You too, *Woolf Woman*."

I'm almost to my car when she calls my name.

"Hey, Jess!"

When I turn to look, she yells from inside her car. "Don't forget to call your sister!"

chapter twenty-eight

For a third time, I dial Ashley's number. But this time, instead of snapping my phone shut, I press send followed quickly by end. Then I pray that the call didn't register.

Shit. Why is this so hard? Why is it easier for me to talk to complete strangers on airplanes or customers at McGinn's than bring myself to call Ashley? She's my sister for Pete's sake. I used to bathe with her and I used to pretend she was the dog I always wanted, throwing her toys to fetch. I laugh, remembering how she used to fetch them, too. If that isn't enough to bond us together for life, I don't know what else could. Besides the fact that we both share our dad's blood, of course. But to me, blood doesn't mean nearly as much as a bond born out of a conscious decision to accept someone as family. Like the way Chloe and I accept each other. It's also sort of what Ashley and I had to do, despite our blood relation. Except Ashley accepted me immediately as the older sister she idolized. For me, it took longer, but I did eventually accept her. Unfortunately, it was too late because my dad died not long after. And then eleven years later, after an insane amount of effort on Ashley's part to stay in touch, which I ignored, I showed up and told her and her mother how much I resented and hated them for taking my father away from me. What kind of person does that?

When my phone vibrates, I glance down hoping it's just Justin calling to say hi or Chloe checking to see how my overnights are going.

"Hello?" Why? Why am I answering as if I have no idea who it is?

"Jess? I thought I recognized your number." So she doesn't have my name programmed into her phone. There must be some residual animosity then. "Jess? You there?"

I cough a little. "Yeah, I'm here."

"Well, I'm glad you finally called. I've left you so many messages. What took so long for you to call me back?"

Does she really not know how much she reminds me of our dad and how guilty I feel when I think about how much I've resented her my whole life? And why do I feel like the younger sister here? *Maybe because of your utter lack of maturity when it comes to this situation?*

"I'm sorry," I whisper.

"Wait . . . what?"

"I said I'm sorry. For everything. For never wanting to bathe with you when we were little. For ignoring you until you'd cry and then cursing you when your mom would make me play with you. For making you fetch things like you were a dog. For never being there to show you how to use makeup, the way a big sister should. For never being there to talk about boys. For resenting you simply because you're your mom's daughter and because you monopolized so much of dad's attention, even though none of that was your fault." I pause but she doesn't make a peep, making me wonder if she hung up. But then I hear her exhale, so I go on. "I'm sorry for . . . telling your mom that I hated her—but only because she's your mom and I'd hate for someone to say that to my mother. And most of all, I'm sorry for telling you I hated *you* and that I wished . . . you'd never been born." I whisper the last part because I'm so ashamed for what I said and tears are streaking my cheeks now. "I didn't mean any of it." Now that my outpouring of emotion is over, the line is silent, except for my own heaving breaths and sniffles.

"Jess . . . I forgave you for saying those things right after you said them. My mom is the one who's holding a grudge."

"But you said you hated me, too. You called me a slut and said I was the worst human being on the—"

"*Jess,* I was seventeen, and I was pissed at you for a lot of things, too. I bet you don't even know how much dad and my mom used to fight about you and your mom. And I had to listen to it. You know I used to lay in my bed at night crying and covering my ears to drown out their yelling? They spent so much time arguing that I felt neglected, too. And I had no one to talk to about any of it. That's why I tried so hard to stay in touch with you, despite the fact that you usually ignored me. From my perspective, *you* were the one who monopolized dad's attention. He might have been with me physically, but he was always thinking about *you*." She exhales forcefully, and I know at that moment just how long she's been holding on to the same type of resentment I've been feeling all these years. However, unlike me—the big sister who's supposed to be older and wiser—she's the one who knew we needed to stick together. I feel like such a fool, and I'm speechless.

After a few calming breaths, Ashley breaks the silence. "So I owe you an apology, too, because I obviously didn't mean the things I said. I was upset and hurt, and I fed off of all of my mom's animosity for you."

I take a deep breath and release it slowly. "Part of me will always hate myself for being such a shit to you."

"Well, like I said, I forgave you for everything a long time ago. Oh, except maybe not for that whole fetch thing. I can't even own a dog because it would bring back bad memories." She laughs.

"Yet another thing for me to be sorry about," I say, cracking a smile.

"I was totally joking! I have a dog actually."

"I had no idea you were such a comedian."

"There's a lot you don't know about me, big sis," she says, the words *big sis* making me smile. "So can we be done with all of this old stuff? It sure would be nice to actually spend time with family once in awhile, especially now that we live so close to each other."

My heart starts beating a little faster at the mention of family. I think it's because I miss my dad and because Ashley is the only thing I have left of him besides the box full of mementos.

"Okay. It's done."

"Oh, one last thing," she says.

"What?"

"You really weren't the worst sister ever, you know. I need you to acknowledge that. I have friends whose big sisters were *way* worse than you. Granted, we didn't get to see each other much after dad died. But still. Do you remember how you used to sing to me at night when I couldn't fall asleep? That "Skinamarinky Dinky Dink" song?

"I do now," I smile to myself.

"And do you remember that time when my mom said I couldn't have dessert and sent me to bed early because the dog ate the broccoli right off my plate but she accused me of feeding it to him?"

"Yeah, and then I got sent to bed for trying to sneak a piece of strawberry shortcake to you."

We both giggle but the laughter is cut short. Probably because we're both remembering what happened after I got sent to bed. The argument my dad and Gwen got into about me being a bad influence on Ashley. How I probably put her up to feeding her vegetables to the dog.

"I'm sorry my mom was always such a bitch to you."

"It's okay. It wasn't your fault. So, we're all good now?"

"I've been good, Jess. That's why I've been trying to get a hold of you for the last few months. Even though you weren't getting back to me, I kept thinking in the back of my mind that dad would want us to have a relationship."

"And what about your mom?"

"Pfft. Let's just say I'm no longer afraid to tell her what I think. As you can probably imagine, it's pretty unsettling to her—me being able to think for myself nowadays. You know? Don't worry about her."

"Sounds good to me," I say, grinning at the thought of Gwen not being able to influence what Ashley does anymore. "So, how are you liking your job?"

Thirty minutes later, I'm lying in the bed of my hotel room going over my entire phone conversation with Ashley as I begin to doze off. I feel like a huge weight has been lifted. Now I don't know why I waited so long to contact her. I guess I was punishing myself. I'm beginning to wonder if Ned was a form of self-inflicted punishment, too.

During our talk, I learned that Ashley loves her job as a special education teacher, and that she's in the running to take on a supervisory role in her department next year. She told me all about her dog, Dinky Dink—yes, after the song—and how they like to go for runs early in the morning before she gets ready for work. I asked her if she thinks that's safe when it's still dark out at five in the morning, my momma hen nature peeking through. She assured me it was with Dink by her side. She also told me that she doesn't miss North Dakota at all, that Wisconsin is where she thinks she's meant to be.

We talked about my life, too. About my schedule as a flight attendant and about my job at McGinn's. I gave her the basics about my love life, not wasting too much breath on my relationships with Ned and Brant, but admitting to the mistakes I've made. She didn't ask a lot of questions when I told her about the past, instead she saved them all for my present online dating endeavors. She even mentioned we might need to sit down and create a profile for her sometime in the near future since she's settled into her new life here in Wisconsin and is ready to start looking for that special someone too. I told her maybe we should wait and see how things turn out for me. Throughout our conversation, it became quite obvious to me that she's a person who believes everyone is capable of good things, a person who gives everyone the benefit of the doubt. The fact that she kept trying to reach me is proof of that.

We would have continued talking much longer I'm sure if I hadn't started to fall asleep. We'd been reminiscing about the sparklers and poppers we used on the last Fourth of July we spent together when my head started to bob. As much as I would have loved to talk to her longer, I told her I had to call it a night.

"Okay, but do you want to do something real quick. For old time's sake?" she asked.

"What?"

"Let's sing "Skinamarinky Dinky Dink.""

"You're joking." We're grown women and she wants to sing a silly song from our childhood?

"No, I'm not." She giggles. "Come on. It'll be good for us. No one can sing Skinnamarink and not feel happy by the end. I sing it with my students all the time."

"Um, okay. If you really want to." I probably sounded indifferent about singing the song, but I wasn't. As silly as it sounds, part of me kind of wanted to sing it.

So we sang "Skinamarinky Dinky Dink"—the song I used to sing to Ashley when we were kids and she couldn't fall asleep. And it was awkward at first, but we kept on singing until the end. As we sang, I closed my eyes and pictured my dad singing it to me before Ashley was born, and strange as it might sound, it felt like my dad was singing with us.

Right before I doze off for the night, I picture Pamela and again I hear her reminding me to call my sister. At least if online dating doesn't end up leading me to Mr. Right, Chloe can revel in the fact that it brought Ashley and I back together.

chapter twenty-nine

I'm standing at the stove stirring pasta sauce when I hear the doorknob jiggling. It's been weeks since Chloe and I have done anything with just the two of us, so I smile knowing we're about to spend some quality time together. I'm also looking forward to kicking her ass at Scrabble.

"Hello! I'm here!" She calls from the hallway. Thudding sounds follow as my cats run toward her familiar voice.

"I'm in here!" I say, covering the sauce pot and giving the boiling pasta a quick stir.

She enters the kitchen, holding Savannah and scratching around her ears. "Mmm. Something smells good."

"The pasta will be done soon," I say handing her the glass of wine I have waiting for her. She puts down Savannah and takes the wine from me. Then we lean against opposite counters, me sipping my wine and Chloe swirling hers.

"So how was work the last few days?" she asks.

"Eh, it was work. You know? *But,* I do have to tell you about something big that happened on Tuesday night."

"What is it?" Her eyes bug out as she sets her wine glass on the counter. Then she folds her arms across her chest and gives me her full attention while I recap my entire conversation with Ashley. By the time I get to the part when we sang "Skinamarinky Dinky Dink" song, Chloe and I are both crying.

"Oh my gosh. I can't believe something so stupid is making me cry," I say, wiping my cheeks with the back of my hand.

"Stop, it is *not* stupid," Chloe says, her voice trembling a little. "I'm so glad you guys worked things out." She leaves the kitchen and returns with tissues for us within seconds. "What made you finally decide to call?"

I barely finish blowing my nose before her question makes me chuckle. "You're not going to believe this, but I went out with a woman on Saturday night."

She gasps before her eyes light up and her lips begin to curl into a grin. Then she suddenly looks confused. "Wait, what does going out with a woman have to do with you calling Ashley?"

Before I tell Chloe about my date with Pamela, I drain the pasta and ask if she's ready to eat. Neither one of us is too hungry yet, so we move into the dining room to set up Scrabble.

Chloe's first question when I get to the part when Pamela reminds me to call my sister is, "So you're definitely not a lesbian?"

"Right. Not a lesbian."

Chloe shrugs and rearranges the letter tiles on her tray. "Can you fire up your computer so I can get a look at her?"

"Why?"

"I just want to see if she's even your type."

"We just established that I'm not a lesbian. Remember? And even if I was, I don't have a *type*. I either think people are attractive or I don't. But again, after last night, I'm pretty sure it doesn't matter how attractive a woman is or how drunk I am. I'm simply not a lesbian."

"Okay, fine." She tacks the word GROOVED onto MU, making MUD. "Then I want to see if *I* find her attractive . . . Sixty-six points."

"Sixty-six? How do you figure?" I ask, retrieving my computer from the ottoman and placing it at an angle on the table between us.

She lifts the D to reveal a Triple Word Score box.

"Crap."

My computer takes so long to boot up that we decide to take a break from Scrabble and eat before I have a chance to pull up Pamela's profile, but Chloe makes me promise to show her before she leaves.

Dinner conversation consists of talk about Sawyer, Justin, and Ned's psychotic episode. Chloe does a lot of eye rolling, teeth clenching, and sighing when I tell her about Ned, but in the end she's relieved to know that he might be out of my life for good. As for Sawyer and Justin, she expresses that she's more torn than ever about who she likes more.

"Chloe, I told you, it doesn't matter who you like more of the two because Sawyer and I aren't dating. He has enough on his plate with his pending divorce and getting back into the swing of things with his business."

She shakes her head and stares at me as she takes a huge bite of pasta.

"I just feel really lucky to be friends with him at this point," I mumble as I stare at my plate and twist noodles around with my fork.

As soon as Chloe finishes chewing, she says, "What about Justin then? Sounds like he might want to date you exclusively. How would you feel about that? Would you stop online dating?"

"I don't know," I say shaking my head and taking a sip of wine. "I've only been online for five weeks and I told you I'd give it a chance for the entire three months of the subscription."

"Yeah, but why do that if you're really clicking with someone? Don't keep online dating for me because I don't care anymore if you stop. I'm just glad you've moved past *The Golfer*." We both laugh at my mom's nickname for Ned.

"Here's the deal, there are a couple people I've been chatting with but haven't met yet. I'm going to see what happens with them before I decide whether I want to keep online dating or not. As for Justin," I shrug, "We're having dinner tomorrow night. That's as far ahead as I want to think about that for right now."

"Sounds like a plan," she says, nodding and polishing off the last bite on her plate.

After we take the dishes into the kitchen, we sit down and finish our game of Scrabble.

Twenty minutes later, Chloe is rubbing defeat in my face. "Boom! Victory is mine!"

"Good game." I smirk and fold my tray, unable to use the final letter. "It's been awhile since you beat me so you really deserve that one. That's why I went easy on you."

"Whatever!" She rolls her eyes and starts bagging the tiles. "Can you pull up your Personals profile now, while I finish cleaning up? I want to see these guys you're still chatting with, and you promised I could see Woolf Woman's profile."

"Fine, but all we're going to do is look. No icebreakers. No messages. And under no circumstance will we send any pokes. No funny shit." I give her my best don't-mess-with-me look. "Okay?"

With a sigh, she covers the scrabble game and scoots her chair next to mine so we're both sitting in front of my laptop. "Hey, I'm on your side, remember?"

Within a few clicks we're staring at my dashboard. "Does it bring back memories?" I ask.

"A little bit. Ick . . . I just had a flashback of the time I logged on and had all those messages from that kooky guy, Drew."

"The one who annihilated you at Scrabble?"

"Whatever. Don't crazy people tend to have really high IQs?"

"The one who had a girlfriend?"

"Well, technically . . ." I raise my eyebrows at her. "Fine, yes. Him."

"The one who—"

"Alright! I know you think you're being funny, but you're not. He was the looniest of the loons. And one hundred dick pics from the firefighter would have been more pleasant than Drew's stalkerish emails."

"Good thing you didn't sleep with him."

"Knock it off. I didn't even come close. Now, show me Woolf Woman's picture and then let's read your messages. I hate to admit it, but now that the nausea I felt at first when the whole Drew debacle came rushing back to me is gone, I'm feeling a bit nostalgic. Not every guy I met was a complete weirdo." She gets a faraway look, and I have a good guess what, or should I say who, she might be thinking about. She's right. Not every guy she met was a complete waste of time.

"Here." I turn the screen toward Chloe so she can get a good look.

"Wow." Her eyes get really big. "She's gorgeous. I'm surprised you didn't take her up on her offer to have sex."

"Why? Would you have sex with her?"

"No! Of course not."

"Then why are you surprised I didn't?"

"You're more adventurous than I am. And you've already messed around with a woman before. You might not be a lesbian, but you could be bi."

"No," I say, shaking my head. "I mean, look at her." I nod toward the screen. "If I was even remotely interested in women, she'd be the one to bring that side out of me. I admit I was mentally and physically attracted to her, though. It's just that the physical part was fleeting. Besides, what does being adventurous have to do with anything? Either you're attracted to someone or you're not."

She shrugs. "Yeah, I guess. But just so you know, I'd be perfectly okay with it if you were something other than straight. Seriously. *Anyone* would be better than Ned." She points into her mouth as if gagging, a childish gesture we used to pull all the time behind the backs of guys we weren't interested in back in the day. "Wow," she says clicking on the photo of Pamela sunbathing while reading a book. "I've never seen a librarian who looks like that. You should set her up with Shelly's friend Cally."

"You're joking."

"I am not! Cally is really nice, and I'm pretty sure she's single. Oh, and she actually *is* interested in women."

"I'm not playing matchmaker. Besides, all I need is for Shelly to hear about it and then she'd have yet another reason to be a total bitch to me."

"She doesn't mean to be a bitch, you know. It's just her personality. That's all."

"So, you're saying having the personality of a bitch doesn't make someone a bitch? That's a brain teaser if I ever heard one," I say, my voice laced with sarcasm. "Let's talk about guys instead." I click on my inbox. I have one message from Scotty and one from someone with the screen name Live2Lift.

"Live2Lift?" Chloe snorts. "Click on it! I need to see what he said. Maybe he wants to Pump," she claps once like she's either Hanz or Franz from the old Saturday Night Live skit, "You up!" She finishes off the routine by pointing at me.

I laugh and click on Live2Lift's message, curious to see what it says.

Hey hottie! Wanna see if I can make you sweat?

Chloe roars with laughter and I stare at the screen. I try to scroll down to see if there's more, knowing full well there isn't. "What an idiot," I say, chuckling and moving to delete the message.

"Wait! Don't you want to at least read his profile?"

I roll my eyes and click on his screen name to view his photo and stats.

"Oh my gosh. He's a neurosurgeon? And a not too shabby looking neurosurgeon at that," Chloe says giving me a few nudges in the arm.

I have to agree with her. He is very nice looking, but I move the cursor toward the X to close his profile anyway. Chloe puts her hand on mine and stops me.

"Wait. Why don't you message him back? I mean, he had to be joking with that message he sent. He's a *neurosurgeon* for crying out loud."

"But I'm not even a fan of working out, and any guy with a screen name like this is obviously obsessed with it," I say, laughing.

"So? You guys might end up hitting it off anyway."

She doesn't remove her hand from mine until I sigh and say, "Fine."

I tap out a quick message to Live2Lift, asking right away if he'd like to get together sometime. As soon as I hit send, Chloe asks, "Who's next?"

"Scotty."

"The claims adjuster?" Chloe asks.

"The one and only."

Hiya Jess,

You know another reason I'd want to read people's minds? Because then I wouldn't have to wonder how often you think about me... I hope that doesn't weird you out. It's just that I've been thinking about you a lot lately. And my friends have been pushing me to have that first date with you. Just get it over with, you know? So, here goes nothing I guess . . . How about Saturday night at Classic Lanes on Oklahoma Avenue?

Sincerely,
Scotty

"Awwww. He sounds really nice."

"Yeah, but, the whole reading people's minds thing kind of creeps me out."

"Oh, stop. Show me what he looks like." Chloe enthusiastically leans in closer to the screen. So I click to enlarge his profile picture, in which he's wearing mirrored sunglasses and a khaki fishing hat with a drawstring under the chin. It's a grainy close-up, so nothing below the chin is pictured, but we can make out the blue collar of a Polo shirt.

"That's it? *That's* his only picture?"

I click around a bit, knowing it is but wanting to make sure so Chloe doesn't badger me to check. "Yep, that's it."

"That's odd."

"Why? Maybe he doesn't want people to recognize him. He is a claims adjuster, you know."

"Right, how could I forget? Makes perfect sense then." She rolls her eyes. "Seriously, there's a good reason he chose that picture. He's trying to hide something. Not necessarily something about the way he looks, but something."

"Oh, knock it off. I'm sure he just wants his privacy but doesn't want to look like a weirdo who doesn't post a picture at all and instructs people to ask for photos by email."

"Knock it off! What if one of my student's parents had seen my profile? *That* would have been weird."

"Why? You're the one who's always telling me online dating is nothing to be ashamed of, that everyone is doing it."

"That might be true *now*, but not when I did it," she says, as if she's some online-dating pioneer.

"Chloe," I look at her, dumbfounded, "it's been less than four months since you met Daran. I don't think things have changed that much."

"Anywaaay . . . back to this guy. Something's weird." She leans in and looks at him more closely. Then she clicks to read his stats. "Wait, you know what? He seems familiar."

"Why?"

"Waaaait a second . . ." Her jaw drops as she reads his introduction.

"What is it?"

" . . . *someone who's down to earth and if you know how to Polka, that's a bonus* . . ." Chloe quietly reads. Then she gasps and clicks to his stats, a ridiculous grin spreading across her face.

~

Scotty – 31
Location: South Milwaukee
Searching for that Special Someone

Relationship Status: Never Married
Kids: No
Want Kids: Maybe
Ethnicity: White / Caucasian
Body type: Athletic
Height: 6' 0"
Religion: Christian
Politics: Middle of the Road
Smoke: No Way
Drink: Social Drinker
Pets: Yes
Education: Bachelor's
Employment: Professional
Income: 60,000-70,000

~

"Oh. My. God!" She begins laughing hysterically.

"What's so funny?"

"Jess . . . Ohmigod . . . that's . . . that's Scott!"

"Yeah, so? Scott, Scotty. What's so funny?"

"No, Jess, that's *my* Scott." She stops laughing for a second and her face contorts. "Ew, that didn't sound right at all."

Then it hits me. Members Only Scott. "Are you sure? I thought he was an accountant?"

"Yeah, well, people change jobs. And didn't you mention he had a black lab? I remember him saying his parents got a dog from the Humane Society a couple months before we met—a black lab. But he said he was more of a cat person." She starts chuckling again. "At least he's not still using his senior picture . . ."

"Are you sure about this," I ask clicking over to my inbox. I begin going through his messages. Do I really care if it is the Scott that Chloe met online? He seems so nice in his messages. Well, except for the whole mind reader dream. Do I really care what he looks like?

"Yes, I'm sure. He used the exact same line about how knowing Polka is a bonus in his intro. And that photo of him . . . trust me. That's him. But, hey, that doesn't mean you shouldn't meet him. Maybe you can go Dutch at Applebee's." She refers to her date with him and grins mischievously.

I sigh. As much as I'd like to meet Scotty in person, I really don't want to endure anything like the awkward date Chloe had with him—if it even is him, that is. Then again, Chloe *is* pretty good with attention to detail, so I doubt she's wrong.

"But I spent so much time messaging him," I whine.

"Well, then go out with him. But I'm willing to bet he'd be just as awkward as he was when I went out with him. Jobs change. Awkward doesn't. Not his kind anyway. His messages to me were always very personable too. That's why I thought I found a winner on my very first try. Boy, was I wrong. But he was part of the process that brought me to Daran, so . . . Hey, I'm kinda hungry again. Mind if I have more pasta?"

I shake my head and type out a quick response to Scotty. Did he used to be an accountant? Is Bernie the black lab mix really his parents' dog? Does he own a Members Only jacket? Chloe looks over my shoulder and laughs. "So much for not sending any messages." I say closing my laptop and standing.

"You think you'll go out with him?"

"Probably not. If it is him, I already know what's in store for me. And now that the seed has been planted—thank you very much, Nancy Drew—even if it's not him, I'll keep thinking it is. So our first date is ruined either way."

"Sorry!" she says as she heads into the kitchen.

"I need more wine," I say shrugging and following right behind her.

Chloe fills a plate with a second helping of pasta as I start loading the dishwasher.

"Hey, are you going to drink that?" I point at the untouched glass of Chianti still sitting on the counter where she left it. I'm shocked when she shakes her head and tells me to go ahead and drink it.

"What, are you pregnant or something?" I scoff as I pick up my glass and finish off the contents. When I reach for Chloe's glass, I realize she isn't laughing. Instead, she's just sitting there chewing and staring at me.

"Sorry, it was just a joke."

Still silent, she sets her fork down and dabs the corners of her mouth with a napkin.

"Wait . . . you're not, are you? Shit. Tell me that's not why you wanted to stay in and cook and play Scrabble tonight. Say something!"

"I'm pregnant." She calmly goes back to eating her pasta.

"Holy shit!" I raise Chloe's glass, and it only takes me a few gulps to down all the contents. "Congratulations! Oh my God! That's wonderful!"

"You really think so?" she asks, wide eyed and looking relieved.

"What are you talking about? Of course I think it's wonderful. You're going to be a mom!" I bend down and wrap my arms around her, squeezing her tight. "Wait," gripping her upper arms, I pull back to look her in the eyes. "Did you already tell Daran? Is he not happy?"

"No," she shakes her head, eyes closed, "I mean, yes, I told him." When she opens her eyes, they're watery. "He's actually really happy about it. In fact, he already booked tickets for us to visit his family. Not that they know yet, but I guess they'll find out soon enough." She sighs heavily. "Do you believe this? I haven't even met his family yet, and I'm pregnant."

"So? Is that what's bothering you?"

"Sort of, but even worse, what are my co-workers going to think? I'm a teacher. I'm supposed to be a role model. What are my students and parents going to think?"

"Chloe, they're going to think you're going to be a great mom. They're going to be happy for you and Daran."

"That's not what I mean."

"What? Because you're not married? Who cares?"

"A lot of people care. It's just how it is."

"Wait, don't even tell me you told Shelly before you told me because that would be some bullsh—"

"Noooo. Of course not. Wait . . . you think she'll have a problem with it? . . . Nah, she'll be happy for us, too."

I disagree but I don't say anything. No need to make her feel even more nervous about the pregnancy. "And what about your mom?"

She shakes her head. "Haven't told her yet."

"Your sister?"

"Just you and Daran so far."

"Well, you're not worried about what your family is going to think are you? I mean, your sister and her husband weren't married when Simon was born."

"No, I'm not worried about them at all. It's just . . ."

"Who cares if *anyone* has a problem with it? It's no one's business but yours and Daran's anyway. Well, and mine, of course, because I'm going to be an auntie!" My proud smile is not reciprocated. "Seriously, you can't be down in the dumps because you're worried about what people might think. What's really bothering you?"

"I'm just scared."

"Well, it's not like you're the first woman to give birth. And you'll have a lot of people to help with the baby."

"I'm scared about Daran and I. What if things don't work out between us?"

"Then they don't work out. You'll still be the little guy's mom and Daran will still be his dad. Doesn't mean you have to stay together. Come on, we both know how that kind of thing works."

"Exactly! What if I end up screwing up this kid just like my parents screwed me up? All because I did something stupid and irresponsible?"

"Oh, my God. Do me a favor and don't ever use the word *stupid* when talking about the conception of your child again. Okay?" I can't help but be frustrated with her. She's come a long way, but she still has issues as a result of being a child of divorce. One positive thing I thought I could say about online dating is that it helped Chloe figure out a lot of things about herself when it comes to relationships. But now I'm left wondering again. Is the pregnancy going to cause her to revert to her old ways and push Daran away out of fear that she'll ruin it anyway? It sounds irrational, but having divorced parents, especially ones who argue like crazy, can really mess a person up. "You're not screwed up. You won't screw up your kid. And you're *not* going to screw up things with Daran either. If there's anything I know about you it's that you always rise to the occasion when faced with a challenge. So, here you go. Take this challenge and run with it. And if you need incentive, think about the little Chloe or Daran growing inside of you. That's amazing."

She cracks a smile. "It is, isn't it?"

"Yep, sure is. So, when are you going to tell your family?"

"Well, I'm pretty sure I'm about six or seven weeks along, so I'm thinking it'll have to be soon because I probably won't be able to hide it much longer. I swear my pants feel tighter already." She sighs and takes another bite of pasta.

"Well, if you keep eating like that . . ."

She cracks a full-mouthed smile and we both laugh. Then I crack a tasteless joke about kinky sex (which makes Chloe frown) as I whip open my laptop again and we start looking up baby names and ideas for nursery themes. Chloe's mood becomes brighter with each new name or idea that inspires her, and suddenly it hits me how much her life is about to change. No more girls' nights out or BAB nights. No more spending the day shopping on a whim or sleeping until noon. No more trying to come up with excuses to push away someone who cares about her. One way or another, Daran is here to stay.

And something tells me this little surprise is a blessing in disguise . . .

chapter thirty

After Chloe left last night, I couldn't stop thinking about how different things are going to be now that she's pregnant. She's already mentioned being tired all the time, so I guess that means no more being a night owl, not until the baby is born anyway. She'll have to give up ladies' night at Home Bar, unless she goes just to eat a Big Ass Burrito. (But let's get real, why would anyone go there just for a BAB?) Another big change for her is she'll eventually have to curb her obsession for Tae Bo. If I know Chloe, though, she won't want to give up exercise altogether, so she'll probably start jogging or walking more. Then it occurred to me that Chloe being pregnant is actually going to be good for both of us. Instead of going out for drinks when we see each other, we can spend more time doing things we used to do before alcohol came into the picture, like window shopping, seeing movies, playing Scrabble or cards, hanging out and listening to music, and going for walks or bike rides. That realization prompted me to set my alarm an hour earlier than normal so I could go for a jog this morning. (Okay, so maybe I only jogged a few blocks, but at least I can say I jogged.) After all, I need to get in shape so I can keep up with Chloe, even when she's pregnant.

When I get home around nine thirty, I'm surprised to see two messages on my cell. The first one is from Molly who says Anne called in sick today so she's wondering if I can stay until eight tonight to help with the dinner crowd. My dinner plans with Justin make me contemplate saying no, but only for a few seconds. I just can't say no because Molly has been so accommodating with my schedule. The least I can do is work a few extra hours when they're in a pinch. So I call her back and tell her I'd be happy to work until eight. Then I text Justin to break the news to him.

Me: Hey, handsome. I hate to do this, but I have to cancel our dinner plans. Molly just called and asked if I can stay late to cover for a sick co-worker. I'll be done at eight . . . Any chance you'd be willing to meet me there for a drink? Then maybe we can still see a movie like we planned?

As soon as I send the text to Justin, I go back into my voicemail to listen to the other message.

"Hey, Jess! It's Ryan. Ryan Cross. I got back from my trip last Saturday but I've been crazy busy ever since, with work and this triathlon I'm training for. But I can tell you about all that when I see you. Anyway, I have an hour for prep time right now, so I figured I better give you a buzz before you start to think I forgot about you. I'm all booked up this weekend already but wondering if you're free next Friday night. If not, I'm not free again until the following weekend. But we'll figure something out. How about if you call or shoot me a text when you get this? Thanks, talk to you soon."

I actually was beginning to accept that Ryan probably forgot about me, but now I'm back to being excited about the prospect of getting together with him. The only problem is I already told Ashley I'd go to a birthday party for one of her co-workers next Friday. She wasn't planning on meeting me at McGinn's until seven, though, so maybe I can ask Ryan to have dinner with me there beforehand. Even if there's overlap, it shouldn't be a big deal.

Me: Hey, Ryan! Good to hear from you. Next Friday works, but only if you can meet me at Molly McGinn's at five. I have plans with my sister at seven.

I send off the text to Ryan, and then rush to get a few things taken care of around my apartment before I need to head to McGinn's. My poor cats follow me around, vying for my attention after having to settle for quick feeding visits from Chloe this week. I don't know what I'd do without her. I refresh the water in their bowls, top off their food (even though both could use a diet), and then I make my way over to clean their litter boxes in the far corner of the living room. After that I unload the dishwasher and eat a banana and a piece of toast before taking a quick shower. While I'm getting dressed, two texts come through within seconds of each other.

> **Sawyer:** I heard you're filling in for Anne tonight. Good. Haven't talked to you for a while. Kinda miss your wiseassness. That's a word, right?

I am not a wiseass. But his text makes me grin.

> **Justin:** I'd love to meet you for a drink. See you at eight, beautiful.

I am beautiful, though. Okay, so maybe I'm a bit of a wiseass too.

"So . . . did you make out with her or not?" Sawyer teases.

"*Sawyerrr,*" I say, exhausted. "Give it up. All you need to know is that I had a nice time, and I'm not going to see her again. And, no, I won't be going out with any more women. Capiche?" I ask, mimicking his use of the word with me the other day in the break room.

"At least tell me if her rack was as nice in person as it looks in her profile picture."

"I should have never let you see my Personals account," I say, rolling my eyes. I grab my order and scurry away from his never-ending questions about my date with Pamela. At least one good thing has come of him giving me shit today . . . it's helping to keep the butterflies at bay, for the most part anyway.

"So who's next? And where are you meeting him?" he asks when I return to the computer next to the window.

"Are you going to keep asking me questions every single time I'm within earshot? Because if that's the case, I quit."

"Does that mean you don't have another date lined up yet?"

"Argh!" I storm off to deliver an order. Then I head to the bar to get a round of drinks for my newest table. While I'm waiting for Bobby to make them, Sawyer peeks his head out of the kitchen.

"Pssst. Jesstine!"

He catches the end of a massive eye roll when I turn to look at him. "You're being annoying. Kind of like I always imagined it would be to have a little brother."

"Last question," he says, putting his hands up as if to surrender. "Promise."

"What?"

"Are you sticking around when you're done? So we can hang out for a while?" He flashes a smile as if he already anticipates my answer will be yes. And out of nowhere, flutters galore. That damn smile of his.

"I can't . . . I mean, yes, I'm staying for a while. But Justin is meeting me." Funny how I cheated on Ned so many times without feeling an ounce of guilt, but for some reason, telling Sawyer about Justin has my stomach in knots. Maybe it's because of the way his smile fades a little, or maybe it's because I've come to consider him such a great friend, and he seems so eager to spend time with me tonight. Whatever it is, part of me wants to cancel on Justin.

"Ahh, so Justin is the lucky guy tonight. What is this, your fourth date with him?"

"Wow, keeping track, huh?" I grin. My turn to give him a little shit.

"Maybe," he says before he disappears back into the kitchen. Then he goes right back to giving me shit every time I go up to the window. I act annoyed, but inside I'm smiling and loving it.

Justin arrives at eight on the dot. He's wearing a fitted turquoise T-shirt and worn-in jeans with dark gray Chucks, and his hair is freshly trimmed, short on the sides and back and a little longer on top. He looks like he walked straight out of a J. Crew magazine, and his subtle, woodsy scent is intoxicating.

"Hey you," I say, standing and wrapping my arms around his neck. He picks me up a few inches off the ground, giving my midsection a little squeeze.

"Hey, beautiful."

I'm starting to like the way he calls me beautiful. It sure does beat the way Ned always used to call me babe.

We hop onto bar stools and situate ourselves, facing each other, his legs flanking mine. I like the closeness of him and the subtle woodsy scent of his cologne, and I wonder if we might have sex tonight.

"If you're hungry, the Reuben rolls here are fantastic. And what would you like to drink? You might as well have my one free drink for the night. I'm sticking with seltzer." I grab the glass I've been continually refilling with seltzer water all day long off the bar and raise it a hair before taking a sip.

"Well, I'll have the same. No need for me to drink if you're not. But I will try some of those Reuben rolls."

And with that, we begin another round of getting to know each other. We're discussing how he met his wife when they were both juniors at the University of Minnesota when Bobby arrives with Justin's rolls.

"So, you two met online?" Bobby glances at Justin and then his gaze falls on me.

I smile and nod, expecting him to turn and leave, considering he has a bar full of customers.

"Justin." He extends a hand to Bobby, and they exchange a manly shake. "And you are?"

"Bobby. Good to meet you. My friend Jess here hasn't been online dating too long. How about you? How long have you been picking up women online?"

Justin chuckles. "About a year. But I wouldn't call it picking up women. Although I suppose it's like that for some."

"Oh yeah? What's it like for you?" I say it as a joke, but he surprises me by answering as if I was serious.

"Well, I think meeting people online is basically the same as meeting them in a bar or at the grocery store. You recognize an attraction and then establish whether or not there's any substance to latch onto. Then you go on some dates to see if anything sticks."

"Whoa, you're one of them intellectual guys, huh?" Bobby quickly refills a few empty beer glasses and then he returns. "Let me guess . . . You wear a monkey suit to work."

I stare at Bobby wide-eyed wondering why he would say such a thing. I even glance toward the kitchen, wondering if Sawyer might have put him up to it as joke. But then common sense kicks in. Why on earth would he do that?

"Nah. Khakis and a polo shirt most days."

Bobby nods, and then he eyes me cautiously. "Hey, Jess, you don't mind me asking your guy here a couple more questions, do you? I'm thinking about giving this online dating business a try myself."

"Sure," I shrug. "Go ahead. But why are you asking me? You should be asking Monkey Suit here if he wants to answer your questions."

Bobby frisbees a coaster at me and Justin laughs and says, "Ask away, brother."

Bobby puts up a finger to let Justin know he'll be back.

"I wonder why he's being so chatty with you about online dating. He hasn't asked me more than a few questions."

"That's because you're not an expert like me." He gives my upper thigh a squeeze.

Bobby reappears. "So . . . how many girls have you met online?"

"Hundreds."

Both Bobby's and my eyes widen. "Hundreds?" we ask in unison.

"Sure," Justin shrugs. "But I didn't meet them all in person."

I finally exhale.

"I only met around . . . oh, I'd say thirty people."

"And how many of those have you . . ."

"Had sex with?" I pipe in.

Now the guys stare at me, Bobby's even wider this time and Justin's twinkling with amusement.

"Geez! Get your head out of the gutter, woman! I wasn't gonna ask that," Bobby says looking at me and then returning his attention to Justin. "How many of those have you dated seriously? Say for a month or longer?"

Who knew I'd be the only one of the three of us with sex on the brain?

Justin taps the bar as he thinks for a moment. "One . . . Just Jess." He winks at me.

Bobby nods, "And you only date people you meet online?"

"No, I still meet people other places. Right before I met Jess, I called it quits with someone I'd been seeing for a few months."

My jaw drops but I recover quickly so the guys don't notice. So Justin was dating this woman while he was busy picking up women online with knock-knock jokes? I think I might need to know more about this.

Bobby finishes interrogating Justin about his online dating experiences, and I continue to wrack my brain trying to remember if he ever mentioned he was seeing someone before we met. And the more I think about it, the more I begin to realize it probably doesn't matter. He didn't say they were serious, he said they were dating. Like us. I wouldn't consider us serious. Plus, I'm seeing other people too, just no one who's been around for three months.

"Jess? Are you sure you don't want something else?"

"Huh?" I ask no one in particular because I'm not even sure who just spoke to me.

"Bobby was just wondering if you're having anything else besides soda water," Justin asks.

"Oh . . . no, I'm good. Thanks Bobby."

"No problemo. Let me know if you change your mind." Bobby nods at Justin. "Thanks for the info, bro."

Justin nods back and then we're alone again at last.

"So, you were seeing someone when we met online?" No point beating around the bush.

"I was wondering if you'd bring that up," he says with a grin. Not an *oops you caught me* kind of grin, though. More like an *I've been meaning to talk to you about that...*sort of grin.

I shrug. "Don't get me wrong, it doesn't bother me. I don't suffer from any illusions about what we're doing here. I know this isn't serious. I'm just curious. And for the record, I didn't bring it up. You did, when you were talking to Bobby."

"Okay, fair enough," He says, laughing and scratching his cheek. "It was just a woman I met at a bar. We only dated on and off for a few months."

"So why'd you stop seeing her?"

"No exact reason, really. We just stopped calling each other. So it was actually a mutual thing."

His answer seems reasonable to me so I shrug. "Okay, good enough for me."

"Now it's my turn to ask you a question."

"Shoot," I say sliding my empty glass closer to the inside of the bar.

"I like you. A lot. And I'm wondering . . . How do you feel about me?"

"Um, I like you too?" I don't mean for it to come across as a question. "I do. I like you," I say, nodding, as if to convince myself. But that's not how I mean for it to come across.

"Well, that's good to hear." He reaches out and runs the backs of a few fingers up and down my cheek, giving me tingles. Then he places his hand on my knee.

"But I should tell you I still have some dates lined up. I just want to be honest." Again, no bushes to be beaten around here.

He sighs heavily. "Okay, but like I said before, I'm on the lookout for something that sticks." He turns me toward him and gives both of my thighs a squeeze. "I hope this sticks."

I smile and place my hands on top of his. "So do you still want to catch a movie or do you want go to a coffee shop . . . or—"

"How about your place?"

"Um, yeah, I guess we could go there. Do you like to play Scrabble?"

He hops off his stool and holds out a hand. "Yes, but I should warn you, I won't go easy on you."

"Good, because I won't go easy on you either," I say, taking his hand so he can help me off my stool.

I'm gathering my things and Justin is putting a few singles on the bar for Bobby when Sawyer appears. "Leaving already?" He asks, hopping onto the stool Justin just abandoned. I glance at the clock and remember what Anne said about Sawyer rarely coming out of the kitchen during his shift. His shift doesn't end for another fifteen minutes.

"Justin, you remember Sawyer, right?"

"Sure, I saw you at Potawatomi with him, from a distance. We were never officially introduced, though." He turns to Sawyer and extends a hand. "Good to meet you. I'm Justin."

Sawyer glances at me briefly before shaking Justin's hand. "Yeah, good to meet you, too," he says, nodding politely. Then he looks at me. "So, where are you two off to?"

Justin raises an eyebrow at me.

"We're going to my place to play Scrabble."

He chuckles and says, "I love Scrabble. We'll have to play sometime." Then he lights up a cigarette and it occurs to me I've never seen him smoke anywhere but at McGinn's. The casualness of his nicotine use makes me wonder why he smokes at all.

"Alright, well, again, it was nice to meet you Sawyer. Have a good night," Justin says. He takes a hold of my hand and begins to walk away.

Sawyer looks over at me and our eyes lock. I sense a certain something between us as we stare at each other but can't pinpoint what it is. Is he wishing I would ditch Justin and stay? Is he wishing he was going home with me to play Scrabble? Whatever it is, I could stand here all night trying to figure out what the something might be. I want to ask him if he feels it too, and I want him to say yes. But I won't because he's still married, and we're just friends. Oh, and Justin is slowly pulling me away.

"See ya, Jesstine." Sawyer gives me that grin of his that makes me want to jump his bones, and then he turns toward the bar, leaving me to follow Justin out the door.

As we walk outside, Justin asks, "Did he just call you Jesstine?"

"Yeah, that's my name."

"Why didn't you tell me? I had no idea."

"It's just that . . . not many people call me that," I say with a shrug.

He stops walking, drops my hand and looks at me. "But Sawyer does." It isn't a question, more like a statement of disdain.

"Oh," I say, shaking my head and putting my hand back in his. I give him a tug to keep moving. "He saw it on my license one night when we were shooting the shit with a few of the regulars. Someone questioned that my birthday falls on April first."

He lets go of my hand again, this time putting his arm around me as we walk to my car. "So I'll follow you to your place then?"

"Sounds good," I say with a nod and smile. Then I get into my car and take a few deep breaths as I try to shake Sawyer from my thoughts. It isn't fair to Justin for me to be thinking about another guy when I'm on a date with him. That's why I cut him a little slack for the jealous reaction he just had to Sawyer knowing my full name when he didn't. Plus, I really do like Justin, and he's been completely upfront with me about wanting more. Sawyer, on the other hand, hasn't given any indication he wants more than friendship from me. Until then, I have to concentrate on Justin.

chapter thirty-one

"Hey, what's up?" This is how Chloe greets me when I call her the next morning.

"I had sex last night."

"Oookay. And?"

"What do you mean *and*? It's the first time I've had sex with anyone since Ned."

"It is not! There was the guy you met at that cocktail lounge we went to on Valentine's Day. Remember? Daran and I left and you stayed with him? Then there was that school counselor you met at Home Bar. And—"

"Chloe, I didn't sleep with any of those guys. I mean, we did other stuff . . . but I didn't have sex with any of them."

"Seriously? I had no idea. I guess I thought . . . I'm sorry."

"Don't be. You assumed I was doing what I would normally do—sleeping with people to cope with my Ned issues."

"Why didn't you say something? You should have corrected me when I assumed you'd gone home with all those guys?"

"Because it didn't matter. And . . . well, I felt guilty . . . because I was still sleeping with Ned."

"Whatever. All I'm going to say about that is thank God that fucker is finally out of your life." She snorts, lightening the mood of the conversation.

"So what's the deal? Who was it? Sawyer?"

"No! Sawyer and I are just doing the friend thing. Remember? It was—"

"*Friends*," she mumbles.

"What?"

"Oh nothing. So, it was Justin then?"

"Wait, why did you mumble *friends* when I said Sawyer and I are just friends. Is that really hard to believe?"

"I don't know. I'm just . . . surprised nothing else has happened between you two since the night you met. I mean, you guys are *always* talking at McGinn's and texting each other. I kind of figured you'd be dating him by now, too."

"You and I talk and text a lot. Should I be dating you?"

"Very funny. You know what I mean. Anyway, how was it?"

"Well, it was fine . . . I guess."

"Hello? Jess? Is it really you? Can somebody please put Jess on the line? What do you mean *fine, I guess*? What's going on with you? I've never heard you sound so blasé about sex before. Does he have an eeny teeny peeny? Or was he a crier or something weird like that?"

"No, no, no. Nothing was off-putting about him at all. He was great actually. And his size is . . . more than acceptable. It's just that I didn't really get that rush of excitement I normally get when I have sex with someone, especially someone new, and it pisses me off. I'm not with Ned anymore. Justin is a nice guy, and I've gotten to know him pretty well. I waited not two, not three, but FOUR dates before we had sex. By all technical standards, as far as doing the deed goes, his performance was expert level. So what's wrong with me? Why weren't there any fireworks?"

"Jess, nothing is wrong with you! I think it might be the opposite. Maybe you're finally ready to find something of substance. Something real. Maybe that's why you didn't feel anything, because you're so used to having sex with people who had no substance at all—not when it came to being relationship material anyway. Maybe it will just take some time for your feelings to catch up with your actions. You should have sex with him again tonight and see if you feel any different."

"Oh, that's a great idea," I say, wondering if she senses my sarcasm. "But I'm on my way to work at McGinn's and he's working tonight."

"Well, whatever. It doesn't have to be tonight. Just keep getting to know him and see if your feelings change. What else can you do? Just don't beat yourself up for not being in an emotional spot it takes most people a while to get to."

"Chloe, it's not so much about emotions. It's about my love for sex. It depresses me that sex with him didn't make me all gooey inside and curl my toes, even though I feel like he's the kind of guy who should elicit that kind of response. I even faked an orgasm."

"No," she whispers, shocked.

"Yeah, tell me about it. Anyway, I shouldn't have even called about this. It's a silly thing to worry about. How are you feeling by the way?"

"Pukey. I saw my OB after work yesterday, and she officially confirmed what five pregnancy tests already told me. I'm close to seven weeks pregnant."

"Have you guys decided when you're going to tell everyone? Can I tell my mom?"

"No way! I, at least, have to tell my mom and sister first. Or . . . I was actually thinking Daran's birthday party might be a good time to break the news to everyone all at once. Nice and convenient, you know?"

Leave it to Chloe to consider what's most convenient when delivering news of an unplanned pregnancy. "You mean at his *surprise* birthday party? Sure, when everyone yells surprise, jump up and yell, *"I'm pregnant!"* Good plan."

"Knock it off," she says laughing.

"Yeah, for sure, that would be an efficient, Chloe-esque way to get the word out. Do you think Daran will be comfortable with you announcing it to everyone like that?"

"He'll be fine with whatever I decide. The party isn't even for a couple of weeks, though, so people will probably suspect by then anyway."

"So, if my mom asks before you announce it . . ."

"Mum's the word."

"Fine," I huff.

"Hey, I gotta get going. If you feel like joining Daran and I for some Band of Brothers after you get off of work, feel free to stop over. Or do you have another date?"

"Wow, another night in, huh?"

"Yep, it's good for the bun."

"Thanks for the offer, but I'm planning on going straight home after work. It's been awhile since I hung out alone at my apartment. I think the kitties could use some love."

She emits a nostalgic sigh. "Alone time. Sounds lovely."

"Bye, momma."

"Bye. Say hi to Sawyer for me," Chloe says before she hangs up.

"How much longer for table seven?" I ask Sawyer. I've been at work for an hour and he seems distracted like he did last week after his business partner Corey contacted him.

"Just have to dish up the Colcannon and you'll be set." He says without making eye contact. Something is obviously bothering him, and his somber mood makes my heart ache.

"I heard you made the Colcannon from scratch this morning. I love cabbage and kale. I'll have to try it." He nods and grins slightly, but doesn't say anything. "Is everything—" I begin but Anne shows up and cuts me off.

"What's going on, sweetie? You seem a bit down today. Anything I can do to cheer you up?" The flirtatious tone of her voice makes me cringe.

Sawyer sets the final dish to complete my order in the pickup window. "Nah, I'm fine, thanks. Life can't always be daffodils and sunshine." He glances at me when he says that last bit.

As the hours tick by, Sawyer becomes more talkative. He begins peppering me with questions about Justin, and they aren't silly questions like the ones he was asking after my date with Pamela. He wants to know serious things like what he does for a living, where he grew up, if he's ever been married, if he has kids and how long he's been online dating. Instead of razzing me, it's as if he's a father figure trying to determine whether dating Justin is a wise decision on my part. It's both endearing and annoying at the same time because I wish I had a father to keep an eye out for me, yet I certainly don't want Sawyer behaving like one to me.

"Jesstine," Sawyer calls out as I pass the window on my way to take a break.

I turn with a smile, glad that he seems to be out of the slump he was in earlier.

"You going outside?"

"Yeah."

"Mind if I join you?"

"Why? So you can continue grilling me about Justin?" I ask with narrowed eyes.

"No . . . just so we can hang out a little outside of this place."

"Helloooo? Sawyer, I need that Guinness stew," Anne chirps, interrupting us and causing me to imagine grabbing the bowl of stew from Sawyer's hands and hurling it at her.

"One sec," he says, sounding a bit irritated. Anne sighs and crosses her arms.

"Sure, I'll be on the bench," I say as I glance at Anne, turning to leave.

Five minutes later, I sense Sawyer sitting down on the bench beside me—the same bench he was sitting on when we first met. Eyes closed, I have my arms crossed and one leg crossed over the other. My head is against the back of the bench so I can enjoy the warmth of the sun on my face.

"Hey," he says. His knee brushes against mine.

"Hey, yourself," I say opening my eyes and looking over at him.

He lights a cigarette and takes a long drag, blowing the smoke straight up into the air.

"How is it that you can go without smoking for long periods of time, like the times we've been at my place? Most real smokers I know have to have one every few hours, at least."

"Real smokers?"

"Yeah, people who buy cigarettes like they buy milk or toilet paper."

He laughs and takes another drag. "Well, I only smoke when I'm stressed, so I guess I'm not a real smoker."

I let out an airy laugh and finally look away and out into the parking lot. "I usually only smoke when I drink."

"What about the day we met? Right here in this spot, you smoked with me."

"That's because I wanted to stay and talk to you," I say laughing.

He laughs too. "So how was Scrabble?" I feel his eyes on me so I glance over at him for just a second, afraid he might see the discomfort in my eyes.

"Scrabble is always a good time."

"Uh-huh," he says, nudging me playfully with his elbow.

I look over at him, laughing, "What? It is." Our eyes lock and he's smiling now too. I study his mouth the way I did the first time we met. The subtle dip at the center of his upper lip . . . his full lower lip . . . "So," I say, snapping out of the spell I usually seem to fall under when Sawyer's around, "is everything okay? You seemed . . . distracted earlier, sort of the way you were last Friday."

"Yeah," he mutters and then he finishes off his cigarette before continuing. "I had a visit from Beth and Corey on Thursday night. They want to sell."

"Then why did they bother asking if you were going to be okay going back to work with them? Isn't your last day here in two weeks?"

He nods. "They weren't expecting me to go back."

"So what are you going to do?"

"I told them there's no way I'm selling. I'll buy them out if I have to," he says with a hint of defiance.

"Sounds like you've got it figured out, so why the funk?"

He sighs and looks at me with a sheepish expression. "Because it would actually be smart to sell, but I'm not sure yet if I want those two assholes to benefit from the work I contributed." Shaking his head, he looks away. "It doesn't feel good to know that I'm behaving like a spiteful child, but I can't help it."

I put my arm around him to give his back a rub and I lean my head against his shoulder. We sit like that, both of us staring at the ground in front of us, until a voice breaks the silence.

"Jess?"

Sawyer and I snap our heads up and find Justin standing in front of us.

"Justin," I say, standing immediately. He glances at Sawyer with a curt nod and then wraps his arms around me. "What are you doing here? I thought you had to work?"

"I do, but I decided to stop by to say hi on my way. How's your day going?" he asks, looking down at me, still pressed against his chest.

"Good. I was just taking a break, but it's just about over, so . . ."

He checks his watch. "Well, since I'm here, I might as well stay for a bite to eat before I head to work. Is that okay?" I follow his eyes as he glances at Sawyer who's getting up to leave.

"Later, Freckles."

"See you inside, Sawyer," I say. Then I look back at Justin. He doesn't say it, but I can tell he's wondering why Sawyer would call me *Freckles*.

"Of course it's fine if you stay and eat. Come on." I hold his hand as we walk inside, secretly wishing he'd called first.

chapter thirty-two

"Good afternoon, Barbara." A muscular guy in shiny athletic shorts and a sleeveless shirt calls to my mom. His flirtatious tone causes me to choke on the water I'm drinking. He continues grinning at my mom as he and his friends make their way toward the basketball courts. Most of his crew is oblivious but a few glance at us, and one elbows him causing laughter among the two.

"Mom, do you really think it's a good idea for you to let your students call you by your first name?" That's not the only thing I don't think is such a good idea, but she'd never take my concerns about the way the barely legal kid was staring at her like a hungry puppy seriously.

"Oh, sweetheart, it's fine," she says shaking her head dismissively, not a hint of appreciation for the young man's obvious attraction to her. "Several of my colleagues allow it as well. I think it makes my students feel less intimidated by the concepts I'm trying to teach them and more invested in my class."

"But don't you think it might make some too comfortable, to the point where they might not take you or your class seriously? Some might even start thinking of you as a friend," or a dating prospect, "and expect special treatment."

She laughs flippantly but doesn't respond, so I shrug off my concerns. If she isn't worried, no need for me to be either, I guess.

"Another roll?" My mom holds out the carryout container of sushi rolls to me. I use my chopsticks to nab a few, placing them on the clear plastic lid I'm using as a plate. "Thanks for picking up lunch, by the way. Remind me to give you some cash before you go."

"No, Mom, that's okay." I lean back against the tree I'm sitting in front of. "You always buy me lunch. I got it this time."

She smiles gratefully, but I know I'll end up finding a twenty slipped into one of my pockets or in my purse. "Sooo," she lowers her chin and eyes curiously, "how's the dating going? Last time we talked you'd been on one pleasant date with a man who has a quirky hiccupping tick, if I recall correctly, two questionable dates, and you were anxious about a third that was coming up. I hope you rose above your apprehensions and put your best foot forward. When you let your personality shine, people are drawn to you, Jess." My mom: the queen of positivity. I can't help but giggle inside because I'm not that great at soaking in compliments, even when they're from my own flesh and blood.

"I did. Let my personality shine, I mean." I smile broadly. "And the date was amazing, probably the best first date I've ever been on." I'm referring to Justin, of course. I plan to stop there but she wants to know more, so I continue with all the details of the date, right down to our kiss afterward and the daffodil he bought for me. Then I tell her about introducing him to Chloe and Daran and a few basics about his background and personal life. The only thing about Justin I completely leave out is the fact that we had sex, and I'm not sure how I feel about it.

"Oh, how wonderful," she gushes, clasping her hands together at her chest. "So you like this young man?"

"I do. But—" I'm about to tell her how confused I feel about my attraction to Sawyer, but I'm not so sure I should. After what my mom went through with my dad and stepdad, I never told her about Brant. I don't care how open-minded she is. Telling her I slept with a married man would probably break her heart. It's bad enough that I told her Sawyer went home with me the first night we met. How can I possibly explain everything that has happened between us since then without telling her he's married? It's all just way too complicated.

"But?"

"But I'm still chatting with a few others from online, too. Oh!" I suddenly remember Ryan Cross. "Guess who I'm getting together with tomorrow night?"

Startled by my sudden enthusiasm, my mom widens her eyes. "Who?"

"Do you remember Ryan Cross?"

"Yes, of course I do. He was a sweet kid and always so polite," she says, nodding. “Remember when he made you that precious Valentine the year you both had Mrs. Johns?”

“Um, yeah.” I say, shocked that she remembers. It sort of feels like I’ve been called out on a deep, dark secret. A deep, dark secret that I keep hidden away in a box in my closet.

“How did you end up running into him?” she asks as she picks up her tea and brings it to her lips to blow on it.

“He’s online dating, too!”

“What a coincidence,” she says before she takes a cautious sip.

“I don’t know. I was sort of thinking it could be more than a coincidence, you know? I mean, there are thousands of profiles online, and I hardly ever look through the matches they send me. What are the odds Yahoo! Personals would pick Ryan’s profile to pop up on my screen at that moment?”

She chuckles. “You and I both know you didn’t get your math abilities from me, Jesstine, but I’d say the odds aren’t all that low.” She continues smiling and shaking her head at me, and I frown at her inability to even humor the idea that it could be something more than a coincidence. “So what do the two of you plan to do?”

“He’s meeting me at McGinn’s when I get done with work.”

“Jesstine, are you sure you want to meet him in a bar? Will you even have time to change your clothes and freshen up before he arrives?”

It never occurred to me that I would want to change and freshen up. I suppose it’s because I’ve known Ryan since I was a kid, and I’ve never tried to impress him before. I shrug. “There’s actually a reason why I asked him to meet me there.”

“What possible reason could you have for asking Ryan Cross to meet you at a bar?

“Ashley and I already had plans for *her* to meet me there before Ryan and I made plans.” I smile, knowing my mom will be pleased.

“Oh, sweetie, that’s the most wonderful news I’ve heard in weeks.” She brings her palms together, clutching them to her chest. “What finally made you decide to call her?”

Perfect segue into telling her about my date with Pamela. “That’s actually an interesting story.”

I'm not sure how my mom will react to me going out with a woman, but I tell her everything anyway. She doesn't even bat an eyelash when I describe the way Pamela came on to me on the bench outside the Putt Putt Club. There might even be a hint of a grin on her face. When I'm done describing the date, my mom smiles and says, "So we learned two things here."

"Yeah? What?"

She holds up one finger. "You're not a lesbian."

I chuckle and nod. "That's what Chloe said."

She holds up a second finger. "You're more prone to taking advice from strangers than people who are close to you."

"What do you mean?" I ask the question even though I know exactly what she's getting at.

"Oh, sweetie, I don't mean it in a bad way. It's good to be aware of your own tendencies. All I'm saying is that I've recommended that you give Ashley a call to patch things up numerous times. So I think this date with Pamela may have been a blessing in disguise. It served a much bigger purpose than helping you figure out your sexual orientation."

"Oh, I wasn't questioning—"

"The date brought you back together with your sister," she continues, holding up a finger to indicating this isn't the final bit of insight she intends to share. "That's a perfect example of the cosmos coming into alignment. Perfect timing. Isn't life amazing? One giant puzzle with pre-made pieces that fit together just so." She smiles at me the way she always does when she thinks we're sharing a poignant moment.

"Yep," I say with as much sincerity as I can muster. "Amazing." While I am grateful that Pamela encouraged me to contact Ashley, I'm not so sure it was the universe that brought us together. I'm leaning more toward crediting Yahoo! Personals for this one. "Speaking of puzzles, Mom, remember me bringing up our puzzle nights the other day?"

"I sure do, sweetie. We had some good mother-daughter talks, didn't we?" She stands and walks over to a garbage can, eyeing a group of male students who are walking by. Instead of sitting back down when she returns, she stands while she takes out a compact mirror and begins freshening up her lipstick. Does she know why I'm bringing it up? Is she trying to deflect my interest in the topic again?

"I've been wondering . . ." I say as I stand so I can be face to face with her. "Remember how you used to say there was one right person for everyone? That just like the pieces of a puzzle, we all have that one perfect match who fits with us perfectly?"

She goes stone still for a second, her lipstick resting on her bottom lip and compact mirror frozen. Then her eyes migrate from her reflection to meet mine, an uncomfortable smile spreading across her lips as she puts her toiletries away. "Jesstine, that was a long time ago. Before Terry made me—before Terry *helped* me realize the idea of soulmates is an illusion. It's something to help people cope with the reality that we're all constantly growing and changing. And since change is such a scary thing to so many people, it's just easier for some to believe that there's only one person out there for them. Because if they find that one person . . . well, then they think they've found something that will never change. It just doesn't work like that though, Jesstine. Nothing lasts forever." She smiles for real now and busies herself packing up her oversized purse.

"Mom?"

"Yes, sweetie?"

"Why do you say Terry helped you realize this? He's wanted you back ever since you found out about the affair and kicked him out. He still thinks you're his soulmate, Mom. He told me so."

She stares at me inquisitively, as if I'm the subject of a case study on denial. "No," she shakes her head, "if I was his soulmate, he never would have cheated. Terry just feels guilty. That's all. He's an easy guy to live with. He'll eventually find someone else."

Now it's my turn to stare at her, my heart deflated. Part of me always believed in our puzzle-time talks about love and soulmates and fate. Even when I was punishing myself with Ned and Brant and all the coaster guys, part of me still believed I'd find my soulmate someday—that one special person whose puzzle piece would match perfectly with mine. I sometimes imagined myself walking down the street and running right into him. Boom. Just like that, I'd know. That's what my mom used to say anyway, that I'd just know.

"Jesstine? Are you okay?"

I shrug. "So, if you don't think there's one person for everyone, then what do you think?"

"Well, I definitely believe in fate. But instead of the idea of one soulmate for everyone, I think maybe we all have multiple people we're meant to meet up with throughout our lives. Honestly, I never should have compared finding love to pieces of a puzzle. It makes no sense," she laughs. "Especially when I neglected to acknowledge that no puzzle piece attaches to the whole on one side only. Every piece has at least two attaching sides. So based on my ridiculous puzzle comparison, we all have at least two matches!" Laughing even harder, she shakes her head. "I don't know what I was thinking filling your little mind with such nonsense."

But I don't laugh because she's just taken one of my fondest memories and turned it upside down. And part of me can't help but wonder if she isn't simply jaded over being burned twice. Can I really blame her if that's the case?

"So I suppose I'm one of those pieces that only attaches on two ends because I'm thinking your father and Terry might have been my only two matches." She laughs again and swings her bag over her shoulder.

"Or maybe you should give Terry another chance? People make mistakes, Mom. You always say it's all about experiences. Well, maybe if you took Terry back you'd both look back on the experiences you've had without each other over the past year, and you'd never question the fact that you're soulmates again."

She lovingly wraps her arms around me. "That's a sweet thought, Jesstine, but . . ." She puts me at arm's length and looks into my eyes. Then she blinks and a tear falls down her cheek. She quickly wipes it away and composes herself before another can escape. "I love you, and I'll see you at Daran's birthday party next Friday."

"Are you bringing Rod?" I ask quietly as I pick up my purse and swing it into place on my shoulder.

"That's the plan," she says cheerfully and a bit too loud. "And Saturday night we're seeing Norah Jones at the Riverside Theater."

"Huh, I never would have taken Rod for a Norah Jones fan."

"Maybe that's because he's not. But he knows I am. And he also knows that her music puts me in the mood for—"

"Uh uh uh, stop right there," I say raising a hand. "I get the idea. Oh, and just so you know, the party might deliver more than one surprise."

"Oh yeah? What's going on? Is Chloe pregnant or something?" She laughs.

"Ha! Good one." I say, turning quickly to leave. "Love you," I say over my shoulder.

She reaches out and gives my arm a quick rub and then turns and rushes off to class.

chapter thirty-three

Today's the day. I get to see Ryan Cross for the first time in five years. I wasn't nervous until this morning when I realized there could still be a small spark for me burning inside of him. That's what prompted me to pack a change of clothes, a hairbrush, deodorant, body spray, and a toothbrush and toothpaste. If Yahoo! Personals showing me Ryan's profile had anything to do with fate, the least I can do is cooperate and be prepared.

After I packed everything, I called and left Ashley a message to let her know that Ryan might be with me at McGinn's when she arrives. When she called me back during her prep time, I happened to be taking a break. She wanted to tell me that she had no idea who I was talking about in my message, so I tried to jog her memory by reminding her of the time when Ryan gave her a candy cane at a holiday program at my elementary school. She was only four at the time of the program, so she still didn't remember who he was, but she did remember that candy cane. She also swore she remembered me talking on the phone with my best friend in second grade, Tracy Miller, and saying that some Ryan kid was gross. I assume it must have been Ryan Cross, because I don't remember any other Ryan going to grade school with me. I guess tonight will determine once and for all what I really think of him.

Since I stupidly asked Ryan to arrive at five, thinking I'd go right from wiping down a dirty table to sitting down with him for a drink, Claire and Jillian tell me to punch out ten minutes early so I have time to change and freshen up. I follow their suggestion, and at five o'clock on the dot, I'm ready and waiting at the same table next to the bar where I started my date with Free Bird. Except, unlike Free Bird, I'm on the stool facing the door, not the TVs.

When I spot Ryan, memories from childhood come rushing back to me, making me feel a little giddy. I hop off my stool and meet him halfway, without looking him over too closely. We both lean into a hug immediately. His back feels taut and muscular through his shirt, reminding me how shocked I was by his rock-hard physique the last time I saw him—the night he snubbed me.

"Jess, you look great," he says looking me up and down. Although I don't get the impression he's doing it to actually check me out. It seems more like he's taking note of how I've changed over the years.

"You too. It's so good to see you!"

We take a seat at the table and get right to chatting. The only break in conversation is when Claire shows up to take our orders. Even when she delivers our drinks, we keep talking about anything and everything —his family, my family, his job, my jobs, people we keep in touch with from school, and gossip we've heard about people we don't keep in touch with. I also learn that Ryan is a competitive triathlete. I almost feel my muscles aching when he describes the training he goes through during weeks leading up to events. He's currently getting ready for an Ironman competition that's happening this July in Racine. Normally, I would crack jokes about how insane a person must be to want to swim, bike, and run over seventy miles, but the passionate way Ryan talks about how much he loves these activities prevents me from sharing my thoughts on the matter.

Conversation slows when our food arrives, and this gives me a chance to figure out how to bring up a topic I've been wanting to talk to him about for years.

"You know, I've always wondered how things would have been different if I'd given you a chance way back when."

He cocks his head. "What do you mean?"

"I mean, sometimes I think if I'd been interested in guys like you back when we were teenagers, I probably wouldn't have ended up dating guys like Toby Johnson as an adult."

"Right, and if I'd been interested in girls like Tabitha Miller back when we were teenagers, I wouldn't have ended up dating women like you as an adult." He chuckles.

"Tabitha Miller? She was the smartest girl in our class. And wasn't she, like, homecoming queen one year?"

He shrugs and nods as he takes a bite of his leafy green salad.

"Wait, are you saying I'm a Toby Johnson?"

"Not anymore. But yeah, you were."

"I wasn't a troublemaker like Toby Johnson," I say dismissively as I take a sip of my Diet Coke.

"You tried to pick the lock on the door of our sixth grade classroom and the bobby pin broke off. Remember? We had to stand in silence against the wall until a locksmith came to get the pin out."

"Oh give me a break," I say rolling my eyes. "It took the guy like ten minutes to get the door open."

Ryan laughs and continues. "But that's not even why you were like Toby."

"Why then?"

"Because Toby didn't care what other people thought of him, and he was more into himself than anyone else."

I'm stunned silent by the insult I *think* Ryan has just given me, for a few seconds anyway. I'm about to let him have a piece of my mind when he continues.

"But none of that really matters now anyway, does it? And I'm sure you're nothing like Toby anymore." He shrugs and eats one bite of salad after another until he finishes it off. While he does so, I poke at the side salad next to my half-eaten Turkey Reuben.

"I'm sorry, Ryan."

"What for?" He looks perplexed.

"For breaking your heart," I whisper.

"What? Are you talking about middle school? That was puppy love," he chuckles, "so don't be. The fact that you never went out to the movies with me has never once crossed my mind."

Now it's my turn to look perplexed.

"Well, what was up with you the night I saw you at that bar on North Avenue? The night I tried to talk to you and you didn't give me the time of day?"

He pushes his empty plate away and dabs the corners of his mouth with his napkin. Then he says, "I'd just found out my girlfriend was cheating on me that day. We'd been dating for three years." To my surprise his solemn expression fades and an amused grin slides into its place. "All these years you thought I was mad at you for not going out with me when we were thirteen? I love ya, Jess, but you always did have a habit of thinking everything was about you."

I want to be mad at him, but I'm not because his perception of me isn't too far off.

"I still have that Valentine you gave me when we were in sixth grade," I say smiling. "You were so cute with your khakis and polo shirts. I can see it now."

"My mom dressed me like a total geek."

When our laughter dies down, Ryan tells me he made plans to meet some friends at the Bradley Center for the Bucks game, since he knew I had plans with Ashley at seven anyway. So we take care of the bill and talk about getting together again soon, but I'm pretty sure it's just a formality. I'm guessing the only way we'll ever see each other again is if we run into each other somewhere. We hug and Ryan is walking out the door when Ashley walks in. They bump into each other, and I see it happen. They fumble around for a few seconds, trying to get out of each other's way and apologizing. Then they lock eyes and smile. Ashley looks over at me and points, and Ryan smiles so big you'd think he won the lottery. A few seconds later, they're both at the table with me. Ashley gives me a hug and we all chat for a few minutes, but before I know it, the conversation shifts to running, biking, and swimming—all things that Ashley loves too. Then they're discussing all the things you only like to talk about if you happen to be a teacher. Forty minutes later, Ashley excuses herself to use the bathroom, and once again, it's just Ryan and me.

He checks his watch as he hops off his stool. "I wish I could stay, but the guys already got me a ticket."

"You should definitely go. We can always get together another time." I glance to my right to see if Ashley's on her way back yet.

"Say, Jess, this might be weird but . . . Would it be okay with you if I asked Ashley for her number? I mean, if it's too weird, then—"

"Of course, I don't care! Ask her. It's obvious she's hoping you will." I glance toward the bathroom again to see her approaching this time.

"Here she comes," I whisper. Then I stand and give Ryan a friendly pat on the shoulder before heading to the bathroom myself. Instead, I check my hair and wash my hands, giving Ryan just enough time to get Ashley's number and ask her out.

It seems fate really was involved here. It just wasn't my own.

Later on, Ashley and I part ways in the parking lot of Majestic Cinema. I get in my car, and a message comes through when I power on my phone.

"Jess! Hopefully this is you, anyway. Wildman here. Or Brock. Pick one and I'll answer. Whatever suits your fancy. In your message, you said to call. Sooooo . . . here I am, giving you a call."

I can hear the smile in his raspy voice.

"My appointment for tomorrow night just canceled, so I'm curious if you might be available for food and drinks. Otherwise, I'm also available Sunday. They have a dynamite ultimate Bloody Mary bar down at Boardman's on Water Street on Sundays. Anyway, give me a call to let me know if this works for you. Enjoy the rest of your night!"

By the end of Wildman's message, I catch myself smiling and wonder if it's possible for me to meet a third great guy. I'm actually starting to think the odds might be in my favor after all.

chapter thirty-four

My Saturday shift at McGinn's flies by in such a flurry, the staff barely has a chance to breathe, likely because it's the first day the patio is open for the season. No one takes a break in fear of getting backed up and causing angry customers. Molly even helps out with delivering orders, and her husband, George, helps out behind the bar. Needless to say, Sawyer and I don't have too many opportunities to say more than a few words to each other. However, we did text back and forth a few times last night because he was wondering how things turned out with Ryan and Ashley.

When I'm in the back punching out, Sawyer peeks his head out of the kitchen, like he usually does. I wonder sometimes how he always seems to know when I'm back here. Then again, he always seems to know where everyone is, even though you'd never guess he was paying any attention. I'm really going to miss having him around here when he goes back to his company in a week.

"Psst . . . Freckles."

I laugh quietly as I close my locker and throw my purse over my shoulder. Then I turn and mimic him. "Psst . . . Sawyer."

"You think you're so cute," he says coming out from around the corner and walking over to meet me in the middle of the back room.

"Nope. I know I'm cute."

"So, Wildman, huh?" I'd asked him last night if he thought I should be worried about a guy with such a screen name. He'd replied *no comment.*

"Yep, he's picking me up outside my apartment at nine, so I need to get moving."

"Alright, well, be safe and have fun. Not too much fun though." He gives me a light tap on the shoulder as he turns and heads back to the kitchen.

"Thanks. I'll talk to you later."

He puts up a hand without looking back before he disappears from sight.

~

At around nine twenty, a black van pulls up in front of my apartment building. I stand slowly, hoping it's not Wildman. Something about a black van on a first date irks me. I'm about to text Wildman to see if it is him, when someone pops out of the driver's side of the van and taps on the roof.

"Hey hey hey! Jess, right?"

"Yeahhh . . ." I say, making my way down the walkway at a snail's pace. "Wildman?"

"Wildman, Brock, whatever floats your boat," he says in his raspy exuberant voice. "Vamonos, chica!" He taps the top of the van a few more times and disappears into the van.

I'm torn between the harmless vibe he's putting out and this ominous van in front of me. But then I notice something as I get closer. The beam from an overhead street light is shining on a graphic on the side of the vehicle. It says *Wildman's Party Squad*. Oh, boy.

Sighing, I get in, and before I even have my seatbelt buckled, Wildman peels away from the curb.

"Whoa," I mutter clicking my belt in and then gripping at my seat.

"Sorry I was late. I had a call come in and had to find someone to take the job last minute. I figured you wouldn't be too keen on bar hopping with strangers on our first date."

"It isn't the worst first date idea I've ever heard," I say, shrugging and relaxing a little in my seat.

"Right on." He peeks over at me, nodding and smiling. "A party girl."

"I wouldn't go that far, but I've done my fair share of barhopping," I say chuckling. "So your business is all about driving drunk people around, huh?"

"You got it." He nods no less than twenty times in quick succession.

"I take it Wildman is a nickname?"

"Nope. It's just ma name. Brock Wildman." He keeps his eyes on the road and continues with the little head bobs, which are starting to make me dizzy.

"Wait, so your last name is actually Wildman?" I grin and suppress a giggle.

"Yep."

"That's perfect."

"I know, right?" He reaches out and turns up the volume on the stereo and we rock out to Led Zeppelin the rest of the way to the bar.

As we drive down Water Street, several people point at Brock's van and a few wave.

"So is this the vehicle you always drive? Or do you have something smaller for errands and stuff?"

"This is it. It's like a billboard on wheels. You wouldn't believe how many calls we get from people after they've seen me drive by. I bet my boy, Dano, who's manning the phones for the night, will get at least one call just from us driving down this road tonight."

I nod, impressed with his business sense.

Brock parks the van in a bank's parking lot, so we have to walk a few blocks back to the long stretch of Water Street bars. Any question I ask is answered with a joke or another question, making me wonder if he's ever serious about anything. He's funny though, so it doesn't bother me one bit.

When we get to the first bar, Brock lays out the plan for me. We're going to have one drink at each bar until we get to the end of the line.

"That's like twelve bars," I say, stunned.

He laughs and opens the door motioning for me to enter, and so my pub crawl with Brock Wildman of Wildman's Party Squad begins. Every time we enter a bar people greet him and want to have a drink with him, and every time we leave, someone tags along with us to the next bar. Even though Brock appears to be looking out for me and always introduces me to whoever he's talking to, it doesn't feel like we're on a date. It feels more like it's 1999, and I'm out whooping it up with my posse from college.

By the time we get to the seventh bar, I've lost count of how many drinks Brock has had. He's managed to down one drink of his choice at each establishment, yet countless people have bought mixers and shots for him as well. I started drinking water at the third bar, so I'm fully alert when Brock nearly falls over on our way out of that seventh bar.

"Whoa, there, big guy," I say, catching him and leaning him against the outside of the building. "It's almost one. We should get going."

"Nah," he slurs, staggering forward. "The night is still young."

"Brock—" I begin to protest, but he unzips his fly and starts peeing right in the gutter, rendering me speechless. *Oh my God, oh my God, oh my God.* I look around, hopeful that he finishes before someone sees what he's doing. That's when I see a cop rushing toward us.

Shit.

Brock has no idea how lucky he is that I'm so well-versed in sweet talking my way out of sticky situations. Because I'm sober, and Brock agreed to let me drive his van, the officer let him go with a citation for public urination. When I first got into the driver's seat, I was shaking I was so nervous, but the van ended up being a lot easier to drive than I thought it would be. Brock? He passed out as soon as a couple of bouncers heaved him onto the back seat. Instead of driving him to my place, I fished his wallet out of his pocket and took him to his place. Then I left his keys on the floor next to him, locked his van doors and started walking. That's when I realized walking was going to take at least an hour.

So here I am, sitting on the stoop in front of a stranger's house in the city of Greenfield. My first thought is to take a bus, but I decide I'd rather walk first. The bus is full of creeps at this hour. My second thought is to call Chloe, but it's a little after two now, so there's no way I'm going to wake her up. Then, on impulse, I whip open my phone and dial Justin only to remember the moment I hit send that he's at a water park with Max. I doubt the call even connected before I closed my phone. I think long and hard for a few seconds before opening my phone again.

"Jesstine?"

"Hey, sorry to call so late."

"Is everything okay?" The slight panic in his voice makes me smile.

"Yeah, yeah, everything's fine. But I need a favor . . ."

Sawyer pulls up fifteen minutes later.

"Thank you so much. You have no idea how much I appreciate you doing this," I say as I get in and buckle up.

"No problem. You can call me for a ride anytime." He looks over at me and smiles. "Wanna tell me how you ended up here?" He asks as he pulls away from the curb.

I sneak a peek at Wildman's van as we pass by and start to laugh. By the time I'm done telling Sawyer about my night, he's had a few good chuckles too.

"That's what you get for going out with a guy named *Wildman*."

I nod and grin out the window as Sawyer turns down a street not far from McGinn's.

"Didn't you say you live near here?"

"Yeah, I can drive by my place if you want. I'm wide awake now."

"Sure, why not."

A few minutes later, he leaves the car idling in front of a large brick duplex with a huge lower front porch. "This is it."

"Are you renting?"

"No," he says shaking his head. "Beth and I have owned this place for ten years now. When we bought our home in Fox Point two years ago, we started renting this one out. Luckily, one of our tenants happened to put in his notice in January, so I decided to move back in. I've always loved this place."

"The brickwork looks beautiful. I mean, it's dark, but still."

"Yeah, I redid all the tuckpointing myself a few summers ago," he says, staring at the house with a faraway look. I can only imagine the memories he must have of this place after owning it for ten years and living here with Beth. "She was pregnant at the time, but she lost it. It was right when we were getting ready to start up the business."

"I'm so sorry," I say putting my hand on his knee.

"Do you want to see the inside?" he asks, his gaze migrating from my hand to my eyes.

"I actually have to get up in a few hours," I sigh. "It's going to be a looong day tomorrow."

"I better get you home then," he says before he slowly pulls away from the curb.

After a few blocks, Justin calls. I debate whether to answer or not, but then I remember dialing his number, so I figure he might think something's wrong if I don't.

"Hey, Justin." I sneak a peek at Sawyer. His eyes are focused on the road.

"I got up to use the bathroom and saw you called. What's going on? Are you okay?"

"Yeah, I'm fine. Long story."

"Well, where are you?"

I hesitate before answering. "I was stranded in Greenfield earlier, so I called you right away forgetting you're in the Dells with Max. Luckily Sawyer was around. He's driving me home as we speak."

The line goes silent long enough that I wonder if we've been disconnected.

"Justin? Are you still there?"

He sighs. "Why didn't you call Chloe?"

"Uhh, because she's a super deep sleeper so she wouldn't have answered anyway." I almost blew it and revealed her pregnancy.

"Well, maybe it's time to think of a different Plan C the next time you need a ride."

I glance over at Sawyer again, and his eyes remain glued to the road. I'm debating whether or not I want to continue this ridiculous conversation with Justin. Who does he think he is? I'll call whomever I want to call when I need a ride somewhere.

"Right, well, have fun tomorrow, and I'll talk to you soon." I hang up before he has a chance to reply.

chapter thirty-five

It takes until Tuesday for me to feel caught up enough on sleep to agree to go out with my co-workers. We're on an overnight in Philly and have a seven o'clock reservation. I've just finished changing into regular clothes when there's a knock on my door. Out of habit, I check the peephole before letting Mindy in.

"Hey? I thought we were meeting in the lobby at quarter to." Mindy scurries in and I close the door as I turn to face her. "What's going on?"

She's sitting on the sofa, her elbows on her knees and her eyes on the floor.

"Mindy, what's up?"

She looks up at me, her eyes glazed with tears. "He won't leave me alone."

Even though she says *he,* I know exactly who she's talking about. I sigh and take a seat in the chair across from her.

"I keep telling him to stop calling me, that it was a mistake and I don't want to be anyone's mistress. He. Won't. Leave. Me. Alone." Suddenly she stands and starts pacing from the bed to the couch. "What am I going to do, Jess?"

I want to ask her why she would sleep with Brant in the first place, knowing he has a wife and kids, and I want to tell her she probably deserves what's happening to her. But most of all, I want to help her, because I know exactly how she feels.

"Have you thought about changing your number?"

"I did that, now he shows up at my apartment at the most random, fucked up times of day. He'll knock and knock *and knock* until I answer the door. And if I don't answer he'll sit out in his car sometimes until I have to go somewhere. He's a fucking psycho!"

Wow, Brant has upped his stalker game with poor Mindy.

"Have you considered finding a new apartment?"

She dismisses me with a shake of her head. "I'm not going to let him run me out of my home."

"Don't take this the wrong way, Mindy, but why did you come to me with this? I'm happy to continue brainstorming ideas with you, but—"

"I'm not asking you to fix this for me." She's standing right in front of me now with her arms folded across her chest. "I just need someone to talk to. Anne told me . . . about you and Brant."

Why, Anne? Why?! I purse my lips and stare at Mindy, refusing to confirm or deny whatever Anne told her.

"She said the two of you were thinking about reporting him. Is that true? Because I'm too scared to do something like that. He has so many friends with the company." She shakes her head and starts pacing again. "I have nobody. I'd probably lose my job."

"What made you realize he was full of shit?" After my talk with Anne, I was seriously considering outing him to his wife, but I kept coming back to the same thought. What if his wife truly is as terrible as he claims she is? Would she even care? So I ask Mindy this because I'm curious to find out if he told her a different story.

"He said he was separated from his wife because she's horrible to him—always saying demeaning things to him in front of their kids, always cutting down his friends and family. He also said she never spends time with their kids and leaves them at her parents' house all the time so she can go out shopping and for dinner and drinks with her friends. He mentioned that she never cooks, so he has to do all the cooking otherwise their kids eat crappy food. I was skeptical, so I drove over to his house one day when I knew he was working, just to try to get a look at his wife. Well guess what? Everything he said about that woman was a lie. She was wearing mom jeans and a hooded sweatshirt, and she looked exhausted. I mean, she was really pretty, but in a plain way, as if she hasn't had her hair or makeup done in decades. And then there were the kids, all smiling and helping her unload the groceries from the back of their minivan. One kid had on a soccer uniform and she was praising him for playing so well in his game. He lied about everything, Jess. *Everything*."

My blood is boiling by the time Mindy finishes rehashing all of

Brant's lies. The same lies he'd told me. At least she had the smarts to call him on his bluff by investigating his claims.

"So did you tell him you saw his wife and kids when you tried to call things off?"

She nods. "He still tried to keep up with his lies."

"That's because he's a psychopath."

"God, I feel like such a fool."

"You and me both, Mindy. You and me both."

Later that night, as I lie in bed holding my phone, I think about all the times Brant sat in his car or in a closet in his house talking to me and all the times he snuck off to my apartment when he said he was going out with buddies. Those weren't even the worst of his actions. The worst was when the asshole would ignore his kids to text or talk to me when he claimed his wife was out shopping or having drinks with her friends. He's just one big lie, and his wife really deserves better. Mindy deserves better. I deserve better. *Every woman* deserves better.

I punch in Brant's home number, which Anne somehow got. I'm about to press send when my phone vibrates.

Justin: I'm glad we worked things out. Sometimes I really put my foot in my mouth. But at least you can count on me to always be honest with you. Sweet dreams, Jess.

Justin and I had a long conversation Sunday night about his suggestion that I need to think of a Plan C the next time I find myself needing a ride somewhere. We both knew what he was really getting at, though, that he didn't like the idea of me counting on Sawyer for anything. I'm pretty sure we've come to an understanding now, though —that I will continue to ask whomever the hell I want for whatever the hell I need—so things are back to normal between us.

Me: I'm glad too. Good night, Justin.

After I click to send the text to Justin, I hold my phone for a few minutes debating whether calling Brant's wife will do more harm than good. Will exposing him cause harm to his children? He might ignore them sometimes, but if his kids are as happy as Mindy said they appeared to be, then he must be a somewhat okay father. I consider how I would feel if my dad had stayed with my mom while continuing to cheat on her. I most likely wouldn't have known a thing about it, and at least my dad would have been there. But would that have been fair at the expense of my mother's dignity and happiness?

My stomach is in knots so I flip my phone shut and place it on the nightstand, shelving the decision for later.

The next day, on our flight back to Milwaukee, a passenger standing near the back flags me over. I assumed she was waiting for the restroom, but neither of the lavatories are occupied.

"Hey, can I ask something?" She backs into the aft galley as she speaks.

"Of course. Is everything okay?"

"How often do you work with Brant Mathis?"

At first, I panic, wondering if she could be Brant's wife, but I recover quickly realizing that Mindy would have recognized her. Next, I study her, doing my best to hide how shocked I am by her question. "Uh, not that often. Maybe . . . oh, I don't know, once a month? Why do you ask?"

She shakes her head sadly, leans in and whispers, "I'm a friend of his wife, Bryn. She just found out he's been cheating on her . . . again." She backs away, suddenly eyeing me with uncertainty. "This time with a flight attendant."

Mouth ajar and slowly shaking my head in disbelief, I clutch my chest. Little does she know that what I really can't believe is the way she's spilling her friend's business to a perfect stranger. A perfect stranger who's a colleague of Brant's at that.

After a few seconds, she sighs and her suspicious expression morphs into one of despair. She just stands there, hugging herself tightly and staring at the floor. I'm about to ask if I can get her anything when she makes eye contact with me again and breaks the uncomfortable silence.

"I've been telling her for years that he's no good, but she's too good of a wife and mom to leave him . . . Even though this kind of thing keeps happening." Her gaze falls to the floor again, but she continues. "First it was a co-pilot back when he worked for Delta. Then it was an old babysitter of theirs who confessed to Bryn that Brant had seduced her when he drove her home one night. He's lucky Bryn shooed the girl away and never reported it to the cops. That girl was only seventeen at the time!" She takes a much-needed breath, pulls a mini bottle of vodka out of her purse, and downs it. Then she holds the empty bottle up and asks, "Can I get a couple more of these?"

That explains her openness.

"Uh, yes, of course. If you'll just head back to your seat, I can—"

"You know what the worst part about all of this is?" She pauses just long enough for me to shake my head once. "He fucked me too. When my divorce was finalized last March. He was always flirting with me and then caught me in a moment of weakness." She looks up at me, matching my wide-eyed gaze before scurrying off to her seat. Despite her inebriated state, I'm guessing she realized she'd said too much.

I never deliver the mini bottles of vodka she asked for, nor do I talk to her or make eye contact with her again. But I do spend the rest of the flight pondering who I feel sorrier for: the drunk woman in 9D or Brant's wife. When all the passengers have disembarked, she pauses and shoots me an embarrassed smile as she makes her way up the jet bridge.

"I wonder what that was about," Mindy says, a fake smile plastered to her face as she waves to the last of the passengers.

"No idea," I say through my smiling teeth, hoping that Mindy's Brant issue has been solved.

chapter thirty-six

"Welcome Home!" Chris hollers to Justin and I when we enter Home Bar.

"Hey, Chris," I say as I crane my neck to scan the crowd gathered for Daran's surprise birthday party. I recognize Shelly, Craig and some of Chloe's family and teacher friends, but I don't see my mom yet, and there are some faces I don't recognize who I assume belong to Daran's co-workers.

"Good to see you again." Justin leans over the bar to shake Chris's hand.

"You guys probably already know there's free Miller for the party. Either of you want one?"

"Sure, I'll take one, and Jess will have aaaa . . ." he looks at me so I can fill in the blank."

"A vodka gimlet, please." I check my phone for the time and Chris gets our drinks. "Hey, do you know exactly what the plan is here?"

Chris shrugs as he adds lime juice to my drink. "All I know about is the beer and to yell *surprise* instead of *welcome home* when Chloe and Daran walk in. They probably know, though." He nods his head to our right and that's when Shelly and Craig greet Justin and I.

"Duuude!" Craig grips Justin's shoulder with one hand and shakes his hand with the other.

"Hi, guys!" Shelly squeals, her voice making me want to walk out the door, as usual. "Isn't this exciting?" She places two empty pint glasses on the bar for Chris to refill.

Why? Why is Daran's birthday exciting to you? So you have an excuse to get shitfaced?

"Yep, it sure is," I say, reaching for Chris to hand me my drink instead of setting it on the bar. "So, what's the plan?" I ask as soon as

Justin finishes answering some question Craig just asked about the Brewers. Then he throws a five on the bar as he grabs his beer.

"Well," Shelly checks her phone, "Chloe is pretending they have a dinner reservation at that little Italian place down the road, and I'm supposed to call her at six fifteen and ask her to drop off my driver's license, which I left in her car yesterday when we went to the gym. So, that's in about twenty minutes." She checks her phone again.

"Huh, that's actually a good plan," I say. Then I look at Justin. "Do you want to head back there?"

He nods and reaches for my lower back as we squeeze by Shelly and Craig.

"We'll meet you back there as soon as Chris fills our beers," Shelly calls after us.

"Oh, goody," I mumble so not even Justin can hear.

The first person who sees me is Chloe's sister Sarah. "Jess!" She rushes over and gives me a hug while her husband Dave shakes Justin's hand. "It's been so long."

"I know. Since you guys first moved back from Vegas?"

"Oh my gosh, yeah, it really has been that long."

Once our greeting winds down, I give Dave a hug and formally introduce Justin to both of them. Then we all walk over to where Chloe's mom, Jan, and her stepdad, Glen, are sitting. Glen's a really nice guy but doesn't talk much. He just smiles and waves. Jan, on the other hand . . .

"Who's this? Your new boyfriend?" Chloe's mom isn't big on greetings . . . or beating around the bush. Sarah rolls her eyes and Dave chuckles as he pretends to watch someone shooting darts.

"Hi, Jan. Nice to see you again," I say, stealing a stiff hug from her. "This is Justin."

Justin jumps right in and outstretches his hand to Chloe's mom and then to Glen. "Nice to meet you, both."

"Whatever happened to that car salesman?"

"We broke up months ago, Jan," I say, plastering on my best pleasant flight attendant face.

"Hmph, you and Chloe," she says shaking her head. "You girls and all your boyfriends." She looks at Justin. "You know, the two of them used to run up my phone bill calling all the boys. They've always been boy crazy. Thank *God* Chloe met Daran." She looks back at me. "Did she tell you I prayed for him?"

"Okay, Mom," Sarah says.

"What?" Jan asks. "I did."

"I know, but nobody here wants to hear about your prayers."

"Actually—" Dave starts to say something but Sarah elbows him.

I glance at Justin wondering if he's at all bothered by Jan mentioning Ned. But he's stifling a grin and seems to be enjoying the conversation that's still going on between Jan and Sarah. He takes a sip of his beer and then glances at me, giving me a little wink.

"Okay, everyone! I'm going to be calling in ten minutes," Shelly announces. "I repeat, *ten minutes*. So get your drinks refilled. Go to the bathroom. Smoke your cigarettes." *Okay, I think we get it.* "Do whatever you have to do, but be back here in *ten minutes*." She holds up her hands, fingers outstretched to emphasize her point, making me want to scream.

I check my phone to see if my mom called or texted to say she's going to be late, but my screen isn't showing any notifications. "Hmm," I say to myself.

Justin puts his free hand on my lower back and leans in. "Everything okay?"

"Yeah, it's just, my mom is supposed to be here. She's never late for things, especially surprise parties."

"I'm sure she's on her way," He says, rubbing my back in circles.

"I hope so," I say, checking my phone again.

As we wait for Shelly to make the call to Chloe, everyone begins to gather in a herd at the end of the bar facing the door. There's a lot of chatter all around Justin and I, but we're just standing, smiling at each other and sipping our drinks. He really is a handsome guy, and the way he's rubbing my back is giving me tiny heart palpitations. It feels good and scary at the same time.

"Ooookayyy, it's tiiime." Shelly steps onto the rungs of a stool and waves her hands signaling everyone to quiet down. Craig makes the same motion from where he's standing next to her, making himself look like her lackey.

"Oh, hey Chloe." She's talking slow like a robot. It's so annoying. "Say, did I happen to leave my *ID* in your car? . . . Oh! I did? . . . We're at Home Bar." She nods her head really fast and grins at everyone. "That would be so awesome of you. See you soon, bye!" As soon as Shelly ends the call, she goes into DEFCON 2 mode, frantically ordering people to stand here or there, hollering to Chris to have drinks ready for Chloe and Daran, and checking the time every five seconds. Justin and I calmly stand there sipping our drinks, and I'm exhausted just from watching her.

When my mom walks in, Shelly's mode is elevated to DEFCON 1. She scurries over to retrieve my mom to bring her over to join the rest of the troops. But my mom shakes her head and gestures toward the door when Shelly tries to get her moving. Rod must be parking the car or something. The poor guy has no idea what he's about to walk into. Shelly's going to be all over him. The door opens and Shelly immediately grabs Rod by the sleeve and pulls him behind her right after my mom who's laughing and already heading toward us. The sight causes a jolt of laughter to travel through the crowd. The next thing I know I'm giving my mom a hug. When we separate I plan to completely ignore Rod and skip right to introducing them to Justin, except when I look up at the face behind my mom, it isn't Rod as I assumed. It's Terry, my stepdad. I stare at him, dumbfounded, while my mom and him stare at me and then at each other. They're all smiles. I give him a quick hug right before Chris whistles, quieting everyone down.

"They're almost here," he says, as he cranes his neck to see from his prime spot at the end of the bar. Then he quickly normalizes his posture, grabs a rag, and pretends to be wiping the bar.

That's when the door opens and Chloe and Daran walk in.

"SURPRISE!"

Daran shakes his head, a bemused look on his face, as people make their way over to where he and Chloe are standing. Before he greets anyone, he gives Chloe a big hug.

After Justin and I say happy birthday to Daran and hi to Chloe, we find a nice, quiet spot in the corner and chat with my mom and stepdad. At first, I wanted to ask how Terry ended up at the party with her, but then I realized there's no need. All I had to do was look at the smile on my mom's face to figure out that her belief in soulmates has been rekindled. That's why Terry's here.

About fifteen minutes after Chloe and Daran's big entrance, Chloe stands up to announce that pizzas are being delivered any minute. She also reminds people that there's free beer until ten. I held my breath at first when she asked for everyone's attention because I thought it was time for the other surprise. I wish I could somehow ask her when she plans to spill the beans, because I certainly hope she isn't planning on waiting until ten after everyone has had their fill of beer. When Chloe finishes talking, Shelly sticks a beer in her face, for the second time since she walked through the door. I watch as Chloe rubs her stomach feigning illness, and I laugh to myself as I imagine what Shelly's face is going to look like when Chloe makes the announcement. Not even five minutes later, when I see Shelly try to push the beer on Chloe again, I decide enough is enough and I excuse myself from the conversation I'm having with my mom, Terry, and Justin.

"Hi, ladies," I say as I set my empty glass on the bar. Chris picks it up and holds it up as a way to ask if I'd like another. I shake my head and mouth *no thanks*.

"What gives?" Shelly asks looking from Chloe to me. "You're done? And Chloe's not drinking at all?"

I shrug. "Not in the mood for liquor. But I am in the mood for cake and ice cream." I smile at Chloe.

"You guys are so boring," Shelly says, rolling her eyes and turning toward the bar to wait for hers and Craig's beers to be refilled.

"Thanks a lot," Chloe says, raising her eyebrows at me a hair and nodding toward the jukebox.

"I'm picking some songs. Wanna join me?' I say to Chloe.

"Sure!"

We travel a few feet to the jukebox and hunch over as we look through the glass and pretend to pick songs even though neither of us has put any money into the machine.

"So when are you going to do it?" I ask.

"I should do it soon, right?"

"No point putting it off."

"All right. As soon as the pizza gets here."

"Speak of the devil," I say as I see the delivery guy walk in with a mountain of pizza boxes.

Everyone is spread out at tables munching on pizza when Chloe and Daran stand next to each other in front of the bar.

"Ahem," Chloe says loudly. "May we please have everyone's attention?"

Chris turns down the background music and eyes throughout the bar migrate to Chloe and Daran.

"We actually have another surprise tonight."

It gets even quieter, but Chloe doesn't say anything She just stands there grinning nervously. Then out of nowhere, Daran, apparently not one for beating around the bush either, says loudly, "Chloe's nine weeks pregnant. We're having a baby. Thanks . . . for all the birthday wishes."

Chloe stares at him, her mouth frozen open in shock, but he just pulls her in for a hug, rubs her back a little, and goes back to the table where his pizza is getting cold.

A mixture of reactions spread throughout our crowd. Justin squeezes my hand, Chloe's sister squeals, her stepdad smiles, Daran's co-workers take turns patting him on the back, my mom makes eye contact with me and golf claps a few times, and Chloe's mom keeps asking people if Chloe and Daran are joking. But the absolute best reaction is from Shelly, who I made sure to watch more closely than anyone. The moment the words left Daran's lips, the sip of beer she'd been taking spilled down her shirt, and now she's standing there holding her beer with her mouth open.

After people have their fill of pizza, we sing to Daran, and cake and ice cream is served. Shortly after that, people start saying their goodbyes to Daran and congratulations to the expectant couple. It seems announcing you're expecting a baby is one way to save money on an open bar because by the time nine o'clock rolls around, the only people left are Chloe, Daran, Shelly, Craig, Justin and me. The guys are shooting pool, and we girls are sitting at a table next to the bar.

"I'm surprised you and Justin are still seeing each other," Shelly says.

Chloe is eating ice cream right out of the tub.

"I know. I can't believe online dating is actually working for me."

Shelly lets out a little laugh. "So just because you've been dating a guy for a few weeks, you think he's the one? How would you even know that?"

"First of all, I didn't say I thought he was the one. I said I think online dating is working for me. Oh, and not that I really care what you think, Shelly, but we've been dating for almost two months."

"Trust me. It's possible to know someone is the one, regardless of how long you've known them." Chloe interjects. Then she goes back to her ice cream.

Shelly glances at Chloe. "Oh I'm not saying it isn't possible for *anyone*. It's just, with all the guys Jess has . . . dated," she looks at me, "nothing ever seems to stick. Except for Ned. But the only reason you kept *him* around so long is because that guy isn't actually available." She puts air quotes around available. "In order for online dating to work I think you have to actually be open to finding *one* person. Look at Chloe."

I bite my tongue because the only things I'm thinking to say to Shelly are things I know I'll regret.

"I think you're wrong, Shelly," Chloe points her spoon a few inches from Shelly's face and I love her for it. "Jess is totally going to end up with someone she meets while she's online dating. In fact, she might have already met him."

I wonder if she's referring to Justin or Sawyer when she says that last bit.

"Hey, ladies," Chris says, leaning over the bar, "Not that I'm listening, buuut . . . okay, so I'm listening. I'd just like to say that I think Jess is going to end up finding someone too."

"Awww, thanks, Chris," I say. Then I blow him a kiss.

He catches it, pretends to slap it on his cheek, and goes back to work. Chloe laughs at our silliness.

"Oh yeah," Shelly calls after him, "I'll bet you a dollar she doesn't."

Chris turns and points at her, "You're on, sister."

Just then, Craig calls out from a few feet away. "How about a round of shots, ladies? Justin's in."

"What are you talking about? Chloe can't do a shot." Shelly gives Craig the fiercest eye roll I've ever seen her deliver.

"I obviously didn't mean *her*," Craig shoots back.

"I could do a shot of seltzer," Chloe offers.

Shelly scoffs at her.

"What is your problem, Shelly? We just told everyone I'm pregnant, and you've been a real downer ever since. Do you even realize that?"

"Can you blame me? You and Daran have known each other for what? Four months? Are you guys sure you're ready to have a *child* together? You don't have to go through with it, you know."

"What the fuck, Shelly?" Chloe asks, her voice more hurt than angry.

"I just think it's a bad idea. You're not ready for a baby." Shelly stands and grabs her purse off the table.

"Thanks a lot. Thanks for the support," Chloe says, nodding. She sounds like she's about to cry.

"Let's go, Craig." Craig looks confused but dutifully follows Shelly out the door.

And just like that, Shelly and Craig are gone. They don't even bother to say goodbye to any of us.

"Well, that was a pretty shitty thing for her to say."

Chloe nods her agreement, but I can tell she probably didn't even hear what I said. She's just staring at the table and running her finger along the side of the sweaty ice cream container.

Not much later, the rest of us decide to call it a night too. We give each other hugs, and Justin and I congratulate Chloe and Daran again for the miracle they've created together. We're all on our way out the door when Justin realizes he needs to use the restroom. Instead of following Chloe and Daran outside, I wait at the bar and ponder what Shelly said about me and relationships. As much as I hate her, she's right. Nothing but my dead-end relationship with Ned has ever stuck.

"Why so glum, Jess?" asks Chris.

"Do you really want to know?" I ask.

"Of course I do," he says, leaning his forearms on the bar.

"I have a feeling Shelly might be right, and I might not end up with anyone at the end of all this online dating nonsense."

He stands with a huff and shakes his head. "Shelly doesn't know what she's talking about. I'll bet *you* a dollar, too, that you're wrong."

I ponder his proposition as Justin makes his way toward us.

"Yeah, sure, what the heck. At least you'll owe me a dollar if I end up single after all of this."

chapter thirty-seven

It's Sawyer's last day at McGinn's. He told Molly he didn't want anyone doing anything special for him, and he didn't want any of the regulars to know. Funny how balloons are everywhere and there's a huge sign hanging above the bar that says *We'll miss you, Sawyer!* Molly even has the new cook, who's taking Sawyer's place, working the dinner shift, so Sawyer doesn't have to focus on running the show. Good thing, too, because everyone's talking to the poor guy today, but he's being a good sport about all of the unwanted attention. Poor me, too. I secretly wish I could have him all to myself.

When I punch out at eight, Sawyer does, too. The fact that I'll never stand with him in this back room again after tonight is driven home when he tosses his time card in the trash. The sense of finality that suddenly overtakes me makes me feel panicked.

"I'm going to miss you," I blurt.

"No worries, Freckles, I don't intend to stop harassing you via text. In fact, you might want to look into purchasing a bigger data plan." Consumed by my sad thoughts, I watch silently as he removes his chef's jacket and tosses it into the dirty bin. "So, what are your plans for tonight? Perhaps a pub crawl? Or maybe some beer pong over at the Kappa Delta Sigma house on Lake Drive?"

"Never again," I say, with a laugh. Leave it to Sawyer to dash my melancholy with a joke at my expense. "If anything good came out of my date with Wildman, it's that I now know I'm too old for that shit."

"Wanna get a coffee at Hi-Fi?"

I balk at his suggestion. "You can't leave. There's still a lot of people out there who want to say goodbye to you."

"Yeah, I know," he says with a sigh. "I suppose I can soldier through another couple hours . . . but only if you soldier through with me." He nudges me as we make our way to the bar area.

"I think our friend here might be needing a ride home tonight," Bobby says, plopping a fresh glass of water down on the bar in front of me. Then he rushes off to a guy waving cash over his head at the other end of the bar.

"Thank you!" I call after him.

Bobby was referring to Sawyer, of course, who has just accepted his fourth farewell shot. He's too nice to say no to all these people who are coming out of the woodwork to say goodbye to him.

Two hours passed before I finally have Sawyer all to myself. I turn to him and we sit grinning a each other until Bobby drops off a Miller Lite. "It's from Mickey," He points over to one of the regulars who always keeps to himself, watching TV and smoking one cigarette after another. The standoffish old man holds his beer up in our direction, and Sawyer does the same, a nod exchanged between them.

"So," Sawyer says.

"So," I respond.

"You like this Justin guy, huh?"

"Like is a vague word. Can you be more specific?"

He looks to the ceiling, searching for a better word. "Do you *fancy* him?" His terrible attempt at a British accent takes me by surprise and I find myself laughing so hard it hurts.

"Hmm, let's see," I say, my laughter tapering off. "How should I put this? I really like banana pancakes with butter—no syrup—but I fancy warm peanut butter brownies with a scoop of homemade whipped cream. I suppose the way I feel about Justin falls closer to the pancakes end of the spectrum, at this point in our relationship anyway. If I never got to eat them again, I'd remember the flavor fondly, and move on. But never being able to eat peanut butter brownies with homemade whipped cream again? That would devastate me to my core."

"But you still plan to go out with him again." It's not exactly a question, simply a benign statement spoken by a guy who's half drunk.

"Well, yeah, of course I do. I don't have any other serious prospects at the moment, and . . . he really is a nice guy." My response is met with a blank stare. Then Bobby shows up again.

"No playboy tonight?" Bobby asks, referring to the conversation Justin and I had with him a few weeks ago about online dating.

"You mean Justin? Nope, he's working." I stifle a yawn.

A wide grin spreads across Bobby's face. "Let me guess," he says, raising his eyebrows, "late night last night with playboy?"

I shrug. "Maybe. Not that it's any of your business."

"Hold up," Sawyer chimes in. "Why do you keep calling him playboy?"

"The guy's an old pro at online dating. Says he's hooked up with at least thirty women."

"Hang on," I say raising a palm. "We don't know that he *hooked up* with all of them. All he said was he *met* thirty women."

"Yeah, okay. Whatever you say, Jess." Bobby gives Sawyer a look that I assume means he thinks I've had the wool pulled over my eyes. Little does he know, a guy sleeping with thirty or more women doesn't faze me one bit. But until now, I haven't even considered that Justin might have a little playboy blood coursing through his veins. "I'll be back." Bobby heads off to do his job.

"So," Sawyer says with a smirk. "It doesn't bother you that he's been with that many women?"

I laugh, rolling my eyes. "I have no idea how many women he's been with. So no, I'm not the least bit bothered. Why? How many women have you been with?"

"Twelve."

"Wow, that was fast."

"Did you expect I'd have to think about it?"

"Well, yeah, I think most guys would take longer than that."

He shrugs. "How about you?"

"You can't ask me that!" I say, giving him my best stink eye.

"Why not? You just asked me, and I told you. So how many?"

"I don't know," I say, shaking my head. No one has ever asked me this question before.

"Ballpark."

"You've seen my coaster collection. Your guess is as good as mine."

Sawyer closes his eyes and taps his chin, as if he's picturing my collection. Just when the thought of him guessing how many guys I've slept with starts to become awkward, Bobby returns.

"So, back to playboy. Brilliant idea using the internet to hook up with chicks. I signed up this morning and already have a date lined up for Sunday night."

"That's great, Bobby. But like I said, I'm pretty sure Justin wasn't using Yahoo! Personals to hook up with chicks. He said so himself that he's looking for something that sticks. Remember?"

"Did you hook up with him?"

"Uhhhm, once again, that's a pretty private question, don't you think?"

"You did! I knew it." Suddenly his expression turns serious. "Wait . . . didn't he say he was dating some other chick too? You're cool with that?"

"Knock it off, Bobby," Sawyer snaps.

Bobby backs off with his hands in the air. "Sooorry. Geez."

After Bobby leaves, I gently backhand Sawyer's shoulder and say, "What was that about?"

"Eh," he waves Bobby off. "Bobby's cool but he can be a real loud mouth. So, does Justin really have his own coaster now?"

I shrug, neither confirming nor denying. "Would you have a problem with that?"

"No, but you did say he was like banana pancakes. So . . ."

"For the record, I'm not collecting coasters anymore."

"Good," he says before finishing off his beer.

"Hey, you two! Mind if I join you for a few?" Anne outstretches her arms around Sawyer and I, creating a weird sort of group hug that she's in the middle of.

"Hey, Anne," I say, moving over so she can squeeze a chair in between Sawyer and me. "I'm actually just having water tonight."

"How about you, Sawyer?"

"Sure, I'll have one more."

I do my best to outlast Anne, hoping she'll leave soon so I can suggest to Sawyer that we leave, but by the time eleven o'clock rolls around, I can barely keep my eyes open, even with Anne's amusing story about a guitar-playing passenger who had everyone singing Bon Jovi tunes for the duration of an entire flight. And neither Sawyer nor Anne appear to be slowing down on the alcohol intake.

"Guys," I say hopping off my stool, "I need to get going."

"Okay, sweetie." Anne wraps her arms around me and gives me a ridiculously long squeeze. "We'll see you next week."

She releases me and turns to the bar to talk to Bobby, and Sawyer slides off his stool to stand in front of me. According to my count, he shouldn't even be able to stand, but he seems surprisingly stable.

"You're leaving."

"Yeah, I'm tired," I say with a yawn. "I'll remind Bobby to call you a cab."

He opens his arms to me and I dive in, more than willing to hug him anytime he offers.

"Stay," he whispers in my ear.

I sigh, haggling with my need to go home and crawl into bed versus my always-present desire to be around Sawyer.

"Sawyer! Come on. Do a shot with me!" Anne pulls Sawyer's arm and he slowly separates from me but maintains eye contact.

"Stay," he mouths, wide-eyed, before turning toward the bar.

I shake my head with a sigh and follow.

While I sit and watch everyone around me become even more inebriated, I repeatedly bring my shirt collar up to my nose so I can take in Sawyer's scent, which rubbed off on me when we hugged. Despite the fact that we're "just friends," it makes me want to hug him close again.

"Kind of ironic how you were teasing me about pub crawls yesterday, and now you need my help unlocking your door. Wouldn't you say?" I joke, as I unlock Sawyer's front door with the third and final key on his keychain.

He surprises me by belting out a few lines of Alanis Morissette's

"Ironic" as we enter his front room. I remove my shoes and turn on the nearest lamp as he stumbles into what I assume is the kitchen, still singing at the top of his lungs.

"You might want to stop or you're likely to attract all the stray dogs in the neighborhood," I say loudly as I take a seat on his couch.

Sawyer's off-key singing stops, and the resulting silence is almost immediately filled with a boisterous laugh I've never heard from him before. He's still laughing a little when he returns with two bottles of water. He takes a seat on the opposite end of the couch and tosses one of the bottles into my lap.

"I'm going to miss seeing you at McGinn's, Freckles." He says before twisting the cap off his bottle and guzzling half the contents.

I nod as I place the water he gave me on the coffee table.

"Not that I won't try to stop in once in a while when you're working," he says, turning to face me, one leg bent and the other hanging off the couch onto the floor. I turn to face him too, and we sit there like that for a moment, staring at each other from opposite ends of the couch. When I lean back and stretch out my legs, he grabs my foot, gives it a squeeze, and then just holds it in his hand.

"I'm going to miss seeing you, too," I say, reaching for the hand he has on my foot. Then out of nowhere, he lunges across the couch and his lips are on mine. I'm pretty groggy so it's like a dream . . . a dream come true that is. Before I know it, we're lying on his bed. Between make-out sessions, Sawyer turns on some blues music and we lie together talking about all sorts of random things until I eventually doze off.

According to the glowing clock in Sawyer's bedroom, it's a little after three when I'm awaken by a dog barking outside. The sound instantly puts a smile on my face because it reminds me of Sawyer's terrible singing from earlier. I reach out, expecting him to be next to me, but he isn't there. I tiptoe out of his bedroom and find my way back to the living room where he's sleeping on the couch.

"Sawyer," I whisper as I give his shoulder a gentle shake. He stirs a little and I continue. "Come sleep in the bed . . . Sawyer."

"Nah, I want to say here," he whispers back.

"Why?" I ask, my stomach dropping a little.

"Because, I just . . . want to do this right."

"Do what right?"

"This," he whispers. "Us."

"Us? Sawyer, I'm—"

"I know, you're dating Justin. I don't care. You'll just have to stop dating him."

I think about the time my mom called alcohol truth serum when she'd found out about my stepdad's infidelity, and suddenly I'm lightheaded as a result of the hundreds of butterflies that swoop into my stomach from out of nowhere, as if they've been multiplying for weeks and trapped inside the invisible friendship net Sawyer and I cast around us. I love what he's saying so much, my heart hurts. In a good way, though. For the hundredth time tonight, I devour his lips. I've never enjoyed kissing someone so much.

"Come lie next to me," I say breathlessly, certain that he'll relent this time.

But he doesn't. And it makes me want him in the bed next to me even more.

Before I crawl back into his bed, I take the liberty of setting Sawyer's alarm clock for six a.m. I really should just go home since I need to be up for work in a matter of hours, but part of me is still hoping Sawyer will change his mind. I doze off almost immediately, and have what I think is a vivid dream of Sawyer climbing into bed next to me and snuggling up as close to me as possible. I moan, waking myself up to find that he really does have his arm draped over my waist. I smile and drift back into unconsciousness, feeling warm and safe.

As I drive home the next morning, I can't help but feel guilty about Justin despite the fact that I haven't made any promises to him.

chapter thirty-eight

It's Saturday night and the end of my shift at McGinn's. I'm crouched on the floor picking up the contents of my purse, which spilled out when I was removing the Coach knockoff from my locker. I guess I forgot to zip it. I pause, a lump in my throat, as I grip the McGinn's coaster that Bobby had written his dating account password on, images of all the filthy, beer-stained coasters in my box at home flooding my brain and making me feel nauseous. He'd asked me yesterday if I could take a look at his profile and give it a tweak for him. As I'm shoving the coaster into my purse, my heart stops when someone enters the break room. I stand, my subconscious hopeful for it to be Sawyer, but at the same time logic reminds me it can't be, and even if it was, things aren't the same between us anymore. It's Molly's husband, George, passing through on the way to their office.

"Hiya, Jess. Have a good one," he says with a wave, barely looking at me as he rushes by.

I happen to have a date with Live2Lift tonight. I'd forgotten all about messaging him the night Chloe told me she was pregnant, and then out of the blue, he contacted me earlier this week asking if I was free tonight. I had every intention of snubbing him, just like I had every intention of cutting things off with Justin. All because I thought something was finally happening between Sawyer and me—something more than friendship, that is.

I spent Sunday, Monday, and Tuesday on Cloud Nine at the prospect of giving my heart to Sawyer. I even told Justin on Sunday that we had to talk as soon as I got back in town on Thursday. I figured the least I owed him was to tell him face to face that I couldn't see him anymore. Except we never had the talk, because there ended up not being a need for "the talk." Instead, when I saw Justin on Thursday night, we made tacos at his place and then had mind-blowing sex. Funny how knowing there's someone else out there that I want more than him made our sex that much better.

Sawyer didn't call me on Monday, and he didn't call on Tuesday either. I didn't think much of it because I knew he was starting back at his company this week. He said he was going to be extremely busy, so he probably wouldn't have much time to do anything other than eat, sleep, shit, shower, work, and repeat. But I missed hearing his voice so much that I called him late Tuesday night when I was tucked into bed in my hotel room. Imagine my surprise when a woman answered. What did I do? I said nothing, allowing only my stunned silence to waft through the phone lines to this mystery woman's ears. *"Hello? . . . Hello? . . . Hello? Who is this?"* I can't get her fucking voice out of my head, and it's killing me.

Sawyer finally called late the next night. The insecure, heartbroken parts in me whispered not to answer, but the hopeful part of me that has been pining for Sawyer since the day we met won out.

"Hey," I'd said sullenly.

"I'm sorry, Jesstine."

"Why, exactly?" I needed to know every little detail so I could stop torturing myself with conjecture.

"It was Beth who answered my phone last night . . . but it's not what you probably think. I was in the bathroom when you called and she just . . ." He'd abandoned his train of thought.

"Yeah? Well, enlighten me then."

"She stopped by to talk . . ." He took a deep breath and let it out slowly. "Because she wants to call off the divorce."

I'll never forget the burning sensation that invaded my chest after he said those words. I wouldn't have been able to speak if I'd tried. So he continued.

"I think I owe it some thought . . ." He emitted a pensive sigh that somehow eased the pain I was feeling, which made me feel like almost as big of an ass as I thought he was being. "Twenty-one years. That's a long time . . . but even if I decide to go through with it as planned, I'd be a hypocrite if I pursued something with you before my marriage with Beth is dissolved."

I didn't know what to say, so I just sat there with my eyes closed listening to his heavy breaths and picturing his heaving chest.

"Can you say something? Anything? Tell me you hate me if you have to. But *please*, say something."

"I can't," I whispered.

"That's a start," he'd said softly, breathing a sigh of relief this time. "I hope this doesn't mean we can't be friends. Because you have no idea how important your friendship is to me. It doesn't make sense, this . . . this bond I feel with you, but it's there, so I can't deny it. But right now, the only thing I can feed it with is friendship. I hope you understand, Freckles."

Freckles.

That's when the tears started falling.

"The other night shouldn't have happened. I'm sorry for that too . . ." And then he muttered under his breath, "God damn it."

At that point, I started crying so hard that my breaths had become choppy, making it impossible for me to hide the fact that I'd lost it. So I hung up.

Since that night, he's texted several times, maintaining that he still wants to be friends. He also clarified that calling off the divorce isn't what his heart wants but that he's never been one to make life-altering decisions without serious thought. And after bawling my eyes out and trying to see things from his perspective, I get it. But that doesn't make it hurt any less, so I'm coping the only way I know how. By continuing to date. What else can I do?

God damn it is right.

I enter Hooligan's and head straight to the bar where Live2Lift said we should meet. I don't have high hopes for tonight, but when I talked to Chloe earlier, she reminded me that sometimes the best things happen when we least expect it. Like how she met Daran after she was technically done with online dating and how she and Daran are now expecting a baby in December. I know she's right, so I'm going to do my best to have a positive attitude tonight in order to move on from the heartbreak of Sawyer.

Twenty minutes later, after sipping down the last of my Diet Coke, I decide it's time to leave because I've most likely been stood up. Whatever. I'd much rather be at home reading a book or doing a crossword puzzle. I turn to leave and nearly run into my date. I know it's him based on his sheer muscle mass.

"I thought you stood me up," I say with a grin.

"I almost did, but my other date fell through."

"What do you mean your *other* date?"

"Just what I said," he says with a shrug. Then he pulls out a stool and sits down sideways as he continues, "I double-booked tonight because the other woman is an ER nurse so she's on call a lot. Anyway, lucky you."

I open my mouth debating how to tell him off, but he interrupts before I have a chance to articulate anything.

"Come on," he waves for me to sit next to him, "Let's have a drink."

I'm torn because he actually seems nice, judging by his demeanor and all. So I decide maybe his *lucky you* comment was a joke and slide onto the stool next to him.

We order drinks, me a rum and Diet and him an Amstel Light.

"You know, if you're trying to lose weight," he eyes me from head to toe, "That probably isn't the best choice?" He points at my drink.

"Excuse me?" I say, wondering if I've misheard him.

"*This* only has five carbs," he says holding up his beer.

"Well good for you," I say leaning away from him slightly. It isn't the most mature comeback, but I'm a bit off my game since this whole Sawyer thing happened.

When he finishes taking a sip of his beer, he considers my face for a good ten seconds, making me widen my eyes at him and ask, "What?"

"You just look . . . different. That's all."

I know it's a mistake the moment the words are out of my mouth, but I ask anyway. "Different how?"

"You're just . . . heavier than you look in your profile picture, and . . ."

He analyzes my face again. "You just look different, that's all. No offense or anything."

To my surprise, I burst out laughing, not because what he's just said didn't sting, but because I'm finally on the kind of date I always expected to be on as a result of online dating. But what did I expect with a screen name like Live2Lift? The laughter is a coping mechanism I guess. I've also just realized I don't even know his real name.

I could insult him the way he just insulted me. After all, he does look like he could be a direct descendant of a gorilla with his huge unnatural-looking muscles. I decide to take the high road instead. "I'm sorry, but I'm pretty sure neither one of us wants to be here. So how about if we just end the date right now?"

"Fine by me," he says shrugging. Then he turns his back to me, but only for a second before he looks over his shoulder. "Are you at least going to pay for your drink?"

Laughing and shaking my head, I dig a five out of my purse and toss it onto the bar. When I turn to leave, I see the worst possible person I could see at this very moment.

Ned has just arrived with some of his co-workers, one of which is a cute, leggy blonde who works at the service counter. She has her arm hooked through his, and I can tell from his posture that he's wasted. I want to leave, but there's no way for me to avoid him if I do. I've just decided the safest thing for me to do is to turn and slide back onto my stool next to the Gorilla Man when Ned makes eye contact with me and his expression turns bitter. Holding my gaze with a smirk, he grabs the blonde and starts kissing her and rubbing her ass. I'm definitely not jealous, but I still can't help but feel slighted. And just when I think I couldn't feel any lower, Live2Lift turns and asks, "Why are you still here?"

"I have no idea," I whisper to myself before slamming my drink like a shot and then marching right past Ned's group toward the door.

As I'm about to walk out, Ned belts out, "Two-timing slut!"

I pause, my back to the crowd, as the immediate area near the door becomes silent. My legs all of a sudden feel like they're made of lead, but

I somehow muster the strength to rush outside just as the first tear trickles down my cheek.

Desperate to not feel so rejected and unloved, I text Justin and ask him to stop over after work. I've decided I'm done. Done with online dating. Done with feeling sad that the stars simply aren't aligned for Sawyer and I. Done allowing things in my life that make me feel bad about myself.

When Justin arrives, I throw myself into his arms and accept the affection he so readily offers me. After all, how will I know if he's the one I'm meant to be with unless I give exclusivity with him a chance?

chapter thirty-nine

"Looking good, pretty lady," I say to myself, hands on hips and turning left to right. The new V-neck Brewers t-shirt I'm wearing fits perfectly.

Ashley and I are finally taking advantage of Justin's repeated offer to see a game as "guests" of his. Translation, he's going to meet us at a top secret location and let us into the stadium for free. I told him it might be a better idea for us to pay for the tickets, but he insisted I shouldn't worry about it. The only catch is Ashley and I have to be wearing team gear, but I've never owned a piece of major league baseball apparel in my life. Hence the shirt I'm wearing, which Justin brought over for me last night.

We've gotten into a comfortable routine over the last two months. If he isn't working, we see each other on Thursday, Friday and Saturday nights. When he is working, whether we see each other or not depends on the start time of the ball games. He's hinted a few times at the possibility of me giving him a key so he can just let himself in on late nights, but I don't feel ready for that yet. Something about a key seems permanent, and I don't want to put that kind of pressure on our relationship just yet. When we're together, Justin likes to stay active doing things like seeing plays, going to festivals and museums, and going out to dinner at trendy restaurants, which is fine. Everything we do is fun and planned—never a dull moment. But sometimes I just want to lie around in a t-shirt and underwear reading books and playing Sudoku. Justin, being the active type of guy he is, definitely needs a few lessons on how to relax. Not only does he need to have everything he does planned (which I understand at times because of Max), but he likes to be kept up to speed on my social calendar too. Again, I get it because he does need to plan his social life around Max, but sometimes his constant checking in to compare schedules can feel a bit stifling.

Don't get me wrong, I like Justin, and so do my friends and family, but sometimes I wonder if we're too big of opposites. Time will tell, I suppose.

I'm about to call Ashley just to make sure she'll be heading out the door soon, when my home phone rings and it happens to be her.

"Hey you. Are you on your way?

"Mmmmm," she groans and then coughs. "Jess, I'm so sorry, but I don't think I can go." She sounds congested and miserable.

"Aww, man. What if I pick you up?"

"Jess, whatever I have hit me like a freight train from out of nowhere." She sneezes and blows her nose. "I really shouldn't be in public. I even left work early today to try to sleep it off, but I feel even worse now. I'm sorry. Maybe Chloe can go?"

"No, she's still busy unpacking. Don't worry about it. You just rest. I'd offer to bring you soup, but I have to figure out what I'm going to do about the game."

"Ryan is bringing me soup." The way she says his name makes me happy, and I'll be forever grateful that Yahoo! Personals brought the two of them together in a roundabout way. Had Ryan Cross and I not connected online, Ashley never would have met him. Come to think of it, if I hadn't tried online dating, Ashley might not even be in my life. I have Pamela to thank for that.

"That's really sweet, Ash. I think he's a keeper," I say cheerfully. She sneezes again. "Well, I better let you get some rest. Call me when you feel better?"

"Absolutely. Love you."

"Love you too."

As soon as I get off the phone with Ashley, I scroll through my contacts as I wrack my brain trying to think of someone who might we willing and able to go to the game with me. That's when I see the perfect candidate's name. Kyle aka Coordinates Kyle aka hiccups.

Even though we haven't talked in months, Kyle is more than happy to go to the game with me because he's never been to Miller Park. He's at my place within twenty minutes decked out in White Sox gear.

"Kyle, you know we're going to a Brewers game, right?"

"Yeah, of course, but the Sox are my team."

I sigh as I step out of my apartment and close the door. "Thanks for going with me on such short notice and for picking me up.

"Thank you for inviting me. I just called Amy on the way here and she's super jealous."

"Of me?" I stop dead in my tracks.

"Oh, no," he laughs. "Not you. She's a big baseball fan so she's jealous that I'm going to Miller Park."

I laugh at the misunderstanding, wondering in the back of my mind how Justin is going to feel about me bringing Kyle to the game with me.

Shortly before the game is about to begin, Kyle and I are waiting where Justin said to meet him. Prompt as usual, he appears at the exact time he said he'd be there.

"What's . . . going on?" He slows his pace when he sees Kyle, making my stomach drop.

"Ashley isn't feeling well, so . . ." I point a thumb at my obviously unwelcome guest. "I brought Kyle," I say.

Kyle hiccups, and I do my best to keep a straight face.

"I can see that," Justin says as he runs his hand through his hair.

"Look, if this is a problem, I can just—" Kyle begins but Justin cuts him off.

"Do you mind if I talk to Jess in private?"

"Sure, no—" Hiccup. "—problem."

Justin gives me a hard stare when I burst out laughing. "What's so funny?" His tone is curt.

"Geez, Justin. Would you lighten up? Kyle's hiccups, that's what's funny." I peek over at Kyle real quick and whisper, "Sorry." He gestures with the raise of a hand that he doesn't mind.

"Who exactly is this guy, anyway?" Justin says, taking my arm and pulling me into him.

The gesture irks me, so I jerk my arm away. "He's a friend of mine. That's who he is . . . and I don't appreciate you being so rude to him." I hiss the last few words.

Kyle hiccups in the background, causing me to grin again.

"I don't have time for this," Justin says, shaking his head. "Come on. I'll show you guys to your seats."

"No. Forget it. We'll pass," I say as I sidestep Justin and walk over to Kyle.

"Fine, I'll stop over when the game is over," Justin calls to me as he starts walking toward the gate.

"I don't think that's a good idea, Justin," I call back.

He pauses and gives me another hard stare, and then he disappears into the stadium. When he does, Kyle let's out one really long breath that he'd been holding, and I can't help it, I laugh. Even though I'm pretty sure I just broke up with Justin, I laugh.

Kyle hiccups.

After Kyle and I grab burgers at a pub and grill near the stadium and he drops me off, I hop in my car and head over to Chloe and Daran's new duplex. They live in the lower and rent out the upper. I haven't seen it since I helped them move in a couple weeks ago, so now seems like the perfect opportunity. I know they'll be home because Chloe is in nesting mode.

"I can't believe he acted like that!" Chloe says as she gently strokes her growing belly.

"Can you feel anything yet?" I ask.

She shakes her head. "Not on the outside. But I can feel her moving around in there, in the mornings especially."

"Her? It's a girl?"

Chloe nods happily and reaches over to grab a folder off an end table. Then she pulls a few postcard size pictures out of the folder and hands them to me. "It's hard to tell, but the doctor assures us she's a girl."

I see the baby's tiny fingers and toes, and suddenly I'm crying.

"Jess, what's wrong?" Chloe scoots closer to me and puts her arm around my shoulder.

"Nothing," I say sniffling and wiping a few stray tears.

"Is it Justin?"

"No," I say, shaking my head. "It's . . . when Kyle drove me home, he took a detour to look at a duplex that him and his girlfriend are thinking about buying, and . . ." I have to pause to catch my breath, and Chloe waits patiently for me to continue. "It's Sawyer's place. It's for sale."

"You're still hung up on Sawyer," Chloe says quietly.

I nod, another tear racing down my cheek.

"Then you should call him. He never wanted to stop being your friend, Jess. You're the one who stopped talking to him."

"I know, but his duplex is for sale. That probably means he decided to move back in with Beth. That's what I'm guessing anyway."

"Come on, you can't assume he's gone back to her just because his place is for sale. How do you know he didn't buy another house?"

I shrug.

"There's only one way for you to find out. You have to call him." She glances down at my purse. "I can give you some privacy if you want."

"No, stay," I say grabbing my phone out of my purse. I have to manually dial Sawyer's number in because I'd deleted him from my contacts. But I memorized it beforehand. I glance up at Chloe and she gives me a reassuring nod before I press send.

The call is picked up on the second ring only it isn't Sawyer who answers. It isn't even a person. Instead, it's an automated message saying his cellular number is no longer in service.

chapter forty

I'm just leaving McGinn's when my phone rings in my hand. I look down and shake my head at the sight of Chloe's name. This is the third time she's called me today to make sure I'm meeting them at Home Bar for a little party that some of the regulars put together for Chris's birthday.

"Chloe?"

"Oh, hey, just checking in to make sure you're still coming."

"For the eighty billionth time, yes, I'm coming. Will you please stop calling me now?"

"Fine, but where are you? You're supposed to be here in less than an hour."

"I'm leaving work. I have to stop at home and change beforehand."

"But you'll be here?"

"Oh my God. Yes! What is up with you?"

"I'm just looking forward to seeing you. Plus, at seven months pregnant, I don't get out much."

"Well I'm looking forward to seeing you too, so I wouldn't dream of ditching out."

"Good. I'll see you soon. Don't be late."

"I'm not the one who's always late, remember?"

"Whatever."

Forty-five minutes later, as I'm walking up the sidewalk to Home Bar, my phone rings again and guess who it is . . .

"I'm here! Okay? I'm right outside."

"Hey, I don't want to be here all by myself. Don't forget Daran's in Virginia for another wedding."

"Isn't this like the sixth or seventh wedding he's gone to since you met him? Is he standing up in this one too?"

"Yep." I can picture Chloe rolling her eyes.

"Wow. Always a groomsman, never a groom. When are you going to help him out with that?"

Chloe laughs.

"Well," I say pulling the front door of Home Bar open. "I'm here. So we can get off the phone now . . . wait, where are you?" With the exception of Chris, who's standing behind the bar smiling at me and a few other patrons scattered about, the bar is empty. "Chloe? . . . Chloe, you there?" She doesn't answer so I assume we got disconnected. I close my phone and walk up to the bar.

"Welcome Home, Jess."

"Do you know what's going on? I thought there was supposed to be a--" And that's when I see him.

Sawyer is standing clear on the opposite end of the bar, and he's holding one yellow daffodil. I glance at Chris again and he smiles. Then I start walking the length of the bar toward Sawyer as he walks toward me until we meet in the middle.

"Hi, Freckles."

"What are you—"

He quickly holds the flower up in front of me, interrupting my question. I slowly reach up and take the daffodil from him.

"What's this for?"

"I ran into Chloe a couple weeks ago."

"Oh yeah? Where?"

"Soup Otzie's," he says, smiling. "She told me you and Justin broke up."

I nod.

"She also told me you tried to call, but I have a new phone, and a new house." He inches a little closer to me. Then he reaches into his back pocket, pulls out a folded piece of paper and holds it out in front of me. "I also have a new lease on life." He nods, prompting me to unfold the paper. It's a copy of his divorce certificate.

The second my eyes snap up to meet his, he pulls another yellow daffodil from behind his back. I was too hyper-focused on the sound of his voice, his familiar scent, and my racing heart to notice that he'd had one hand behind his back the whole time.

He takes the piece of paper from me and I take the second flower from him, so now I'm holding two yellow daffodils.

"You know what those represent, right?" Sawyer asks as he stuffs the paper back into his pocket.

"No, why don't you tell me," I say, smiling broadly.

He takes one last step toward me, completely closing the distance between us and says, "It means we're going to begin again."

The next thing I know, I'm in Sawyer's arms and he's kissing me even more passionately than he kissed me that night at his place. And again, just like that night, I feel like I'm dreaming. Only this time I'm wide awake.

Just as we're about to walk out the door, Chris says, "Hey, Jess."

Sawyer and I both turn. "Yeah?" I say.

"You owe me a dollar."

acknowledgments

First and foremost, I want to thank *you*, the reader, for the time you devoted to my characters. I hope you got something more out of Jess's story than just a little entertainment. I hope you came to love her as much as I do and that you were able to relate to her in some way, despite all of her flaws.

A HUGE thank you to my beta readers: Bria Starr, Jamie Biggins, Marnie Ide, Sarah "Eagle Eye" Fluegel, Suelynn Spersrud, and Alica Flechner. Whether you provided feedback on the original first draft or the new and improved first draft (or both), your time and efforts are greatly appreciated. You've all helped make this story better, not just with your feedback and suggestions, but also with your constant support.

Bria – Without you, I don't think I ever would have finished writing this book. Thank you for being there for me: to listen, to give advice, to offer words of encouragement, to provide a voice of reason, to talk me off ledges, and to bounce ideas off of. You're one of the most selfless people I know, and I feel so blessed to have you in my life.

Jamie – I can't even express how grateful I am to have you in my life and for all that you've done to support me, not just with my writing endeavors, but through life in general. Thank you for utilizing your many talents, such as your gift of snark and your charming ability to tell it like it is, to help me with this book. I don't know what I would have done without your input regarding various topics and situations!

Thank you to all the individuals who helped piece this book together: Leah Campbell (developmental editing), Barbara Malmberg (copy editing), Amy Queau (cover & promo materials), and Carl Ann Eastman (blurb).

To all of my author, blogger, and book friends who've been there to support me, I can't imagine navigating this book world without you. A special shout-out to: Jennifer Hanson, Elise Widrig and Polly Langel Barreto (Romance Rendezvous Book Blog), Sarah King, and Tess Woods.

Jesstine – Thank you for letting me use your beautiful name!

Last but not least, thank you to my husband and children for your continued love and understanding, even when I'm engrossed in writing. Dante, I appreciated these things more than you know: when you lent your ear (whether you were really listening or not), when you worked hard all week long and then spent weekends making meals and taking care of our children so I could write, when you worked from home so I could sleep in after being up all night, when you didn't balk at the cost of everything it took to bring this book together, and when you provided words of encouragement when I felt lost and frustrated. You guys are my motivation, and I love you.

more. *books*. by k. j.

Click Date Repeat

Don't Call Me Kit Kat

A Case of Serendipity

Visit kjfarnham.com for more information.

ALSO AVAILABLE BY K. J. FARNHAM

click. *date*. repeat.

These days, finding love online is as commonplace as ordering that coveted sweater. But back in 2003, the whole concept of internet dating was still quite new, with a stigma attached to it that meant those who were willing to test the waters faced a fair amount of skepticism from friends and family.

Such is the case for Chloe Thompson, a restless twenty-something tired of the typical dating scene and curious about what she might find inside her parents' computer. With two serious but failed relationships behind her, Chloe isn't even entirely sure what she's looking for. She just knows that whatever it is, she wants to find it.

Chloe's foray into online dating involves a head-first dive into a world of matches, ice breakers and the occasional offer of dick pics, all while Chloe strives to shake herself of the ex who just refuses to disappear. Will she simultaneously find herself and "the one" online, or will the ever-growing pile of humorous and downright disastrous dates only prove her friends and family right? There's only one way to find out... Click. Date. Repeat.

about.*the*.author.

K. J. Farnham was born and raised in a suburb of Milwaukee. She graduated from UW-Milwaukee in 1999 with a bachelor's degree in elementary education and went on to earn a master's degree in curriculum and instruction from Carroll University in Waukesha. She then had the privilege of helping hundreds of children learn to read and write over the course of twelve years. Farnham now lives in western Wisconsin with her husband and three children.

Connect with K. J. at kjfarnham.com

www.ingramcontent.com/pod-product-compliance
Lightning Source LLC
Chambersburg PA
CBHW030351120726
47901CB00007B/1984
9780692113721